W9-BRB-142

Everybody *loves* Carolyn Brown

"I know when I read a book by Carolyn Brown, I'm in for a treat."

—*Long and Short Reviews*

"Carolyn Brown is a master storyteller who never fails to entertain. Her stories make me smile, they make me laugh, and sometimes I cry a few tears."

—*Night Owl Reviews*

"The most difficult thing about reading a Brown book is putting it down."

—*Fresh Fiction*

"Hilarious… A high-spirited, romantic page-turner."

—*Kirkus Reviews*

"Brown's writing holds you spellbound."

—*Thoughts in Progress*

"If you love small-town stories with wonderful characters and witty dialog…Carolyn Brown will thrill you!"

—*The Reading Café*

"Brown will warm your heart, and bring you characters so real, you'll swear they're flesh and bone!"

—*Love Romance Passion*

"Delightfully fresh and unique… Brown's writing has such a down-home country feel that you will feel like you are right in the heart of Texas."

—*Book Reviews and More by Kathy*

Also by Carolyn Brown

The Shop on Main Street
The Sisters Café

Lucky Cowboys
Lucky in Love
One Lucky Cowboy
Getting Lucky
Talk Cowboy to Me

Honky Tonk
I Love This Bar
Hell, Yeah
My Give a Damn's Busted
Honky Tonk Christmas

Spikes & Spurs
Love Drunk Cowboy
Red's Hot Cowboy
Darn Good Cowboy Christmas
One Hot Cowboy Wedding
Mistletoe Cowboy
Just a Cowboy and His Baby
Cowboy Seeks Bride

Cowboys & Brides
Billion Dollar Cowboy
The Cowboy's Christmas Baby
The Cowboy's Mail Order Bride
How to Marry a Cowboy

Burnt Boot, Texas
Cowboy Boots for Christmas
The Trouble with Texas Cowboys
One Texas Cowboy Too Many
A Cowboy Christmas Miracle

What Happens in Texas
A Heap of Texas Trouble

the Sisters Café

CAROLYN BROWN

sourcebooks casablanca

Copyright © 2013, 2019 by Carolyn Brown
Cover and internal design © 2019 by Sourcebooks
Cover design by Dawn Adams/Sourcebooks
Cover image © Elektrons 08/plainpicture

Sourcebooks and the colophon are registered trademarks of Sourcebooks.

All rights reserved. No part of this book may be reproduced in any form or by any electronic or mechanical means including information storage and retrieval systems—except in the case of brief quotations embodied in critical articles or reviews—without permission in writing from its publisher, Sourcebooks.

The characters and events portrayed in this book are fictitious or are used fictitiously. Any similarity to real persons, living or dead, is purely coincidental and not intended by the author.

All brand names and product names used in this book are trademarks, registered trademarks, or trade names of their respective holders. Sourcebooks is not associated with any product or vendor in this book.

Published by Sourcebooks Casablanca, an imprint of Sourcebooks
P.O. Box 4410, Naperville, Illinois 60567-4410
(630) 961-3900
sourcebooks.com

Originally published as *The Blue-Ribbon Jalapeño Society Jubilee* in 2013 in the United States of America by Sourcebooks Landmark, an imprint of Sourcebooks.

Library of Congress Cataloging-in-Publication Data

Names: Brown, Carolyn, author.
Title: The Sisters Café / Carolyn Brown.
Description: Naperville, Illinois : Sourcebooks, Inc., [2019]
Identifiers: LCCN 2019022906 | (trade paperback)
Subjects: GSAFD: Love stories.
Classification: LCC PS3552.R685275 S57 2019 | DDC 813/.54--dc23
LC record available at https://lccn.loc.gov/2019022906

Printed and bound in Canada.
MBP 10 9 8 7 6 5 4 3 2 1

To all the folks at Sourcebooks who took this book from a dream to a reality!

Dear Readers,

Welcome to Cadillac, Texas, where the gossip is more accurate than a DNA test. It's small-town Texas where everybody knows what everybody has done, is doing, or is thinking about doing. The only reason they read the local newspaper is to see who got caught.

Come on in to Miss Clawdy's Café and get to know the Andrews twins, Cathy and Marty, as well as their friends Jack, Trixie, and Darla Jean. Draw up a chair and sit a spell. And if you are really lucky, maybe Agnes will come in to visit.

Stick around for the Jalapeño Jubilee. The Blue-Ribbon Jalapeño Society sponsors it every year, and it's the biggest thing in the state. They celebrate their forty years of growing the hottest jalapeño in Texas and winning the competition at the Texas State Fair. It's always in November after the State Fair is over, and they've hung their new blue ribbons up out at the Prescott mansion. It kicks off with a parade at mid-morning and doesn't end until every cowgirl and cowboy has danced all the leather off their boots at the street dance at midnight. Don't forget your sweater. It can turn cool when the sun sets.

Since this is my debut novel into a new area, I would like to thank several people. Thank you to my agent, Erin Niumata, for giving me that extra push to write in this genre. Thank you to Sourcebooks for publishing the book and to everyone behind the scenes at Sourcebooks who has taken this from a dream to reality. But most of all, I want to extend an extra big thanks to Deb Werksman, my editor, for hours and hours of working with me on making this book what it is today and for believing in me.

Here's hoping you have fun reading about the goings-on in Cadillac and that you enjoy *The Sisters Café*.

All my best,
Carolyn Brown

Chapter 1

If Prissy Parnell hadn't married Buster Jones and left Cadillac, Texas, for Pasadena, California, Marty wouldn't have gotten the speeding ticket. It was all Prissy's damn fault that Marty was in such a hurry to get to the Blue-Ribbon Jalapeño Society monthly meeting that night, so Prissy ought to have to shell out the almost two hundred dollars for that ticket.

They were already passing around the crystal bowl to take up the voting ballots when Marty slung open the door to Violet Prescott's sunroom and yelled, "Don't count 'em without my vote."

Twenty faces turned to look at her and not a one of them, not even her twin sister, Cathy, was smiling. Hell's bells, who had done pissed on their cucumber sandwiches before she got there, anyway? A person didn't drop dead from lack of punctuality, did they?

One wall of the sunroom was glass and looked out over lush green lawns and flower gardens. The other three were covered with shadow boxes housing the blue ribbons that the members had won at the Texas State Fair for their jalapeño pepper entries. More than forty shadow boxes all reminding the members of their history and their responsibility for the upcoming year. Bless Cathy's heart for doing her part. She had a little garden of jalapeños on the east side of the lawn and nurtured them like children. The newest shadow box held ribbons that she'd earned for the club with her pepper jelly and picante. It was the soil, or maybe she told them bedtime stories, but she, like her mamma and grandma, grew the hottest jalapeños in the state.

"It appears that Martha has decided to grace us with her presence once again when it is time to vote for someone to take our dear Prissy's place in the Blue-Ribbon Jalapeño Society. We really should amend our charter to state that a member has to attend more than one meeting every two years. You could appreciate the fact that we did amend it once to include you in the membership with your sister, who, by the way, has a spotless attendance record," Violet said.

Violet, the queen of the club, as most of the members called it, was up near eighty years old, built like SpongeBob SquarePants, and had stovepipe jet-black hair right out of the bottle. Few people had the balls or the nerve to cross her, and those who did were put on her shit list right under Martha, aka Marty, Andrews' name, which was always on the top.

Back in the beginning of the club days, before Marty was even born, the mayor's wife held the top position on the shit list. When they'd formed the Blue-Ribbon Jalapeño Society, Loretta Massey and Violet almost went to war over the name of the new club. Loretta insisted that it be called a society, and Violet wanted it to be called a club. Belonging to a club just sounded so much fancier than saying that one belonged to a society. Loretta won when the vote came in, but Violet called it a club anyway and that's what stuck. Rumor had it that Violet was instrumental in getting the mayor ousted just so they'd have to leave Grayson County and Loretta would have to quit the club.

Marty hated it when people called her Martha. It sounded like an old woman's name. What was her mother thinking anyway when she looked down at two little identical twin baby daughters and named them after her mother and aunt—Martha and Catherine? Thank God she'd at least shortened their names to Marty and Cathy.

Marty shrugged, and Violet snorted. Granted, it was a ladylike snort, but it still went right along with her round face and three-layered neck. Hell, if they wanted to write forty amendments to the charter, Marty would still do only the bare necessities to keep her in voting standing. She hadn't even wanted to be in the damned club and had only done it because if she didn't, then Cathy couldn't.

Marty slid into a seat beside her sister and held up her ballot.

Beulah had the bowl in hand and was ready to hand it off to Violet to read off the votes. But she passed it to the lady on the other side of her and it went back around the circle to Marty, who tossed in her folded piece of paper. If she'd done her homework and gotten the numbers right, that one vote should swing the favor for Anna Ruth to be the new member of the club. She didn't like Anna Ruth, especially since she'd broken up her best friend's marriage. But hey, Marty had made a deathbed promise to her mamma, and that carried more weight than the name of a hussy on a piece of paper.

The bowl went back to Violet and she put it in her lap like the coveted jeweled crown of a reigning queen. "Our amended charter states that only twenty-one women can belong to the Blue-Ribbon Jalapeño Society at any one time, and the only time we vote a new member in is when someone moves or dies. Since Prissy Parnell got married this past week and moved away from Grayson County, we are open for one new member. The four names on the ballet are: Agnes Flynn, Trixie Matthews, Anna Ruth Williams, and Gloria Rawlings."

Even though it wasn't in the fine print, everyone knew that when attending a meeting, the members should dress for the occasion, which meant panty hose and heels. Marty could feel nineteen pairs of eyes on her. It would have been twenty, but Violet was busy fishing the first ballot from the fancy bowl.

Marty threw one long leg over the other and let the bright red three-inch high-heeled shoe dangle on her toe. They could frown all they wanted. She was wearing a dress, even if it only reached mid-thigh, and had black spandex leggings under it. If they wanted her to wear panty hose, they'd better put a second amendment on that charter and make it in big print.

God Almighty, but she'd be glad when her great-aunt died and she could quit the club. But it looked like Agnes was going to last forever, which was no surprise. God sure didn't want her in heaven, and the devil wouldn't have her in hell.

"One vote for Agnes," Violet said aloud.

Beulah marked that down on the minutes and waited.

Violet enjoyed her role as president of the club and took her own sweet time with each ballot. Too bad she hadn't dropped dead or at least moved to California so Cathy could be president. Marty would bet her sister would get those votes counted a hell of a lot faster.

There was one piece of paper in the candy dish when Beulah held up a hand. "We've got six each for Agnes, Trixie, Anna Ruth, and two for Gloria. Unless this last vote is for Agnes, Trixie, or Anna Ruth, we have a tie, and we'll have to have a run-off election."

"Shit!" Marty mumbled.

Cathy shot her a dirty look.

"Anna Ruth," Violet said and let out a whoosh of air.

A smile tickled the corner of Marty's mouth.

Saved, by damn!

Agnes was saved from prison.

Violet was saved from attending her own funeral.

The speeding ticket was worth every penny.

Trixie poked the black button beside the nursing home door and kicked yellow and orange leaves away as she reached for the handle. She heard the familiar click as the lock let go and then heard someone yell her name.

"Hey, Trixie. Don't shut it. We are here," Cathy called out.

Trixie waved at her two best friends: Cathy and Marty Andrews. Attitude and hair color kept them from being identical. They were five feet ten inches tall and slim built, but Cathy kept blond highlights in her brown hair and Marty's was natural. In attitude, they were as different as vanilla and chocolate. Cathy was the sweet twin who loved everyone and had trouble speaking her mind. Marty was the extrovert who called the shots like she saw them. Cathy was engaged, and Marty said there were too many cowboys she hadn't taken to bed to get herself tied down to one man.

Marty threw an arm around Trixie's shoulder as they marched down the wide hall. Trixie's mother, Janie Matthews, had checked herself into the nursing home four years before when her Alzheimer's had gotten so bad that she didn't know Trixie one day. Trixie had tried to talk her mother into living with her, but Janie was lucid enough to declare that she couldn't live alone and her daughter had to work.

"Congratulations, darlin', you did not make it into the club tonight. Your life has been spared until someone dies or moves away and Cathy nominates you again," Marty said.

"Well, praise the Lord," Trixie said.

"I know. Let's string Cathy up by her toenails and force-feed her fried potatoes until her wedding dress won't fit for even putting your name in the pot." Marty laughed.

"Trixie would be a wonderful addition to the club. She wouldn't let Violet run her around like a windup toy. That's why I keep nominating her every chance I get," Cathy said. "Anna Ruth is going to be a brand new puppet in Violet's hands. Every bit as bad as Gloria would have been."

Trixie stopped so fast that Marty's hand slipped off her shoulder. "Anna Ruth?"

"Sorry." Cathy shrugged. "I'm surprised that she won and she only did by one vote."

Trixie did a head wiggle. "Don't the world turn around? My mamma wasn't fit for the club because she had me out of wedlock. And now Anna Ruth is living with my husband without a marriage certificate and she gets inducted. If she has a baby before they marry, do they have a big divorce ceremony and kick her out?"

"I never thought she'd get it," Cathy said. "I don't know how in the world I'm going to put up with her in club, knowing that she's the one that broke up your marriage."

Trixie paled. "Who's going to tell Agnes that she didn't get it again? Lord, she's going to be an old bear all week."

"That's Beulah's job. She nominated her. I'm just damn glad I have a class tonight. Maybe the storm will be over before I get home," Marty said.

Cathy smiled weakly. "And I've got dinner with Ethan back at Violet's in an hour."

"I'm not even turning on the lights when I get home. Maybe she'll think I've died." Trixie started walking again.

"You okay with the Anna Ruth thing?" Marty asked.

Trixie nodded. "Can't think of a better thing to happen to y'all's club."

"It's not my club," Marty said. "I'm just there so Cathy can be in it. I'm not sure Violet would let her precious son marry a woman who wasn't in the al-damn-mighty Blue-Ribbon Jalapeño Society. I still can't believe that Violet is okay with her precious son marrying one of the Andrews' twins."

Cathy pointed a long slender finger at her sister. "Don't you start with me! And I'm not the feisty twin. You are. I can't see Violet letting Ethan marry you for sure."

"Touchy, are we? Well, darlin' sister, I wouldn't have that man, mostly because I'd have to put up with Violet." Marty giggled.

"Shh, no fighting. It'll upset Mamma." Trixie rapped gently on the frame of the open door and poked her head inside a room. "Anyone at home?"

Janie Matthews clapped her hands and her eyes lit up. She and Trixie were mirror images of each other—short, slim built, light brown hair, milk chocolate-colored eyes, and delicate features. Trixie wore her hair in a chin-length bob, and Janie's was long, braided, and wrapped around her head in a crown. Other than that and a few wrinkles around Janie's eyes, they looked more like sisters than mother and daughter.

"Why, Clawdy Burton, you've come to visit. Sit down, darlin', and let's talk. You aren't still mad at me, are you?"

Marty crossed the room and sat down beside Janie on the bed, leaving the two chairs in the room for Cathy and Trixie. It wasn't the first time Janie had mistaken her for Claudia, the twins' mother, or the first time that she'd remembered Claudia by her maiden name, either.

"I brought some friends," Marty said.

"Any friend of Clawdy's is a friend of mine. Come right in here. You look familiar. Did you go to school with me and Clawdy?" Janie looked right at her daughter.

"I did," Trixie said.

Janie's brow furrowed. "I can't put a name with your face."

"I'm Trixie."

Janie shook her head. "Sorry, honey, I don't remember you. And you?" She looked into Cathy's eyes.

"She's my sister, Cathy, remember?" Marty asked.

"Well, ain't that funny. I never knew Clawdy to have a sister. You must be older than we are, but I can see the resemblance."

"Yes, ma'am, I didn't know you as well as"—Cathy paused—"my little sister did, but I remember coming to your house."

"Did Mamma make fried chicken for you?"

"Oh, honey, I've eaten fried chicken more than once at your house," Cathy said.

"Good. Mamma makes the best fried chicken in the whole world. She and Clawdy's mamma know how to do it just right. Now, Clawdy, tell me you aren't mad at me. I made a mistake runnin' off with Rusty like that, but we can be friends now, can't we?"

Marty patted her on the arm. "You know I could never stay mad at you."

"I'm just so glad you got my letter and came to visit." Janie looked at Trixie and drew her eyes down. "You look just like a girl I used to know. It's right there on the edge of my mind, but I've got this remembering disease. That's why I'm in here, so they can help me." She turned her attention back to Marty. "You really aren't mad at me anymore?"

"Of course not. You were in love with Rusty or you wouldn't have run off with him," Marty said. They had this conversation often so she knew exactly what to say.

"I did love him, but he found someone new, so I had to bring my baby girl and come on back home. How are your girls?" She jumped at least five years from thinking she and Claudia were in school to the time when they were new mothers.

"They're fine. Let's talk about you," Marty said.

Janie yawned. "Clawdy, darlin', I'm so sorry, but I can't keep my eyes open anymore."

It was always the same. On Wednesday nights, Trixie visited with Janie. Sometimes, when they had time between closing the café and their other Wednesday evening plans, Marty and Cathy went with her. And always after fifteen or twenty minutes, on a good night, she was sleepy.

"That's okay, Janie. We'll come see you again soon," Marty said.

Trixie stopped at the doorway and waved.

Janie frowned. "I'm sorry I can't remember you. You remind me of someone I knew a long time ago, but I can't recall your name. Were you the Jalapeño Jubilee queen this year? Maybe that's where I saw you."

"No, ma'am. They don't crown queens anymore. But it's okay. I remember you real well," Trixie said.

Less than half an hour later, Trixie parked beside a big two-story house sitting on the corner of Main and Fourth in Cadillac, Texas. The sign outside the house said *Miss Clawdy's Café* in fancy lettering. Above it were the words: *Red Beans and Turnip Greens.*

Most folks in town just called it Clawdy's.

It had started as a joke after Cathy and Marty's mamma, Claudia, died and the three of them were going through her recipes. They'd actually been searching for "the secret," but evidently Claudia took it to the grave with her.

More than forty years ago, Grayson County and Fannin County women were having a heated argument over who could grow the hottest jalapeños in North Texas. Idalou Thomas, over in Fannin County, had won the contest for her jalapeño corn bread and her jalapeño pepper jelly so many years that most people dropped plumb out of the running. But that year, Claudia's mamma decided to try a little something different, and she watered her pepper plants with the water she used to rinse out her unmentionables. That was the very year that Fannin County lost their title in all of the jalapeño categories to Grayson County at the Texas State Fair. They brought home a blue ribbon in every category that had anything to do with growing or cooking with jalapeño peppers. That was also the year that Violet Prescott and several other women formed the Blue-Ribbon Jalapeño Society. The next fall, they held their First Annual Blue-Ribbon Jalapeño Society Jubilee in Cadillac, Texas.

The Jubilee got bigger and bigger with each passing year. They added vendors and a kiddy carnival with rides and a Ferris wheel, and people started marking it on their calendar a year in advance. It was talked about all year, and folks planned their vacation time around the Jalapeño Jubilee. Idalou died right after the first Jubilee, and folks in Fannin County almost brought murder charges against Claudia's mamma for breaking poor old Idalou's heart. Decades went by before Claudia figured out how her mother grew such red-hot peppers, and when her mamma passed, she carried on the tradition.

But she never did write down the secret for fear that one of the Fannin County women would find a way to steal it. The one thing she did was dry a good supply of seeds from the last crop of jalapeños just in case she died that year. It wasn't likely that Fannin County would be getting the blue ribbon back as long as one of her daughters grew peppers from the original stock and saved seeds back each year.

"If we had a lick of sense, we'd all quit our jobs and put a café in this big old barn of a house," Cathy had said.

"Count me in," Marty had agreed.

Then they found the old LP albums in Claudia's bedroom, and Cathy had picked up an Elvis record and put it on the turntable. When she set the needle down, "Lawdy, Miss Clawdy" had played.

"Daddy called her that, remember? He'd come in from working all day and holler for Miss Clawdy to come give him a kiss," Marty had said.

Trixie had said, "That's the name of y'all's café—Miss Clawdy's Café. It can be a place where you fix up this buffet bar of southern food for lunch. Like fried chicken, fried catfish, breaded and fried pork chops, and always have beans and greens on it seasoned up with lots of bacon drippings. You know, like your mamma always cooked. Then you can serve her pecan cobbler, peach cobbler, and maybe her black forest cake for dessert."

"You are making me hungry right now just talkin' about beans and greens. I can't remember the last time I had that kind of food," Marty had said.

Trixie went on, "I bet there's lots of folks around here who can't remember when they had it either with the fast-food trend. Folks would come from miles and miles to get at a buffet where they could eat all they wanted of good old southern fried and seasoned food. And you can frame up a bunch of those old LP covers and use them to decorate the walls. And you could transfer the music from those records over to

CDs and play that old music all day. You could serve breakfast from a menu and then a lunch buffet. It would make a mint, I swear it would."

That started the idea that blossomed into a café on the ground floor of the big two-story house. The front door opened into the foyer where they set up a counter with a cash register. To the left was the bigger dining area, which had been the living room. To the right was the smaller one, which had been the dining room. What had been their mother's sitting room now seated sixteen people and was used for special lunch reservations. Their dad's office was now a storage pantry for supplies.

Six months later and a week before Miss Clawdy's Café had its grand opening, Trixie caught Andy cheating on her, and she quit her job at the bank to join the partnership. That was a year ago, and even though it was a lot of work, the café really was making money hand over fist.

"Hey, good lookin'," a deep voice said from the shadows when she stepped up on the back porch.

"I didn't know if you'd wait or not," Trixie said.

Andy ran the back of his hand down her jaw line. "It's Wednesday, darlin'. Until it turns into Thursday, I would wait. Besides, it's a pleasant night. Be a fine night for the high school football game on Friday."

Trixie was still pissed at Andy and still had dreams about strangling Anna Ruth, but sex was sex, and she was just paying Anna Ruth back. She opened the back door, and together they crossed the kitchen. He followed her up the stairs to the second floor, where there were three bedrooms and a single bathroom. She opened her bedroom door, and once he was inside, she slammed it shut and wrapped her arms around his neck.

"I miss you," he said.

She unbuttoned his shirt and walked him backward to the bed. "You should have thought about that."

"What if I break it off with Anna Ruth?"

"We've had this conversation before." Trixie flipped a couple of switches, and those fancy no-fire candles were suddenly burning beside the bed.

He pulled her close and kissed her. "You are still beautiful."

She pushed him back on the bed. "You are still a lyin', cheatin' son-of-a-bitch."

He sat up and peeled out of his clothes. "Why do you go to bed with me if I'm that bad?"

"Because I like sex."

"I wish you liked housework," Andy mumbled.

"If I had, we might not be divorced. If my messy room offends you, then put your britches back on and go home to Anna Ruth and her sterile house," Trixie said.

"Shut up and kiss me." He grinned.

She shucked out of her jeans and T-shirt and jumped on the bed with him. They'd barely gotten into the foreplay when a hard knock on the bedroom door stopped the process as quickly as if someone had thrown a pitcher of icy water into the bed with them. Trixie grabbed for the sheet and covered her naked body; Andy strategically put a pillow in his lap.

"I thought they were all out like usual," he whispered. "If that's Marty, we are both dead."

"Maybe they called off her class for tonight," Trixie said.

"Cadillac police. Open this door right now, or I'm coming in shooting."

Trixie groaned. "Agnes?"

Andy groaned and fell back on the pillows. "Dear God!"

And that's when flashing red, white, and blue lights and the mixed wails of police cars, sirens, and an ambulance all screeched to a halt in front of Miss Clawdy's.

Trixie grabbed her old blue chenille robe from the back of a rocking chair and belted it around her waist. "Agnes, is that you?"

"It's the Cadillac police, I tell you, and I'll come in there shooting if that man who's molesting you doesn't let you go right this minute." Agnes tried to deepen her voice, but there was just so much a seventy-eight-year-old woman could do. She sounded like a prepubescent boy with laryngitis.

"I'm coming right out. Don't shoot."

She eased out the door, and sure enough, there was Agnes, standing in the hallway with a sawed-off shotgun trained on Trixie's belly button.

The old girl had donned her late husband's pleated trousers and a white shirt and smelled like a mothball factory. Her dyed red hair, worn in a ratted hairdo reminiscent of the sixties, was crammed up under a fedora. Enough curls had escaped to float around the edges of the hat and remind Trixie of those giant statues of Ronald McDonald. The main difference was that she had a shotgun in her hands instead of a hamburger and fries.

Trixie shut her bedroom door behind her and blocked it as best she could. "There's no one in my bedroom, Agnes. Let's go downstairs and have a late-night snack. I think there are hot rolls left and half of a peach cobbler."

"The hell there ain't nobody in there! I saw the bastard. Stand to one side, and I'll blow his ass to hell." Agnes raised the shotgun.

"You were seeing me do my exercises before I went to bed."

Agnes narrowed her eyes and shook her head. "He's in there. I can smell him." She sniffed the air. "Where is the sorry son-of-a-bitch? I could see him in there throwing you on the bed and having his way with you. Sorry bastard, he won't get away. Woman ain't safe in her own house."

Trixie moved closer to her. "Look at me, Agnes. I'm not hurt. It was just shadows, and what you smell is mothballs. Shit, woman, where'd you get that getup, anyway?"

Agnes shook her head. "He told you to say that or he'd kill you.

He don't scare me." She raised the barrel of the gun and pulled the trigger. The kickback knocked her square on her butt on the floor, and the gun went scooting down the hallway.

"Next one is for you, buster," she yelled as plaster, insulation, and paint chips rained down upon her and Trixie.

Trixie grabbed both ears. "God Almighty, Agnes!"

"Bet that showed him who is boss around here, and if you don't quit usin' them damn cussin' words, takin' God's name in vain, I might aim the gun at you next time. And I don't have to tell a smart-ass like you where I got my getup, but I was tryin' to save your sorry ass so I dressed up like a detective," Agnes said.

Trixie grabbed Agnes's arm, pulled her up, and kept her moving toward the stairs. "Well, you look more like a homeless bum."

Agnes pulled free and stood her ground, arms crossed over her chest, the smell of mothballs filling up the whole landing area.

"We've got to get out of here in a hurry," Trixie tried to whisper, but it came out more like a squeal.

"He said he'd kill you, didn't he?" Agnes finally let herself be led away. "I knew it, but I betcha I scared the shit out of him. He'll be crawling out the window and the police will catch him. Did you get a good look at the bastard? We'll go to the police station and do one of them drawin' things and they'll catch him before he tries a stunt like that again."

They met four policemen, guns drawn, serious expressions etched into their faces, in the kitchen. Every gun shot up and pointed straight at Agnes and Trixie.

Trixie threw up her hands, but Agnes just glared at them.

"Jack, it's me and Agnes. This is just a big misunderstanding."

Living right next door to the Andrews' house his whole life, Jack Landry had tagged along with Trixie, Marty, and Cathy their whole growing-up years. He lowered his gun and raised an eyebrow.

"Nothing going on upstairs, I assure you," Trixie said, and she wasn't lying. Agnes had put a stop to what was about to happen for damn sure.

Trixie hoped the old girl had an asthma attack from the mothballs as payment for ruining her Wednesday night.

"We heard a gunshot," Jack said.

"That would be my shotgun. It's up there on the floor. Knocked me right on my ass. I forgot that it had a kick. Loud sumbitch messed up my hearing." Agnes hollered and reached up to touch her kinky red hair. "I lost my hat when I fell down. I've got to go get it."

Trixie saw the hat come floating down the stairs and tackled it on the bottom step. "Here it is. You dropped it while we were running away."

Agnes screamed at her. "You lied! You said we had to get away from him before he killed us, and I ran down the stairs, and I'm liable to have a heart attack, and it's your fault. I told Cathy and Marty not to bring the likes of you in this house. It's an abomination, I tell you. Divorced woman like you hasn't got no business in the house with a couple of maiden ladies."

"Miz Agnes, one of my officers will help you across the street." Jack pushed a button on his radio and said, "False alarm at Miss Clawdy's."

A young officer was instantly at Agnes's side.

Agnes eyed the fresh-faced fellow. "You lay a hand on me, and I'll go back up there and get my gun. I know what you rascals have on your mind all the time, and you ain't goin' to skinny up next to me. I can still go get my gun. I got more shells right here in my britches' pockets."

"Yes, ma'am. I mean, no, ma'am. I'm just going to make sure you get across the street and into your house safely," he said.

Trixie could hear the laughter behind his tone, but not a damn bit of it was funny. Andy was upstairs. The kitchen was full of men who worked for him, and if Cathy and Marty heard there were problems at Clawdy's, they could come rushing in at any time.

"Maiden ladies my ass," Trixie mumbled. "I'm only thirty-four."

Darla Jean had finished evening prayers and was on her way back down the hallway from the sanctuary to her apartment. Her tiny one-bedroom apartment was located in the back of the old convenience store and gas station combination. Set on the corner lot facing Main Street, it had served the area well until the super Walmart went in up in Sherman. Five years before when business got too bad to stay open, her uncle shut the doors. Then he died and left her the property at a time when she was ready to retire from her "escort" business. She had been worrying about what to listen to: her heart or her brain. The heart said she should give up her previous lifestyle and start to preach like her mamma wanted her to do back when she was just a teenager. Her brain said that she'd made a good living in the "escort" business and she would be a damn fine madam.

The gas station didn't look much like a brothel, but she could see lots of possibilities for a church. It seemed like an omen, so she turned it into the Christian Nondenominational Church and started preaching the word of God. Main Street ran east and west through Cadillac and north and south streets were numbered. The church sat on the corner of Fourth and Main streets, facing Main. Straight across Main was the Cadillac Community Building, and across Fourth was Miss Clawdy's Café.

She hadn't even made it to her apartment door when the noisy sirens sounded like they were driving right through the doors of her church sanctuary. She stopped and said a quick prayer in case it was the Rapture and God had decided to send Jesus back to Earth with all the fanfare of police cars and flashing lights. The Good Book didn't say just how he'd return, and Darla Jean had an open mind about it. If he could be born in a stable the first time around, then he could return in a blaze of flashing red, white, and blue lights the second time.

She pulled back the mini-blinds in her living room. The police were across the street at Miss Clawdy's. At least Jesus wasn't coming to whisk her away that night. There was only one car in the parking lot, like most Wednesday nights, and she knew who drove that car. Hopefully, the hullabaloo over there was because Trixie had finally taken her advice and thrown the man out.

God didn't take too kindly to a woman screwing around with another woman's man. Not even if the woman had been married to him and the "other woman" wasn't married to him yet. Maybe it was a good thing that Jesus wasn't riding in a patrol car that night. She'd hate for her friend Trixie to be one of those left behind folks.

"Got to be a Bible verse somewhere to support that. Maybe I could find something in David's history of many wives that would help me get through to her," she muttered as she hurried out a side door and across Fourth Street toward the café.

"Holy Mother of Jesus, has Marty come home early and caught Andy over there and murdered him?" Darla Jean mumbled.

Had the cops arrived in all the noisy fanfare to take her away in handcuffs?

Then she saw a policeman leading Agnes across the street. So it hadn't been Marty but Agnes who'd done the killing. That meant Trixie was dead. Agnes had never liked her, and she'd threatened to kill her on more than one occasion. Now the policeman was leading her across Main Street to her house, probably so she could get out of that crazy costume and back into her regular clothes. Lord, have mercy! The twins were going to faint when they found out.

It looked like an old man, but it had to be Agnes. There wasn't another person in the whole town of Cadillac that had red hair like that. Darla Jean stopped so quick in the middle of Fourth Street that she pulled the toe piece out of a flip-flop, got tangled in the rubber strap, and fell right on her butt, with the fall leaves from the trees around Clawdy's blowing all around her. She shook her head and didn't blink for several seconds. What in the world was Agnes doing in that getup? It wasn't Halloween for another three weeks.

The minute the police were out of Clawdy's kitchen, Trixie melted into a chair and slapped both hands over her ears. Was she doomed forever to hear pigs squealing every time her heart beat? A shotgun blast in the small confines of a hallway was worse than the noise from the local boys' souped-up stereo systems in their fancy little low-slung pickup trucks chasing up and down Main Street on Saturday night.

"Shit!" she mumbled, but even that word sounded like it came out of a deep dark tunnel.

When she looked up, her ex-husband was standing at the bottom of the stairs wearing a sheepish grin. He was fully dressed in his dark blue policeman's uniform, gun holstered, radio on his shoulder, and bits of her last scrapbook paper job stuck to his shiny black shoes. His hair was a nondescript brown and he wore it short; his eyes hazel with flecks of gold; his build solid on a five-foot-ten-inch frame. He'd missed being handsome by a frog hair, but he made up for it in pure sex appeal and charm. When he walked into a room, he brought a force with him that said, "Look at me and just wish you were with me," and when he poured on the charm, there wasn't a woman in the world who wouldn't drop her under-britches for him.

She bent down and swiped the paper remnants from his shoes. Anna Ruth would go up in flames if he tracked paper into her perfect house.

"You could vacuum," he said.

"Yes, and you could have been a good husband and not cheated on me." She followed him to the back door, picking more paper from the butt of his uniform.

He brushed a kiss across her forehead. "See you next week," he whispered before he slipped out the back door and quickly blended into the mass of milling men in uniforms.

"What happened around here? I was on my way home. Heard it on the radio. Parked over in the church lot since everything was full here," Andy asked Jack.

Jack shook his head slowly. "Agnes thought she saw someone up there fightin' with Trixie, but it wasn't nothing. Agnes told my officer that she could see shadows behind the window shades and the man threw Trixie down on the bed and was raping her."

Trixie made out every word even though it was muddled. So it had been the candles that had brought the mothball queen across the street with her fedora and shotgun. Lord, Agnes Flynn was a meddlesome old witch. Claudia Burton Andrews had taken care of Agnes like she was her mother instead of her aunt, and she'd passed the legacy of looking after her on down to Cathy and Marty. But Trixie damn sure hadn't taken on the job of taking care of the nosy old toot, so she could keep her red hair, stinky getup, and shotgun across the street.

"She wasn't defending a damn thing for me. She was just making sure nobody was getting something that she couldn't. If it had been a rapist, she would have probably insisted I share with her," Trixie muttered.

Next week she was buying black-out drapes. No telling what would happen if Anna Ruth, Andy's live-in girlfriend, found out he spent Wednesday nights in Trixie's bed. And if Agnes ever discovered it, heaven help everyone, because the whole town of Cadillac, all 1,542 people, would know about it by breakfast the next morning. Agnes had a gossip hotline that worked faster than a sophomore boy his first time.

Trixie heaved a sigh of relief when all the cop cars and the ambulance were finally gone. She'd deal with the shotgun and the hole in the ceiling later. Right then she needed a good stiff drink. She pushed the chair back, rustled around in the cabinet, and found the whiskey. She poured two fingers of Jack Daniels in a jelly glass, added one ice cube, brushed plaster dust from her chenille robe and hair, and sat back down at the table. It was a poor substitute for a bout of good old passionate sex, but at least it warmed her insides.

Chapter 2

ANDY WAS ALMOST ACROSS Fourth Street when, from the corner of his eye, he saw someone smack in the middle of the pavement. Surely some bum hadn't passed out cold. It was Wednesday, not Saturday when all the drunks came out of the mesquite and woodwork. Dammit! Had there been someone hiding in the attic and Agnes's shotgun blast wounded them? Then the person sat up and brushed leaves from their hair and clothing.

Tall and thin, she had dark hair that fell to her waist and brown eyes. In her best earning days, she'd been the cream of the crop, but gravity had begun to work on her face, and at forty, she had hung up her hooker shoes and her suitcase of sex toys.

"Good evening, Andy," Darla Jean said.

Andy extended a hand. "What in the hell are you doing sitting there? I thought you were a drunk or a dead man."

She reached up and took his hand. "I was on my way to see if you were dead and I fell down."

He pulled her up. "Why would you think I'm dead?"

"Thanks for the hand. Figured Marty came home early from her classes, caught you, and killed you."

The woman had always intimidated the hell out of Andy. He cleared his throat. "It was Agnes, and she shot the ceiling. I got away without a scratch. I got to admit I ducked when that blast went off, though."

Darla reached out and brushed a bit of paper from his shoulder.

"Trixie all right?"

"She might appreciate you dropping by," Andy said.

"That's where I'm headed." Darla Jean kicked off the other flip-flop, leaving them both on the street.

"That is littering, and it's too late in the year to be wearing flip-flops," Andy said.

"What you were doing might be adultery, and what kind of shoes I wear is none of your business," Darla Jean said.

"I'm not married to Anna Ruth," Andy said defensively.

"But you were married to Trixie when you started sleeping with Anna Ruth, weren't you?" Darla Jean shot over her shoulder.

Andy picked up the flip-flops and tossed them in his trunk before he drove out of the church parking lot.

Trixie poured a second shot. She couldn't remember when she didn't know Marty and Cathy Andrews. Their mothers had grown up in Cadillac and were friends. Then she and the twins—and Jack Landry—had grown up together. First as toddlers in church, then as rambunctious kids, and later as teenagers. After graduation, Jack went into the Army, leaving Trixie, Cathy, and Marty to share everything: joys, tears, PMS, boyfriend troubles, divorce, sex stories, and everything in between.

Through it all, they had each other. They'd been her bridesmaids when she married Andy right out of high school. They'd been her support system when she divorced him. And now they were business partners.

Marriage to Andy had not been easy for either of them, but they'd been young and foolish. If they'd been older and wiser, they would have known that his obsession toward neatness and her I-don't-give-a-shit-about-keeping-things-in-order attitude would never work. The only thing that kept their marriage together was wild, passionate sex, and his affair with Anna Ruth was the thing that ended it.

A month after the divorce was final, Trixie had run into Andy at the Walmart store in Sherman, six miles north of Cadillac. His hand brushed hers and it was all downhill from there. They couldn't keep their hands off each other anymore than they could back when they were in high school.

Yep, she'd shared everything with her friends—except for Wednesday nights with Andy. Marty would kill him graveyard dead if she ever saw him in the house. Cathy was sweet enough that she'd provide the shovels to bury his sorry old ass out under the crape myrtle bushes in the backyard, and they could probably get Darla Jean to say a prayer over his body. But it was Marty who'd do the actual murder because she'd never trusted him. She said from the beginning, back when he and Trixie started dating her senior year in high school, that he'd been a player since he was old enough to talk a girl's skirt up over her belly button and he'd never change. And he'd damn sure proven her right.

"Sorry sumbitch. I'm not going to sleep with him anymore," she declared.

Darla Jean didn't knock. She never did.

"You all right, girl? I just ran into that SOB, and I did hear you say you weren't sleeping with him, didn't I?" she asked as she pushed the door open.

"You did, but I won't stick with it. You know I won't. I never do." Trixie shook her head from side to side. "The blast is still ringing in my ears, but it's getting better. Did the sirens or the shot get your attention?"

"Honey, my first thought was that the Rapture had come. I even said a prayer in case Jesus returned," Darla Jean said.

Trixie looked down at Darla's feet.

"Lost 'em out on the street, but Andy couldn't leave them there to litter." She laughed. "The pavement was still warm, and the grass felt pretty good on my feet. October in Texas don't mean a person has to wear shoes, does it?"

"What would you have done if it had been the Rapture?" Trixie asked.

"Well, I wouldn't be standing here if it had been. I'd have been on my way to glory. Evidently the good Lord needs me to stay here a spell longer and take care of all y'all over here at Clawdy's. Now tell me what happened and how in the world you got Andy out so slick and how come Agnes looked like she was trick-or-treating."

Trixie raised her head. "That woman is going to be the death of all of us! Agnes was the one who called the cops and the ambulance. She thought I was being attacked in my room. I swear the old girl has a camera trained on the house. And she had a shotgun, I'm tellin' you, a real, honest-to-God loaded gun. There's a hole in the landing ceiling to prove it. And that's not even the worst of it! She dragged her dead husband's old clothes out of a mothball trunk and put them on so she'd look like a police officer. She had a fedora on top of that ratted-up red hair. You should have seen her!"

Darla Jean poured a cup of coffee from the pot and heated it in the microwave while she nibbled on a leftover hot roll from lunch.

"I did see her," she giggled, "while I was sitting on the street where I fell."

"Are you all right?" Trixie asked.

"I'm fine. Just my pride was hurt and your cheatin' husband even gave me a hand up. Who was she trying to shoot? You or Andy?" she asked.

"She blew a hole in the ceiling, and half the attic floated down on me. But it might have been a different story if I'd been holding that shotgun. We'd moved past the foreplay and were getting ready for the big production when the red, white, and blue strobes hit the window right along with the sirens."

"I wondered what all that dust was doing on you. Figured you'd taken up another hobby. You've got to start giving Andy a brushing before he leaves. He had your scrapbooking bits and pieces on him. They were shinin' on that dark uniform out there in the moonlight. You can bet if I can see them in the dark, they won't get past Anna Ruth." Darla Jean sat down at the table. "You havin' sweet tea?"

Trixie held up her glass. "I've got J.D.'s special brand of tea."

"Whiskey and another woman's man. Been there. Only difference was I got paid," Darla Jean told her.

"Oh, honey, I'm getting paid in more ways than one. I get good sex once a week, and I'm getting back at Anna Ruth at the same time. Why would he want to marry her? She can't be good in bed because if she was, he wouldn't be having sex with me every week," Trixie asked.

"Men marry for reasons other than sex. He don't need it from her long as you are puttin' out. Lord don't look kindly on a woman givin' it away to a married man."

"But it's okay if you sell it to him?" Trixie asked.

Darla Jean smiled, her big brown eyes twinkling. "Don't reckon he looks too kindly on that either or else he would have steered me in the direction of bein' a madam rather than a preacher when I quit the business. But this ain't about my past sins, Trixie Matthews! You almost got caught, girl! God is talkin' to you pretty strong. He's sayin' that if you don't give up your wickedness, he's goin' to stop talkin' and let Agnes take care of things. You want that?"

"Hell no! I'd rather face off with the devil as that old girl. But I'm not giving up my Wednesday nights, either. I'll just be more careful." Trixie giggled and felt some of the pressure release in her ears.

"There's lots of men you can have sex with. Why Andy?" Darla Jean asked.

"He drives me crazy. I make him nuts. I'm messy; he's a neat freak deluxe. Perfect is barely good enough for him. Anna Ruth is the same way. But put me and Andy in a bed and, honey, it's worth taking the risk for."

Cathy was sitting in the back booth of the Rib Joint, a little barbecue joint in Luella, Texas, when her phone rang.

"Shoot!" she mumbled. She was right at the end of the novel that just came out by Candy Parker, and it was so hot that she actually felt the heat coming through her e-reader. She'd discovered the author four years ago and pre-ordered all her books the day they were available. She always bought them in e-book format. She couldn't have faced Trixie or Marty if they'd known she was reading smut.

Agnes would pitch a hissy if she picked up one of Candy's books. Lord, she might have a coronary and it would be laid to Cathy's charge. Yes, ma'am, it was much easier to keep them on the e-reader. Agnes wouldn't even know how to access a book on it if she did find it lying about.

The phone rang four times and then there was a pause before it started ringing again. Someone must be in big trouble to need to talk to her that badly.

"Hello," she said sweetly.

"This is Beulah. I called Violet and she said you were already gone, and I called Marty but she's not answering, and there's not an answer at Clawdy's. And I'm worried plumb out of my mind. There were shots fired and the police cars, the ambulance, and the fire truck are all over at your house. I'm afraid to go outside and Jack won't answer my calls. I can just feel my blood pressure risin'. If someone has shot Jack, I don't know if I can stand it. I'm looking out the window now, and there are policemen everywhere and they're takin' Agnes…my God, what is she wearing? Cathy, she's shot Jack. And I'm afraid his black suit will be too small. Do you think they'll let me bury him in his uniform?" Beulah's voice cracked and she began to sob.

"I'll be home in five minutes, Beulah. Did you tell Agnes about the vote?" Cathy asked.

"Oh, honey, it was awful, just awful. She cussed and carried on and threatened to shoot Violet. Oh my God! Do you think she went over to Clawdy's and shot Trixie? I told her that Anna Ruth got chosen, but she was rantin' about so much that she might've thought it was Trixie who kept her from getting in the club."

"Agnes wouldn't do that even if she was mad. I'll call you. Don't worry, sweetheart—Jack is fine."

Cathy put her e-reader inside her oversized purse and headed for the door. Her high heels sunk into the gravel, and just as she got to her car, one popped clean off. She grabbed the hood to keep from falling. She hobbled around the car, crawled in, and looked longingly at her purse. A few more minutes and she'd have finished reading the chapter. She hated to stop in the middle of a scene, but it would have to wait.

She started up the car and sighed. If only her fiancé, Ethan, could be as passionate as the men that Candy Parker wrote about. It didn't matter if they were cowboys, firemen, navy SEALS, or even mechanics. They all had one thing in common. They knew how to turn a woman on until all she could think about were their hands and lips on every part of her body.

She muttered as she drove, "So Ethan isn't passionate. He is respectable and he has morals. After we are married, he'll show more emotion. He just doesn't want to get all involved when we've agreed not to have sex until we are married."

Actually, she could read about it every chance she got, but the real thing scared the bejesus out of her. In today's world, women were not virgins at thirty-four—but Cathy was. Marty lost her virginity at the age of fifteen and came home that night to sit on her twin bed and tell Cathy every single detail.

It had all started in high school right after Marty's first bad boy cowboy talked her into a hayloft and Andy talked Trixie into the backseat of his car. It had been easy for Cathy to let them think that she had been doing it as long as either of them. It was the one thing, possibly the only thing, she kept secret from them. Well, that and her appetite for erotic romance. At first it was easy just to let them think she was bonking the guy in the library where she went every night. She never actually said that she had sex, but a little insinuation can go a long way. Like telling them that they should try doing it in between the back two bookshelves because the danger of almost getting caught was so exciting.

Then when she was thirty and they'd gone to a male strip joint in Dallas to celebrate, she'd let them believe she was going home with Butch, the stripper cowboy in chaps, boots, and a barbed wire tat on his bicep. The next morning she just rolled her eyes and measured out about a foot between her hands when they asked her how things went with him in the motel room. Sometimes it wasn't what you actually said but what they thought they heard.

She held her breath as she turned off State Highway 11 and down Main Street. She didn't see flashing lights or hear sirens anywhere near the café. Everything was as quiet as it was every Wednesday night when she pulled up in the driveway. She parked her car and hit the back porch in a jog, threw open the door, and there were Trixie and Darla Jean sitting at the table, cool as cucumbers.

Trixie looked at Cathy's feet. "Is this barefoot night?"

"I broke a heel getting here. Beulah called and thought someone had shot Jack in this house. She said there were police cars and even the ambulance. Please tell me they didn't park on the lawn and ruin my flower beds. In the dark I couldn't see a blessed thing and I just put the pansies out last week. They've not even had time to get adjusted to the ground."

"Your lawn is fine. The flower beds didn't lose a single petal, and the trouble was Agnes," Trixie said.

"There were police cars, the ambulance, and the fire truck. But they kept it all on the curb," Darla Jean said.

Cathy's eyes went to the glass Trixie was holding. "Tea with no ice?"

"Jack Daniels, neat. Want one? You might need it before you go upstairs. Agnes brought her shotgun and blew a hole in the ceiling."

Cathy shook her head. She should be glad that no one was hurt and it was all a crazy mix-up, but she wasn't. She'd wanted to sit in the Rib Joint and finish her book. She'd even begged off from dessert at Ethan's, saying that she had to make sweet potato pies for Clawdy's lunch the next day and she'd best get on home to get a head start on them.

She pulled out a chair and sat down. She pushed the sleeves of her baby blue sweater up to the elbows, reached in her purse for her phone, and poked in some numbers. "I've got to call Beulah before y'all tell me the story. She thinks Jack is lyin' over here dead, and she's frettin' about whether his black suit is goin' to be too tight."

"That's Beulah," Trixie said.

Cathy finished her call and looked up. "I smell mothballs."

"Agnes called in the troops when she thought she saw someone molesting me. I had candles lit and the shades drawn. Who knows what she saw. Probably me putting on or taking off my big chenille robe, and she came over here smelling like rat piss and mothballs," Trixie said.

"Smelling like what?"

"You heard me. You should have seen her, Cathy. She pulled her husband's old clothes out of a mothball trunk and put them on so the rapist would think she was the Cadillac police." Trixie reached for the whiskey to refill her glass. "Sure you don't want one?"

"After tonight it looks tempting, but no thanks," Cathy said.

"Agnes would drive a holiness preacher to whiskey. Want me to see if Andy can fix that hole in the ceiling over the weekend?"

Cathy grabbed the whiskey from her hands and put it back in the cabinet. "You stay away from that man! He cheated on you and broke your heart. I won't let him drive you into alcoholism. I mean it, Trixie!"

Darla Jean snorted when she giggled.

Trixie shot her a look that said the night wasn't over and the shotgun had not gone home yet. "Hey, don't punish me because you couldn't get me into your club shit. I wouldn't have gone to the meetings anyway, even if they had voted me in. Why in the hell would I put myself into a situation where I had to be in the same room with Anna Ruth?"

"But if you'd won, she wouldn't be there." Cathy rolled her big blue-green eyes toward the ceiling.

Trixie changed the subject. "So did you and Ethan finally get in the horizontal position tonight?"

"I told you Ethan is a gentleman. We are saving sex until our wedding night when I fully well intend to get pregnant with a son, Ethan Prescott the fifth. Doesn't that sound classy? Ethan's middle name is Edward so we'll probably call him that and he's going to have blond hair and big blue eyes. "

"It'll be a girl and look and act just like Marty. One of those McCleary genes might surface and she'll have red hair and look like Agnes," Trixie whispered. She could hear better and her hands weren't shaking anymore. Thank God for Jack Daniels.

"I've waited..." Cathy hesitated before she spit out anymore.

"Waited for what?" Darla Jean asked.

"A man I can trust. Someone who loves me and won't cheat on me."

Trixie held up the glass with only a few drops of whiskey in the bottom. "Touché, Cathy."

"I'm sorry, that was mean. I'm tired and cranky. I didn't sleep well last night, and I don't want to be in a club with Anna Ruth."

Trixie nodded. "You are forgiven, darlin'. I'd be pissy if I had to go out to that museum called the Prescott house and spend time with Violet every week and had to face off with Anna Ruth once a month."

Cathy fidgeted in the chair. "Violet's not so bad. She just wants the very best for her son. As bad as I want a baby, I can almost understand her, but I'm tellin' you, I'll be glad when Ethan and I are married, have our own place, and don't have to deal with her every time we are together."

"You are a pushover, girl." Trixie removed her arm.

"No I'm not. I just try to be fair."

"And do you understand Anna Ruth too?" Trixie asked.

"She is enough to drive me to the whiskey bottle with you."

"And Andy? Do you feel sorry for him?" Trixie pushed.

"He doesn't deserve to be understood. He cheated on you, and I'm not going to like him. I don't want to talk about him or Agnes anymore. You promised to help me plan this wedding even though you aren't fond of Ethan. I helped you plan yours, and I didn't care much for Andy even then. At least I don't have to worry about Ethan cheating on me."

"Bravo," Darla Jean said.

"I'm so sorry. That was ugly. What is the matter with me tonight?" Cathy groaned.

"But it was true. Your mamma and y'all girls did help with my wedding. Besides, Ethan will have his hands full with two women. He wouldn't cheat on you, because that would involve a third woman in his life. He'd stroke out if he tried three," Trixie said.

Cathy raised a perfectly arched eyebrow. "Three?"

"You and Mommy Dearest are about all he'll be able to handle, especially with his campaign going on. No way would he bring in a mistress." Trixie's hearing was almost normal and the whiskey was mellowing her out. "And, honey, even if I do think he's a stuffy old fart, I intend for you to have one helluva wedding. Three months from now you will have the biggest splash Cadillac, Texas, has ever seen. We'll even hire guards to keep the paparazzi back. It'll be bigger than the Christmas Ho-Ho-Ho. I mean, after all, you are marrying Ethan Prescott the fourth, the richest bastard in Cadillac, Texas."

Cathy smiled. "Not the richest and not a bastard. His mamma and poppa were married."

Marty looked over the top of her laptop computer at the students in her Adult Basic Education class. She only had to lean a little to the left and there he was in the flesh: Derek, the young cowboy who was the hero in her newest work in progress. His hair was dark, his chest was broad, and those biceps were made to hold a woman. She shut her eyes just long enough to get a good solid image of him naked and then she opened them and began to type.

It had begun as an outlet while she was still teaching full time. Nowadays, she used the time she was monitoring her ABE class to catch up on writing. Her students were all full-grown adults brushing up their skills to take the GED test.

That required little actual teaching. She stacked booklets on the end of her desk, and her students picked them up at the beginning of class. They worked at their own speed and raised a hand when they needed one-on-one help. If they finished early, they put their name on the front of the booklet and gave it back to her to grade. If they didn't get it done by the time class ended, they put their name on the front and left it on the other end of her desk so they could work on it again the next week. Eight weeks to complete the class and then they took their GED test. If they passed, she never saw them again. If they didn't need a lot of help, she could get the biggest part of a rough draft done in that time.

When her first book sold and her editor asked her if she was going to write under her name or an assumed one, she made the decision to use the pseudonym Candy Parker. She didn't intend for anyone in Cadillac ever to know that she was writing erotic romance. She'd never do anything to embarrass her sister. So Candy Parker, the erotic romance writer, was her second secret. The first being keeping Aunt Agnes out of the social club, no matter what the cost.

Class had ended, and she was standing on the sidewalk outside the college classroom building, watching Derek's cute little butt get into his truck when her phone rang. If she was ten years younger she might have a little sample of that cowboy. She didn't mind if her flings were slightly younger, but nineteen was just too damned young.

She answered the phone on the fourth ring just before it went to voice mail. "Hello."

"Marty, I just passed Clawdy's, and something has happened. There's police cars and the ambulance and the fire truck all there," said Christopher Green, a regular at the café.

"Thanks, Christopher. I'm on my way home," she said.

"Sure thing. Hope everything is all right."

"You sure it was my place or Aunt Agnes's? She lives right across the street."

"No, it was yours. They were leading Agnes back across the street. I had to stop and wait for the officer to get her across. Wouldn't have known the old girl, but that red hair can't be missed. She was wearing some kind of weird getup. Reckon she's gone off the deep end?"

"I don't have any idea, but I'm going home to see about it," Marty said.

Dammit! Agnes had never liked Trixie or Janie. Had the old girl snuck in the café and killed Trixie in her sleep? Marty didn't need a second speeding ticket in the same night so she kept a close watch on the speedometer. But when she left the main highway and entered the Cadillac city limits, she stepped on the gas. Andy or any of his town policemen wouldn't stop Marty. Most of them had lunch at Clawdy's on a regular basis and she was the cook. They'd be afraid to give her a ticket.

She hit the back door in a dead run. "What in the hell happened here? I got a call that there was an ambulance here."

"You done missed the excitement," Darla Jean said.

Marty looked at Trixie.

Trixie shrugged. "Aunt Agnes."

"Dammit, Cathy! We ought to put her in a nursing home. What'd she do—get mad as hell over that stupid club vote and come over here to start a fight with Trixie?" Marty asked.

"She threw a fit about the club, but that wasn't the problem. And she ain't never goin' to a nursing home," Cathy said. "Mamma made me promise after Daddy died so sudden that if she went like that, we'd take care of Aunt Agnes."

Marty pulled a cold beer from the refrigerator. She'd promised her mother something about Aunt Agnes too and had gotten a speeding ticket that night, so she knew something about promises, but she damn sure didn't have to like them.

"And you're marrying Mr. Hoity-Toity and leaving me with the job. I didn't make a promise, so my way of putting up with her is to poison the old witch and then shed a fake tear at her funeral. What'd she do?" Marty leaned against the counter and looked at Trixie. "You look like hell rained down on you."

Trixie told the story for the third time while Marty drank two beers and swore the whole time.

Trixie pointed to the cabinet. "Cathy won't let me have another two fingers of Jack and I deserve it. It rained plaster dust, insulation, and who knows what from the attic. I might die from some kind of antique dust mite poisoning unless I wash all the stuff out of my system with whiskey."

Marty melted into the last chair around the table. "When you start telling jokes that aren't funny, you've had enough. I hope Aunt Agnes is constipated all day tomorrow and can't even come over here. I don't want to see her for a week."

"Marty! She was protecting Trixie. I'd say she gets a gold star for that because she doesn't even like Trixie," Cathy exclaimed.

"Oh, stop being so nice. You know she's a meddling old woman," Marty said.

"I'm tired of this whole thing. I'm going to bed," Cathy said.

Before she could stand up, the kitchen door flew open without even a knock and Anna Ruth blew into the room like a whirlwind. She grabbed Cathy around the neck and hugged her so tightly that Cathy's eyes bugged out and then she headed toward Marty.

"I was so excited that we're going to be club sisters that I had to rush over here and tell you. Isn't it just the most exciting thing ever?" She beamed.

Trixie and Marty locked gazes somewhere between the table and cabinet. It was one of those times when two lifetime friends could speak without using a single word. Marty would help Trixie mop up Main Street with Anna Ruth. All Trixie had to do was nod.

"Anna Ruth, I hardly think it's appropriate for you to be—"

Anna Ruth interrupted before Cathy could finish the sentence. "Oh, don't be silly. Trixie knows that she never had a chance at the club, don't you?"

Marty stepped to one side. "What she's saying is that Clawdy's is closed."

"But we are club sisters now. I have the right to come in the kitchen and talk to my sisters," Anna Ruth protested.

"No, you don't," Trixie said.

"Tell her, Cathy. She's just mad because I won and she lost."

"Well, there is something about breaking up my marriage. Of course, it's a little thing," Trixie said.

Anna Ruth shrugged. "That doesn't count. This is about the club, for God's sake."

"I'm going back to the church. Anna Ruth, I'll walk you out." Darla looped an arm around Anna Ruth's shoulders. The small woman had no choice but to let herself be led outside. "Y'all remember to lock the door," Darla Jean said over her shoulder. "We've had enough excitement for one night on our block."

"Now I'm really going up to my room." Cathy disappeared up the stairs.

"Lord, have mercy! How many times did she shoot the ceiling? It's a mess up here," she yelled in a few seconds.

"I'll clean it up," Trixie called up the stairs.

"Go on to bed. You fended off Aunt Agnes and didn't pick up a butcher knife and kill Anna Ruth. I'll do the clean-up," Marty said.

Trixie covered a yawn with the back of her hand. "Guess I'm off to bed."

Marty nodded. When she was alone, she retrieved her laptop from her truck and opened it at the kitchen table. She only had another five thousand words and she'd have the rough draft done, but nothing came to mind without her sexy cowboy muse.

She sat there another ten minutes before she shut the laptop. It was all Agnes's fault. She was a busybody who spied on everything that went on in the whole town of Cadillac and especially at Clawdy's. But if Agnes said she saw two people in that bedroom, then she probably did. So who in the hell was Trixie having sex with?

Chapter 3

If Agnes really would have shot someone in Clawdy's the night before, they would have had to hire another cook and two more waitresses. Thursday wasn't usually a busy day at Clawdy's, but that morning Marty couldn't keep up with the orders. Cathy had to help in the kitchen, leaving Trixie to do all the waitressing and payouts at the cash register. A ruckus involving a shotgun would have been the talk of the town no matter where it happened, but Miss Clawdy's Café offered a place to sit, damn fine food, and unlimited refills on coffee. And it also gave the folks in Cadillac the opportunity to weasel more information out of Trixie. Not a bad deal for less than five dollars.

Rumor had it that Trixie and Agnes got into an argument over the voting at the social club and Agnes tried to kill her. Beulah said the cops and the ambulance were called out and that she feared that her precious son, Jack, had survived two tours of Iraq only to come home and be killed—and all because Agnes Flynn thought Trixie had gotten into the social club and she had gotten left behind for the twentieth time.

That morning, Clawdy's customers went through two extra pans of biscuits and a second gallon of sausage gravy, and Marty completely ran out of bacon and ham steaks. Everyone left full and unsatisfied, because all Trixie would say was that Agnes thought she saw someone hurting her and rushed across the street to protect her. Now that was a big crock of bullshit. Everyone knew there wasn't a smidgen of love lost between Trixie and Agnes, and there was no way in hell she would protect Trixie from anything or anyone. No, sir, that was a lie, but never fear, the gossipmongers would ferret out the truth if it absolutely killed them.

It was ten thirty when Trixie finally had time for a five-minute break and poured herself a cup of coffee. She sat down at the kitchen table with Cathy and Marty and buttered a leftover biscuit. She'd barely gotten the first bite when the back door slung open and the faint aroma of mothballs filled the room.

"Good mornin', Aunt Agnes," Cathy said. "You had breakfast?"

"Hell yes, I've had breakfast, but that was hours ago. I wish y'all had the buffet up and ready. Now I'm ready for fried chicken."

"It's not ready, but I've got some leftovers from yesterday. You want me to pop them in the microwave?"

"Got beans and greens?" Agnes asked.

"Maybe a cup full of each."

"Two pieces of dark chicken and whatever beans and greens you've got with pepper jelly on the side for my corn bread," she said.

"You're not mad at me? I figured you'd still be mad because you were wrong last night," Trixie said.

"I don't like you enough to be mad at you and I wasn't wrong. Somebody was in that room with you. I'm mad at Cathy," Agnes declared.

"What did I do?" Cathy asked.

"You're the one who put Trixie's name in the pot for the social club. If you hadn't done that fool thing, then there would have been the six votes for me that she got."

"And I didn't even want to be in the damned old club," Trixie said.

"How did you vote?" Agnes pointed at Marty. "I figured Cathy wouldn't betray me, but she did. I guess you did too."

Trixie waved to get everyone's attention. "Okay, Agnes, how did you vote in the last presidential election?"

"That is not one damn bit of your business," Agnes huffed.

"Point proven then," Marty said. "Voting is private."

"And Beulah should not have told you how many votes went which way," Cathy chimed in.

Agnes shook her finger at the lot of them. "I'm going to be in that social club before I die. Speakin' of which, Violet is about to put in a miserable year. It'd be in her best interest to shoot a member"—she looked right at Marty—"or find a way to make one move."

"Why don't you shoot Violet? She's the one who doesn't want you to be a member," Trixie said.

"Because I want her to be alive and well the day she has to give me that little club pin to put on my lapel that says I'm a member. Put my food in a to-go box, Marty. I've had all of y'all I want for one day. It's a cryin' damn shame when a woman's nieces treat her this way."

"You can have my pin," Marty said.

"Those are the gaudiest damn things I've ever seen! I don't know why you'd want one of the ugly things," Trixie said.

"I know! Back when Violet and Mamma designed them, they were to show the Fannin County women's club that they had bragging rights to the hottest jalapeños in the whole state. Did you know they only had twenty-one of them made and that's the reason there can't be any more members in the club than that?" Cathy said.

"I thought the original charter said twenty." Marty raised an eyebrow.

"It did, but Grandma wanted an extra one made just in case someone lost theirs. That's why they had the extra one so that we could both get in."

"Hmph," Agnes snorted. "Nobody ever lost one of those ugly things. Hell, Violet would stand at the Pearly Gates and kick them into hell if they lost a club pin."

Trixie giggled. "BR—Bitches Rule—in ruby red letters. Then the little emerald green jalapeño, which must stand for hot as hell. And after that S in rubies. I heard that in the beginning there was a big argument and the S should be a C for club instead of an S for society."

"It stands for 'stupidity,'" Agnes said.

Brenda Lee was belting out "Sweet Nothin's" when the front door opened, and Trixie left Agnes still fussing, Cathy trying to calm her down, and Marty unloading the dishwasher. Customers had to be waited on no matter what the kitchen drama of the day was.

"What in the hell are you doing here?" Trixie hissed when she saw Andy.

Andy bypassed the cash register counter and sat down at a table in the old dining room. "A piece of sweet potato pie and a cup of coffee. That's not a very nice line for a waitress. It won't get you a tip, even if you do look like a young version of the woman singing that song. And would you please pour the coffee and cut my slice of pie? Marty might do something evil to it. I figure if Anna Ruth is welcome here, her being a club sister and all, then I should be able to get a good meal here at Clawdy's. Right?"

"The sweet potato pie won't be ready to serve until noon. All we have left from yesterday is pecan cobbler," she said.

"My favorite. Add some of y'all's whipped cream to the top. Not any of that stuff out of the tub or the can, either. I know the difference in fake and the real thing," he said.

"Don't bet on it, buster," Trixie said.

Trixie filled a bowl with cobbler, warmed it in the microwave, and then topped it off with the last of yesterday's whipped cream. She poured a cup of coffee, put both on a tray, and carried them out to Andy's table.

Damn the club anyway! She could wring Cathy's neck for putting her name on the ballot. And who in the devil *did* Marty vote for? If she had cast her vote for Anna Ruth, Trixie was selling her part of the business and moving plumb out of Cadillac.

Clawdy's only served breakfast and lunch. Most days the lunch rush was over and done with by two and the café cleaned up by three, but that day, it was four straight up when Marty turned off the music. When the sisters got serious about converting their parents' home into a café, they used their mother's record covers for decoration and played the old music from them all day. It made a lively conversation starter when folks heard the song and tried to find the cover hanging on the wall that went with it. Thank goodness many of the old records had been remade into CDs. After that it was just a matter of buying a fancy player that held multiple CDs and changing them every night.

Marty shucked out of her jeans right in the middle of the kitchen floor and carried them to the utility room. She peeled her shirt over her head and threw it in the basket beside the washer and found an old grease-stained sweatshirt in the dryer and a pair of gray sweatpants that were stained up just as bad.

"See y'all later. I'm off to the garage. Trixie, give me your keys and I'll get the oil changed in your car before we start on the Caddy."

Trixie fished keys from her purse and tossed them. "Thanks a bunch."

Marty caught them midair. "You've got that Chamber meeting, so I'll get it done while you're over at the community center. What are you doing this evening, Cathy?"

"Soon as I get out of these clothes, I'm going to make sure my flowers are all right, prune the crape myrtles, and harvest another crop of peppers before it frosts. I've got seeds, but I swear the people coming in here to eat can put away two quarts of pepper jelly a day."

"You always plant the peppers right where your grandma and mamma did?" Trixie asked.

"Oh, yes. I'd be afraid to move them anywhere else for fear they wouldn't do as well."

"I bet the secret to raisin' them hot devils is in the soil then, not in the pepper seeds."

Cathy put a finger over her lips. "Shh. I figured that out a while back, but we can't let the Fannin County women know it or they'll be digging up my dirt. I don't know what they put in that dirt, but it grows some fine jalapeños. What are you doing until Chamber time?"

"I'm going to tally up today's receipts and get a bank deposit ready to put in the night drop. After the meeting, I'm going to work on my scrapbook. Mamma's birthday will be here soon, and I'm hoping the pictures will jog her memory so she'll be herself that day," Trixie answered.

"I'll see y'all later." Marty waved from the back door. She jogged from the house to the garage, a freestanding building at the back of the lot where her vintage Caddy was kept. She inhaled deeply at the door. Oil, grease, tires, and car wax. It was the most exciting thing in the world, next to a naked cowboy in a hayloft.

"Hey, you're here!" Jack's head popped up from under the hood. He already had grease on his nose and a smear across his forehead. "Must've been one helluva busy day, but then it's not every day that Agnes almost kills me, is it?"

Jack wasn't the hunky material for a hero in her book, but he was a good-looking man. His brown hair was kept in a military cut, his shoulders were wide, and the spare tire around his waist wasn't too awfully big. His hazel eyes were kind, and he'd never, not one time, let her down when she needed a friend. Like her, he could fix anything under the hood of a car. And he was a whole hell of a lot better at bodywork than she was.

"How'd you get into the story?" Marty asked.

"Mamma called Violet since you weren't answering your phone and told her that shots had been fired and I was dead. Rumor has it that Agnes was doin' the shootin' and that I got shot protecting Trixie. Trixie was the dirty culprit, and the whole thing had to do with y'all's club stuff."

"It's like that game we played when we were kids and someone whispered a sentence in your ear. By the time it got to the end of the line, it was so far removed from the original that it was just plumb crazy." Marty giggled. "We need to change the oil in Trixie's car before we start on the Caddy."

"That because you feel guilty that you voted for Anna Ruth and not Agnes or Trixie?" Jack asked.

Marty sputtered and stammered, "What did you just say?"

"Mamma said that you folded your ballot and that you came in late and was the only one who put a folded one in the bowl. Don't worry, I'm not telling, and if Mamma hadn't thought I was dead, she probably wouldn't have let it slip either. She's afraid that if any of the club members find out that she let the cat out of the bag they'll kick her out. Must be something sacred goes on at those meetings. Do y'all kill a fatted calf or what?"

Marty opened the old rounded refrigerator with rust around the door and pulled out a beer. She jerked the tab off and guzzled a third of it before coming up with an unladylike burp.

"Not bad for a skinny-ass girl." Jack laughed. "Come look at this belt. Think we ought to replace it? You going to tell me about the fatted calf?"

"I wouldn't know. The only time I show up is to vote. We'll change the belt if it needs it. Which one?"

"The long one right here," he said.

Six months before, one of the belts had blown, and Marty lost control out on a country road. A tree stopped the car and Marty wasn't hurt, but the Caddy suffered severe front end damage. Jack had been helping a couple of nights a week.

She carried her beer to the pegboard where belts, small spare parts, and tools were neatly arranged. She picked out the right one and laid it on the fender.

"Where's your beer?" she asked.

"I just got here a minute before you did. Alarm didn't go off when it was supposed to. Here. You put on the belt, and I'll get one," he answered.

She took a screwdriver from his hand, deftly removed the old belt, held it up to the light, and pointed at the split. "Another mile and we'd have had a real problem. Can't have the old girl breaking down right in the middle of the Cadillac Jalapeño Jubilee parade, can we? She's been leading the pack for more than forty years."

She was putting the new belt on when the wrench popped off and her knuckles hit the engine. She jerked her hand back, shook it, and yelled, "Son of a bitch!"

"Hurt?" Jack asked.

"What the hell do you think?"

He took her hand in his, and before she could wiggle, he poured the rest of her beer right on the open cuts. "That'll heal it. You want me to put the belt on?"

"Hell no! My hand is busted up now, and I'll make a damn believer out of it all by myself. Some friend you are, pouring beer on my poor hand."

"Bubbles will clean it out. Stop your whinin' and let's get this damn thing on."

"Soon as this belt is on, we need to change the oil in Trixie's car. Should have done it to begin with and I might not have busted my knuckles. Wipe that grin off your face. Some friend you are," Marty said.

"Ah, you know you've loved me forever," Jack teased.

He had lived right next door his whole life and he'd moved back home two years before. He'd planned on staying with the military the full twenty years, but after that last tour in Iraq, he'd had enough.

The yards were split by a white picket fence with lantana on Cathy's side and miniature roses on Beulah's side. A gate was located right in the middle of the long expanse of fence and still squeaked on its hinges like it did when Cathy, Marty, Trixie, and

Jack had run back and forth between the yards and houses all their growing-up years.

"What are we going to do in the evenings when we get the Caddy completely finished?" Jack asked.

"Well, I expect we can drink beer and just sit back and enjoy our work. Long as I can prop up my feet, talk to my friend even when he teases me, and smell oil and transmission fluid, I'm a happy woman."

That time the belt slipped on as slick as if she'd greased the posts with hot butter.

"We could go over to my house and watch movies," Jack said.

"Your house don't smell like oil and transmission fluid. And I bet Beulah would pitch a hissy if we took beer in the kitchen door."

"Yes, ma'am, she would. Speakin' of kitchens?" He waggled his eyebrows.

"There's some cold fried chicken and a plate of fried fish left."

"Any Cathy's sweet potato pie?"

"Couple of pieces and I think there's a little bit of loaded mashed potatoes left in the refrigerator."

He nodded. "I'll have both slices of that pie and I want pepper jelly for my biscuit. Ain't nobody in the world can make pepper jelly like y'all do. It's my favorite."

"With whipped cream and lots of it on the pie, right?" Marty smiled. Jack had always liked eating at her house better than his mamma's. Beulah, bless her heart, knew her way around a kitchen, but what she produced couldn't compare to Claudia Andrews's cooking.

Trixie darted upstairs, took a fast shower, and dressed in black slacks, a red shirt with black lace on the scoop neck, and black high heels. She was the Chamber of Commerce delegate for Miss Clawdy's Café. The Chamber and the City Council both helped with all the festivities in Cadillac, and that night they were discussing the craft festival, which was always held the weekend before Halloween. After that there would be the Jalapeño Jubilee in November and finally the big Christmas Ho-Ho-Ho Parade and Carnival in the middle of December. Then there was the town musical in the spring between Easter and Mother's Day and the July 4th festival. Cadillac was one busy little town.

Each partner at Miss Clawdy's had a community job. Trixie had been on the Chamber roster when she worked at the bank, so she was familiar with all the members and kept that place. Cathy was a member of the club and they were always big in the Jalapeño Jubilee. Marty was the secretary of the local Kiwanis Club and they did the Christmas Ho-Ho-Ho. So they all had a holiday responsibility.

Trixie looked up at the clock. She still had fifteen minutes. She might have time for a piece of cold fried fish if she ate fast. They'd have finger foods at the committee meeting. The Lord would strike Beulah Landry dead if she didn't bring her deviled eggs to every single function and Beulah, like Violet Prescott, was one of the grand matriarchs of southern Grayson County. And Annabel would bring fancy cookies. Someone else would have those little tidbits with ham and cheese rolled up in flour tortillas and cut into bite-sized pieces. In Cadillac, folks brought food to everything. It didn't matter if it was a Chamber meeting, a funeral, or a baby shower. The catch was that the food wasn't served until the function was over and Trixie would starve if someone got long-winded at the Chamber meeting.

Trixie grabbed a piece of fish and was about to take a bite when Agnes pushed into the kitchen. "I'm hungry. Y'all got any fish or chicken left? And I want a piece of that sweet potato pie, too."

"Got some fish and a few pieces of chicken. The pie is gone. Marty carried the last two pieces out to Jack."

"Well, shit. She's probably bribin' him to keep his mouth shut about the vote." Agnes pulled down a to-go box and loaded it with chicken strips and fish.

"How would he know anything about that stupid club?"

"His mamma talks too much. Put this on my bill. I'm still not talkin' to you."

"You would have talked to Anna Ruth if y'all were in club together, though, wouldn't you? And she's not a bit better than my mamma."

"No, she's not, and when I get into the club she'd best be married to that philanderin' son-of-a-bitch you couldn't hang on to or I'll vote that we kick her sorry ass out. I'm leaving now because I'm not talkin' to you."

"You going to fix the ceiling?" Trixie called out when she was on her way out.

"Hell, no! I was protecting you so you can get someone to come fix the ceiling. Besides, the twins need to update the upstairs anyway. I'll never understand why they'd sink all their money into a café, for God's sake. And namin' it such a stupid name. Don't be askin' me to bail you out when it goes belly-up in this economy. Folks ain't interested in good food. They want something fast and easy," Agnes said.

"Oh, we have a backup plan, Agnes. If the café fails, we're going to change the sign to Miss Clawdy's Brothel, and underneath it's going to say, *Y'all come on in and check out our menu.* You want a job answering the phone for us?" Trixie asked.

Agnes narrowed her eyes and clucked her tongue like a hen gathering chickens in a thunderstorm. "I knew when they let you move in here there would be trouble. I swear to God you are a bad apple, girl. Only one over here worth a dime is Cathy, and that's because she's kind like her mother was. I can't believe that Claudia took one look at those two little babies and named the wrong damn one after me. Catherine should have my name. Not Marty!"

"Why thank you, Aunty Agnes, but I disagree about the names.

Marty is just like her Aunty Martha Agnes, so I think they were named right," Trixie said.

Agnes shook her bony finger at Trixie. "I'm not your aunt and if I was, I'd take you to the river and drown you."

Cathy was in the yard pulling weeds away from the sweet williams and the marigolds on the east side of the house when her phone rang. She didn't even check the ID before she pulled it out of her bibbed overall pocket and answered it.

"Hello," she said sweetly.

"Cathy, what was going on there last night?" Ethan said.

"Agnes thought someone was in the bedroom hurting Trixie." Cathy sat down and pulled the sleeves to her sweater down to her wrists. "I was coming home when Beulah called me. She was afraid that Jack had been shot."

"Okay, then. I just had a few minutes and wanted to check on you. I've got another campaign meeting this evening. It's a busy time with the last weeks of the election. I'll see you on Saturday night."

"I love you, Ethan," Cathy said.

"Me too," he answered.

Why was it so hard for him to actually say the words, *I love you*? He had to love her, didn't he? He had proposed and they were getting married in less than two months.

Cathy put the phone back in the bib pocket and leaned back on her elbows.

The phone rang again and she bit back a string of cuss words that would have scorched the hair out of a bullfrog's nostrils when she saw that it was Anna Ruth.

"Hello?" she said tersely.

Marty would have loved it if she'd lost her temper and actually said all the words about to explode in her head.

"I just had to touch base with you since we're club sisters now. Are you involved with the craft show this fall? Violet called and asked me to be at the Chamber meeting tonight and I wondered if we might get a cup of coffee afterward."

"I'm not involved with that," Cathy said.

"Marty?"

"No?"

"Don't tell me Trixie is."

Cathy sighed. "Anna Ruth, Trixie is my oldest and dearest friend. I'm not talking about her to you."

"Well, I'm your club sister, so that card trumps a friendship," Anna Ruth shot back.

"I don't think so."

Anna Ruth could suck the energy out of a Jehovah's Witness in thirty seconds flat.

"Well, I'm a better friend because I've worried myself sick all day that Trixie might have caused you to have a heart attack last night."

"Why would I have a heart attack? Healthy people don't have heart attacks at thirty-four," Cathy said.

"Well, you do have to deal with a drunk friend, and there is the stress of the wedding," Anna Ruth said. "I've got to go now. I'm in front of the community room. Oh, I can see you across the street. I'm waving at you. About that coffee afterward. We could still go."

"As you can see, I'm busy, so no, thank you." Cathy disconnected and put the phone back in her pocket.

A fat robin flew down from a tree and pulled a nice big juicy earthworm from the earth where she'd been digging. She sat very still and watched him. And then it dawned on her that Trixie had already left for the Chamber meeting and Anna Ruth was on the way. She should at least warn Trixie!

She sat up so fast that it startled the robin. He flew away and dropped the worm on her bare foot. She flicked it off and grabbed the phone out of her pocket. She hit the speed dial button for Trixie and tapped her foot as she waited. On the fifth ring it went to voice mail. She tried a second time and it went straight to voice mail.

Too late.

She couldn't get dressed in time to go support Trixie in the meeting where Anna Ruth was headed. And she sure couldn't show up at a town meeting in her overalls. Lord, Violet would stroke out right there in front of everyone.

If Trixie wasn't home in an hour, Cathy would call the police station and ask what Trixie's bail was for strangling Anna Ruth until her big blue eyes popped out of her head. Cathy would hock everything, including Miss Clawdy's and Marty's Caddy if it was necessary to get Trixie out of jail. She just wished she had had time to get cleaned up and see the fireworks.

Trixie held a paper plate with three small thumbprint cookies. They weren't bad, but one bite said they weren't from Annabel's kitchen. That night Annabel had brought a dip with horseradish sauce and cream cheese and Trixie hated horseradish. She should have volunteered for refreshments and brought Marty's pumpkin tartlets. At least people wouldn't be wrapping them in the cute little purple napkins and tossing them into the trash can like they were doing the thumbprint cookies.

Violet Prescott, Cathy's future mother-in-law, popped the wooden gavel on the podium twice. The room went silent and everyone proceeded to find a chair like little windup toys. Trixie turned her paper plate upside down in the trash can to cover up the cookies and the horseradish dip that had nearly sent her into a gagging fit. Violet shot a look her way that said she'd best get in her seat, so she hurriedly slid into the last chair in the front row. She looked up at the clock and got another ugly stare from Violet. No one questioned her ability to start a meeting right on time! The first thing a Cadillac citizen learned was Violet was the queen bee in Cadillac. The second was that you never ever crossed Violet. The third was that you never approached her unless she held out the golden scepter—that being her forefinger, which was, honest to God, adorned with a fourteen-carat gold fingernail.

"If everyone is seated, we will begin our meeting." Violet's double chin wobbled like a bobble-head doll every time she moved. Trixie bit her lip to keep from giggling. Laughing at the queen could get her in big trouble. She might have to eat that horrid horseradish dip as punishment.

It wasn't until she was seated that Trixie realized she was elbow to elbow with Anna Ruth Williams. She couldn't move. She couldn't kill her. That was against the law. And her ex-husband sure wouldn't cut her any slack when he threw her in jail. Now that was an interesting idea. Sex in a jail cell with him handcuffed to the bars.

Anna Ruth realized who had sat down beside her and gasped. Trixie kept her eyes straight ahead. There was no justice in the world or it would not be a sin or against the law to shoot a cheating husband's new bimbo. Finally, curiosity got the best of her and she looked right at Anna Ruth. But the woman's eyes were on Violet as if she were God.

"This meeting is called to order. Old business?" Violet asked.

No one said a word. Someone did cough in the back row, but he cut it off short when Violet gave him an evil glance.

"Okay, we'll get right on to the new business. Anna Ruth Williams is representing the City Council tonight and is here to ask us to support them in a decision about zoning. Anna Ruth, honey, come right on up here. You have five minutes and then we're moving on to the next item on the agenda." The gold fingernail indicated that Anna Ruth could leave her seat and take her place behind the podium.

Anna Ruth stepped right on Trixie's toe when she stood up. "Oh, dear. I'm so sorry. How clumsy of me."

She pranced up to the front of the room in her tight little pink skirt, matching tight sweater, and pink high heels and threw her blond hair back over her shoulder with a flick of her hand. Freshly manicured pink fingernails with cute little diamond accents glittered under the fluorescent lighting. Lord, she was another Violet Prescott in the making. When the old girl died, she'd probably leave that gold fingernail to Anna Ruth in her will.

"Hello, everyone. As you all know, there are several historically old houses on the three hundred block of Main Street. When the town was laid out, two blocks, the fourth and fifth blocks to be exact, were declared commercial lots. All others were zoned residential so that people wouldn't have cafés or coin-operated laundries right next door to their beautiful homes. The three hundred block has four houses on the south side that are at least fifty years old and five on the north side of the street that are that old or older. We need to remember that our town is steeped in history. I'm here to ask you to support the Council that the old Andrews' home be zoned from commercial back to residential. It's come to our attention that another business has petitioned for a rezoning on that block, and we simply cannot have our old homes being destroyed."

Trixie was on her feet in an instant. "Why would you do that? We were given a commercial zone for that corner that was supposed to be good indefinitely. We are a contributing business to Cadillac. Our café brings in tax dollars, and all three partners participate in community affairs."

"The lawyer for the Council, Clayton Mason, has reviewed the papers, and he says that it does say that you have commercial zoning, but it does not state a time limit. So we either need to zone the whole block or revert your zoning. We either stop it now or pretty soon the whole town will be ruined." Anna Ruth dabbed at her blue eyes with a tissue she pulled dramatically from under the podium. "I just can't bear to see those old historical homes with businesses in them. If I'd been on the Council, Miss Clawdy's…" she snarled her nose before going on, "would have never gotten a commercial license to ruin such an old house in our quaint little town."

"You have my support," Violet said. "I always said those old houses on that street are of historical value to the area and should not be made into businesses."

Trixie was still on her feet. "Everyone in this room eats at Clawdy's on a regular basis. Why in the hell are you all in such a tizz about the house now?"

"You leave one bad apple in the barrel and pretty soon they're all rotten. If this keeps on, there could be a McDonald's buying up one of our precious old houses and razing it for the space to put in a fast food place. How many of you want that right next door with that kind of noise and traffic? And we'd thank you to keep your comments clean, Trixie," Anna Ruth said.

"I want to talk after she gets her five minutes," Trixie said.

"Then get your name on the agenda for the next meeting," Violet said. "Now all of y'all be thinkin' about what Anna Ruth has proposed, and when we meet again, we'll discuss it then. I'll be expecting a vote in November. The people wanting to put a business in the old Shambles' place need an answer by then. But personally, I believe that we should rezone it back to residential."

"I should get to state my opinion if she gets to do hers," Trixie pressed on.

"You are not on the agenda. Sit down, Anna Ruth. I'll close things." Violet took over the podium again.

Trixie did not sit down. "I thought we were here to discuss the Craft Fair, not a zoning issue."

"That's next week, Trixie. You need to read the memo that Clayton Mason emailed everyone."

Trixie slumped back into her chair. She hoped that God would strike Violet dead before the next meeting. Hell, she might even help Agnes make her life miserable.

"Now any more new business?" Violet asked.

No one said a word.

Trixie jumped when Violet hit the gavel on the podium and said, "The next meeting will be next Thursday to discuss the Craft Fair, for those who don't bother to read the memos. We are adjourned."

Anna Ruth smiled smugly as she walked right in front of Trixie on her way to the refreshment table. Trixie stuck her throbbing toe out and didn't even try to catch Anna Ruth as she tumbled ass over teakettle, knocking down the chair she'd been sitting in on her way to sprawl out on the floor. Amazing! The woman wore white cotton granny panties!

"Oh, my!" Trixie bent to tug Anna Ruth's tight little skirt down over her thighs. "Those heels are demons to walk in, aren't they?"

The house had been occupied by Andrews since it was built in the '30s. It was a charming two-story white frame house with big pillars holding up the wide porch, a driveway on the west side, and flowers blooming everywhere Cathy could plant them, but it didn't have enough parking space to support a business. That's where Darla Jean first came into the picture. She offered them the use of her parking lot right across the street for a free dinner every so often.

The first Andrews had owned a cotton gin in town. They left the house to their son, a lawyer, who left it to his son, also a lawyer. When those folks were gone, their two daughters, Marty and Cathy, inherited the place and turned it into Miss Clawdy's Café six months later. Marty quit her job as a full-time teacher at the Grayson County College in Sherman but stayed on to teach adult basic education classes once a week. Cathy quit her job as a home economics teacher in Tom Bean, just south of Cadillac. And just before the café opened, Trixie quit her job at the Cadillac Community Bank to join them.

Getting the right zoning and all the legal papers to put in a business had taken time and money, but now it was not only up and running—it was a thriving business. The only reason Violet and Anna Ruth were so eager to shut them down was that Anna Ruth was afraid Andy would kick her out and go back with his ex-wife. Little did she know that Trixie was still way too pissed at him to take him back.

"I don't want him for anything but a romp in the hay, Miss Granny Britches," Trixie said aloud as she angled across Main Street to the café.

She expected to go right to her room and work on her scrapbooking the rest of the evening, but Cathy was waiting on the front porch in one of the rocking chairs. One look at her said volumes. Cathy could never play poker because everything she thought showed on her face.

"Did Agnes die?" Trixie asked.

She could hope, couldn't she?

"I tried to call but you had your phone off. Was it awful?"

"What?" Trixie asked.

"Anna Ruth was at the meeting, right?" Cathy asked.

"How did you know?" Trixie asked.

"She called me on the pretense of being worried," Cathy said. "I couldn't be ugly to her. We're in the club together. She told me that she was coming to the meeting. I tried to call you but it went straight to voice mail and I didn't want to crash the meeting by showing up out of the blue, so I kept pulling weeds and deadheading plants and worrying my head off."

"Well, you might not be in the club together very long, darlin'," Trixie said. "She was there to propose taking back our rights to a commercial zoning. Another business wants to buy the old Shambles place next to Agnes and now the Council is thinking about sending us back to a residential status."

The rest of the color drained from Cathy's face. "No!"

Trixie sat down in the other rocker. "She's just mad at me and trying to run me out of town. She's afraid Andy will come back to me for some decent sex. I can't imagine anyone as prissy as her liking sex, but I guess she does since she was able to talk him into bed in the first place."

"I don't think she did as much talking as he did, Trixie. Blame Andy. He's as guilty as she is, maybe even more so," Cathy said.

"How's that? It took both of them," Trixie asked.

"He was married and she is so young. Now tell me about the meeting. Why didn't you tell them what you think? I can't believe you didn't storm up to that podium and rant and rave."

"Sorry suckers wouldn't let me talk because I wasn't on the agenda. So I tripped Anna Ruth and enjoyed watching her fall on her face. She wears white panties."

Cathy slapped a hand over her mouth. "You didn't!"

"I did, but she deserved it. She stepped on my toe and it's still throbbing. I think it may be broke," Trixie said.

"I'm so sorry," Cathy said.

"Hey, it wasn't your fault and it's worth the pain to get to deliver the payback. Let's go in. I need a drink."

They circled the house and went in the back door. Trixie went straight for the cabinet and grabbed the Jack Daniels.

Cathy was still pale as a ghost when she slumped down in a chair.

Trixie poured an inch of whiskey into each of two glasses. "Tip it up, darlin', and drink it like a cowboy in an old Western movie. It'll put some color back in your face. We aren't going to lose our business. We'll put Agnes to work for us."

Cathy shook her head. "It's not you they're after. It's me. Ethan doesn't want me to work when we are married. I wouldn't tell him that I'd sell out or quit my job so he and Violet are going after it a different way. If I sell or quit, they'll drop this thing. If I don't tell them I will, then they'll shut us down. I wouldn't even be surprised if Violet wouldn't burn us out to get her way."

Trixie threw back her whiskey and poured another shot. "Could be it's both of us they're after. Remember the line in that old movie? 'They haven't seen trouble, but it's coming.' Well, they'd better not mess with us because we've got Marty on our side."

"And Agnes. Don't forget her." Cathy picked up the glass and sipped. She shivered and said, "This stuff is vile. How do you drink it?"

Darla Jean opened the door and stopped in her tracks. "I don't believe it. I'm going out and coming back inside. Has the devil done claimed your soul, Cathy Andrews?"

"Come on in. It's just a shot to get her color back," Trixie said.

"Who died? Oh, Lord, don't tell me that Agnes done passed on," Darla Jean asked.

"No one died, but the lines have been drawn. Violet and Anna Ruth have spit on their knuckles, but we aren't afraid of them. Agnes has a gun so there could be blood on the field." Trixie laughed. It wasn't so bad now with two shots of Jack warming her. She replayed the story for Darla Jean.

"They might come after your church next," Trixie said.

"I don't think that's possible since it was a gas station before I inherited it so it's already zoned commercial," Darla Jean said. "But if they do, they better get prepared to fight a long uphill battle because I've got God on my side and he's got a lot more power than Violet Prescott."

Cathy put her head in her hands. "It's going to be horrible."

"Don't tell God how big the storm is. Tell the storm how big God is," Darla Jean quoted.

"You tell him for me," Cathy said.

"I'm going. I just wondered how the meeting went." Darla Jean headed for the door and met Marty halfway across the yard.

"Hey, no leftovers to take home?" Marty asked.

"Let's sit on the bench and I'll tell you what's going on. Cathy is still pale and blaming herself, and Trixie thinks it's her fault. Neither of them need to hash it out again."

Marty sat down on a bench beside the crape myrtle bushes. "Now you are scaring me."

Darla Jean told her the whole story and then added, "Marty, if you need money to beat this, I've got it."

"Thanks. If it gets deep, I might. We could move the café on the other side of your church. There are plenty of vacant buildings, but it's the principle."

"I agree," Darla Jean whispered. "So if they want war, let's load up our slingshots and take it to them."

"David and Goliath." Marty laughed.

"That's right."

"Still makes me mad as hell, though." She went on inside the house.

Darla Jean wiped the sweat from her forehead and headed over to the church. So the almighty Prescotts did not want Cathy to work at the café when she was married. What on earth Cathy, with her beauty and looks, saw in that man was a mystery for sure, and he was a big mamma's boy to boot. Cathy had to be marrying Ethan because she was afraid her biological clock was about to blow up in her hands. She talked more about having a baby in nine months than she did about being in love.

Twins were a strange sort. It wasn't uncommon for one to be a hellcat and the other a pious saint. And Marty and Cathy proved that point. Marty was a free spirit, a coyote running wild in the plains. Cathy was the complete other side of the coin—grounded, rooted in traditions. And yet, there was something about Marty that wanted a taste of Cathy's personality and something in Cathy's eyes that craved a taste of Marty's wildness.

Darla Jean had never had time for real friends, not until she got acquainted with Cathy, Marty, and Trixie. And even with their faults, she'd gladly give them everything in her bank account if they needed it to keep their café going. And that bank account was even bigger than Darla Jean's good heart.

Chapter 4

Most of the small towns in the area had been named for either cotton barons, the oil boom, or else their names had something to do with the railroad. Cadillac was right there with them. It had sprung up as a cotton town in the '30s, then oil was discovered and people started flowing into the town. Its first name was Cornwall and that stuck until somewhere in the fifties when rumors surfaced that General Motors was looking at a plot of land between Cornwall and Tom Bean. According to the grapevine gospel, they were going to produce Cadillacs right there in Grayson County. It didn't take the town council long to petition that the town's name be formally changed. The plant never materialized, but the new name stuck firmly.

The Prescotts lived between Cadillac and Luella in a lovely old red brick two-story house that had been built at the height of the cotton industry. Violet had dubbed it the Prescott Plantation. Cathy squinted at it from her car window and though it was a lovely home, thought it lacked the wide veranda and the big white pillars that she imagined when someone said plantation home.

She didn't want to go to the Prescotts' that night. Her stomach knotted up and her head hurt thinking about confrontation. But if Violet started in about the zoning issue, Cathy would stand up for Clawdy's and that could cause an enormous problem between her and Ethan.

One time, just one time, she'd like to have dinner with Ethan without his mother. They'd done that before they were engaged.

They'd go out to a restaurant for dinner and talk for hours. He'd discuss his campaign strategies and ask her what she'd do differently.

"Hmm," she mused.

Compared to the books she'd read and the relationships that Marty and even Trixie had had, theirs had been more like a business arrangement from the beginning.

She walked past two brand new white Lincolns parked in the circle driveway on her way to the door. Violet said that even the color of their cars had to be considered, and didn't the good cowboys always wear white hats?

The idea of a white hat brought on a visual of the cook at the Rib Joint. He wore a white baseball hat turned around backward and had a cute little soul patch like the hero in Candy's second novel. Did that mean his touch might make her melt like hot barbecue sauce? Would he do unspeakable things to her body?

"Hush!" she scolded. "I'm engaged. I shouldn't be thinking about another man, even if he does have a cute little soul patch."

Cathy pushed the doorbell, squared her shoulders, and counted.

One, two, three.

Violet was getting slow on the uptake. Normally she didn't reach three before the door swung open and Violet did a once-over.

Cathy always felt like she was being scrutinized to make sure she was presentable enough to step over the threshold. Sometimes she envisioned showing up in her gardening overalls and no shoes just to see the expression on Violet's face. But she kept telling herself over and over that in a few short months, she and Ethan would have their own house and they'd only have to deal with Violet occasionally.

Four.

The door swung open and Violet started at her toes and traveled upward until she got to Cathy's face. She finally smiled and stepped to one side. "Come in, Catherine. We've been expecting you. Did you get a late start?"

"No, ma'am. Just didn't realize I was driving slow, I guess."

Cathy checked her watch. She was five minutes early.

"Always remember punctuality is the key to success. Ethan, honey, Catherine is here."

Cathy hated to be called Catherine. It sounded cold as a tombstone compared to Cathy.

She flashed on a picture of her tombstone. Cold, gray granite with the words *Catherine Andrews Prescott* in block letters and *wife of Ethan Prescott IV* underneath her name. She didn't want to live her whole life only to be remembered as the *wife of.* She had things to offer, even if it wasn't any more than *part owner of Clawdy's* or *mother of* or even *twin sister of.*

Ethan stuck his head out of the parlor and crooked his finger. "Come on in. I've got the tea poured. Supper isn't for half an hour."

It was what he said every Wednesday and Saturday night. Word for word. They weren't in bloody England, and Cathy would have much preferred hot chocolate or even a Diet Coke than weak hot tea with a cube of sugar (that's right, a cube, not a spoonful) and a splash of fat-free milk.

Violet led the way. "Clayton has joined us tonight. Won't it be wonderful to have a fourth when we set up the Scrabble board after dinner?"

Cathy wanted to grab her purse and run away to the Rib Joint. She'd rather have a root canal with no deadening as spend a whole evening with Clayton, who was the family lawyer as well as the manager for Ethan's political campaign. And now, from what Trixie had told her, he was also the lawyer who was in charge of rezoning Clawdy's.

She'd just that day finished the latest Candy Parker novel and had downloaded a new one. What would she rather be doing right at that moment? Clayton on one hand; hot romance on the other. Hot romance would win, hands down. They could even engrave *Cathy*

Andrews, avid reader of erotic romance on her tombstone if she could get away from the chill of his glare.

Cathy put on her best fake smile. "How nice to see you, Clayton."

"I'm glad to be here," Clayton said.

His eyes were the color of mud, that cold kind that freezes over in the winter and then turns to slush when it warms up. His angular face, pointed nose, and pinched mouth reminded her of Sunday school pictures of Lucifer. She always wondered if he tucked a long forked tail up behind that high-dollar custom-made suit coat.

Ethan gave her a dry peck on the cheek and led the way to the settee. "Hello, sweetheart."

She did remember once when his kiss had a bit of warmth. It was the night she had accepted the engagement ring. He was so happy that they'd gone straight into the house from the front porch and told Violet that they were engaged. The three of them had shared a glass of expensive champagne before Ethan drove her home. Of course, Violet went along that night and Cathy would always remember the occasion well. It was the last time that Violet sat in the backseat.

"How was your day?" Cathy asked.

"Clayton and I've been very busy with the campaign."

Clayton picked up the conversation as if on cue. "I was just telling Ethan that he will be riding in the lead car at the Jalapeño Jubilee parade. It will be the Saturday before election so it's a big thing. We have rented a Cadillac limo with a sunroof so he can stand up and wave at the crowd. Maybe toss candy out to the little children. Of course you and Violet will ride inside, windows down so you can wave and show your support. You should wear white gloves and practice your wave so that it looks graceful."

Cathy was speechless.

Marty's Caddy had always been the lead car in that parade. Since it was a convertible, the most important person in the parade got to ride in it and this year Ethan had been elected as the Cadillac Celebrity of the Year because he was running for State Representative. Adam Andrews had driven the Caddy right up until the year he died. Marty had kept up the tradition by driving it the past four years.

"I know that Martha drives the lead car in the parade. Well, this year she will bring up the rear and she will be carrying last year's celebrity in her car," Violet said.

Marty was going to go up in mile-high, scalding red-hot flames. There wasn't a jalapeño in the whole world as hot as the hissy she'd throw when she got that news. Last year's celebrity had been Andy for having put in ten years on the Cadillac police force and he'd ridden in the Caddy. A week later, Trixie caught him cheating with Anna Ruth, and Marty threatened to put the car up for sale since Andy had touched it. There was no way she'd ever let Andy sit in her car again. For the first time since Adam Andrews bought that car, it would not be in the parade.

Ethan slung an arm around her shoulder and gently squeezed. "You'll take care of telling Martha that for us, won't you?"

She couldn't make words come out of her mouth. The night couldn't get a bit worse.

Ethan squeezed Cathy's shoulder again, harder this time. "Are you off in la-la land, sweetheart?"

"No, I'll tell Marty as soon as I get home," she whispered.

"Good!" Clayton opened his leather-bound folder to go on to the next item.

Yak. Yak. Yak. Blah. Blah. Blah.

Cathy didn't hear a word.

"You will need to be here at ten o'clock," Clayton said.

And we'll invite Violet to dinner on Sunday evening once a month. That is enough to be polite. That's what she was thinking when she felt Ethan staring at her.

"Clayton is talking to you," Violet said shortly.

"I'm sorry. I was thinking about the wedding cake. There's a fair in Dallas this weekend, and Trixie, Marty, and I are going. Forgive me. I should have been listening," she said.

"Well," Clayton glared at her, "I said…" he shot a cold look her way, "I have a press release ready for the area newspapers. It will come out in full color on the week before Halloween. Timing is everything. And they've asked to come here for a photo shoot next Saturday. You will join Ethan in one picture and you will need to be dressed appropriately."

Should my gloves be wrist or elbow length? she thought.

"And plan to stay for lunch because we will be entertaining the press staff from all the newspapers. Wear a business suit and panty hose are a must." Violet snarled at Cathy's dress as if she'd bought it from the clearance rack at the Goodwill store.

Ethan gave her another dry peck on the cheek. "It might seem picky, but it's all important, Catherine. It takes more than a brilliant political mind to win an election."

What happened to Cathy? Or is that reserved for the bedroom and I will always be Catherine in this house?

"The press conference is when we will announce that you two will be living in this house," Clayton said.

Cathy gasped.

She liked the house, but she didn't want to live in it. She had her heart set on a small three-bedroom frame house on the east side of Cadillac. It had the cutest little picket fence around the yard and roses were already blooming in the flower beds. It had been on the market for a year and the price was right for a couple just starting out.

Violet clapped her hands and squealed. "I know it's a great surprise and I've saved it for this very night."

"You are giving us your home?" Cathy whispered.

"In a sense, but not until I'm dead and then the will says it belongs to Ethan, of course, since he's my only child. But Catherine, you do realize that the prenup will state that you have no right to it should you ever leave him. But, oh dear, that is such foolishness. You would never leave Ethan. Look at him. He's perfect."

Cathy glanced at him. Perfect? Not by a long shot. Kind and sweet? Definitely. His nose was a bit small and his lips just a little too wide to consider him ruggedly handsome, but he was a gentleman and he loved her. That was enough for Cathy.

"And she's not actually giving anyone this house since she'll continue to live here too," Clayton said. "Now, I do believe our time is up. Dinner should be on the table, right, Violet?"

"Yes, it is." She smiled.

When Cathy stood, Violet hooked her arm through hers and led the way to the dining room. "Don't worry about that fair, Catherine. Annabel is my best friend and she makes the most gorgeous wedding cakes and she's agreed to make Ethan's. We are going to talk to her a week from tomorrow at four thirty. I should've told you before now, but she just confirmed that she'll be available. Put it on your calendar, but don't worry, I will remind you two days in advance. I was thinking rather than the plain old white wedding cake that we'd have red velvet cake and do the flowers in blue. Isn't that a lovely idea for a politician who has just won the election? And your bridesmaids can wear red velvet dresses and carry miniature versions of your red, white, and blue bouquet."

That was the proverbial icing on the cupcake.

Cathy might not even go home that evening. She had her e-reader in her purse. She might just point her mother's old Chevy Lumina toward California and not stop driving until she hit water. There she'd live in her car and become a beach bum who picked up soda cans and redeemed them at the supermarket to make money to buy more erotic books.

Trixie was usually the last one to arrive at the scrapbooking group on Friday nights, but that night she arrived in plenty of time, got her materials out, and was already working on putting a fancy border around a picture of her and her sister when they were preschoolers. Her mother's birthday was in February and every year she made her a scrapbook in hopes that it would help her to remember. It hadn't for the past four years, but Trixie still held out hope.

Two other ladies of the six-member group arrived and got their supplies set up. When the last three claimed their spaces, Beulah stood up and said, "Girls, I brought my famous sugar cookies to go with our coffee tonight. And I also brought someone who has never done any scrapbooking. Everyone, make Anna Ruth welcome."

Trixie remembered a raunchy story that her mother told years before. It had to do with two young southern girls. One married a poor farmer and one a rich banker. The poor girl went to visit the rich one Sunday afternoon. The rich one said, "When we married, my husband gave me that Porsche out there in the driveway. When we were married a year, he built this mansion for me. When I had my first child, he gave me this five-carat diamond. When I had my second son, he gave me a trip to Paris and an unlimited credit card to shop."

At the end of each sentence, the poor girl said, "Ain't that nice."

Finally the rich girl asked, "What has your husband done for you?"

The poor girl said, "He sent me to finishing school."

"Why would he do that?" the rich girl asked.

"So I'd learn to say, 'Ain't that nice' instead of 'Screw you, bitch.'"

The story flashed through Trixie's mind in a nanosecond as she looked up to see Anna Ruth smiling smugly across the table from her.

"Well, ain't that nice," Trixie said.

And it was. Andy could blame any bits of paper on Anna Ruth from now on and Trixie wouldn't be a paranoid worrywart about brushing every square inch of his uniform before he left her bedroom.

Not!

As afflicted with OCD as Anna Ruth was, she would lick the floor to keep from leaving the faintest whisper of a paper lying about like that, so forget the only perk to having the woman in scrapbooking with her.

"Trixie?" Anna Ruth continued to smile like the cat that ate the canary and didn't even leave a single feather as evidence. Of course she wouldn't! It would be clutter.

"Anna Ruth, did Andy tell you that I love scrapbooking?" Trixie asked.

"Oh, no, he never mentions you, but I did have to clean up that hobby room of yours when I moved in so I figured it out. Thought I'd never get all those little bits of paper out of the carpet. Didn't you ever clean house?"

Molly, the queen bee of scrapbooking in all Grayson County, gasped.

Trixie had a smart-ass remark on her tongue, but she couldn't ruin Molly's night, not when the elderly woman had taught her so much about the craft.

"Well, ain't that nice," she said, the words saccharine sweet.

Trixie ignored Anna Ruth and fanned out a two-hundred-sheet assortment the size of copy paper in the middle of the table. "I found some lovely paper on sale at Hobby Lobby this past week. I bought two packages. Help yourselves. I'm sharing. I saw the red plaid on top and had to have it for a picture I'm working on it for my mother's birthday book, but so much of the rest doesn't go with anything in the book."

"That is the sweetest thing," Molly said. "You are always doing something nice for us who don't get up to Sherman to the store very often. Oh, my! I want that pink gingham check. I'm working on a memory book for my niece's high school graduation next year and it'll be perfect for her baby picture."

Trixie felt a chill pass over her body and looked up to see Anna Ruth glaring at her.

The Dairy Queen logo in Texas is referred to as the Texas stop sign. It's where the old farmers and ranchers go for their morning coffee and to gather around the smokers' tables to talk about crops, politics, and religion. Women met there in the morning for an hour of gossip, and when school was in session, the kids had lunch and hung out after school to flirt and drink half-price soft drinks during happy hour.

The first sign that a Texas town is headed for the ghost town registry is when the Dairy Queen shuts its doors and boards up the windows. Down through history when the Dairy Queen closed, it wasn't long until the post office and the school were both gone and there are only a few diehards left, waiting to fill their plots in the cemetery.

So far the Dairy Queen in Cadillac was doing a booming business, and their peanut parfait sundaes were on sale for ninety-nine cents on Saturday evening from five to eight o'clock.

Marty arrived ten minutes before the deadline. She was third in line and kept a watch on the big clock above the ice cream machine the whole time. It was one minute to eight when she hurriedly gave the lady her order for the peanut parfait sundae special that night.

"Make that two, and I'll pay for both of them," Anna Ruth's squeaky voice said right behind her.

Marty looked over her shoulder and down into Anna Ruth's face. She held her hands tightly to keep from smacking the woman. She'd looked forward to a chocolate sundae all day, and now it wouldn't even taste good.

The waitress set the sundaes on the counter and Marty pulled out a dollar and a few pennies to pay for hers. No way was Anna Ruth spreading all over town that she'd bought Marty a sundae. Trixie would disown her for sure.

She hoped that paying for her own ice cream would keep Anna Ruth from sitting with her in the booth back in the far corner.

Not so!

The brazen hussy sat down across from her and smiled brightly. "I wasn't teasing. I intended to pay for our ice cream. I owe you for your vote for me to get into the social club."

Marty hadn't blushed in years and she sure didn't appreciate Anna Ruth for making it happen that night.

"I know you voted for me," Anna Ruth whispered.

"And what gave you that dumb-ass notion?" Marty asked.

"Aunt Annabel saw you put your ballot in right at the end and it was the only folded one in the candy dish. And Violet pulled it out last so Aunt Annabel said it was your vote that got me into the club. I owe you big-time, Marty. I'm just so tickled that you voted for me. I would have never thought you would since…well, you know."

A piece of folded paper was going to be the undoing of more than thirty years of friendship, and it could even shut down Clawdy's. Why in the hell had she folded her ballot?

So no one could see the check by Anna Ruth's name, she reminded herself.

Fat lot of good that did. Now she was in a pickle, and all over a fold in a piece of paper. Shit-fire!

"Don't worry, I won't ever tell. What happens in the club stays in the club. Just because I'm a new member don't mean I don't know the rules. Aunt Annabel told me exactly what would be expected of me before she even nominated me. But I did want to thank you for your vote. Next time, the ice cream is on me," she continued to whisper.

Marty nibbled at the beautiful parfait while Anna Ruth rambled on about how excited she was to be in the club and how she intended to make every single meeting. Why, she'd just be tickled as punch to stop by Clawdy's and take Marty with her since it was right on the way and all. And it would make Violet so happy if Marty came to more meetings.

She had barely come up for air when she looked at her watch. "Oh, honey, would you look at the time? I swear we've wasted half an hour just goin' on about the club, and now I'll have to rush through Andy's supper. See you real soon, and remember the next sundae is on me."

Marty wanted to bang her head on the table just to get the words and vision of Anna Ruth out of it. Jesus would have trouble keeping from strangling the woman, and Marty did not have an ounce of his patience.

"What was she doing here?" Darla Jean slid into the place Anna Ruth vacated.

"Trying to kill me with words. What are you doing out tonight? I figured you'd be getting ready for services tomorrow morning," Marty said.

"Sermon is ready. Sanctuary is swept and ready. I ordered a hamburger. Want one?"

"No, I got the special." She pointed toward the half-eaten parfait.

Darla Jean's cell phone rang, and she held up a finger. "Hello, Trixie… At the DQ. Marty is here too… Okay."

She flipped it shut and put it back in the pocket of her jeans. "Trixie says we aren't to leave. She's on her way."

"Guess scrapbooking is over."

Marty barely got the sentence out before her phone rang.

"What's up, Cathy?"

Darla Jean listened and then said, "Yes, ma'am."

Darla Jean looked across the table at her. "I'm to go home. I'm to call Trixie and tell her to come home. I'm to bring you. I'm not to ask questions. Looks like big problems. Cathy doesn't ever sound like that."

"Number thirty-two," the lady called out.

"That's my burger. You walkin' or drivin'?" Darla Jean asked.

"I drove."

"I walked. I'll ride with you and call Trixie on the way."

Agnes was sitting at the table, a fork in her hand and what was left of half a pecan pie in front of her, when Marty and Darla Jean arrived. First she'd seen Marty walk toward the Dairy Queen. Agnes couldn't believe she was walking right down Main Street dressed in her grease-stained sweatpants and shirt. It was an abomination, and besides, why in the hell would a woman want an ice cream when there was half a pecan pie sitting there for the taking?

Then she had seen Trixie leave with that suitcase of paper shit; she knew she'd be gone until at least eight thirty. If Molly could keep her eyes open, that stupid little club she'd formed that had grown women cutting and pasting paper would keep going even longer.

Cathy had driven off to Violet's house—thinking of her blood kin about to marry into that family was enough to make Agnes cuss. She prayed every night that Ethan would drop dead of some dreaded disease and his mother would catch it when she kissed his dying lips good-bye, and most of all that it would happen before the wedding.

She and Violet had actually been friends when they were girls, right up until Violet got her under-britches in a wad when she lost Bert Flynn to Agnes. She and Agnes had drawn a line in the Texas dirt and declared out-and-out war on each other. The battle had been going on for more than sixty years.

Darla Jean smiled when she saw Agnes. "Got hungry, did you?"

"Aunt Agnes, you'll be sick if you eat all that rich pecan pie," Marty scolded.

"It was eat or cuss, and it's Saturday night. I got to go to church in the morning and face off with God so I figured I'd eat. You look like shit," Agnes said.

"Now you've cussed so don't eat all that pie. I don't want to drive you to the emergency room with a bellyache in the middle of the night."

"You made me cuss. Why are y'all home anyway? Y'all were supposed to stay out for another half-hour at least. And don't you roll your eyes at me, young lady. I'm old, and I'll eat what I want and die when I'm supposed to. All this worryin' about eating healthy is for the birds. I might have the rest of that chocolate cake over there before I go to sleep tonight just to prove it."

Trixie pushed through the back door. "What is going on that we've…oh! It must be important if you called her too."

"Nobody called me for anything, but I'm staying now that I know something is happening. Is Cathy all right?"

"I'm fine." Cathy rushed inside. "But thank God you are all here."

"Did he die?" Agnes asked.

"Who?"

Agnes threw up her hands. "Ethan the fourth!"

"No!"

"Well, damn! Sometimes God takes his own sweet time in answering prayers," Agnes said.

Trixie dropped her scrapbooking case with a thud and sat down in a kitchen chair with a plop. "Anna Ruth joined my scrapbook club. She's trying to force me out of town. But that's not what's going on, is it?"

"No, I called the summit," Cathy said. "Marty, darlin', promise me you will not say anything until you count to ten."

"Do I need to run across the street and get my shotgun?" Agnes asked.

"Maybe," Cathy said.

"Oh my God! It's serious, isn't it?" Darla Jean crossed herself and looked up. "Sorry about that, God. I didn't mean to take your name in vain. It just slipped out."

Agnes shook her head in disgust. "Hooker changed to preacher, my ass. You can't change a leopard's spots or think God is listening to you just because you make a cross on them big boobs! God bless! This whole area of town has gone to hell in a handbasket."

And that's when the whole room went deadly quiet.

Cathy made sure everyone was seated and had a tall glass of sweet tea before she started, and then she told them the whole story.

Trixie couldn't even get a cuss word to come out of her open mouth.

Darla Jean's mouth moved in a silent prayer. She didn't care what Agnes said. Prayer didn't hurt and it just might help.

Agnes hadn't promised anything about counting to ten or holding her temper, either. "That bitch! You can't marry that spineless piece of shit she produced, Cathy. I won't allow it. Your parents are dead, and you have to pay attention to me now."

Marty held up one finger. "One."

She pushed back her chair. "Two."

She headed for the door. "Three."

She slammed it so hard that the coffee pot rattled.

"Four," she yelled.

They heard the Caddy's engine fire up and the tires squeal when she backed out of the driveway. A minute passed and then a horrible noise sent them all running out the back door.

Marty was standing beside her prized Caddy with the front end wrapped around the pecan tree in Beulah's yard. "Ten. Now can I talk?" she asked.

Cathy nodded.

"Andy can ride in a wagon pulled by a mangy jackass, but he's not putting his feet in my car."

"But you didn't have to wreck it. You just got it fixed," Cathy said.

"And it'll be fixed by fall again. Me and Jack will have a good time doing it, and Andy will still be a first-class sumbitch. And you've got a good excuse for Violet without having to get yourself in hot water with the almighty damned Prescotts."

Jack came running out of his house to see what the noise was all about and slapped his leg. "What in the hell have you done, Marty? We just got her fixed up."

"And we can fix her up again, but not in time for the Jalapeño Jubilee parade."

Chapter 5

Violet Prescott and Beulah Landry were the only two remaining charter members of the Blue-Ribbon Jalapeño Society, and their word was as good as written in stone and carried on the shoulders of the newest members to every club meeting. In the original charter, it was decreed that only twenty members could be in the club at any given time, and there had only been one amendment since it was written, and that was to allow a one-time addition to the twenty members so that both Martha and Catherine Andrews could be inducted.

The iron-clad rules of the club involved the limit on membership, the fact that members must live within the borders of Grayson County and that the only way a new member could come in was if someone died or moved away. The unspoken ones included dressing up for club, always wearing the pin given at the first meeting by Violet, and staying on Violet's good side.

Prissy Parsons' moving away had paved the way for Anna Ruth. Before that, an open spot had been given to Anna Ruth's Aunt Annabel when poor Edna Smith was laid to rest under an oak tree in the Cadillac Memorial Cemetery.

When Prissy left, Annabel had called Violet and asked if she could put her niece's name on the ballet and Violet had told her that she'd have to take some time to think about it. After all, Anna Ruth's mother had been from the wrong side of the tracks, so to speak. Annabel's brother probably wouldn't have married the poor girl if she hadn't gotten pregnant, so it wasn't a cut-and-dried case. And there was that little bit about her living with Andy, but he was the chief of police, which in Cadillac meant he had standing and could be useful to the club. And at that time the only other name on the ballet was Agnes Flynn, put there as usual by Beulah, who declared that Agnes was her neighbor and things would be very sticky if she didn't nominate her.

The next day, Violet had decided that it would be un-Christian to punish the girl for the mother's deeds. She had, after all, married the father and stayed with him unlike Trixie's mamma, who came home with a baby that had her maiden name.

The club was held the second Tuesday night of every month, and Violet always hosted it at her house. She usually chose a Halloween theme for the October meeting, but with the election just weeks away, she'd gone with red, white, and blue for patriotism. The table was laid with finger foods. Plates were red, cups were blue, and the saucers were white. The centerpiece, sitting between two tall red vases of red, white, and blue flowers, was petit cheesecakes. Some were topped with blueberries, some with cherries, and some left plain, but they were arranged to resemble the flag. Ethan would be the speaker that evening, and Violet had even borrowed the podium from the Cadillac Baptist church for him to stand behind. Clayton would introduce him, of course, and Violet would sit in a chair right behind him, symbolic of her undying support. She'd thought about a second chair for Catherine, but the woman wasn't in the family yet, and until she was, she'd didn't really have a place.

Anna Ruth was the first to arrive. She was such a pretty little thing in her bright red slim skirt and matching jacket. Her blond hair was twisted up, and her eyes had just enough makeup to bring out the color.

She came in gushing. "Everything is beautiful, Miz Violet. You've outdone yourself. Those little cheesecakes are so fitting with the red, white, and blue floral arrangement. And Ethan is speaking? I'd just be delighted to help with his campaign in any way I could. Remember my name when you need help stuffing envelopes or when you need someone to go door-to-door passing out cards."

Violet wished just one time that Catherine would show that kind of emotion. If she'd had her way, Ethan never would have asked that woman out on the first date, but Clayton assured her that the Andrews came from old stock and it would be a good thing for his campaign.

Violet hugged Anna Ruth. "Why, now, isn't that the sweetest thing ever? I'll write your name down in my book, Anna Ruth, and I will definitely be calling you."

"I know he's just swamped with his classes at the school and trying to make every single function right here close to election time. I swear I don't know how he keeps up with the professor duties at the college and do all that he has do to with the election."

"Yes, that's right. And *when* he is elected." Violet winked at her. "And yes, I did say when, and not if. I'm sure the college will miss him dreadfully."

"Oh, I know they will," Anna Ruth said.

The doorbell rang, and Violet opened the door. "Come right in, Catherine. Could you be a dear and man the door for me tonight? Members can be seated in the parlor for the meeting and to hear our guest speaker. Ethan, Clayton, and I have to go over a couple of the fine points of his speech in his study. Anna Ruth, you can come with me. Catherine will take care of the guests as they arrive." She draped her arm around Anna Ruth's shoulders, and together they headed for Ethan's office.

Cathy stood beside the credenza and waited for the doorbell.

"What's wrong with this picture?" she muttered.

Anna Ruth is the fair-haired glory girl, and I'm the butler. Violet scowls at me and hugs her. What in the hell is going on? That did sound like Marty, didn't it?

The doorbell sounded. Beulah was standing on the porch. A large-boned, gray-haired woman in the same black suit she wore every month to the club, she looked nervous.

"Hi, Cathy. I'm not late, am I?"

"No, darlin', you are not a bit late. We are sitting in the parlor for the meeting. Just go on in and save me a seat beside you. Marty won't be coming tonight."

"Oh, dear." Beulah wrung at her hands. "That puts Violet in a stew."

"Not tonight. She's all worked up over Ethan's speech," Cathy whispered.

When everyone was seated in the parlor, Violet made her entrance between Ethan and Clayton, walking down the aisle between the folding chairs like a queen. She sat between Anna Ruth and Annabel and beamed while Clayton gave the introductory speech and glowed while Ethan spoke of his plans to improve the whole district.

Anna Ruth got all misty-eyed and flushed at several places in his speech.

Beulah kept stealing glances through the door at the cherry cheesecakes.

And Cathy was so busy thinking about whether to top out the crape myrtles or let them get taller for another year that she didn't hear a word of what he said. She thought he might introduce her as his fiancée at the end of his speech, but he didn't. And she'd worn her brand new navy blue straight skirt with the little short jacket to match and her mother's pearl necklace. She'd even shaved her legs for the second day in a row and put on panty hose.

"And now before we go to the refreshment table, we have to pin our newest member. Anna Ruth, would you please come forward and accept the pin that says you are a member of the Blue-Ribbon Jalapeño Society?"

Anna Ruth dabbed at a tear. "Thank you for voting me into the club. I can't tell you how pleased I am or how much I will slave for this club."

Violet fastened the pin to the lapel of her jacket, and everyone clapped. Cathy felt guilty putting her hands together, but she managed a few claps before settling them back in her lap.

The refreshment and gossiping stage of the club lasted thirty minutes and then everyone was expected to go home. Anna Ruth kept watching the clock and was the first to air-kiss Violet and gush on and on about what a lovely time she'd had. Evidently, she had no intentions of making a mistake at her first formal club meeting.

She shook Ethan's hand for the third time and offered again to support him and stressed "in any way." Cathy hung back until they were all gone and waited until she caught Ethan coming out of the kitchen alone.

"I'd like a word, in private," she whispered and laced her fingers in his.

He nodded toward his office and almost shut the door, leaving it open by two inches in case his mother came searching for them. A politician couldn't be too careful, not even with his future wife. He planted one of those dry kisses on her forehead and said, "You look very pretty today, sweetheart."

Her chin quivered. "Thank you, but I want to tell you something and it is very difficult for me to say."

He dropped her hand and touched her chin. "What is it, sweetheart? Please don't tell me you are getting cold feet about the wedding."

"No, but I will not live in the same house with your mother. I want us to have our own house. I don't care how small it is at first. I just want to be like a normal newly wedded couple and—"

Ethan dropped her hands. "That's unreasonable."

"But—" she said.

The door swung open and Violet came into the room like an unwanted odor. "Here are the love birds sneaking away for a moment together. That's so sweet, but Clayton needs you in the parlor to go over the next speech you'll be giving on Friday night. And before I forget, Catherine, we are to see Annabel about the cake Friday night. She just told me that she would be ready for us then. Now Ethan, you go on to the parlor and I'll walk Catherine to the door."

He made a hasty escape out the door.

Violet tucked her arm in Cathy's and led her into the foyer and toward the front door. "Darlin', you did fairly well today with your outfit, but please don't wear that on the press day. I'm thinking maybe something in a royal blue would be good with your hair and eyes. Pearls are so out, especially the ones that are aged. Maybe a scarf instead of a necklace and a flag pin on your lapel would be just the thing. Oh, and we need to make a date soon for your wedding dress. I'm thinking old-fashioned with a high collar and pointed sleeves. That would show the voters that you are serious about your job as a politician's wife."

Cathy was on the porch and the door had shut behind her before she could say a single word.

Trixie parked her car beside Andy's at the far end of the Walmart parking lot, threw her bags into the backseat, and got into the passenger's seat.

"I've got a surprise," he whispered. Charm oozed out of him like filling from a Hostess chocolate cupcake. He leaned across the seat, tilted her chin up with his left fist, tangled his fingers in her hair with his right hand, and kissed her in a clash of hot passion that came close to fogging the car windows.

He kissed his way to her neck and nuzzled there, inhaling her perfume. "God, I missed you. It's been too damn long. I'm so glad that Anna Ruth went to her aunt's after the meeting."

That's where he went wrong the first time. He should have never brought up Anna Ruth, not when they were about to spend time in a motel room getting super satisfied with passionate sex. But if he was very, very good, she might forgive him one mistake.

He drove for a while, made a few turns, and caught Highway 75 south. "We are going out to dinner, to a movie, and then to the motel."

"But…"

"No buts." Andy glanced over at her. "By the way, you look beautiful tonight, honey. I always did like you in that shade of blue."

She wore black slacks and a pale blue sweater set and black high heels. Gold hoop earrings dangled from her ears, and a silver clunky necklace with a silver heart pendant dropped just to the top of two inches of cleavage created by a Victoria's Secret push-up bra.

"No, we are not. We are going to a motel, having mind-boggling sex, and going home," she said. "I've already eaten. I don't want to sit in a movie. I want sex, and then I want to go home. I'm not going out on a date with you, Andy."

Andy's mouth set in a firm, hard line, and his jaw worked like he was chewing gum.

Trixie had seen that look before. Many, many times. So what had set him off this time? Then it dawned on her like a flash.

Anna Ruth was pressuring him to get married. He wanted to be seen with Trixie so that it would get back to Anna Ruth and she'd break up with him. Of course it would all be that bitch Trixie's fault.

"Why?" Andy growled.

"Because I might not like you, but I love the sex we have, and Marty will kill you dead if she finds out we are together," she said.

"Marty! You put her ahead of me?"

That was his second mistake and three was his limit, so he was treading on thin ice.

"So when does Anna Ruth want to get married?" she asked.

The jaw worked harder, and his mouth disappeared. "I have no idea what you are talking about."

Bleep!

Number three! Andy was out.

No sex for you tonight, feller.

She pointed her finger at him. "You are lying."

He slapped her finger away.

And that's where Andy Johnson really went wrong.

"Pull over in that parking lot right there. The one by the Big Lots store."

"I don't see a motel or a restaurant," he said as he stopped the car.

She got out and stomped her way to the bench in front of the store with him scrambling to get the car perfectly into a parking spot with exactly the same amount of space on each side.

He finally got it parked, got out, slammed the door, and sat down beside her. "What in the hell is the matter with you?"

"You wanted someone to see us together, didn't you? She's pressuring you to get married because of that damned club shit, and you want her to be the one to break it off instead of you. How close am I?"

He ran his finger up her thigh. "Come on, Trixie. Don't be mad."

She slapped it away. "I'm mad because I didn't want a damn date. I just wanted a motel room and to have sex on a Tuesday night because our Wednesday nights have been interrupted the past couple of weeks. I'm mad because nothing has changed and won't change. Go home and leave me alone." She took her cell phone out of her purse.

Darla Jean answered on the first ring. "Trixie?"

"I'm in Sherman on the bench in front of the Big Lots store. Will you please come get me?"

"I'll be there in a few minutes," Darla Jean said.

Andy threw up both palms. "What set you off tonight?"

"We got a divorce because you were bonkin' Anna Ruth. I took the blame because if I'd picked up the damn towels or made sure there were no wrinkles in the sheets when I folded them and put them in the drawer, maybe you wouldn't have gone out and screwed another woman. But when you slapped my fingers, it hit me. Dammit all to hell, I didn't bonk another man because you made me so damn mad with your freakin' OCD, so you had no damn right to screw around on me then or to slap my fingers tonight. Go home or I'm callin' the cops and havin' you arrested for harassment."

"I won't leave you on a park bench at night," he said through clenched teeth.

She poked three numbers into her phone and waited.

"You wouldn't dare!" he said.

She looked him right in the eye and said into the phone, "My emergency is that I'm sitting on a park bench in front of Big Lots and my ex-husband is harassing me. He already slapped me once tonight, and I need a police officer to come down here."

"Put that damn phone away," Andy seethed.

"No, ma'am, he's not threatening me. It's not me that you need to come down here and save. It's him. I've got a .38 in my purse, I've got a license to carry a concealed weapon, and I intend to shoot him in the balls if you don't send someone to get him away from me. No, ma'am, I will not stay on the phone. You've got five minutes and his cute little balls are going to be hamburger meat. And FYI, I'm a damn fine shot."

She flipped the phone over in her purse and waited.

"You did not just do that!" Andy said.

"I hear the faint sound of sirens. You better get on out to your car and head north. It wouldn't look too good for you to have your name in the paper for sexual harassment of your ex-wife. But then maybe that would be a good thing. Anna Ruth would leave you and you'd be free to sleep with someone else," she told him.

Andy jogged out to his car and had already pulled out onto the highway when her phone rang. One look said that it was Darla Jean so she answered it.

"Where are you?" Trixie asked.

"On the way to get you. What happened?"

"It all came to a boiling head tonight and I just now called 911 and threatened to shoot Andy's balls off if they don't come make him leave me alone," Trixie said.

"I told you that you was messin' with fire. Did you really call 911?"

"Hell no, but he thinks I did."

"What set you off anyway? I thought that man was so good in bed that you'd walk through hot coals to have sex with him. But you told me after the shotgun thing that you were finished with him," Darla Jean said.

"Tonight the coals were hot and the weather is hot and my feet are tender and I figured out he was using me to break up with Anna Ruth, and anyway, I'm right here on the bench waiting and he's on his way home."

Darla Jean didn't say anything.

"No lecture?" Trixie asked.

"No, you just sit there and simmer awhile. We'll talk when I get there."

"I'll simmer away, but I'm already over my mad spell."

"Don't sound to me like you're over nothing. I'm on my way. Don't be lettin' anybody pick you up. Just sit right there and fight off the Johns."

"Why? I could be a hooker," Trixie said.

"If you ain't sittin' on that seat when I get there, I'll turn around and come back home and you can walk." Darla Jean hung up.

Trixie looked at the phone a long time before she put it back in her purse. It barely hit the bottom before it rang again. She groaned and hoped to hell it wasn't Cathy or Marty. She couldn't tell them that she'd gone out with Andy, not on the phone. She'd have to come clean about it eventually, but definitely not on the phone.

It stopped ringing when she finally got her fingers around the thing but started again when she dropped it. That time she fished it out and answered without looking at the ID.

"Are you ready to talk about this?" Andy said tersely.

"Are you ready to drop dead?"

He hung up.

She stuffed the phone in her bra.

Thirty seconds later he called again.

"This is ridiculous, Trix. Hell, you didn't act this bad when I admitted I was having a fling with Anna Ruth."

She hung up.

A minute went by and she checked to make sure the phone didn't need recharging. Another minute and it rang again.

"I'm not staying in town forever," he said.

"Go home."

"I'm not leaving you stranded, Trix. Shit! Cathy and Marty were ready to kill me when I cheated. They'd really do it if I left you sitting on a damn park bench after dark this far from home."

"I thought the affair was my fault because I'm messy. I was pissed but I didn't even know what anger was until right now. Guess I hit the next step in the process of getting over a cheatin', lyin' son-of-a-bitch of a husband. How many were there before Anna Ruth?"

"Don't go there."

"Why? Because you can't count that far without taking off your shoes?"

It was the pause that sent her to the totally pissed off stage. She hadn't even thought about there being other women until that minute. He'd said that it was a midlife crisis thing and she'd believed him.

"Who was the first, Andy? And how soon did it happen after we got married?" she hissed.

He hung up and she called him right back.

"Got that name ready for me? When you do, we'll talk. Oh, and tell Anna Ruth we can make her wedding invitations at scrapbook class. I wish Marty had killed you," she said.

"Well, if she hadn't voted for Anna Ruth to be in that damn club I wouldn't be in this position," Andy said coldly. "Now that she's in the damned almighty social club, she's scared to death they'll kick her out if we don't get married."

"Marty did not vote for her!" Trixie yelled.

"Oh, honey, she did. This is all her fault so blame her, not me."

He hung up again and she heard the screech of tires as he pulled out from the end of the building and headed back north.

She didn't have a thing sorted out and she was still severely pissed when Darla Jean parked right in front of her and honked.

"You simmered long enough?" Darla Jean asked when she got into the car.

"I've never been mad like this. Did you know that Anna Ruth wasn't the first?"

Darla Jean drove to the nearest McDonald's and got out. "I didn't know anything, but I'm not surprised. Andy is who he is and he's always looking around at the women in the room."

Trixie followed her across the parking lot. "How do you know that?"

"Let's just say that I know men," she said.

They ordered and carried their food to the back of the café.

"Talk to me," Darla Jean said.

"We might be here until morning."

"I ain't got to be nowhere tonight." Darla Jean popped a hot fry into her mouth and fanned her lips with her hand. "Hot, hot, hot. Right out of the grease."

"I wish my ex-husband was boiling in that grease right now. I hope he does marry Anna Ruth. That's the best damn revenge on her I could ever get." Any man that would cheat on his wife would lie about her friends, too. There was no way in hell that Marty would have voted for Anna Ruth.

Darla Jean nodded and mumbled, "I hope you mean it, Trixie. I've been prayin' that you'd come to your senses and see that sorry man for what he is."

Agnes meant to slip inside the house, do a snatch and grab of the roast that had been on the special that day, and tote it over to her house for a late night snack. But she heard music and laughter in the garage on the back of the property and kept going that way instead.

Jack had his head under the hood and Marty was sitting in a white plastic lawn chair with her feet propped up on a wooden box. She had a beer in one hand and a cigarette in the other.

"Put that out this minute. You promised your sister that you would quit," Agnes yelled from the doorway.

Marty dropped it so fast that the red tip didn't even dim. Agnes beat a path across the garage floor and stomped on it like it was an evil spider. "I catch you with one more and I'm telling Cathy."

"It was the first one in months, I promise. I'm so angry about the way Violet is treating Cathy that I could just spit. I had to have something to calm my nerves. It was either that or picking up a cowboy on the side of the road and having sex with him in the nearest hayloft. Which one do you think is worse?"

Agnes didn't even bat an eye when she slapped Marty on the shoulder. "You don't talk like that in front of Jack!"

"Jack is my best friend, next to Trixie. He knows I like cowboys."

Agnes drew back her hand. "Then don't talk like that in front of me."

Agnes knew exactly how Marty felt. That blasted Violet looked so smug at church every Sunday morning, sitting there between Cathy and Ethan like she was afraid they'd have sex right there on the church pew and ruin his chance at election. Agnes had thought about standing up in the middle of the sermon and dropping the F-bomb on Violet just so God would send down lightning streaks. She would hide under the pew, and the lightning could fry Violet right there in church. It would be death by natural causes and not murder, so Agnes wouldn't have to spend a single day in jail.

Agnes had wanted to be invited to join the Blue-Ribbon Jalapeño Society back when Jane Slidell died in 1960, but Violet wasn't having any part of that idea. Then in 1972, Gladys Overton broke her hip and moved to Louisiana to live with her daughter. Before poor Gladys unpacked her knickknacks in her new bedroom at her daughter's house, Violet had Lizzy Beechman's name on the club roster. In 1980, Edith Walton suffered heat stroke and Agnes just knew when Edith passed on she'd be asked to join. Violet sponsored Inez Green that year. In 1991, Ruby Dantrell dropped dead from a heart attack and fell right into her rosebushes, and be damned if Violet didn't sponsor the twins' mother instead of Agnes, just to lord it over her even more. Then three years ago, Clovis Richman died, and the twins' mother put her daughters' names into the pot for consideration. Agnes heard later that Beulah had nominated her again, but she'd only gotten three votes. After that, everyone knew that as long as Violet had a breath left in her body, Agnes Flynn would never get into the Blue-Ribbon Jalapeño Society.

Agnes would far rather see Cathy hooking up with Jack as Ethan. At least Beulah had nominated her and didn't act like God's throne wasn't good enough for her to park her fat ass on.

"Hey, y'all. What's going on with the Caddy?" Cathy asked.

Agnes kicked the cigarette butt under the car. "They're fixin' it again but it's goin' slow. How did the club go?"

"I told Ethan I didn't want to live with his mother."

"Good for you. Your mamma's pearls look nice," Agnes said.

The compliment startled Marty so bad that she dropped her beer and it sloshed on Cathy's shoes. She jumped up, peeled off a fist full of paper towels, and dabbed at the shoes. "Dammit to hell! I'm sorry, Cathy. You just bought those shoes for that press shit this next weekend."

"They are knockoffs, and I didn't spend that much. Besides, my whole outfit is wrong. I should wear a royal blue suit and a scarf because they are in fashion. The pearls aren't the in thing, and by all means, I must have a flag on my lapel."

"I suppose that bitch told you to do that?" Agnes said.

Cathy nodded. "She means well, Aunt Agnes. She wants everything to be perfect for Ethan. I guess that makes us working toward the same end, doesn't it?"

"She wants to be God, and honey, she does not mean well. She's training you to obey her every whim and wish. Your life is going to be pure hell. Did Ethan say you could have your own place?" Agnes asked.

Cathy shook her head slowly. "He didn't, not really. But I might have persuaded him if Violet would have given us another few minutes alone."

"I can fix it so you can live your whole lives alone," Marty said. "Soon as we get my Caddy fixed, I can pretend she's my third tree to hit head-on."

Jack chuckled.

Cathy hadn't realized he was in the garage. "Hello, Jack. I thought you'd be at work this time of night."

"Mamma was at the club meeting, and I had some time I had to take or lose. So I took tonight off to help Marty, but we aren't going to have this fixed in time for the Jubilee."

"Thank the Lord," Cathy exclaimed. "If you did, she'd wreck it again to keep Andy from touching the door handle."

"Ah, Andy ain't that bad. He's a fine boss," Jack said.

"But he's a horrible friend and a worse husband," Marty said.

Chapter 6

Picking out the wedding cake was supposed to be joyous, second only to the day she'd chosen her dress, but Cathy was a nervous wreck from morning until Clawdy's closed. Getting in her car and nonstop driving until she hit the ocean was getting more and more appealing by the second. East or west, it didn't matter.

Her gorgeous white dress hung on the door of her closet. Violet wasn't going to like it. Ethan was going to be appalled when she came down the aisle toward him. She touched the plastic bag protecting the frothy confection of tulle over white silk, off the shoulder, fitted to the waist with a sewn-in bra and bones hidden away in the seams, and a billowing skirt.

She had a raging headache when she reached the Prescott house and Clayton opened the door. "Come in, Catherine. I would like a few words with you before you and Ethan, and of course Violet, go to Annabel's to order the cake."

Every hair on her arms stood straight up. Her stomach knotted into a pretzel. It was prenup time and she hated the whole idea. For goodness sakes, this was Grayson County, Texas, not a big city. Sure Ethan would inherit an estate someday, but it wasn't millions, and besides, she wouldn't have agreed to marry him if she wasn't serious about staying married. Two people were supposed to have enough love to carry them through the bad times.

Clayton's eyes were icy cold. His side glances as he walked beside her sent waves that chilled her skin even though the first chill of winter hadn't hit yet. His touch would probably freeze her to death, so she kept her distance. No one else was in the office, and he sat in Ethan's chair like he was judge, juror, and executioner. He motioned for her to sit in one of the two chairs facing the desk. "Sit down, please. I've drawn up a prenup according to what Violet and Ethan have requested. Basically it says that what you bring into the marriage is what you take out when you leave it, if you should. It also says that what Ethan brings he keeps. That means, in layman's terms, that you will not be able to sue him for part of this estate or his present trust fund."

"I'll take it home and read it," she said.

Clayton handed her a pen. "Reading it won't change a thing, Catherine. It's standard, so just sign it."

She looked down and her eyes came to rest on the words *Miss Clawdy's Café*. "It says that I have to sell my part of the café or give it away."

"That's part of the prenup. A politician's wife or a professor's wife or a Prescott does not work in a café," Clayton said.

"I'm not signing it right now. I want to read it."

Ethan, bless his heart, chose that moment to poke his head in the door. "All done? Let's go to Annabel's and look at cakes, sweetheart. Mother is already waiting in the car."

She picked up the papers and shoved them down in her purse with her e-reader and smiled at Ethan. "I'm ready."

Ethan laced his fingers in hers and they went out to the car where he opened the door for her. She had the whole backseat in the big white car to herself since, as always, Violet was up front in the passenger seat.

The doorbell had barely stopped buzzing when Anna Ruth opened the door to her aunt's house. "Hello. Come right on in. Aunt Annabel is in the dining room. We have coffee and cookies for you while you are looking at the wedding cake book."

"I'm so excited that I could be here to help pick out the cake," Anna Ruth said.

Cathy wondered how long she could live on what was in her savings account if she slept in her car and ate bologna sandwiches and generic chicken noodle soup.

Annabel motioned for them to join her at the dining room table where refreshments awaited, along with *the book*. It was covered in white satin with little gold bells sewn to the ribbons that tied it shut. It looked as ominous as the one that St. Peter reportedly had on a pedestal right outside the pearly gates.

"I've kept a picture of every wedding cake I've ever made. That way you can see my work," Annabel said.

Ethan pulled out a chair on Annabel's right and Cathy slid into it.

Surely it wouldn't take long to flip through the book, pick out the style, and tell Annabel that she didn't want any color on it. White wedding cake, white icing, and a few white sugar roses. The cake topper, a gorgeous crystal bride and groom she'd found in the spring, would sit in a bed of white rose buds and greenery that she'd have arranged at the florists.

Violet wasn't going to like it, no matter what she chose, but Marty was right. It was her wedding and her cake.

Annabel pointed at the chair on her left. "You sit here, Ethan, so you can both see everything."

Violet stood behind Annabel. Anna Ruth put her hands on Ethan's shoulders and leaned in for a better look when her aunt opened the book. Annabel stroked the first page with the loving fingers of a mother showing off pictures of her children.

"I made this for Anna Ruth's mother's wedding. It was my very first."

Hmm. I wonder if Marty had a book like that with all the cowboys she's slept with if she'd treat it like a national treasure.

"And this is my second cake. Everyone thought I did such a beautiful job on the first one that I started getting orders. Look at the little rosebuds. I'd just learned to make them."

"They are just beautiful, Aunt Annabel. I swear you've always had the touch," Anna Ruth said.

By the time they reached page twenty, Cathy was ready to yank her hair by the roots and paint her bald head purple.

"Annabel, they are all lovely, but we'd like a simple cake. White cake, white icing, only a few white sugar roses," Cathy said.

Annabel, a small slip of a woman with salt-and-pepper hair and a long face, wiped at a tear and shut the book, picked up a pen, and pursed her thin mouth. "Well, if you know what you want, I'll start taking notes."

"I'm just not one for pillars and bright colors," Cathy said.

Violet threw up her hands. "Nonsense! The cake is important. It makes a statement, and Ethan's wedding will do just that. A plain old white cake would just say that he was plain. We have to get the message out that he's bold. After all, he will have just stepped into office. We have to think about the future of his career, Catherine. Now, Annabel, we want it to be like that big one you made last year for the Smith-Gilbert wedding. Remember, it was this tall." Violet held her hand up beside her waist.

Annabel perked right up and flipped the book to one of the back pages.

It was the exact opposite of the elegant cake she had in mind, but the way Violet's eyes were lighting up said she wasn't backing down. It was just a cake, for God's sake. It wasn't a statement, and Cathy was too jittery to argue the point.

Violet pointed but didn't touch the book. "Like that one. Red velvet inside with white icing and lots of piping. Then we want bright blue flowers on it."

Annabel smiled brightly. "Oh! Morning glories? I've been dying to make a cake with morning glories. They are so pretty and I've never gotten to do them before. I'll make them in life-sized sugar flowers and we'll put the cake on a mirror so when it is cut it will reflect all the colors of the flag. If it's agreeable to you, Violet, we will use your gorgeous red crystal vases on either side of the table with an arrangement of the same flowers. And maybe we can even find some good quality silk morning glories to use on the guests' tables."

"Doesn't she just have the best ideas ever?" Anna Ruth threw her arm around Ethan and hugged him in her happiness. "I can't wait until she and I can start preparations for my wedding."

"I'm sure that Annabel will design everything beautifully," Ethan said.

The monstrosity in the book hurt Cathy's eyes. She blinked, looked down at her feet, and spotted the e-reader. Right next to it was the prenup document. She couldn't call off a wedding after she'd already bought the dress, could she? How had things gone so far astray? She was so excited to be engaged, and now she'd rather be in the Rib Joint with her e-reader or weeding her flower beds than ordering her wedding cake.

"Well, I guess that covers it," Violet said. "We really must be going since tomorrow is our press day."

All eyes were on Cathy.

No one had listened to her about anything, so why should she say anything? Violet was a mother-in-law-zilla, but her time was fast coming to an end. When the wedding was over, Cathy and Ethan would only have to see her once a week, if that. Cathy would live through the wedding and the absurd wedding cake. Someday when her son was getting married, she'd use the experience as a guide in what not to do.

Violet tapped her foot. "Well?"

"Nothing I can think of," Cathy said.

Violet cocked her head to one side and looked at Annabel.

Cathy's eyebrows knit together and promised a raging headache. "Thank you so much, Annabel. I appreciate your doing this for us."

"I'm glad to get the business. You could have paid a bakery to do it for you, but I'm so glad that you chose me to have a little part in your wedding. It will be great for my business, and because you've been so kind, I'm going to give you a ten percent discount," Annabel said.

That was it! Cathy was supposed to pay the woman? The way Violet had talked, Cathy was under the impression that Annabel was making it as their gift. How stupid of her! She picked up her purse and took out her checkbook.

"Thank you for the discount, but I'm glad to pay full price," Cathy said.

"Oh, honey, that is so sweet of you. Just having the business would be enough, but I'll make sure I do an extra special job on it since you won't even let me give you the discount," Annabel said as she pushed a piece of paper toward Cathy. "Violet said five hundred people. This cake easily feeds three hundred, but I'll have sheet cakes in the back if we run out."

Cathy blinked twice. A thousand dollars for a cake! And she was supposed to quit work, according to the prenup?

She made out the check and put it in Annabel's hand. "Once more, thank you."

"Well, we are definitely going now." Violet ushered Ethan and Cathy out the door with Anna Ruth and Annabel right behind them.

Cathy heard the chatter between them, but she couldn't utter a single word. A thousand damn dollars for a cake that was going to look like shit!

Trixie hadn't meant to get involved with the work in the garage when she'd wandered out to check on the Caddy's progress. Ten minutes and a beer later, her head was under the hood with Jack's and she was working as hard as Marty. Without a father around in her life, Trixie's mother had made her learn to change tires and change oil before she was allowed to drive the family car. So a car engine wasn't completely foreign to her, but she couldn't tear one down and put it back together the way Marty or Jack could.

Jack Landry had quit from the Army and come back home to Cadillac. An opening came up for a night shift at the police department and he applied. He had meant to stay with his mother just long enough to find his own place, but a month stretched into six, and a year stretched into two.

The girls kept telling him that he should buy his own place, but now it had gotten complicated. Beulah was going to have a fit and make a big issue out of it after all this time.

"You are awful quiet tonight." Trixie poked Jack's arm.

"Got a lot on my mind."

"Finally thinkin' about moving out of your mamma's house?" Marty asked.

"Maybe, but I'm not ready to talk about it yet," he said. "What's the newest scuttle on the wedding plans?"

"Did Cathy tell you what Violet wants us to wear as bridesmaids in the wedding?" Marty looked at Trixie and winked.

"Something to do with red, white, and blue because she thinks that Ethan will be a couple of weeks away from taking oath in his new office. Wonder how she'll feel when the wedding is all arranged and he don't win that election. I can't see him really winning, can you?" Trixie asked.

Marty didn't act any different. If she had really voted for Anna Ruth to get into the club like Andy said she did, there would have been a big difference, right?

"Hell, no! He's not going to win. I don't even know why he's all up into politics anyway," Marty answered. "What about you, Jack?"

"I don't see it happening. I just hope it doesn't disappoint Cathy," he answered.

"Did I hear my name again? I swear, every time I come home, y'all are gossiping about me," Cathy said.

"Did you pick out the cake?" Trixie asked.

"I paid for a cake." Cathy's voice did not give off happy vibes.

"I didn't ask if you paid… what? I thought Annabel was making it for a present." Trixie frowned.

"Annabel would charge Jesus for a cup of water," Jack said.

"You got that right, Jack, and she'd make him pay double," Trixie said.

"She does make pretty sugar flowers but…" Cathy let the sentence dangle.

"But what?" Marty asked.

"Can you imagine a red velvet cake with big, blue, life-sized morning glories all over it?" Cathy moaned.

Trixie slapped a hand over her mouth to keep the giggles back.

It didn't work.

Marty guffawed and held her ribs. "Stop thinking, Trixie. I can see your thoughts. At least she didn't want you to have fake jalapeños all over the thing. I bet she does figure out a way to put at least a few peppers somewhere in the decorations."

Jack chuckled. "Sounds more appropriate than morning glories to me. At least they're hot!"

"Well, hot damn!" Trixie giggled harder.

Cathy popped her hands on her hips. "It's not funny! It's horrible. I hope when you two get married that you get a mother-in-law who's twice as bad as Violet."

Trixie wiped her eyes. "Had one and am grateful that she moved to Florida the second year of my marriage or there wouldn't have been a third year. Well, shit! If she'd have stayed, I wouldn't have wasted all those years. She could have broken us up instead of Andy's cheating."

"And I don't intend to ever get one. I'm learning my lessons from you, sister," Marty said.

See there, Trixie thought. *Andy had been lying about Marty voting for that hussy. No way would she vote for Anna Ruth and then call me sister!*

Chapter 7

"Lawdy, Miss Clawdy" was blaring from the CD player when Jack walked into the café that morning. He grabbed a table in the smaller room and nodded at Trixie.

She filled a mug with coffee and carried it to him. "You just gettin' off work?"

He covered a yawn with the back of his hand. "I am and it was a boring night. Hey, I forgot to tell you. Couple of days ago a guy stopped out front and asked directions to Dallas from here. He'd taken the wrong highway out of Sherman. Anyway, he asked me which one of y'all was Miss Clawdy."

Trixie smiled. "Had he been in here?"

"Had beans and greens with y'all that very day. I told him about the café being named for the twins' mamma. He said it was the best food he'd ever eaten, so pass that on to Marty."

"I will," Trixie said. "Hey, did your mamma mention the voting at the social club the other night?"

The music stopped and then Elvis started singing "Suspicious Minds."

Heat inched its way up the back of Jack's neck. "Why would you ask that? You know that what goes on in their club is so secret that they have to sign their names in blood just to get inside Violet's house. That's probably why Marty don't go very often. You remember how she acted when she saw blood when we were kids?"

The door opened and eight people trailed in together.

"You won't be able to sleep if you leave before you have breakfast," Trixie said as she turned away from Jack's table.

"You are probably right. But this is my supper since I'm just getting off work. What's in the fridge from yesterday? I've had my mind on beans with a big chunk of corn bread, greens on the side, and maybe a piece of fish."

"Got enough beans and greens for you, but the fish is all gone. Pork chop do? You could have picante or pepper jelly with it."

"Oh, yeah! Both. A side of picante and pepper jelly with my corn bread." He exhaled slowly. He'd barely escaped that bullet, but Trixie really did have a suspicious mind, and she would find out about that damned vote. He just hoped he wasn't the one who told her.

Cathy could scarcely believe that Violet was smiling when she opened the door that morning. At least until her gaze dropped to the same suit Cathy had worn to the club earlier in the week. The smile faded and her highly arched brows shot up another inch.

Cathy breezed past her into the house. "Thank you so much for your advice on what to wear, Violet. But I didn't have time to shop and I didn't have a thing in royal blue. Trixie did have this gorgeous scarf she picked up last week at Walmart that matched so I borrowed it and didn't wear Mamma's pearls. What do you think?"

"It'll have to do. You're too tall to wear one of my better suits, or we could whisk you up to my bedroom and change you. The scarf is cheap, but it does match."

Cathy ignored her and asked, "Where is Ethan?"

That's when Violet noticed that Cathy wasn't wearing panty hose and sucked up enough air to blow her lungs right out of her rib cage.

"I told you to wear hose. Now they'll have to take the picture from the bust up and I wanted a less personal one. What's the matter with you, Catherine?"

"I shaved my legs," Cathy said.

Violet shook her head. "I just hope no one got a picture of you at the club and puts it in the *Cadillac News* this week. There will be a big spread in the Sherman newspaper, and it would be tacky if you were seen in the same suit in both papers on the same day." Violet shut the door with enough force to rattle the pretty crystal vase on the credenza. "Ethan and Clayton are in the study. I'm hoping that gigantic purse of yours has the prenup in it and you've signed it?"

"Not yet. I didn't have time to read it last night. I'm not very smart when it comes to legal papers, so after church tomorrow, Darla Jean is bringing her lawyer to the house, and he's going to explain all the fine points to me."

Violet turned beet red and looked like she was about to explode. Cathy thought for sure she'd fall on the floor any minute, grasping at her throat and rolling her eyes back in her head. The doorbell rang, but she didn't hear it until Cathy pointed.

"What?" she snapped.

Cathy pointed over Violet's shoulder. "Press is here. Right on time. I'm going to duck into the study so that Ethan and I can make an entrance together. Don't you think that will be a nice campaign move?"

Violet spun around. Her voice was sugary sweet when she opened the door for the press. But Cathy had no doubt that she would pay for her little rebellious streak. Violet would make sure that fitting back into the perfect mold was very painful.

Clayton could never sit in the chair he had coveted his whole life, which was the one in the Oval Office in the White House. His background would never stand up under the pressure. But he could make it to that office in a slightly less public position if he was a patient man. Ethan Prescott the fourth, with his perfect background, was just the person who could get him on the first rung of the ladder.

There wasn't even a parking ticket on his record. And Catherine was a perfect choice of a wife. She was poised, kind, and he could already see her making a big splash for education and children. Oh, yes, he would enjoy managing Ethan's campaign for this election and then moving right on up to the big one in a few years. Everyone started on the bottom rung and it took lots of grooming to get them to the top.

He'd had a few misgivings when he researched Catherine Andrews. Her sister's reputation wasn't nearly as sterling. But then it could be used to his benefit. Other politicians had relatives with less than stellar reputations and it made for excellent press coverage. Drop the right little tidbit in the right place and suddenly Catherine and Ethan were in the news. His file on Catherine was an inch thick and there wasn't one bad word in it.

He looked up from behind Ethan's desk and smiled when Catherine walked into the room, but it did not reach his brown eyes. She barely glanced his way and went right to the chair where Ethan sat and braced a hip on the arm. When Ethan looked up, she brushed a kiss across his lips.

"You were supposed to wear a blue suit. Ethan has dressed accordingly, so you would match and make a statement, and where is your lapel pin?" Clayton asked.

The woman had the audacity *not* to answer him. She brushed a piece of lint from Ethan's shoulder and said, "Darlin', you look very handsome. If the polls were open today, I'd vote for you. Shall we go on out and make our entrance for the press?"

Clayton's eyes grew an extra layer of ice. "Did you bring the prenup?"

Finally, she looked at him. "No, we'll talk about that later. Today is Ethan's big day. We don't want to ruin it. Besides, my lawyer couldn't get away until tomorrow to go over it with me. Ethan?"

For the first time Clayton wondered if he'd chosen the right woman. It was salvageable if she didn't shape up. She could always die. The press from that would be wonderful. Clayton could just see Ethan at her funeral, touching the casket, tears rolling down his cheeks onto his black suit, and at the cemetery laying flowers on her tombstone. Oh, yes, the public loved to support a poor bereaved widower.

Ethan had a lovely honest smile, and he flashed it at the camera when he and Catherine walked out of the study, her hand tucked away in his. She was a beautiful woman, and he was grateful to Clayton for being instrumental in getting them together. It had all started so innocently. Clayton had told him that the woman he had been seeing was not the wife of a politician and that if he was serious about the election he had to think past his selfish desires. He needed a woman who had a spotless past and a good name. Ethan had mentioned Cathy, and Clayton stayed on his back until he finally did ask her out. Now they were standing in the foyer with the press cameras lighting up the room.

Catherine kissed him on the cheek and said, "It's your turn to shine. You'll make them all vote for you. Call me when you are ready for the picture of us together." Then she quietly faded back into the study.

Like his mother, Catherine knew what to do, and she did it. She was a lady, and she'd bring grace to his life and office. Too bad he didn't love her, but then, like Clayton said, "Love is one thing, marriage is another, and sex gets the top billing with neither love nor marriage being a factor."

Marty had a gorgeous blue suit that she had worn to her father's and mother's funerals. Cathy had planned to borrow it, but when she awoke that morning, the first thing she saw was that danged prenup on the desk with her e-reader right beside it. Symbolically, they represented what she wanted and what she was going to get.

That's when she had decided to wear the same suit she'd worn to the club. The scarf was one that she'd received from a fellow teacher when she quit teaching. The lie about the scarf had slid off her tongue so slick that she wondered if she and Marty had really switched spirits that morning.

Clayton rounded the end of the desk on his way out as she entered the office. He was a nice-looking man. Nothing he could do short of plastic surgery would ever make him look less like the devil to Cathy, but maybe there was good in his soul… somewhere.

"I'm on my way out to the conference, Catherine," he said.

"I'm sure you are. This won't take long. That prenup is on my desk at home. My lawyer is really coming tomorrow, and we're going to read it together. That is, if you call off the dogs on this zoning law. If not, I'm going to shred it."

"When the prenup is in my hands, I'll call them off. It's up to you how much damage gets done before that," he said.

She wasn't backing down this time. Violet could have her way with the stupid cake, but her dress was bought, and she wasn't going to sign that blasted prenup until Clayton backed down on the zoning issue. She didn't want Ethan's inheritance or Violet's house, but she was not giving up her job or her mother's car. That much was as reasonable as she planned to get.

"There's a meeting tonight. You know who to call to make it go away, Mr. Mason. I can look at that prenup favorably tomorrow, or I can tear it up and you can start all over. We're pretty close to the election for problems, aren't we?"

She sat down on the arm of the same chair where Ethan had been sitting moments before. "Trixie is going to the meeting. When she comes home with the news, I'll know what to do. Oh, and I want that whole block, both sides, zoned commercial. That way, if Aunt Agnes decides to sell her house, she'll get more for it. Now run along so you can be in the pictures. Don't forget to smile. It makes your features less harsh. And tell Violet that I'm in here waiting for her summons when I'm needed."

He flashed a look over his shoulder that sent shivers down her spine as he left. Cathy fell over into the chair, threw her head back on the chair, and took six long breaths. Where on earth had she gotten the courage to say that? And what had she just done? Clayton could kill her by staring at her ten whole seconds with those icy eyes.

"One for e-reader. Zero for prenup," she said, wishing she had a shot of Trixie's Jack Daniels.

It was not possible to take off deodorant that was applied in the morning and leave only the sweat smell of a whole day's work in its wake. Trixie would have done so if she could, and then, when Anna Ruth sat down beside her at the meeting of Council and Chamber committees that evening, she would give her a big hug.

Trixie didn't change from the jeans and T-shirt with Clawdy's logo on the front. She just laid aside her scrapbook papers, dusted what bits of paper she could see from her jeans, and walked kitty-corner across the street.

The awkward silence that met her said that she'd been the topic of conversation, but she didn't care if they were painting her as the smelliest villain in all of Texas. She wasn't there to model the newest fashions. She was there to keep that damned zoning dispute from closing Clawdy's.

"Am I late?" she called out.

Violet's glare was probably meant to shrivel her up into nothing but a sweaty prune, but it made Trixie giggle.

Violet shook her chubby finger at Trixie. "And what is so funny?"

The woman looked like she'd just eaten a cow-pie sandwich. What had happened at the press thing that day anyway? Cathy had said that it went well, but the look on Violet's face didn't back up Cathy's story.

"Were you looking out the window and talking about how tacky I look?" Trixie answered with a question. "That's what it looked like when I came in and the whole place went quiet as a tomb."

"Of course not!" Anna Ruth blushed.

Violet edged her way to the front of the room and everyone else found a seat. "We have better things to discuss than the ex-wife of one of our policemen, Trixie. Now that we are *finally* all here, let's get on with the meeting. This is informal so we aren't calling it to order. We're here to discuss the Craft Festival. The Blue-Ribbon Jalapeño Society usually takes the job of the concession stand at the football field, but this year we are in charge of our very own table with handmade items. Of course, Ethan will deliver the speech and we'll be passing out little flags to everyone to wave after Ethan gives his speech and we play the National Anthem. So the Chamber will take the concession stand and work along with the police department. Anyone have a problem with that?"

So much for it being informal. The queen was in the room.

Trixie raised her hand. "That's from six to nine, right?"

Violet smiled. "Yes, it is."

"Then as spokesman for the Chamber, I'll agree. How many policemen can I have for the concession stand?"

"That's up to you, Trixie. I can't imagine you'd want to work with your ex-husband, but I'm sure you can persuade enough of the others to help you. Now on to the next thing. The Blue-Ribbon Jalapeño Society would like to take charge of the booth spaces at the Jalapeño Jubilee. We'll make sure their fees are paid and everyone is set up to their best advantage. And this year instead of roping off a side street, we have gotten permission from Andy to use Main Street."

"Which two blocks?" Trixie asked.

"The block to the west of Miss Clawdy's and the one to the east."

"Are you planning to use the Christian church lot for extra parking?" Trixie asked.

"I'm sure that the preacher won't mind," Violet said and started to go on.

"I'd get her permission first and ask Andy if he's willing to clean up the mess that will get made," Trixie said.

Anna Ruth cleared her throat.

She could ahem until there was a snowstorm in Cadillac in July, but Trixie wouldn't stop talking about Andy. She'd been married to him fourteen years, and she knew him better than Anna Ruth did.

Violet held out the golden fingernail to Anna Ruth. "Put that in your notes. I'm sure *you* can talk Andy into doing that for us and *you* can go talk to the preacher over there."

"Darla Jean," Trixie said.

Someone in the back snickered.

"What?" Violet raised an eyebrow.

"The preacher is Darla Jean. It might go better if you know her name. And I'd like to know what's been decided about the zoning issue."

Violet's mouth clamped shut so tightly that Trixie wondered if she'd gotten her lip gloss and superglue mixed up. It took a while but finally Violet quit working her jaws and held up a hand. Trixie figured that meant they'd be talking to Darla Jean's lawyer about more than a prenup the next day.

"That has been resolved. Clayton Mason has reviewed the papers for all parties involved. It appears that the Council is willing to rezone that block into a commercial status. Now on to the next thing. How many food vendors at Cadillac's Jalapeño Jubilee this year? And do they all have to have some form of jalapeños as in salsa, pepper sauces, or jellies to sell?"

A person at the back said that the food vendors brought in a lot of business so it was decided they'd let whoever wanted to sell Indian tacos, baked goods, chili, or whatever at the Jubilee. However, the only way they could get the coveted Jubilee Award for best booth was to serve jalapeños in some form.

Trixie's mind was running in circles like a hamster on an exercise wheel. They'd gotten their zoning status, but it had been too easy. It had something to do with that press conference. What in the hell had Cathy done?

"And the last thing is, I understand Martha Andrews has damaged her Caddy again. It's a shame that she drives like a drunk teenager, but what are we to do?" Violet smiled at Anna Ruth.

"So," Violet drug the word out dramatically, "we won't have the vintage Caddy to bring up the rear of the parade. We need one for Andy to ride in as last year's celebrity, so y'all be thinking of one by the next Council meeting."

"Doesn't Marty always head up the parade? It's tradition," someone asked.

Violet puffed out her chest and turned on her best smile. "We are changing things this year. Ethan will be riding in a brand spanking new Caddy limo at the front of the parade. Now I don't think we have anything else, but Annabel has made her famous pecan sandy cookies, and we have coffee for anyone who'd like to stay and visit."

Trixie didn't want to visit with anyone so she beat a path across the street. She expected to find Cathy in the kitchen wringing her hands in worry. But the whole house was empty. No Marty, Cathy, Darla Jean, or even Agnes. There was a note on the refrigerator that said Cathy and Marty had made a run to Walmart and to call them if she got home before they did.

"Hello," Marty answered on the first ring.

"Tell Cathy thanks."

"For what?"

"I don't know how she did it, but the zoning law is good for the whole block, and Violet didn't want to talk about it. I just hope she didn't sell her soul for us."

Agnes didn't give a damn if the whole town of Cadillac was zoned commercial. She intended to leave her house feet first in a body bag. She'd be stone cold dead, but she did want Cathy to get a fair price for the place so she kept a watch on the cars down the street at the Community Center.

She would have gone to the meeting herself, crawled up on the stump, and went to preaching about bringing business into town if the fools would stop their politics and do things right, but if she had, Violet Prescott would have dug her heels in tighter. Damned old stubborn bitch thought she was taking Cathy away from her to make her pay for marrying Bert. Well, there hadn't been a wedding yet and Agnes would fight it right up until Cathy walked down the aisle.

Just how much money would she have to lay out to have someone kidnap Cathy and hold her captive until she came to her senses? Maybe Trixie knew someone who'd do the deed. No, never! Agnes wouldn't ask Trixie to help her with jack shit. She'd get it all wrong, but maybe if Trixie kidnapped Ethan and terrorized him, he'd be too traumatized to get married or take office. Violet would have a heart attack and die. And Trixie would go to jail. Solve lots of problems that way.

Agnes didn't like Trixie. Never had. Never would. The woman was an idiot and Agnes had no time for fools. Andy Johnson had been a womanizer from the time he was old enough to chase a skirt and any woman who married him was a complete moron. To stay married to him meant she was a fool. Not catching him in his philandering just meant she had her head up her ass in all that craft shit and that made her an idiot.

Add to it that Trixie had lied about the man in her room that night and it really made Agnes angry. Agnes was old but she had perfectly good eyesight. Never bought a damn pair of glasses in her entire life and she saw what she saw. There was a man in that room and if he wasn't molesting Trixie then by damn she was allowing him to pin her down on that bed. If the latter was the case, then Trixie had no business living in the house with Cathy and Marty.

She waited until she saw Trixie jog kitty-corner across the street before she put on her house shoes, tucked the key to the back door of the café in the pocket of her chenille robe, and started across the street.

Bless Claudia's heart for giving her a key to the house before she died. Marty might have wanted it back when they put in the café, but Cathy would never let her ask. For that alone, Cathy deserved to inherit everything Agnes owned. Besides, if she did go through with the wedding, later she might need the money to buy a divorce.

The door wasn't locked so Agnes let herself in to find Trixie pouring a shot of whiskey in a water glass.

"What are *you* doing here?" Trixie asked.

"I got more right to be in this house than you. What happened at that meeting?"

"If you want to know then attend." Trixie downed the shot and poured another one.

Agnes frowned at the smell but Andy would drive any woman to drink. Maybe he had an agreement with the liquor store out at the edge of town. He'd use his charms to get a woman into bed, leave her, and she'd turn into a drunk. The liquor store was probably paying him a nice little check each week on their profits.

"Anna Ruth there?" Agnes asked.

"Oh, yeah. Wearing her spike heels and all dressed up fit to kill."

Agnes chuckled.

Trixie frowned. "What's so funny?

"Bet you she's throwing back a few too. I heard about her and

Andy at the Sunday school meeting last night… we was discussing Bible school, whether to have it or not this year. I think it's a big waste of time. Kids used to think it was a treat to get to go to Bible school and they'd endure the learnin' about Jesus part if they could have refreshments and do craft projects. Nowadays they've got video games and music in their ears and—" She stopped. "Where in the hell was I? You made me lose my train of thought. It's probably that nasty smell of liquor."

"Sunday school meeting. Andy and…" Trixie started.

"That's right. That new woman they hired to be the part-time dispatcher down at the police station. Andy is sleeping with her."

The blank expression on Trixie's face was priceless.

Agnes went on, "He's always had a thing for the women. You just had your head too deep in all that shit you do with paper and ceramics to see it, girl. Wake up and smell the bacon frying. He's a sumbitch. He's been screwing around on you ever since y'all got married."

"They agreed to let the new business come in and they've zoned the whole block commercial," Trixie said in a hollow voice.

Agnes did not feel sorry for her. She should have put her paper dolls and ceramic roosters away years ago and figured out that she'd married a cheatin' man that wouldn't ever be faithful to her.

Jack removed the front grille of the Caddy and set the mangled chrome mess to one side. It would be two weeks before the new one arrived and he'd had a devil of a time finding a salvage yard with one. He could have bought one from the restorer's catalog, but Marty wanted to keep everything authentic. His head was under the hood again. He had one hand slipped down beside the radiator and the other working at removing it so he could see if it could be repaired or if they'd need to order another one. He heard the fizz of a beer can opening and eased up.

"I promised sandwiches and beer," Trixie said.

She handed him the beer and collapsed on a chair, her head in her hands, sobs wracking her body.

"Did Marty die?" Jack asked.

"No, and not Cathy either."

"Agnes?"

"I'm crying, not laughing."

"One more. Darla Jean?"

"Nooo," she said. "I need a friend and they're all gone or busy. I can't bother Darla Jean when she's working on tomorrow's sermon, and besides," she hiccupped, "she'd tell me to forgive and forget and I want to kill him, not forgive his sorry ass."

Jack sat down in the other chair and threw his arm around Trixie's shoulders. "I'm your friend, Trixie. I've always been your friend."

She leaned over and cried on his shoulder until she didn't have any more tears. "I'm sorry. Agnes just told me that Andy is cheating with the dispatcher down at the station."

"I can't talk about Andy, Trixie. He's my boss," Jack said.

"You are my friend, not his, tonight. And I've been your friend longer than he's been your boss anyway."

"I'm your friend but I can't talk about my boss. It's not right."

He wanted to tell her. God only knew how much he wanted to name names, places, and times that he was positive about, but he couldn't. It went against everything he'd been taught about respecting the chain of command and protecting your officers.

She wiped her cheeks with the back of her hand. "Everyone in town knew about his flings, didn't they?"

Jack patted her on the shoulder. "It's over, Trixie. Don't worry about it."

"Why didn't someone tell me? Did you all think I knew?"

He hugged her tightly.

"Agnes wasn't just trying to rile me up, was she?"

"Agnes doesn't like you, but she's not trying to rile you up," he said.

There. He'd given her an answer, but he hadn't said a word about his captain.

She reached over to the workbench beside her, peeled off two paper towels, blew her nose, and tossed the soiled towel into the trash can. "Thank you. You are a good friend. My fifteen minutes of whining is up. Show me how I can help."

Trixie wiggled out of his embrace and flipped the tab off a beer can. She took several long gulps and nodded toward a plate of roast beef sandwiches.

"You eat and then we'll work," she said.

Jack smiled. At least she hadn't asked him about the voting shit. There would be nothing left of Clawdy's but ashes and jars of picante—that damn stuff was hotter than flames—if Trixie found out that Marty had voted for Anna Ruth. For the life of him, Jack couldn't figure out why in the hell she'd done such a thing anyway. Marty had wanted to put out a hit on both Andy and Anna Ruth when Trixie caught them in bed together. And then she'd gone and voted for Anna Ruth to be a member of the club. That was the ten-thousand-dollar question that didn't seem to have an answer.

Chapter 8

DEREK CAME INTO CLASS all dressed up that Wednesday night. The Stetson was strong enough that she knew he'd shaven not long before, and a couple of water droplets still glistened on his black hair. He sat down at his desk, picked up the booklet, and began to work after he flashed her a brilliant smile. Evidently, the cowboy had a date as soon as class was over.

Marty opened a brand new page on her laptop and got ready to write. Maybe the next crew that came through her class would have a fireman or a weight lifter in it, but right now she worked with the muse she had and that was Derek. She put her hands on the keyboard and started typing, the words flowing from brain to keys as she imagined what her female character would like to do to that cowboy and have him do to her.

When the class ended, she gathered up her things and was locking her door when her cell phone rang. She groaned when she saw Agnes's number. If someone was attacking Trixie, Agnes had a damn gun; she could take care of it and hopefully she hit her target this time and didn't shoot a hole in the ceiling.

"Hello," she said cautiously.

"There are no leftovers from today's lunch? I thought you had pecan tarts on Wednesdays. There's always a few left and I wanted them to serve at my Sunday school class meeting tomorrow. Where are they?"

"We sold out," Marty said.

"Where are you? It's time you were home. If you were here, you could make a dozen for me tonight," Agnes told her.

"But I'm not home, and I'm not going to make pecan tarts at this time of night. Grab a package of Oreos from the pantry and serve them at your meeting," Marty said.

Cathy had donned her overalls that Wednesday, glad that Ethan, Violet, and Clayton were at a Kiwanis or maybe it was a Masons group meeting so he could speechify about his campaign. She needed to unwind, to stop worrying about that damned prenup.

The weatherman said there was a cold snap coming the next week with frost, so it would be the last of the yard work for a few months. She would always maintain the beautiful lawns at Clawdy's, but she looked forward to landscaping her own yard when she and Ethan got married. And she wasn't visualizing the Prescott place, either!

She dumped the bag full of clippings into her compost pile at the back of the garage and stirred them down into the mulch with a garden rake. She gathered up her small tools to dig about in the small garden with the pepper plants on the east side of the house. They'd almost quit producing, but she'd kept a jar full of seeds to plant the next year and maybe by then she'd figure out what kind of fertilizer her mother used.

Cathy really was ready for a long soaking bath when she put away her tools and went into the house. She wanted to read, but unlike a paper book, an e-reader could not go to the bathtub. Dropping a book into the water would ruin it. An e-reader slipping out of Cathy's hands would be equivalent to losing a whole library of hot erotic books.

It was either take a long bath without a book, since she seldom bought anything other than ebooks anymore, or a quick shower and curl up and read until bedtime. The shower won. Afterward, she donned her favorite old worn cotton-knit nightshirt and locked her door.

She piled the pillows up against the headboard of her bed, picked up her e-reader, and started reading where she'd left off. She'd barely gotten a page done when her phone rang.

"Hello," she answered.

"This is Agnes. I'm downstairs and I called Marty, but she won't come home and make me a dozen pecan tarts for tomorrow's committee meeting."

"Aunt Agnes, there are a couple of bags of Oreos in the storage room. Help yourself to however many you need. I'm reading," Cathy said.

"Well, hell! You ain't goin' to make me any either, are you? You'll be sorry when I leave my house to the church. I swear to God, I never thought I'd see the day when you'd act like your sister."

"Call Trixie. Maybe she will make them," Cathy said.

"I'd rather eat dog biscuits as ask her for shit. She's up there cutting out paper dolls or painting some gawd-awful ceramic owl or something. Read your damned old book, and I'll take what I can find," Agnes said.

"Good night, Aunt Agnes. Lock the kitchen door on your way out."

"The hell I will. You want it locked, you come do it. It was open when I got here, and I'm not locking it."

"Now Aunt Agnes, don't be angry."

"I ain't angry. I'm pissed because I wanted pecan tarts and there ain't a one down here. Next week you tell Marty to make an extra dozen in case I need them."

Cathy started to say something else, but the phone went dead.

One more page and the phone rang again.

"Aunt Agnes, I'm not making tarts," she said without looking at the ID.

"I'm not Agnes." Ethan laughed.

He had a nice deep laugh that went with his voice. That, with his brilliant smile, would go a long way in his campaign. But neither made Cathy's heart race like reading about good old hot sex.

"Hello, darlin'. Did the meeting go well?" she asked.

"Hasn't started yet. I had five minutes, and Clayton wants to know what you and your lawyer decided about the prenup. I really want this thing out of the way so we don't have to think about it anymore and can concentrate on the wedding. Did you see the newspaper?"

"No, not yet. Do we look good?"

"Yes, we do. Now about the prenup. Can I expect you to bring it all signed on Saturday night? Mother has invited Clayton to supper and we can take care of it before we eat. After that maybe I'll whip you at Scrabble and we'll all have a good time."

Her idea of a good time involved time spent with him alone, not sitting at the table with Violet finding fault with everything she said, did, or wore. And surely not freezing to death under Clayton's ice-cold glares.

"Well?" Ethan asked.

"Tell you what, darlin'. There are a couple of issues I'd like to visit with you in private about. So how about you meet me at the Dairy Queen tomorrow night. We'll have a cup of coffee on neutral grounds and make a few adjustments, then Saturday night it will all be done," she answered.

"I suppose that's doable," he said. "Until tomorrow night then. Sleep tight."

Oh, yeah, like that was going to happen after finishing the book she was reading.

Two more paragraphs and the back door slammed. She must have made a believer out of Agnes.

Then Marty's high heels rat-a-tatting on the steps stopped at her door and she heard sobs. She bailed out of bed and heard what sounded like a dying cat on the landing crying, "Caaathhhy! Open your door. I need a friend."

Marty would never sound like that. Neither would Trixie, and Agnes cussed when she was upset; she did not cry. She opened the door carefully and Anna Ruth fell into her arms, sobbing and flailing around like she was going to faint dead away.

Trixie looked at the scrapbook. Should she use the heart punch or the scalloped scissors for the wiggly piece on the side of the picture? A heart appliqué was on the hip pockets of her jeans so it made better sense to use the heart punch.

Cathy's phone had rung and she could hear her talking but couldn't make out the words since both of their bedroom doors were shut. Then Marty came home.

No, those weren't Marty's footsteps. She'd worn flats to her class that night. Black ones with cute little stones glued to the front. Trixie had commented on them. What she heard was the definite rat-a-tat-tat of high heels.

She had the paper lined up just right and was about to push when she heard the pitiful wailing in the hallway. She put all her might behind the punch so the edges would be crisp and pinched a blood blister on her forefinger.

"Son of a bitch! Whoever the hell you are, you'd best be dead when I open this door." She stuck her finger in her mouth, and when that didn't help, she slung it around, stopping long enough to look at the blood blister on the way across the floor.

Nothing helped the throbbing, and the sobbing got louder and louder. She slung open the door to find Cathy in the hallway, holding Anna Ruth up as she carried on like a wounded banshee.

It was a beautiful sight!

Anna Ruth caught sight of Trixie and pointed. "I thought you were screwing him on Wednesday nights."

Lying was a mortal sin, so Trixie shrugged as if she didn't have any idea what Anna Ruth was talking about.

Anna Ruth wailed even louder. "I blamed the wrong woman. It's been that tart with the bubble butt down at the station all along. I'm so stupid. Aunt Annabel said if I could steal him away from his wife, then someone could steal him away from me. And the sad part is I just did it to prove that I could love a man other than… oh, no!" She slapped a hand over her mouth and rolled her eyes.

Poor Cathy! She was wedged in between a rock and a hard spot with no place to crawl out. Trixie felt sorry for her but not enough to help hold up that weeping bag of bones.

She did not have an ounce of pity for Anna Ruth. She'd already cried her tears over that cheatin' son of a bitch. Anna Ruth could cry hers all on her own. At least Anna Ruth had only given Andy a few months of her life and not fourteen years.

Suddenly Anna Ruth stopped moaning and her blue eyes flew open so wide that they looked unreal. She untangled her arms from around Cathy's neck and pointed toward Trixie's bedroom door.

"God Almighty!" she whispered.

"Yes, he is," Darla Jean said from the top of the stairs. "The back door was open and I heard someone cryin' their poor little soul out. What is going on up here?"

"Would you look at that mess?" Anna Ruth raised her voice and shook her finger toward Trixie's bedroom. "No wonder Andy kicked you out of the house. He was right! You are a slob."

Trixie forgot all about her own throbbing finger. "Want to come in for a better look? I just sprayed yesterday so the roaches should all be dead by now and surely six mice were all there was holed up under my bed."

Anna Ruth shook her head. "How could he ever live with you? I was an idiot to think he'd ever screw around with you. He couldn't stand to be in that room long enough to have sex."

Trixie opened her mouth to name times, places, and positions but clamped it shut.

Cathy managed a weak smile. "Let's go downstairs and have some coffee. Darla Jean will be glad to visit with you."

Bless Cathy's heart. She would befriend a rabid skunk.

Anna Ruth swung her pointed finger around to stop just inches from Trixie's nose. "I hate you. I thought if I was the opposite of you, he'd love me and I'd learn to love him as much as I do…"

Trixie slapped her hand away. "As you love who?"

Anna Ruth let out a scream that echoed off the walls worse than Agnes's shotgun blast. If there hadn't still been a hole in the ceiling for it to escape up through, it would have scared the hell out of Trixie and made an angel out of her right there in the crowded landing.

"Don't you ever touch me!" Anna Ruth yelled as she yanked a fist full of Trixie's hair with one hand and scratched her upper arm with the other one. Her skinny arms flew every which way as she tried to get a hold on anything that belonged to Trixie's body.

Trixie had a blood blister on her finger, a bleeding arm, and now was about to be snatched bald. No way was she letting Anna Ruth do any more damage. Trixie opened up her hand and slapped the woman right across the face.

Lord, it felt so good that she had the other hand open and on the way to put a matching red print on the other side when she checked herself and said, "Get a hold of yourself. Andy is rotten but you are acting like it's the end of the world. It's not, believe me. The sun will come up tomorrow morning."

Anna Ruth went back into wailing and flailing, falling into Darla Jean's arms that time. Darla Jean looked at Trixie who said, "Watch those fingernails. They're sharp as knives."

Agnes pushed past Darla Jean right into the middle of the mess. "What in the hell is going on up here?"

Anna Ruth straightened up when a new audience entered the tiny landing. "Oh, Agnes, he's cheated on me."

"Well, hell, woman, what did you expect?"

"And Trixie hit me right in the face," Anna Ruth said.

"Can't say I blame her," Agnes said.

Trixie grinned. Some days couldn't get any better. She winked at Darla Jean. "She's all yours. I've got scrapbooking to do."

Cathy fidgeted.

Suddenly, Trixie could have kicked the woman down the stairs for putting Cathy in such a spot. Poor Cathy didn't need all this drama added to what she was enduring at the hands of Ethan and his mother.

Agnes threw up her hands. "I'm going home. I thought someone had died and hoped it was Trixie."

Trixie sighed. Good times don't last forever. You had to seize the moment and enjoy the memory of it after it was gone. She turned around and went back into her room. "Cathy, I'd like your opinion on something I'm working on for Mamma. I bet Darla Jean can take care of Anna Ruth and her soul."

Darla Jean nodded toward Trixie and led Anna Ruth down to the kitchen.

Trixie pulled Cathy into her room and shut the door firmly behind them.

"Lord!" she said. "What a night! Too bad the whiskey is downstairs!"

"Amen to that," Cathy said.

Marty hummed all the way home, but it changed into a cussing fit when she saw Anna Ruth's new little bright red Mustang sitting in front of her house. Nothing that had a thing to do with Andy was welcome to visit her house. She might get away with eating at Clawdy's, but she'd best keep her sorry ass away from Trixie after hours.

Agnes met her at the truck door. "I had to come break up a fight between your friend who is going to ruin your place with her reputation and that sleazy niece of Annabel's. I don't know what they were fightin' about, but I'll tell you right now that sorry Andy Johnson ain't worth Trixie getting scratched up. I'm not a bit surprised there's fightin' and carryin' on in the house, but it's a shame to see a couple of grown women acting like hookers fightin' over a dick."

"A John, Aunt Agnes."

"I said what I meant," Agnes told her.

"And what does Anna Ruth look like?"

"Darla Jean's got her in the kitchen and she's got a pretty red handprint on her cheek. She deserves it just because she made me put on my house shoes and rush over here. I was ready for bed already when I heard the screamin' goin' on."

Marty threw up her palms. The great night was over.

She grabbed the doorknob and Anna Ruth ran out so fast that Marty had to step aside or get knocked down.

She pushed right past Marty without so much as an apology and said, "Forgive, hell! I'm not forgiving him and I'll never forget this. He's ruined my reputation. I thought he'd marry me. Aunt Annabel and I were already planning the wedding. Your friend in there can go preach to someone else. I'm not interested," she fumed.

There wasn't nearly enough light for Marty to see the red print on Anna Ruth's face. Sometimes a woman just couldn't catch a lucky break.

There was a method to the madness in Trixie's room. Ceramics on the right side, paints organized on one side, brushes on the other. Scrapbooking on the left side of the room, spread out over a folding eight-foot table, but when Trixie wanted something all she had to do was reach and grab. That it was always right where she grabbed amazed Cathy.

She sat on one side of the bed with Trixie on the other.

"The poor woman doesn't have friends and thinks just because we are in the club together that I'm her buddy," Cathy said.

"It's hard for me to feel sorry for her, Cathy, but I wouldn't trade places with her. I can't imagine how she must feel. When I found out he was cheating on me, I had you and Marty and Darla Jean."

Someone rapped on Trixie's door before Cathy could say anything. Trixie bounced off the bed like a boxer coming up off the ring. "If she's back up here, I'm going to drag her inside this room and make her sit on the floor with all the mess. That'll kill her dead in ten minutes."

She swung the door open to find Darla Jean giggling. "I heard that remark. I reckon it would be murder by mess, but I don't think it would be considered homicide. I'm not sure how God would write it up, though."

Trixie left the door open and motioned for Darla Jean to come inside.

Darla Jean had barely settled into the rocking chair at the end of the ceramics table when Marty poked her head in the door.

"Agnes met me in the driveway and said I missed the show."

Cathy moved down and Marty sat beside her. When Cathy finished telling the way it had really gone down, Marty slapped a pillow. "Dammit! I would've driven faster to see that."

Trixie held up her arm. "See what she did to me?"

"What can I say? She's a crazy bitch." Marty turned toward Cathy. "Weren't you supposed to be at Ethan's tonight?"

"He had that campaign thing, remember? But he called to ask about the prenup."

"Cathy, darlin', you are thirty-four years old, and I realize your clock is ticking loudly, but you cannot sign that piece of trash," Marty said. "Let me go with you out there. I'll tell them exactly what we will and will not put up with."

"You have to love him because I do and because he's going to be your brother," she said.

"He won't be my brother. I hope he's not even your husband. And I wouldn't love that man if he was Jesus," Marty said.

Darla Jean frowned.

"Well, maybe," Marty said, "but he ain't, so I don't have to love his sorry old ass. Any man that would let a lawyer put that shit in a prenup should have to marry Anna Ruth."

"I like it! Ethan and Anna Ruth," Trixie said. "She even likes Violet."

"That is absolutely perfect!" Marty giggled.

Cathy held up her hands. "I'm going to talk to Ethan tomorrow night at the Dairy Queen and we're sitting down all alone. We're going to settle all this. I'll concede to a few things and he can do the same. It's called compromise and it is supposed to work in marriage. And all of you are staying at home. It's just the two of us."

Marty threw her arm around Cathy's shoulder. "No Violet?"

"No, and no Clayton."

"You better take a condom. You might get a chance to sneak off and do some hanky-panky." Trixie laughed.

Darla Jean giggled.

"What is so funny? We aren't having sex now, but we will eventually, and it will be really hot," Cathy said.

"My thoughts had nothing to do with you and hanky-panky. I was thinking that maybe we should go stand guard outside the Dairy Queen. I can't imagine Violet letting Ethan out of her sight. We might need to restrain Violet so you and Ethan can have some time alone. You bring the rope; Marty and I'll bring the gag."

The moment froze as if Cathy had pushed a pause button on life.

Friends! Sometimes they were kin and interfered like Marty.

Some weren't kin but looked out for you anyway like Trixie and Darla Jean. Sometimes they had shared so much it was hard to believe they weren't kin.

Chapter 9

It wasn't that Darla Jean liked Cathy better than Marty or Trixie. Cathy was just so gullible. She had a wonderful, kind spirit just like Jesus, but even the son of God couldn't be pushed too long. He'd done some damage when he found out there was a big sale in the temple. And when the time was right, Cathy would take care of that prenup. Knowing that didn't keep Darla Jean from worrying about her, though.

Darla Jean hummed the hymns she'd picked out for the congregational singing the next Sunday as she swept the sanctuary floor with a wide dust mop. Doing her own cleaning helped her think about her sermon, and living in the church wasn't so bad. She had a couple of rooms behind the sanctuary that she'd converted into a bedroom and a kitchen/living room. She'd known building up the congregation in a church would be every bit as tough as building a clientele list in the escort business, so she hadn't gone into it blind. She'd set aside four years of salary out of her savings and had given up her swanky Dallas apartment when she retired.

She scooted the dirt into a dustpan and sat down on the front pew. Her Christian church had come a long way in three years. An average of fifty people a week dropped in for services and twenty tithed regularly.

"Help me, please," a voice said behind her.

Darla Jean turned, expecting to see Cathy. It had been Darla Jean's business to know men and she'd been right about Ethan. His heart was kind, but his mother was strong. The prenup was going to stand, and Cathy could take it or fight. Too bad she'd gotten blessed with a soft heart instead of Marty's temper.

But she wasn't facing Cathy when she looked down the aisle. It was a small woman or a medium-sized teenage girl dressed in jeans with holes in the knees, barefoot, and a hooded sweatshirt.

Darla Jean held up both hands. "Whoa, now! This is a church. There's nothing here worth killin' over."

The girl removed her hands from her pockets and held them up. One was empty. The other held a cell phone. "I need a place to hide."

Darla Jean motioned her forward. "Take that sweatshirt off. It's too hot to be wearing a coat."

The woman shook her head, hurried forward, and sat down on the front pew and rolled up into the fetal position as racking sobs shook her body. "I can't go back. He's going to kill me."

Darla Jean put her arm around the girl. "Nobody is going to kill you in my church. You are safe here, child."

"My name is Lindsey. I'm not a child. I'm almost twenty; next month is my birthday." She pulled the hood back to reveal a purple face, one eye swollen shut, lip split with dried blood crusting on the outside of the wound, and bruises the size of a man's fingers on her neck. When she removed the sweatshirt her arms were a palette of purples and yellows, old bruises, new ones, and red marks where fresh ones would start tomorrow morning.

Darla Jean was aghast. "Who did this to you? Your pimp?"

Lindsey shook her head. "I'm not a hooker."

"Go on."

"I got married six months ago. I thought he loved me and that's why he was so possessive. But…"

"But it turned bad, didn't it?"

She nodded. "If he thinks I look at a man too long in the grocery store, I catch hell. If the towel isn't hung exactly even in the bathroom, that's grounds for six lashes with the belt. If his supper isn't on the table and everything perfect, then that's ten lashes. If I talk to my girlfriends on the phone and he finds out…"

Darla Jean nodded toward the phone she held tightly. "That's what happened tonight?"

Lindsey nodded. "One of them gave me a burn phone. He found it. I waited until he went to sleep and snuck out the back door. I can't go back. He said if I left him, he'd hunt me down and kill me."

"Are you from here in Cadillac?" Darla Jean asked.

She shook her head. "Up near Denison. I hitched a ride, but this is as far as I got, and I don't have money, and I'm terrified of him. Leaving him is instant death. It's written on a piece of paper and taped to the mirror in our bedroom."

"Family?" Darla Jean asked. "I'll take you to them."

"I went home the first time it happened and showed them the belt whelps on my legs. He followed me and told them I'd fallen down the stairs. They believed him. He's very charismatic."

"I've got a place I can take you where you'll be safe. What is his name?"

Lindsey whispered, "Walter Cranston."

"That is the last time you'll have to say that name. Monday morning, you'll become Lindsey Jean. I know some people who will take care of things for us, and we'll get you a brand new driver's license along with new credentials. What kind of work skills do you have?"

"I was studying early childhood development at college at night and working at an oil company, but when we married I had to quit school and work. He was just so jealous," Lindsey said.

"What made you come to my church?"

"A light in the window and I'm so tired."

"I'll lock the door and we'll go out the back way. You are going to my sister's place in Blue Ridge. Ever heard of that town?"

"No, I grew up in Durant, just over the river in Oklahoma."

"Well, Blue Ridge isn't nearly that big."

"I don't even know your name, and you believed me and you're helping me."

"It's Darla Jean. No middle name and Jean is my last name. There were six Darlas in my school so they had to do something to know which one was which. I been Darla Jean ever since."

Lindsey's phone rang.

She held it like it was a poisonous snake, out from her body. "It's him. He talked my friend into giving him the number," she whispered. "What do I do?"

Darla Jean took the phone from her, slammed it down on the floor, and stomped it to bits. Then she swept up the remains in the dustpan and put them into the small trash can behind her podium.

"You are through with that phone and with him." She held a hand out to Lindsey.

The imagination is both a wonderful and a cruel thing, and some things are just better left unknown. For years, Betty Jean had worried about her younger sister, Darla. What kind of job paid the kind of money she made? Was she into drugs, or was she living in sin with a rich sugar daddy?

Don't ask the question if you don't want to know the answer, her mother had often said, so she didn't ask. And then, praise the Lord, Darla had come to Blue Ridge three years ago and announced she was starting a church in Uncle Joseph's old service station building.

Darla's birth had been a difficult thing for Betty to accept. She was twenty and her mother forty-two that year, and a new baby in the family should have belonged to Betty, not her mother. But Betty's fiancé was killed in Vietnam, and she had a sister instead of a wedding and a baby of her own. She figured she'd wind up raising the girl, but her mother had lived long enough to get Darla through high school and packed off to college in Dallas before she died.

Betty had been antsy all day, so she wasn't surprised to hear from her sister that evening. "I thought you might come by today or call," she said.

"I was about to hang up. It rang four times."

"I was talking to Lottie about the clothes closet duties. Are you coming down here tonight? I made a cake," Betty said.

"I'm on my way. But I've got this big favor."

"Yes."

"You didn't even let me tell you what it is."

"I don't care what it is. If you need help and I can provide it, the answer is yes. How far away are you?"

"Five minutes."

"I'll put the coffee on," Betty said.

Betty could not ever remember her sister asking her for anything. She'd gone to college right out of high school but never finished. And then she got a really good job in Dallas that she never discussed, but she was always generous with her money. So if she needed help, Betty would do what she could. She filled the Mr. Coffee and met Darla on the porch.

"It's a big favor." Darla bent to hug Betty, who was six inches shorter than Darla and fifty pounds heavier. Her salt-and-pepper hair was cut in a bob and her face was as round as a pumpkin. She wore a caftan with bright red roses on a black background and her house shoes.

Betty didn't even hesitate when she nodded. The young girl with Darla looked like she'd barely survived a car wreck, but Betty knew what had caused all that damage and it had nothing to do with an automobile. She'd seen it before and she'd helped a couple of women escape men who did such things.

"Let's go to the kitchen and have some coffee. Are you hungry?

I made Mamma's vegetable soup for supper. We could heat some in the microwave," Betty said.

"That sounds wonderful. This is Lindsey and this is my sister Betty." Darla made introductions.

Betty was already bustling around in the kitchen. "Darla, you get the crackers and slice some cheese. There's a lemon Bundt cake under the dome. I was hoping you would come so I made your favorite. Lindsey, darlin', just sit down there at the table. We'll have something to eat ready in no time."

Darla Jean told the story, keeping it short.

"Well, darlin'," Betty laid a soft hand on Lindsey's shoulder, "you'll be safe with me. And in a few weeks, if you want, you can move over next door in Mamma's house. It's been settin' empty for years and I can't bear to rent it out, but I'd just love to have a neighbor."

Darla Jean hugged her sister again and whispered, "I'll send money to help and come around to check on things every week."

"You always have," Betty whispered back.

Ethan could give a passionate speech that would bring tears, or he could incite an audience to chanting his name and waving tiny red, white, and blue flags. But going into that Dairy Queen to talk to Catherine about the prenuptial agreement was just downright aggravating. It shouldn't be happening. She should have signed it the first day and not made such an ordeal about it. But he *would* take the thing home signed that evening. He could control a group of people with his words, so surely he could sweet-talk his fiancée into signing the papers. He even had the pen in his shirt pocket, ready to do the deed.

Hopefully when it was done, his mother would stop carrying on like someone had died. And Clayton would lose that horrible scowl.

She was waiting in the back booth in the nonsmoking section with the folder in front of her. He slid into the opposite side before he remembered that he should have kissed her first. It was too late to go back to the door and start over, so he laid a hand over hers and squeezed.

"Been waiting long, sweetheart?" he asked.

"Only a few minutes. I ordered coffee." She pointed. "You want something?"

He shook his head, took the pen from his pocket, and laid it on the folder. "Please sign those papers so we can get on with our marriage plans. This is frustrating Clayton and worrying Mother. We need to get it settled, Catherine."

She picked up the pen and handed it back to him. "Yes, we do."

That was definitely not a good sign.

"Why won't you sign it?"

"Because I'm not going to give up my part of Clawdy's or my mother's old Lumina. I like that car, and I like to work."

"But both make me look bad," he said. "I will buy you a new Caddy, and you can help Mother with all the charity work and fundraising. That will get some of the pressure off her and give you something to do."

"Do you love me?" she asked right out of the blue.

He hesitated. "I asked you to marry me, didn't I?"

"If you love me, you will throw this in the trash and trust me." She tried to remember the last time he'd told her that he loved her. A frown worked its way across her brows but no memory came. She tried to remember the first time. Was it when he proposed? No, he'd said she made him happy, but he hadn't said he loved her. Was he saving that for their honeymoon too? What if he didn't say the words? She didn't want to live her whole life hearing her husband tell her that he cared deeply for her or was fond of her. She wanted to hear the three magic words every single day of their lives.

"I can't do that, Catherine," Ethan said.

"It's going in the trash, Ethan. Either you do it or I do."

"Which means?"

"Well, look who's out and about this hot, hot evening." Anna Ruth slid into the booth beside Ethan. "I just ordered a big old hot fudge sundae to celebrate getting all my things out of Andy's house. I've moved in with Aunt Annabel until I can find a place of my own. I've been thinking about finding an apartment in Sherman. It's closer to Bells where I teach anyway. I'm ready for a change, to get away from small-town politics and into a big city."

"Does that mean you're not going to be in the club?" Catherine asked.

"Oh, no! Bells is still in Grayson County. I'd never move so far away I couldn't be in the club."

Ethan sucked air when Anna Ruth laid a hand on his thigh. He was there to sweet-talk Catherine, not get felt up by Anna Ruth, but if he said anything, there would be a big argument and the papers would not get signed. He couldn't go home without them.

Anna Ruth's hand moved up two inches. "So tell me, Ethan, where are you all planning to live once the election is over?"

"In our home, of course. When I win, I'll be away a great deal of the time, but Catherine will live in our house with Mother."

Anna Ruth looked over at Catherine and sighed. "You are so lucky."

"Yes, I am." Catherine smiled sweetly. But she didn't feel lucky, not with her fiancé sitting beside another woman.

Anna Ruth blinked her big blue eyes until tears formed on the ends of her eyelashes, thick with layers upon layers of black mascara, and ran in muddy-looking streaks down her cheeks. "I wish I could be so lucky."

Good grief, what was Ethan to do with a crying woman arousing him and an angry one close enough to scratch his eyes out?

Catherine jerked a paper napkin from the dispenser in the middle of the table and handed it to Anna Ruth. "So you've moved out of the house? That was fast."

"Oh, well, off with the old and on with the new." She sniffled as she moved her hand up an inch more and squeezed Ethan's thigh. "That's the way I see it. I'm not letting him hold me back another minute. I was only living with him because I couldn't have the one I truly loved." Another squeeze.

Ethan slapped a hand over his mouth and coughed to cover the groan.

"Are you getting sick?" Catherine asked.

"No, just got a whiff of smoke from the smoker's section." He reached under the table and removed Anna Ruth's hand.

When his phone rang, he grabbed it from his pocket and said, "Excuse me, ladies. It's Clayton and we are discussing more yard signs tonight, so I'd better take it."

Anna Ruth slipped out of the booth first, but when he stepped a few feet away, she sat back down.

"Is it done?" Clayton asked bluntly.

Ethan smiled at Catherine. "Not yet, but we're working on it."

"Damn! Do I need to come down there?"

"I'm on my way right now. Be there in ten minutes." He put the phone back in his pocket.

Anna Ruth was out of the booth instantly. "I'm going to see why my sundae isn't here. I just bet that girl forgot all about me. She was flirting with her boyfriend at the window. I don't blame her. If I had a chance to flirt with the man I was interested in, I'd take it no matter what."

Ethan couldn't keep his eyes off the way her waist nipped in above a well-rounded butt as she headed back to the counter. Anna Ruth had been flirting with him, there was no doubt about it, but he couldn't think about that with his mother's fretting, his campaign manager's demands, and that damned folder.

Catherine tapped the folder. "So back to this."

"I'm not trashing it," he said. "I'll talk to Clayton about your issues, and we'll discuss them Saturday evening when you come to dinner."

He started toward the door. Catherine did the same but sped up so she was a step ahead so he could see her shove the folder into the trash can with her coffee cup.

Courage to do the right thing was supposed to give her a big surge of self-confidence. It didn't. Cathy's hands trembled as she gripped the steering wheel. It was over. She'd stood her ground and delivered what she promised. The folder with its contents would be covered with cold, greasy French fries, leftover last bites of hamburger or chicken nuggets, and empty packets of picante sauce for tacos. But had she just thrown out her future marriage with it?

She looked down at her engagement ring, sparkling in the last rays of the setting sun. Her phone rang and she answered without even looking, hoping it was Ethan telling her that he regretted not throwing the thing in the trash. That he was on his way home to tell both his mother and Clayton that they were buying the little house in Cadillac and she could work at the café as long as she liked.

"I can't believe you did that right in front of the whole world," Ethan said.

"I can't believe you didn't," she said.

"I'll have Clayton draft another one for you to sign Saturday night. I'll make it plain that you can keep your mother's car. There's plenty of room to park it in the garage and you won't be driving it all that much anyway," he said.

"And working?" She held her breath.

"I'm not budging on that. Your sister…"

Cathy snapped the phone shut.

It rang again immediately but she didn't answer. She drove through town to the house she'd imagined living in with Ethan and parked on the front curb under a big pecan tree. Her son was supposed to ride his tricycle up and down that sidewalk. She was supposed to sit on the porch and laugh at his antics after a long day at work she loved.

A car pulled up behind her and she looked up in the rearview mirror, hoping to see Ethan. But Jack Landry got out, lit a cigarette, and leaned against his back fender, staring at the place.

Cathy rolled down the window. "Hey, Jack, what are you doing here?"

He rounded the back of her car, put his cigarette out, braced his hands on the car door, and leaned down to talk to her. "Hey, yourself. I'm waiting on the real estate agent. I'm a little early but she should be here soon. Get out and come with me to check out the place."

"You buyin' it?" Cathy asked.

"Thinkin' about it. Price is right and it's time I get out of Mamma's place before one of us shoots the other one. Never thought I'd live there as long as I have, but it worked, what with me working nights. But there's a day shift open that I'm going to take and I need my own place. Why don't you come on in with me and give me a woman's point of view?"

"I'd be glad to," she said.

They were sitting on the porch when the agent arrived with the keys. It was just like Cathy imagined. Small foyer, a living room to the left with a kitchen/dining area on past that, and a hallway with doors leading into a linen closet, a coat closet, a bathroom, and three bedrooms. The master bedroom had a big closet and a really nice master bathroom.

"So from a woman's point of view, what do you think?" Jack asked.

"I would love to live here," Cathy said.

"Really?"

"Oh, yes. It's cozy, just the right size for a family. The backyard does need to be fenced. I'd put up a wood privacy fence and maybe later a deck. The trees are wonderful. They'd provide shade in the summertime," she said.

"Okay, that settles it. Ten percent for escrow?" he asked the agent.

"That's more than enough. We can have the papers ready to sign in a week. The owners are really ready to close a deal," she said.

Jack wrote a check.

Cathy waited for him on the porch.

"You got a good deal, and it's far past time for you to have your own place, but Beulah isn't going to like it," she said.

"I know, but it's time I owned a house." He chuckled. "Thanks for helping me out, Cathy."

"Hey, that's what friends are for. When are you telling your mamma?" she asked.

"Guess it had better be soon. You want to do it for me?"

Cathy shook her head. "Not me. She's going to pout and cry."

"Think Marty will go talk to her?"

"No, but we could send Darla Jean. She could calm down a suicide bomber, I swear she could."

"Well, then tell Darla Jean to bring her Bible and get ready to work some magic tomorrow morning."

When Marty was worried, she cussed.

She started pacing the floor when Cathy left, and if cuss words could have peeled the flesh off Ethan's bones, nothing but a skeleton would have left the Dairy Queen that night.

When Trixie was worried, she joked. Her attempts to stop Marty's pacing and cussing failed. Marty didn't even laugh at her "ain't that nice" joke.

When Agnes was worried, she ate and gave advice. Within thirty minutes of the time Cathy left, both Marty and Trixie could have yanked all of Agnes's curly red hair out of her scalp and glued her lips shut with superglue.

The back door opened. Trixie stopped in the middle of a joke.

The swearing ceased. And Agnes looked up from an enormous wedge of banana nut cake.

And Darla Jean came into the house instead of Cathy.

"Well, shit!" Agnes forked a bite of cake into her mouth.

Marty resumed her pacing. "Dammit! Where is she? They said she left the Dairy Queen half an hour ago, and she isn't answering her phone."

"Maybe she's driving out to the Prescott place to shoot Violet," Trixie said.

"I take it that Cathy isn't back yet?" Darla Jean said.

"Yes, I am." She breezed into the kitchen, opened the cabinet door, and took out the Jack Daniels.

"Is Ethan alive?" Trixie asked.

Cathy poured two fingers in the glass. "Oh, yes, and so is Anna Ruth."

Marty took the whiskey bottle from her and downed two big gulps straight from the bottle. "What in the hell has she got to do with this?"

"She was in the Dairy Queen."

"And?"

Cathy told the rest of the story.

Agnes slapped the table hard enough to rattle the lid on the sugar bowl. "That hussy came in there on purpose. I bet that Violet was whining to Annabel about the pre-dump and she sent Anna Ruth there just to cause trouble."

"Prenup, not pre-dump," Cathy said

"I didn't stutter. I can damn well hope it's a pre-dump and you get rid of that man. Marry Jack if you've got to have a man in your life. He's buying the very house that you wanted to live in with Ethan."

"Jack is my friend," Cathy said. "And Ethan and I will work this out. It might take a couple of weeks. And how did you know about that house?"

"I know everything that goes on in Cadillac," Agnes said.

"Where is that folder?" Marty asked. There were a couple of things Agnes didn't know. If she did, she'd be in jail eating beans and bologna rather than banana nut cake.

"In the trash can at the Dairy Queen under a bunch of leftover food and soaked through with coffee and Coke," Cathy said. "I told him he could throw it away or I would. Ethan loves me. He'll forget about it."

Darla Jean patted her hand. "He might love you, but his mamma isn't going to let him marry you without your signature on those papers. You hold out for what you want, darlin'. And remember, whether you like it or not, you are marrying Violet as well as Ethan."

"Run, Cathy! Run away and don't ever look back," Agnes raised her voice. "God sent Jesus in human form to save our souls, right, Darla Jean?"

"Basically," Darla said.

"The devil sent Violet in human form to drag you down to hell by your ankles. Living in hell would be a picnic compared to living with her," Agnes said.

"Sitting here, it doesn't look as formidable as it did with Anna Ruth over there pressed up so close to him that they looked like Siamese twins." Cathy tipped up the whiskey bottle and took a drink.

"Pray for her, Darla Jean. My poor little Cathy has done sold her soul to the bottle." Agnes shook her head and shoved more cake in her mouth.

"I've been telling you a little shot of Jack will put a new perspective on the whole world," Trixie said. "Whiskey has kept me from killing Andy."

Cathy held up the glass. "To new perspectives. Now, can we talk about something else? Jack is buying a house, and Darla Jean, you've got to go talk to Beulah tomorrow and make her understand it's time for him to have his own place. Take your Bible and quote all kinds of scripture to comfort her."

"For real?" Trixie asked.

"For real. He's got to tell his mamma first, but that'll be done by tomorrow morning. You will go over there and talk to her, won't you, Darla Jean? I know she's not a member of your church, but she does live right down the street from you," Cathy asked.

"Of course I will, but right now I've got a story to tell y'all," Darla Jean said.

Chapter 10

Cathy felt like Daniel from the Bible story and the lion's den lay on the other side of the Prescott doors. She took a deep breath and pushed the doorbell. No one answered, so after a full minute she hit it again. Had the devil come to collect Clayton's soul? Were Violet and Ethan in so much shock that they couldn't come to the door? Or maybe the three of them were getting the hungry lions ready to devour her.

The door opened and Clayton stood there, smug as Lucifer. Violet and Ethan probably weren't weeping in shock after all if he was still alive.

"Catherine, please come with me into the den. Ethan is waiting," he said formally.

Den?

He walked fast enough that he kept at least two steps ahead of her all the way across the foyer and into the office. Ethan was sitting in one of the two burgundy leather chairs facing the desk. He didn't even look at her. Clayton sat down behind the desk and pushed one single sheet of paper toward her.

Where were the lions?

"Sign this, please," he said.

Please did not make it any less of a barked out order.

She stared at Ethan long enough to force him to look at her. When he did, he barely shrugged and looked at the bookcases behind Clayton.

She hoped that the twenty-page legal jargon had been replaced by a few sentences stating that she could not sue him for his family estate in case of an estrangement.

Not so. It didn't say anything except that she agreed with all the aforementioned conditions and she would abide according to those agreements, yada, yada, yada. Sign. Date. Get screwed without even a kiss or foreplay.

"And what is on those aforementioned pages?"

"The very same thing except for that hideous car," Clayton said.

Ethan stood up. "I'm not a hard man, sweetheart. I gave you the car. Work with us."

It was that word, *us*, that did it. She was marrying Ethan. She was not marrying *us*. Before she married *us*, she'd die a virgin and be content with her e-reader and raunchy stories that she read in the back booth of the Rib Joint.

"Now!" Clayton barked. "This has gone far enough."

Ethan handed her a pen. "Annabel and Anna Ruth are in the parlor with Mother. They'll be waiting on dinner."

"What are they doing here?" she asked.

Ethan frowned. "Mother invited them. Poor Anna Ruth is disgraced by the way your friend's husband has treated her."

"Ex-husband," Cathy said.

Ethan smiled. "Let's not keep our guests waiting."

She could spend the evening with Anna Ruth gushing over Ethan and Violet, with Clayton's evil glares on the side, or go to the Rib Joint and read. The e-reader looked better by the minute.

"What if I told you that I read erotic romance on my e-reader and I'm not going to stop reading the stories? Would you make me get rid of that too?" Cathy asked.

Ethan's eyes popped wide open. "Do you?"

Clayton held up a hand. "What you do in private is your own business, but you cannot have that thing in public. A politician's wife can't be caught delving into pornography."

Ethan stood up. "Let's not discuss something like that right now. Our guests are probably hungry and dinner is getting cold. Sign the paper and let's go, sweetheart."

She took a step forward and got so close to Ethan that he had to look at her. "I want you to tell me that you love me."

"Good grief, Catherine. I asked you to marry me, didn't I?"

"That's not what I want to hear."

Ethan's face turned scarlet.

"It's three words, but when you say them I want to hear that you mean them," she said.

He opened his mouth and nothing came out. He didn't even look embarrassed, just frustrated.

Cathy carefully put the sheet of paper down on the table and laid the pen on top of it. Then she pulled off her engagement ring and put it right beside the pen.

"What are you doing?" Clayton blanched.

She looked at Ethan. "If I'd known about the prenup, I would have never accepted this ring. And besides, if you can't tell me you love me in this room, how are you going to promise to love me in a church full of people with God watching over the ceremony?"

"But..." Ethan sputtered.

"Good-bye. I wish you well on your campaign, but I'm not going to marry you."

She let herself out the door.

The Rib Joint had a neon sign out front but it was not a new building. Made of rough, weathered wood, it resembled an old feed store. Country music floated out the doors, right along with laughter and loud talking.

She marched across the parking lot and stopped in her tracks when she reached the porch. The cook was standing right in front of her. He had a thick mop of blond curly hair, a cute little brown soul patch under his sexy mouth, wire-rimmed glasses with thick lenses, and a barbecue-sauce-stained bibbed apron with his logo on the top.

"Are you my new waitress and beer girl?"

She shook her head. "No, I just come here to read."

But you have been playing the part of the sexy hero who knows how to put out the fires in a woman's body.

"That's a new one! Reading in that noise? You interested in drawing beer and hollerin' out order numbers? I can't cook and run the front too. By the way, I'm John. I own this place."

"Yes, I am interested." She heard the words come out of her mouth but couldn't believe that she'd said them.

"What's your name?" John asked.

"Cathy. It's Catherine, but I really like Cathy better," she said.

"Me too. It fits you. Come on in. You got any experience runnin' a cash register and drawin' beer?"

She nodded again. What could be the difference between putting money in the drawer for plate lunches or for ribs, or drawing beer or Cokes?

The place was as rough inside as out. Décor was old car and truck license plates from every state and year, funny sayings painted on rough boards and hung with baling wire, and rusty tools that she couldn't even identify. Buckets of peanuts were in the middle of the tables, and the shells crunched under her feet as she walked across the wood floor. Booths lined the north and south walls and were full of people laughing, talking, and eating barbecue or tossing shells as they waited on their orders. Bright lights flashed from a jukebox, and country music echoed off the walls.

"We sell ribs and brisket. Prices are up there." John pointed to the menu above the counter, items stenciled in block letters. "Both come with an order of fries and a chunk of Texas toast to dip up the barbecue sauce. My buddy, Jamie, was supposed to send his niece to work tonight. My regular waitress can't work on Wednesdays and Saturdays. That's why I thought you were my new waitress. Prices are also listed right here." He tapped a menu taped to the counter beside the cash register.

Toby Keith's voice came through the jukebox with "Beer for My Horses," and a group of women formed a line dance in the middle of the floor, their stomping boots and shuffling feet creating even more noise. Every so often they'd yell, "Bull…shit," and slap their butts.

She'd barely gotten settled in behind the cash register when the song ended and thirsty dancers lined up in front of the bar.

"Two Coors," the first one said.

The handles were marked Coors, Budweiser, Miller, and Busch instead of Coke, Dr Pepper, and Sprite, but it worked the same way. She filled two mugs, took their money, made change, and looked up at the next person in line.

"Six Buds."

She grabbed three mugs, filled them, set them on the counter, filled three more, rang up the amount, made change, and turned to look at the next one in line.

"You'll do fine." John went back to the kitchen.

At midnight, he pulled the plug on the jukebox, announced that they were closed, and the last four people left. He locked the door and opened the bulging cash register, handed her two twenties and a ten, and drew up two beers.

"Might as well sit down and have a drink before you go home. You took to it like you knew what you were doin'."

She shook her head and followed him to a booth. "I've worked with a cash register and ran a machine like that, only it wasn't beer. Not much difference."

He set the beers on the table and pushed one over to her.

It was better than the champagne she and Ethan had the night he proposed and a helluva lot better than Trixie's whiskey.

John waved a hand in front of her face. "Hello!"

"What?"

"I was talking to you."

"I'm sorry. My mind was off in la-la land."

"Interested in working a couple of nights a week? Any tips are yours to keep. And I pay minimum wage. It ain't much, but it'll help out while you are in college. You are twenty-one, aren't you?"

She smiled. "And then some."

"Long as the law don't come down on me, I don't care if you are twenty-one, one day, and one hour, darlin'. I only need someone on Wednesday and Saturday, though."

"I'm free those two nights," Cathy said. Funny how things worked out, wasn't it?

"So do you want Cathy or Catherine embroidered on your work shirts? That fancy shirt and those high-dollar-looking slacks are classy, but I'd rather you wore jeans or denim shorts and a company shirt to work in. You'll mess up a lot of good clothes if you don't."

"Cathy is what I want on my shirts," she explained. "One is enough since I'll only be here twice a week."

"Finish your beer and I'll walk you out to your car. You'll be late for classes if you oversleep."

Her car was the only one left in the parking lot. One streetlight dimly lit the parking lot and the smell of smoking ribs and brisket still floated around in the hot night air.

"That Lumina belong to you?" John pointed.

"It does now. It was my mother's and I inherited it when she died. Twelve years old and only 20,000 miles on it," Cathy said.

"I used to have one of those. Loved that car. Had plenty of leg room, got good mileage. I told the dealer when I traded it in that they quit making them because they were too damned good. Nothing ever went wrong with them," John drawled.

His deep Texas drawl went with the romantic hero in her

imagination. Candy Parker should take a research trip to Luella and eat John's barbecue. She'd have a whole new hero, and a setting like the Rib Joint would make a new book sell like hotcakes.

Why didn't his wife help out at the restaurant? Could be that she was his regular waitress and they couldn't find a sitter on Wednesday and Saturday nights for their kids, or that she was a nurse who worked the night shift.

He opened the car door for her and said, "You might want to lock the doors. I get all kinds out here and I'd sure hate to see a car in this good of shape messed up."

"I will do that from now on. Thank you for the job," she said. "I'll see you Saturday. What time?"

"I open at six. If you could be here then, I'd appreciate it. Close at midnight every night. I live behind the joint in a trailer house. Maggie Rose is waiting for me, so good night, Cathy, and I'm glad you took the job."

"I'll be here when you open," she said.

It was all surreal. Had she really broken up with Ethan? Shouldn't she be crying? Had she really gone to work at a glorified beer joint?

Chapter 11

Good food.

Good friend.

Jack had it all right in front of him.

But Marty was worried about something. Her mind wasn't on the tray she'd brought out to him from the leftovers of the buffet bar. And it wasn't on restoring the Caddy all over again, either.

"Okay, honey. What's on your mind? You poutin' because I'm moving away from next door?"

"Well, there is that, but I'm worried about Cathy, Jack. You know that we're total opposites and yet I feel it when she's in trouble or hurting."

"One completes the other?" He crumbled corn bread into the greens and tasted them, then added pepper vinegar, tasted again, and really settled into his supper.

"That's exactly right. She's as nice as Jesus. Honest to God, she is. And it just comes natural. I'm her opposite. I say what I think and to hell with feelings. And the thing I'm worried about is that I don't feel anything horrible down in my gut. It's at peace for the first time since she got engaged to Ethan," Marty said.

"Maybe she's come to her senses," he said.

"I hope so." She sighed.

"That sigh says something is wrong," Jack said.

"It's Trixie. She's not quite herself. Do you think she knows about the vote shit?"

"She was asking me about it," Jack said honestly. "I was able to steer her away from it, but I wouldn't be surprised that she's gotten downwind of some gossip."

"Dammit!"

Cathy pulled into the driveway and took a deep breath before she even went into the house. Marty and Trixie had stood beside her, tried to get her to see the light, and she'd fought them the whole way. They deserved to know that they had been right all along.

Trixie had a beer and a plate of fried catfish in front of her. "What took you so long to get home? I've been worried."

"But Mamma, look at the clock. It's only twelve thirty and that means I'm making curfew." Cathy pulled a Diet Coke from the fridge. She hadn't eaten since lunch and the fish looked good. She sat down beside Trixie and picked up a piece from her plate.

"That's all you get. Warm up your own fish. You could have called," Trixie said.

"I needed some time."

Marty pushed through the door and joined them at the table. "Okay, talk."

Jack was right behind her. He set his tray with empty bowls and plates on the countertop, got a beer from the refrigerator, and looked up. "Anyone else?"

"I had one already," Cathy said.

"In Ethan's house? He has something like beer in that house?" Marty asked.

"No, at the Rib Joint."

Trixie sniffed the air. "Is that what I smell? You and Ethan went to the Rib Joint. Was *he* drunk? I didn't think he'd ever go to a place like that. I figured he'd have to be in a wine and white tablecloth joint."

Marty leaned against the cabinet. "You smell like barbecue and beer, sister."

"Nice change, isn't it?"

That's when Trixie noticed Cathy's left hand and squealed, "Look, Marty, no ring!"

"Well, hot damn and halle-damn-lujah! Get on with the story, sister. Now I know it's got a happy ending."

Cathy started at the beginning when she had to ring the doorbell twice and ended with, "And Anna Ruth was there in the parlor with her Aunt Annabel the whole time. Ethan was more worried about their feelings than mine, and he would not tell me that he loves me. I feel like I'm back in high school, coming home in the evenings to tell y'all the details of my life."

Marty laid a hand on Cathy's shoulder. "Is this just the calm before the storm? Are you going to fall apart?"

Cathy shook her head.

"I heard the good news!" Agnes burst in the back door dressed in a bright red sweatsuit, red house shoes, and red hair sticking up like a worn-out mop that dried sitting on the back porch.

"What good news?" Marty asked. "Did you hear something about me being out with a sexy cowboy?"

"Hell, Marty, you've been to bed with half the cowboys in the state of Texas. And I know you've been out in the garage with Jack all night. I just got a phone call from Liddy Jo who heard it from Beulah who got it from Annabel who was at the Prescotts' tonight that Cathy gave the ring back to Ethan because of that damned pre-dump. I told you I called it the right thing, didn't I? It made you dump him, didn't it? Make me some of that stuff Trixie is eating. I'm ready to celebrate."

"Aunt Agnes! I might have broken his heart," Cathy said.

"I don't give a shit! At least yours won't get broken." She bent down and peered into Cathy's eyes. "Nope, I don't see a broken heart. I see relief. What made you finally change your mind?"

"Guess I figured out that I'm a beans and greens and fried chicken girl, not a prime rib and red wine lady." Cathy's perfectly arched eyebrows knit together into one line. “Does that make me a horrible person? Oh my God!”

“Well, if that don’t sound just like Marty takin’ the Lord’s name in vain,” Agnes said.

“What brought on the OMG?” Trixie asked.

“The cake! That blasted cake! I’ll have to cancel it and I already paid her for the thing and I broke the engagement and she’s Violet’s friend and she’s in the club and it’s going to be a nightmare!”

Agnes reached for the phone hanging on the wall and punched in several numbers. “Sorry, Annabel, did I wake you? No, well, that’s real good. Cathy and I want to cancel that cake order since there ain’t going to be a weddin’.”

A long pause.

“You can write her a check back, minus ten percent for your trouble,” Agnes finally said.

Another long pause.

“Okay, then she’s paid for the damn cake, so make it, and if you skimp on one of those morning glories, we’ll tell all over the county that you did a lousy job. On the day the wedding was supposed to have been taking place at the Baptist church, I want it delivered to the Christian church across the road from Clawdy’s.”

Agnes pursed her lips and drew her eyebrows into a solid line across narrowed eyes. “I don’t give a flying rat’s ass, Annabel. My niece paid a thousand damn dollars for a cake. We’ll feed it to the congregation over at Darla Jean’s or we’ll sell tickets for people to run and jump in the middle of it like on one of them damn television shows. It’s our cake. Cathy paid for it and we want the damn thing. First Saturday in December, two o’clock. There better be a cake there or I’ll make sure your business does a nosedive.”

She hung up the phone with a loud bang. “Stupid woman thinks she’s going to keep your money and not produce a cake. She’s crazy as hell. I’ll freeze the whole damn thing in portions and take pieces of it to committee meetings before she does a dumb fool stunt like that. Who in their right mind puts morning glories on a wedding cake anyway?"

"Morning glories on a wedding cake? Aren't you supposed to use roses?" Jack asked.

"Or something exotic like calla lilies," Marty said.

"Don't have to worry about it now, do we? Darla Jean's congregation is going to have red velvet cake with sugar morning glories for refreshments the first Sunday in December." Agnes grinned.

Following the heart was Darla Jean's sermon topic that Sunday morning. It had come to her when she'd talked to Beulah. Poor woman had been distraught over her son buying a house when someday he'd inherit the one she lived in. Darla Jean had quoted scripture about a man following his heart. She had assured Beulah that God was probably using Jack to complete his will and that wonderful things would come to pass because Jack had his own house. They'd had a moment of prayer, and before Darla Jean left, Beulah was already talking about asking the club to host a housewarming for Jack.

The congregation was sparse with only thirty people sitting in front of her. Marty, Cathy, and Trixie sat on the back pew. Jack had slipped in right after the hymns and edged his way in beside Trixie. Darla Jean didn't care if there were ten people or a thousand sitting in the pews, if they were poor or rich, or if they were clean or slightly dusty. She just hoped that she was preaching to listening hearts.

Cathy listened intently. She didn't suppose God would approve of her reading material, but she didn't feel a bit guilty. It was the e-reader that had finally given her the courage to take that ring off. If a man couldn't make her pant as much as words, then he couldn't be the right man. Listening to the heart was tough when a woman's biological clock impaired her hearing. She'd wanted a husband and a baby, but after thinking about it, she hadn't loved Ethan any more than he'd loved her. They were both marrying for all the wrong reasons and her heart had been trying to make her understand that for a long time.

Marty had a heavy heart that morning. She just knew that Trixie had found out about the vote. She needed to tell her why she'd voted that way, but she'd promised her mother it would stay a secret.

Oh, don't be silly. I just didn't want Agnes to know. You can tell Trixie if it means keeping your friendship right. Besides, she'll help you protect the secret. I trust her.

Marty stole a glance over her shoulder. Claudia Andrews was not sitting on the seat behind her, but she could have sworn that was her mother's voice whispering in her ear.

Trixie had never seen Jack at the Christian church before that day. He might not have a choice about moving out when his mamma found out. Beulah, along with Agnes and Violet, were dyed-in-the-wool Baptists. Nothing could ever make them switch churches. It had been hard on Agnes when Marty and Cathy started going to Darla Jean's church. It would come nigh onto giving Beulah a Texas-sized stroke.

Trixie tuned everything out so she could hear her heart, but it wasn't saying anything. Evidently, it was happy with things just the way they were.

Angels straight from heaven's open portals would tremble at the thought of stealing Agnes's seat on the fourth pew on the east side of the Baptist church in Cadillac. Her grandmother sat in that pew in the days when it was the only church in the area. That was back when there was no town but just a wide spot in the road with a Baptist church and a few farmhouses. Her mother sat in it back when the town was Cornwall, and now it was Agnes's spot. Even though it didn't have her name written on a brass plate, nobody ever had the nerve to sit in it, not even when she was absent. It was as much a part of Agnes as her DNA and red hair.

The first hymn had already begun when Violet and Ethan paraded down the center aisle and sat in front of Agnes. Leave it to Violet to wear a swishy red, white, and blue striped dress with a big flowing skirt and a wide belt around her thick middle. The dress looked like it had been made of leftovers from a circus tent, and wide belts didn't look good on anyone but a runway model. What in the hell was she thinking? She might as well have made a poster board that said *Vote for my prissy-assed son Ethan* and stood in front of the congregation while the preacher sermonized.

The Good Samaritan was what the preacher talked about after the hymn. He flipped open his Bible to the parable and read the whole thing and then began to preach, saying that we should love our neighbors even with their faults and always offer a helping hand.

That preacher could pucker up and kiss Agnes's naturally born white ass if he was preaching to her about being nice to Violet Prescott. It wasn't happening; not in this life or the one to come. Agnes wouldn't piss on the woman if she was on fire. Violet had been a dagger in her side since they were teenagers. She'd pushed the blade deeper and deeper with her power and money, and then when she was forty years old and had Ethan, she'd stabbed it all the way to the hilt with her honey-coated arsenic remarks about how sorry she was that poor Agnes could never have a darling baby like her Ethan.

Agnes was not feeling one bit of the Good Samaritan attitude when services ended. And she couldn't even get away from Violet with the traffic jam at the end of the pews. The narrow aisle between the pews and the outer edge of the church was as congested as the center aisle so there was no escape there, either. She tiptoed forward to get a better view of just who was causing the holdup.

Beulah Landry had plugged up the whole line and was weeping on the preacher's shoulder as he patted her back. She was probably having some kind of major breakdown about Jack going to Darla Jean's church. Agnes had seen him all dressed up and walking that way that morning and figured Beulah would have a stroke over it, especially coming on the heels of him buying a house. Great God Almighty, the man was past thirty! It was time for him to have his own house. But Beulah could have waited until everyone had a turn at shaking the preacher's hand before she started carrying on like that.

The sound of tongues clucking up and down the human traffic jam sounded like hens scratching in the barnyard. News of what caused the line to come to a standstill filtered back through the people, but Agnes wasn't up to clucking. She didn't give a damn where Jack went to church or even if he did. She just wanted to get away from Violet before the woman started something.

Agnes expected to see Violet in funeral black, no makeup, and red eyes. But she'd fooled her by showing up all flamboyant, which meant she had a plan. Agnes figured it was a conspiracy between her and Beulah, since she kept tiptoeing so she could see the exact moment Beulah hugged the preacher one more time and then moved on outside.

Violet took a handkerchief from her purse when the line moved an inch or two and began to sob. Ethan threw his arm around her and patted her on the shoulder.

"Oh, Agnes," she cried in a loud voice, "how could your niece trick us like that? It's horrible, simply horrible."

The buzz of conversation stopped so quickly that a feather floating down from the church rafters would have sounded like an atomic bomb. Everyone strained their ears toward the two old ladies in the middle of the church. The silence was just plumb eerie.

When Agnes ignored Violet, she sobbed louder, her bright-colored dress shaking like a circus tent in the wind. "I just can't understand why Catherine would do that to us when we all loved her so much. She's done my poor son so dirty."

Agnes whipped around to face Violet. "My niece didn't do a damn thing. You shouldn't have tried to make her sign that damn pre-dump." She rolled her eyes toward the ceiling. "You made me cuss in church. God should lay that one up to you."

"Oh, Agnes darlin', you don't know? Ethan caught her with another man. Of course, I'm not one to spread gossip so I won't call names, but he's a prominent man in Cadillac and a member of the police force. Oh, dear, I hope I don't get him fired. My poor Ethan is just heartbroken."

Agnes looked up at Ethan. He looked smug, not heartbroken.

Violet wiped at her eyes and the clucking around her grew in volume. "I'm so sorry to break the news to you. I realize that since you could never have children that you've always favored Catherine, but you shouldn't have put your trust in her. She's a sneaky, devious person."

Damn! Where was that shotgun when Agnes needed it anyway? Well, a woman worked with what she had and since her shotgun was at home, she doubled up her fist and decked Violet right there in front of the people, the preacher, and even God. The clucking stopped and dead silence reigned. It damn near broke her knuckles, but it was worth every bit of it.

"You hit me, you old witch." Violet grabbed her eye. "You've blacked my eye."

"Now you got something to really cry about, and we are both seventy-eight so don't be calling me old! My niece wasn't with another man and you know it. Think twice before you ever say a bad word about her again."

The line parted like the Red Sea, and Agnes walked out of the church on burgundy carpet like a celebrity going out to meet the paparazzi.

Chapter 12

The concession stand offered hot dogs, hamburgers, chips, candy, nachos, and cold drinks. Two firemen grilled hamburgers and hot dogs out back between the building and the chain-link fence, but only Trixie and Jack had shown up to run the concession stand where they'd sell their wares. Jack propped up the front window to a long line of people already waiting to buy food.

"Whew!" Trixie said.

"Ah, we can do it," Jack said. "You are Wonder Woman and I'm Superman."

"Really?" She laughed.

"Oh, yeah! I put our capes in a safe spot. Wouldn't want to get mustard all over them."

Agnes brought a tray of hot dogs in the back door. "Capes. We got to wear capes. Nobody told me we had to get dressed up. I could've gotten into Bert's trunk and found his fireman's outfit."

Trixie's day just turned from bad to worse. "What are you doing here?"

"I come to poison Violet," Agnes said.

"Shh. Someone will hear you," Trixie said.

"I'll take the money then," Agnes said. "Cathy is right behind me. She's got a box of pecan tarts from Clawdy's. She can take the orders. People can pay me. I'm damn good at the money business. Then you two can make the orders and Cathy can deliver them."

Trixie lowered her chin and looked over the top of her sunglasses. "No poison?"

Agnes giggled. "Don't you know a joke when you hear one? I left the arsenic at home, but that don't mean I wouldn't do it."

"And you can't hit her," Cathy said.

"My fist is still sore and her black eye ain't healed yet. But I'm tellin' both of you, if she starts it, I ain't backin' down."

Cathy patted her on the shoulder. "Violet wouldn't start anything today. She'll be on her best behavior because Ethan is speaking tonight. Here's a stool for you to sit on and there's the money box."

"Thank you both for showing up," Trixie said. "I appreciate the help."

Agnes settled in at the end of the serving shelf. "No thanks necessary. I came to help Cathy. Don't think I came down here to help you."

"Ah, come on, Agnes. You know you love me," Trixie said.

"Of course she does. Everyone loves Trixie." Jack chuckled.

"If everybody jumped off the cliff, I would not join them," Agnes snapped. "And if Jesus loved Trixie, I still wouldn't."

"Aunt Agnes, be nice. What can I get you, Darla Jean?" Cathy asked the first customer.

"Nachos with an extra spoonful of picante if it came from Miss Clawdy's, but if it didn't, then leave it off and a cup of hot chocolate. It's getting cold out here."

Her order was ready by the time she reached Agnes with her money.

They quickly fell into their roles and a dozen customers later, Cathy looked up to see Violet staring right at her. "What can I get you today?"

Violet tilted her chin up two notches and looked down her nose at Cathy. "I'll have two hot dogs, two Diet Cokes, and those last two pecan tarts. I suppose Marty made them, right?"

"Yes, ma'am," Cathy said. "Pay Agnes and that will be right out."

Violet lowered her voice so that the people around her would have to strain to catch the words. "Catherine, honey, I don't carry grudges. Ethan and I both hope you are very happy in your new relationship. We just wish you would have been honest and not played him along so long. He's heartbroken."

Trixie yelled from the workstation in the middle of the stand, "Hello, Violet. Did I hear you say that Ethan is very happy in his new relationship? Cathy always knew that he and Anna Ruth had a thing for each other and now they can be together. Ain't that nice?"

"Did I hear my name?" Anna Ruth said from two people back down the line.

"Yes, we were just saying how wonderful it is that Cathy was willing to give the ring back when she found out Ethan was in love with you," Trixie hollered over the crowd.

"Oh, my!" Anna Ruth gasped.

"Well crap, now I've let the cat out of the bag. I'm so sorry. I guess he was waiting until after the election to declare himself." Trixie lowered her voice, but only slightly.

Jack's shoulders rocked as he held in the laughter. Trixie was Wonder Woman, in the flesh!

Violet clamped her mouth shut and moved down to Agnes. She threw a bill on the counter and Agnes counted out her change. Cathy set the order in front of Violet, and Agnes removed the tarts.

"Those are my tarts. I already paid for them so you can't have them. All we got left is two pieces of fudge and I will promise you that I did not put poison in them even though it crossed my mind."

"Ethan doesn't eat fudge. It's too sweet for him. Give me both pieces though and don't you dare charge me double for that fudge. I'm not paying a penny more for it than I would a pecan tart," Violet said through clenched teeth.

Agnes pulled two thick pieces of fudge wrapped in cellophane from under the counter and put them on the tray for Violet. "Honey,

I'm giving you the fudge since I'd already spoken for the tarts. Now you be sure that tray gets brought back here and don't leave it settin' on the bleachers or the cleanup crew will throw it away."

Violet didn't even answer.

"You said you wouldn't poison her?" Trixie asked.

"I didn't!" Agnes protested.

"Why did you only bring two pieces?" Cathy whispered.

"It's all I had left in the pan and I know how she loves fudge. I didn't even spit on it, I promise. Remember what your mamma taught you about catchin' flies with honey? Maybe that fudge will sweeten her up."

The new bathroom facilities were supposed to be finished in time for football season to start in September. But on the last Saturday in October, they were still nothing more than pipes sticking up out of a concrete floor surrounded by block walls about four feet high. Even though the existing facilities were in bad repair and entirely too small, they had to work for one more football season. Marty had been at the tail end of a dozen people waiting in line in front of the ladies' room when Violet Prescott rushed around the field, her high heels making holes in the grass along the way.

Gossip had already solidified the whole rumor about Ethan and Anna Ruth into the gospel truth. Seeing Anna Ruth right smack beside Ethan, handing out little flags while he handed out his cards, just put more meat into the story. Everyone forgot all about the rumor that Cathy was sleeping with a policeman. Now they focused on Ethan and wondered if he'd marry Anna Ruth before the election. Would he give her the same engagement ring that he'd given Cathy or would she get something even bigger just to show the world that he loved her more than he had Cathy? Would Anna Ruth sign the prenup?

Violet fidgeted and even moaned a couple of times as the line moved slowly forward. Marty tried her best to ignore the woman, but that wasn't happening.

"This is ridiculous. I never realized how bad we need bigger restrooms," Violet said.

"This is the last season we'll have to use these bathrooms. The new ones should be finished for next year," Marty said.

Violet whimpered and crossed her legs. "Why is it taking so long?"

Marty nodded toward the door. "A lady took six little girls in. Here she comes out now."

"We're only going in to freshen up our makeup. We'll let y'all cut in line," a young teenager offered.

Violet and Marty moved up closer to the front.

"I'm sorry to take up space. We were waiting on our kids. They went in with Scarlett. You can move on up here," another person said.

When Scarlett brought those little girls out of the bathroom, Violet took off like a teenager on a cross-country run. She threw the door open to the first stall and disappeared in a blur.

"You okay in there?" Marty asked while she washed her hands.

"Must've been those hot dogs. I bet they've been sitting out all day and they're tainted. I knew we should have manned the concession stand as well as our own table of homemade gifts. You can't trust Chamber and the fire department to get things done right," Violet said weakly.

After the things she'd tried to spread about Cathy, Marty figured she deserved more than an upset stomach. Marty wouldn't have blamed Cathy if she did poison her, but her sister was too nice to do that. Now Agnes was a different story altogether.

"Anything I can do to help? Should I get Ethan so he can take you home?" Marty asked.

"No, I wouldn't ruin his evening for anything. This is our day of glory to be at home court and let all his constituents get to know him," Violet said. "I do believe it is just a case of nerves."

"Constituents are what he has after the election," Marty said.

Violet swung open the door. Marty squirted more soap in her hand and washed them again. "He will win this election. And if he doesn't, it's all your sister's fault."

"Mrs. Prescott," Marty lowered her voice to a whisper, "I would be careful what I spread about if I was you. Agnes loves me, but I would not cross her. You, on the other hand, she would gladly kick right out in front of a semi. And Cathy is her favorite."

The cloud that Anna Ruth floated on was hundreds of feet above the earth and Ethan was the only other person on it. He loved her! The whole town knew and Trixie, bless her heart, had let the cat out of the bag.

When Beulah relieved her, she handed over her flags and winked at Ethan. They'd have to be discreet until the election, but that didn't mean they couldn't meet in private. By the first of the year, she'd be living in that big house with Violet and Ethan. Cathy didn't know how good she could have had it, but Anna Ruth was so glad that she'd refused to sign those papers. Anna Ruth would have signed them in a heartbeat. Just let him ask her if she'd give up her teaching job to be his wife.

She was standing in the line at the bathroom when Violet came trotting across the field—again.

"Oh, hello, Violet. Come on up here and take my place in line, honey," Anna Ruth said.

"Get out of my way!"

"Are you not feeling well, Violet?" Anna Ruth sputtered.

"I'm feeling just fine but don't you be getting any cute ideas about the rumors Trixie started tonight. They are not true. Ethan is heartbroken about Catherine breaking up with him over that policeman down at the precinct. It's horrible that she threw my son over for a womanizer. It's more than he can take. Finally, it's my turn," Violet said.

Anna Ruth stepped aside and Violet rushed inside again.

Business had slowed down to a crawl and Agnes got bored with her job just before it was time for Ethan to crawl up on the flatbed trailer and do his speechifying. She'd eaten the two tarts that she wouldn't sell to Violet and had a hamburger. Her butt was numb from sitting on the bar stool too long. She'd done her duty to her niece and given Violet those pieces of fudge. Now it was time for her to go take her place at the edge of the parking lot where she could hear all about why she should vote for Ethan.

Should was the word. Wouldn't was the truth. She wouldn't vote for that pansy-assed politician if the only other candidate on the ballot was Anna Ruth, and she hated her for taking her spot in the social club.

She popped out her lawn chair and set it right smack over the extension cord bringing electricity from the field house to the flatbed trailer.

"Hey, Marty." She motioned her over. "I'm tired and I want to get situated before Ethan tells us all his bullshit. You can finish up my shift."

"What if I had a mind to get my chair situated?" Marty asked.

"I'm older than you are and it won't hurt you to help your sister," Agnes said.

"Okay, what do I do?"

"Ask Cathy."

"Cathy, what has Agnes been doing?" Marty opened the back door. "She sent me to finish her job."

"She's been taking money, but we're only a few minutes from closing down. I bet all the crafts are already picked over, but it wouldn't be nice to leave without hearing Ethan's speech," Cathy said.

"That old girl is brilliant." Marty laughed.

"How's that?" Cathy asked.

"She got to play, doesn't have to pick up her toys, and now she has a front row seat to probably throw tomatoes at Ethan. She's got her lawn chair right up next to the platform," Marty said.

"Oh, dear God. We'd better get on over there and stop her from doing something crazy. I figured she'd want to be as far from Violet as possible."

"That woman always has an agenda. If she's sitting there it's because she's planning something wicked. We're all three in here and Darla Jean is out there somewhere. I saw her buying some items for her sister's Christmas presents. Want me to call her and see if she'll go babysit?" Marty asked.

"No, Agnes promised she wouldn't start a fight," Cathy said.

"But she didn't promise to be good if she could agitate Violet into starting one first," Trixie said then moaned. "Well, shit! Look who is on duty tonight."

"Who?" Marty saw Andy the minute the word was out of her mouth.

"Andy will be introducing Ethan's campaign manager," Jack said. "And then the campaign manager introduces Ethan. It's a big affair, you know."

"Seems like a lot of introducing to me," Trixie said.

"It is what it is. This is small-town Texas where everything is a big splash, including the fall Crafts Festival."

"Hey," Darla Jean came around the end of the concession stand, "don't close up yet. I need another cup of hot chocolate. The wind has shifted from the south to the north. Looks like we're in for a cold snap after all."

Cathy poked her on the arm. "I'll get one ready for you but then we've all got to go keep Agnes out of trouble."

Darla Jean peeked around the end of the concession stand at the football field parking lot. Craft tables were set up in two long lines. The football field had been roped off with yellow tape with signs saying that no walking on the grass was permitted. The back gate was open so folks could use the bathrooms, and the front gate was open so folks could get to the concession stand.

"She's just sitting there waiting for Ethan's speech."

"Not Agnes. She's got something up her sleeve," Marty said.

"It's time to shut the place up if we're going to hear the big speech. We'll come back and clean up afterward." Jack unhooked the chains and locked the flap.

Agnes shivered when the wind did a turnaround. Her orange sweatshirt was warm enough in the concession stand where there was heat from the grill, but outside it wasn't keeping her warm. However, she'd bet dollars to horse shit that she fared better than Violet right then.

Violet had to be chilly in that straight navy blue skirt and lightweight sweater. She should have turned around backward and looked in the mirror before she went out in public wearing that sweater. The fat rolls on her back looked like a couple of piglets under a navy blue blanket as she trotted back and forth to the bathroom. And she had on high-heeled shoes. She had made so many trips in those high heels that she would probably have to have her knees replaced before Christmas.

Agnes giggled at that vision. Life couldn't be a bit better.

The flatbed trailer, all decked out in bunting, sat waiting ten feet from her. Andy stepped up to the microphone and tapped it. The buzz of the crowd dropped enough that he could introduce Clayton Mason, the campaign manager for Cadillac's own future Representative.

Shit introducing more shit!

Both of them probably thought that the applause was for them, but folks were clapping because the festival would be over soon and everyone could pack up their wares, get the hell out of the cold wind, take their rowdy kids home, give them a bath, and put them to bed.

Clayton said a few words and then Ethan took the platform.

The clapping and whistling was louder that time. The crowd must like Ethan more than she did.

He got out two sentences before she bent down to tie her shoes and unplugged the long extension cord bringing electricity from the field house to the flatbed. They might find the problem, but just to make sure it wouldn't work if they did, she kicked half a can of lukewarm Coke over to spill on both ends.

His mouth moved. People close to him caught a few words.

Someone yelled, "We can't hear!"

"Who cares?" Agnes yelled back.

Andy ran over to beat on the microphone but nothing happened. He grabbed the cord and followed it, asked Agnes to move to one side, and quickly found the connection.

"Got it," he yelled and snapped it together.

Sparks flew.

Andy threw it down and jumped backward.

Fire blazed up from the dead grass that had sprouted up in the cracks in the asphalt covering the football field parking lot.

Agnes picked up her lawn chair and moved it back five feet more so Andy and Ethan could stomp the blazes out with their pretty, shiny black shoes. When the ruckus was over, Andy went back up on the platform and cupped his hands around his mouth. "Sorry about this, folks. We'll have to catch Ethan's speech at the next big thing in town, which will be the Blue-Ribbon Jalapeño Society Jubilee, just a week before the big election day."

He turned to Ethan and shrugged. "Sorry about that. Some kid must've run past and tripped over it and then someone else spilled soda pop on it."

Agnes was so glad that she was looking right at Violet at the very moment it dawned on the old girl what had happened. It was the most beautiful sight in the world.

It only took ten steps—Agnes counted them—to bring Violet and all her anger to Agnes's chair. She'd promised she wouldn't start a fight, so she couldn't say or do one thing until Violet made the first move.

Violet shook her fist and yelled, "You bitch! You dosed that fudge and now you've ruined Ethan's night in his hometown. All because you are mad over your slutty niece? God, Agnes, I thought you had more class than that."

The comment about Cathy brought Agnes up out of the chair. "You done made a big mistake. I won't stand still and let you call Cathy a slut."

Violet's open hand made contact on Agnes's jaw, jerking her head to one side.

Agnes came at her like a bull elephant and grabbed a handful of hair to hold her steady while she kicked her shins a dozen times.

Violet pushed Agnes and they both went down on the concrete, rolling around through the burned out place, collecting dead grass and ash on their clothing and skin. It was a blur of flying fists and red and black hair. Agnes caught one on the arm, but she landed a solid right to Violet's good eye. One of Violet's damned old spike heels got Agnes on the arm and the blood ran to her fingertips, but Agnes used that wicked right to bloody Violet's nose the next chance she got.

Arms circled about her waist and more were suddenly around her legs, but she kept throwing punches, landing a couple more on Violet's arms before they dragged her away. Even then she managed to get in one more kick.

"Turn me loose, damn it! I'm not finished. She done stepped over the line when she called my niece a slut," Agnes yelled.

Trixie had her arms wrapped firmly around Agnes's waist and held on for dear life. Cathy hugged her from behind, pinning both of those wicked fists to her side. Marty was flat on the ground with both her arms around Agnes's legs. Darla Jean was in front of her, keeping Violet at arm's distance.

Ethan, Clayton, and Andy finally corralled Violet. They carried her kicking and screaming toward the flatbed with Ethan and Andy holding her back and Clayton scowling as usual.

She got one hand free and rocked Andy's jaw, got a foot free, and was on her way back to Agnes when Andy slapped cuffs on her wrists.

"You need my extra set?" Andy yelled at Trixie.

"I think we got her," she hollered back.

Violet yelled above both of them. "You take these things off me right now. It's her fault and I'm pressing charges. Andy, take *her* to jail."

Ethan handed her his sweaty handkerchief to hold against her bloody nose. "Mother, settle down!"

Agnes finally relaxed, stopped trying to get free, and yelled across the distance. "She hit me first, Andy. I was minding my own business and she went crazy. I should've got the first hit in since it's my boyfriend she's sleeping with. I told her she'd better leave him alone or I'd black that other eye. Take *her* to jail. Or turn me loose and you can take her to the damn morgue."

"She's got a boyfriend?" Trixie gasped.

"Hell no! She's just pestering Violet," Marty said breathlessly.

"Do you?" Trixie looked Agnes in the eye.

Agnes winked.

"Okay, okay! Jack!" Andy motioned to his off-duty deputy to help him.

"Yes, sir?" Jack took a step forward from behind Agnes's corner.

"You stay here to supervise everyone getting their stuff out of the parking lot. I'm taking this whole bunch down to the station to cool off. Y'all can ride with me." He pointed at Violet's crew.

He turned to his ex-wife and raised an eyebrow. "Trixie, can I trust you to get her down there?"

"Oh, we'll be there, all right! I'm filing assault charges against her. Look at my arm and this is my best shirt. She's going to pay for it, too," Agnes said.

Agnes went from raging to giggling to laughing like a hyena on the way to the station. Her mind had finally snapped and Marty would put her in a nursing home. There wouldn't be a thing she could do about it because not even Darla Jean could live with a raging lunatic.

"When did you get a boyfriend?" Darla Jean finally asked.

"Hell, I ain't got a boyfriend and there ain't a man alive that'd take on Violet. Not after she bitched Ethan's poor old daddy into the grave. I always felt sorry for him," Agnes said.

"Then why did you rant about Violet sleeping with your boyfriend?" Trixie asked.

Agnes sat between Marty and Darla Jean in the backseat. Cathy drove and Trixie rode shotgun. She leaned forward, propped her arms on the back of the front seat, and said, "You gave me the idea when you said that about Anna Ruth and Ethan. I don't give a shit what anyone thinks of me, but she's always had to be perfect."

"You may have just ruined Ethan's election," Cathy said.

"No, he'll do that on his own. I just had a bang-up good time. Paybacks ain't bitches; they're wonderful."

The Cadillac jail, like the restrooms at the football field, had been built fifty years before, but unlike the restrooms, the only use it got was an occasional Saturday night drunk. It had two cell blocks separated by bars, each with a long bench on one side and a stainless steel commode in the corner.

Violet was sitting on a bench in one cell, but the door was open when Andy ushered Agnes into the other cell.

"You all can wait outside," he told Trixie.

"Not me. Agnes sits in the can; I sit with her," Trixie said.

"But you don't even like her," Andy said.

"You really think those bars will keep her from snatching Violet bald-headed?" she whispered. "Remember the shotgun?"

"Me too." Darla Jean went inside with Agnes and sat down stoically on the bench.

Andy shook his head. "Only one person. You can't both stay."

"She is my spiritual adviser," Agnes said. "And I want my nieces too. They're my bodyguards. That woman is crazy. She'll eat her way through those bars and kill me."

The other three women filed into the cell and sat down beside her.

"No one is going to hurt you in my jail," Andy growled.

"I know it because I have my spiritual adviser and my bodyguards. Violet can have four if she can roust up that many friends. I don't imagine she can, and Lord only knows her spiritual adviser is Lucifer and he's got his hands full making deals with politicians right now."

Violet jumped up and was out the door before Andy could get to it, but he did manage to slam the door to Agnes's cell.

"I want my lawyer and my son and I want Agnes Flynn locked up a whole year for assault."

Agnes stood up. Cathy and Marty got between her and Violet, who had both hands stuck through the bars trying to reach Agnes. Trixie grabbed one of Agnes's hands and Darla Jean got the other one.

"Sweet Jesus, but you are strong," Darla Jean said.

"Jesus ain't got a damn thing to do with it. You two leave me alone. I'm not getting that close to her. She might give me rabies.

She might already have given them to me when she tried to cut my arm off," Agnes said.

"You *are* going to jail," Violet said.

"You hit me first so I was just defending myself."

"You put stuff in my fudge!"

Andy ushered her back to her cell and quickly slammed the door.

"Aunt Agnes, you said you didn't poison her!" Cathy exclaimed.

"I didn't!"

Violet started a high-pitched moan like she was dying for sure. "You poisoned me? What did you use? Now I'll never live to see Ethan in office."

Agnes shook a finger at her. "Stop your caterwauling. I didn't poison you. I just used five bars of Ex-Lax in a pan of fudge. And I mixed Miralax with the milk so I wouldn't have to put in that pinch of salt. It was guaranteed to start working in one hour or less. Didn't miss it by much, did it? If you die tomorrow morning, we can bury you in a shoebox, Violet Prescott, because you won't be full of shit no more."

Violet snarled and growled. "You are a mean, jealous witch."

"That'd be the pot calling the kettle black. Ain't it nice that they've got a potty in your cell, though? You sure you want your son in there with you?" Agnes asked.

Andy opened the door and Ethan preceded him into the hallway in front of the jail cells. "Mother?"

"You can't come in here. It's too horrible. What if the press saw you sitting in a jail cell? It would ruin our chances at election."

"I didn't come to sit with you. We've paid the city fine for aggravated assault and we are taking you home," he said.

"Well, shit!" Agnes whispered. "I really wanted to see if she'd use that pot."

"Aunt Agnes!" Cathy and Marty chimed in together.

"Just get me away from that woman," Violet said.

"Don't you dare go home and sleep with my dear Herman," Agnes yelled.

"Go to hell!" Violet screamed back.

"Nope! I keep tellin' you that I ain't spendin' eternity with you."

The door slammed and Agnes cackled. "We showed her, didn't we? Bet she thinks twice before she calls Cathy a slut again."

Marty bristled. "She did what?"

"I took care of it real good so don't get your dander up. That felt so good that I wish I'd done it fifty years ago."

It was thirty minutes before Andy came back. "Okay, Violet is at home now so I'll let you go. Fifty-dollar fine for public disturbance, Agnes."

"Pay him, Marty."

"Why me?" she argued.

"Because I took up for your sister and kept you from a murder charge. You'd have killed her for calling Cathy a slut," Agnes said.

Chapter 13

Agnes appeared the next morning with gauze wrapped around her arm from wrist to elbow and carrying it in a sling that smelled like mothballs. A bit of overkill for a scratch, but Trixie wasn't saying a word.

Cathy hugged her gently. "Oh, Aunt Agnes, does it hurt?"

"Violet probably had rabies up under her fingernails. You reckon I need to take those horrible shots in my belly?" Agnes was able to use the arm very well to dip sausage gravy over the tops of two big buttermilk biscuits.

Cathy giggled. "We're never going to live this down."

Agnes's sparkling eyes and tight little smile told Trixie that they'd not seen the end of the fifty-year-old cat fight.

"Sweet Nothin's" was playing in the café when the chimes on the doorbell let everyone in the kitchen know the first customer of the day had arrived. Trixie went through the swinging doors backward, tying her apron. She stopped so fast that she almost pitched forward when she came face to face with cameras and a microphone pushed into her face.

"Miss Andrews?" The lady with the microphone took a step closer and a cameraman started filming.

"No, I'm Trixie. Which Miss Andrews do you want?"

The camera clicked off.

"Clawdy, of course," the woman said.

"There is no Clawdy. The café is named for Claudia Andrews,

but she passed on a while back. Would you like to speak to Cathy or Marty Andrews—they are her daughters?" Trixie asked.

"Either one will do fine," the woman said.

"Hey, Cathy, you better take this one," Trixie yelled toward the kitchen.

Cathy was stunned to see a cameraman with Sherman's television station logo on the side. "What is this all about?"

The little red light flashed on the camera.

Agnes pushed her way in front of the cameras. "You want to know about the fracas at the football field last night, you ask me, not her. That was all my doings and she had no part in it."

"We are here to ask you how you feel about this zoning business. We all love this cute little café in this area and would hate to see you have to sell out. Will you think about relocating to a bigger place, like Sherman or Denison, if your zoning laws are changed?"

"That was resolved at the last Council meeting," Cathy said.

"It's been reopened for review. The company that was looking at the house across the street decided to buy property in Sherman. And we have it from a good source that the Cadillac City Council is once again trying to decide if they're going to rule that your house isn't zoned for a business."

"We thought it was taken care of. We'd have to discuss our options before we could make a statement. I'm in business with two partners," Cathy said.

"This is all Violet Prescott's doing," Agnes said.

"Ethan Prescott's mother?" The lady reporter gave the cameraman a sign to keep the cameras rolling.

"That's right. It's a long story, but she attacked me at the fireworks show last night. See?" Agnes held up the arm. "I might have to take rabies shots."

"She bit you?"

"Who knows what she did, but just to be on the safe side, I'm on my way to the doctor's office to see if a human bite can cause rabies." Agnes limped out of the camera's view into the kitchen.

"Well, Miss Andrews, thank you. We are doing a piece on the economy and how rezoning portions of our small towns might bring more business into them. Would you sign a release form giving us permission to air this?" the lady asked.

"Yes, ma'am, I will. Anything to help the small businesses," Cathy said.

Damn that Violet Prescott. She should have left well enough alone. Now they'd have to watch Agnes like a hawk. Violet had no idea what kind of shit storm she'd just kicked up.

It was not what Darla Jean expected when Agnes opened the door and motioned her inside her home. It did not smell like mothballs but like bacon and biscuits. It didn't have doilies and knickknacks everywhere, but was nicely decorated in earth tones.

"What the hell do you want?" Agnes asked.

"I'm your spiritual adviser and I'm advising you to ride down to Blue Ridge with me today," Darla Jean said.

"Why would I do a fool thing like that?"

Darla Jean gave her a brief account of Lindsey, but she didn't tell her that Cathy had called after the camera crew had left. The café was suddenly swamped with customers who seldom ever went out to lunch. And none of the three could watch Agnes so they'd enlisted Darla Jean's help in keeping her out of meanness.

"Well, why didn't you say so? Does this Lindsey and your sister know you are a hooker?" Agnes asked.

"I'm a preacher in the Christian Nondenominational Church and I'd just as soon not broadcast my past," Darla Jean told her.

"Yes, but you used to be a hooker."

"And you were pretty ornery yourself last night. I understand that you and Violet are sleeping with the same man. He must have a lot of stamina for an eighty-year-old man."

Agnes laughed. "Okay, I'll go with you. Cathy sent you to keep me out of trouble, didn't she?"

Darla Jean smiled. "A spiritual adviser is bound by the same laws as a lawyer and his or her client. I'm sworn to secrecy, and if I answer that question, then God might not even let me dust off the clouds in heaven."

"Honey, you'll have to pray until there's calluses on your knees 'fore God lets a hooker into heaven."

Darla Jean said, "Way I figure it is if Jesus loved that woman at the well and she was a prostitute, he could love all of us, even you, Agnes."

"He told her to go and sin no more," Agnes said. "I reckon you are trying to do that part. Well, what in the hell are we waiting for? We can't have Cathy worrying and burning the red beans or scorching the turnip greens. I heard she was making one more batch of pepper jelly today with the last of the jalapeños from her little garden. It would be a damn sin if she didn't get it done up right. So you are my babysitter and I promise to be a good little girl today. Just don't expect it every day."

Agnes settled into Darla Jean's vehicle and said, "I never thought about you having family. Your sister got any kids?"

"No, she never married. She was engaged to a fine young man and he was killed in Vietnam. She never got over it, but she's really taken to Lindsey like a mother hen."

"I wanted kids," Agnes said. "Didn't get them and Bert died when the twins were small so I kind of adopted them. You know they're named after me and my sister. Martha Agnes and Catherine Francis."

"They sure named them right. Marty is just as mouthy as you are," Darla Jean said.

"Be careful now. At my age I can claim that I don't remember promising to be good!"

"Okay, right three blocks down and then a left. I see it right now."

"What do you see? I don't see jack shit. This place hasn't even got a McDonald's," Agnes said.

"No, but Betty's church is having a dinner, so we're eating lunch there."

"Who died?" Agnes asked.

The parking lot was small but there were at least a dozen cars angled in toward the church.

"No one. It's the monthly ladies' auxiliary meeting and they have food. Hungry?"

"Starving, and I love church dinners. They are the best."

Darla Jean settled Agnes in right beside Lindsey at the end of a long table. Agnes lowered her chin and whispered, "Tell me his name that hurt you and that sumbitch won't never see the light of day again."

Lindsey's smile lit up the room.

"If you'll tell me your story, I'll tell you about the fistfight I got into yesterday. I'm wearing this so people will feel sorry for me and hate Violet for giving me rabies," Agnes said.

"Violet is a dog?"

"She's a bitch, but she's only got two legs."

Lindsey giggled. "You go first."

"Nope, I'm hungry and you already got to eat so you talk first," Agnes said.

Lindsey had barely smiled in the past week and hadn't even opened up to Betty, but in less than two minutes she was talking to Agnes.

"Look, Betty." Darla Jean tilted her head toward the other end of the table.

Chapter 14

A BLAST OF BITTER cold wind hit Cathy in the face when she opened the door and she almost ran back to the nice warm restaurant. It wasn't just the cold. She didn't want to go home. But it was midnight, closing time, and John had to get home to his wife, Maggie Rose. He talked about her a lot. She loved ribs. She liked a walk before bedtime. She loved to watch television.

He followed Cathy outside and to her car. He crawled into the passenger's seat. "Turn on the heat and talk to me a while. Tomorrow is Sunday. You don't have to open your café and I'm closed so we can sleep late."

Imagining him as the hero in her romance stories was one thing. Sitting in the car with him when his wife might come around the corner and get the wrong idea was another. She liked her job at the Rib Joint. It put her in the midst of a very different bunch of people than she saw at Clawdy's. They were exciting, wild, and loud. She darn sure didn't want to get fired because the wife was jealous.

He sighed. "I'm in a Jesus mood. I could use some company."

"A what mood?"

"A Jesus mood is what my grandma called it when I got like this. She said that I wouldn't know what I wanted, and if I got it, I wouldn't want it, and Jesus couldn't even live with me. Talk to me. Tell me why you were in that fracas on the football field parking lot the other night at the craft show."

Cathy blushed scarlet. "You were there?"

"I was for a little while. I ran out of Coke syrup and my friend at the convenience store had a spare. I drove by in time to see a fight going on. You do have a twin sister. I could hardly tell you apart from a distance. The elderly lady who was fighting? The one you were having trouble holding back, what's her name?"

"That would be my Aunt Agnes who is actually my great-aunt, my mother's aunt."

"What happened?"

"It's a long story."

"It takes a lot to get me out of my Jesus moods, and I've got all night."

"You want me to start with 'In the beginning, God made dirt,' or just jump into the fight scene?"

He chuckled. "I want the whole thing from the day of the dirt manufacturing."

"Okay, but remember you asked for it. Won't Maggie Rose be worried?"

"Give me just a minute to go make things right with her. It won't take long. If you leave, you'll be responsible for whatever I do when I'm in this mood."

"I'll wait," she said.

Reading erotic fiction. Working at a place that sold beer. Talking to a married man after midnight. Aunt Agnes would take away her good twin crown.

He was only gone a minute and when he opened the car door, a small bundle of black and tan fur bounded inside, bounced up into her lap, and looked up at her with big brown eyes.

She rubbed the dog and it licked her hands. "Well, hello, pretty baby. Do you live here or are you lost?"

John reached out and touched the Pomeranian on the head. "I'll be damned. She doesn't usually like anyone but me. My friends can't get close to her. She only weighs five pounds but she acts like a pit bull."

She laughed as the dog licked her chin. "I'm a pushover. Dogs know it. You know what they say about not being able to fool dogs and kids."

"You got that right. Cathy, meet Maggie Rose, my muse and best friend."

The Lone Star Restaurant on Main Street in Cadillac did something that Clawdy's didn't, and that was opening for business on Sunday. They closed on Monday instead. That Sunday, Cathy, Marty, Darla Jean, and Trixie claimed the last table in the place. They were still looking over the menus when Agnes hollered from the front of the café.

"Get me a chair, Myrtle. I'll eat with the girls," she said.

The gray-haired waitress pulled a chair from a side wall and Agnes settled in beside Darla Jean. "So y'all beat the Baptists, did you? Must not take y'all as long to save, sanctify, and dehorn as it does us. If it wasn't for not lettin' Violet win, I'd change my membership just for that reason."

Marty nodded toward the door. "Speak of the devil."

Violet and Ethan stepped inside the door and looked around.

Violet and Agnes both saw each other at the same time. Violet shot evil looks across the café and Agnes fired them right back at her. If their stares had had sound effects, folks would have been running from machine gun fire.

Cathy reached out and touched Agnes on the shoulder. "Aunt Agnes, you stay right here."

Agnes held up a palm toward Cathy. "I'll go home and eat cat food before I let her sit at our table even if we do have room. You will not be that nice today, not after the things that bitch said about you."

"I wasn't going to suggest that. I just didn't want you to go up there and antagonize her," Cathy said.

"Well, I damn sure don't want Ethan sitting here," Marty said. "That would be as bad as letting Andy join us."

"Wow! I didn't know anything was that bad in your eyes," Trixie said.

Darla Jean tilted her head toward the front of the café. "Guess if she can't run you out of church, then you aren't allowed to run her out of this place on Sunday. Are we going to have to split the church in two like Solomon was going to do with that baby?"

Agnes shrugged. "Y'all going to the Council meeting about this zoning shit tomorrow night?" She changed the subject.

"Oh, yeah!" Trixie said. "Are you going this time?"

"Damn tootin' I am. Anywhere Violet is, there I'll be from now on. She don't like it then she can leave town."

"Aunt Agnes, you wouldn't show up at the club, would you?" Cathy gasped.

"Hell, no! She can have that one, but only if she's nice to your sister. One smart-ass remark about you and I'll use her to wipe up her driveway and let the whole damn club watch. Hell, I might sell tickets."

"Aunt Agnes, didn't you listen to the preacher this morning?"

"I always listen. Sometimes I don't agree."

"Move over." Jack grabbed an extra chair from a table for four with only three people at it.

He sat at the end with Trixie on one side of him and Darla Jean on the other. "I only got an hour. Don't have time to wait for a booth or table. I'll get y'all's dinner since you are letting me sit by you."

"Well, thank you, Jack. That's sweet," Agnes said.

"Missed you at church," Trixie told him.

"You did?"

"Sure. There were old scrooges this morning. I could have used a smiling face."

Ethan touched Violet on the wrist. "Don't look at them. Pretend like you don't even know they are there."

"She just makes me so mad," Violet whispered.

"Well, hello!" Anna Ruth sat down beside Violet. "Are you okay, honey? That was horrible the way Agnes treated you."

"It was, wasn't it?" Violet whimpered just enough for effect.

Anna Ruth patted her on the leg. "Y'all are waiting for a table, I guess?"

"Yes, we are. Looks like… oh, no!" Violet's eyes almost popped out of her head.

"What? Are you ill? Can I get you some water?" Anna Ruth asked.

"Mrs. Prescott, we have a table for you," Myrtle said.

It was the table right beside Agnes's. She simply could not be that close to the redheaded witch. But Myrtle was already leading the way. It was follow or lose—those were Violet's options, and she damn sure wasn't going to forfeit to Agnes, especially when Lone Star was the only place open on Sunday. She stood up, back ramrod straight, and followed Myrtle to the table right beside Agnes.

"Speak of the devil," Agnes said.

When Violet and Ethan had gone three steps, Ethan turned back and said, "Anna Ruth, come join us. It's a table for four and there's only two of us."

"Ethan!" Violet hissed.

"It's just being polite, Mother."

"Didn't you hear the gossip?"

"No, I was too busy taking care of your fight, and you were asleep when Clayton finally left."

"They said that you are in love with her and that's why you and Catherine broke up."

"That explains a lot," Ethan said.

"You *are* going to be good. I mean it. No more public scenes," Marty whispered to Agnes.

"There will be plenty of time to be good when I'm dead. I have to seize every moment in this life, but I promise I won't throw the first punch," she whispered back.

Then Agnes said loudly, "We were discussing these zoning laws, weren't we? I've been thinking about making my famous fudge to sell to the public. If you girls can make a buck with red beans, your mamma's famous pepper jelly, and turnip greens then I should be able to make a quarter with my fudge. I make other kinds than chocolate, you know. And it has so many wonderful uses."

Marty was glad that she was sitting between the two old women. Maybe she and Jack together could separate them if food or dishes started flying.

"Hey, guess what? John, my boss, isn't married," Cathy blurted out to get Agnes on another subject. "I thought his wife was Maggie Rose. He talked about her all the time, but I found out that's his dog. She's this cute little Pomeranian. I could just put her in my purse and bring her home, but the inspectors would have a conniption if we had a dog in the house with the café."

"All bitches don't have four legs," Agnes said.

Violet took that comment like a slap to the face and made a motion to push her chair back, but Ethan laid a hand on her arm. "Don't make a scene."

Marty wrapped her arm around the back of Agnes's chair and dropped a hand on her shoulder. "Be still."

"So what does your boss look like, Cathy?" Darla Jean asked.

"He wears glasses, has blond hair that is too long, wears a baseball cap backward, and cooks in cutoff jeans, a company T-shirt, and flip-flops. Real laid back and nice as he can be to me. Makes some fine barbecue. Y'all should come out and have some."

"We'll have to get a party together and do that," Jack said.

Violet hissed something toward Ethan and he removed his hand. She stood up and deliberately held her skirt to one side as she passed by Agnes on her way to the ladies' room at the back of the café. Agnes hid her giggling behind the menu.

"What's so funny?" Jack asked. "You don't want to go to the Rib Joint with us?"

"Nothing to do with the barbecue joint. I was just thinking about some right fine fudge," she said loud enough for Violet to hear.

Trixie whispered in Jack's ear, "I'll tell you later. It has to do with the fight."

His eyes got big. "Oh!"

"You understand now?" Trixie asked.

"Oh, yeah! And I wish I didn't right here at dinnertime."

The waitress arrived and everyone at their table ordered the Sunday special: chicken and dressing, mashed potatoes, cranberry orange sauce, green beans, and hot rolls. It came with sweet tea and pumpkin pie for dessert.

"And put it on one bill," Jack told her.

Trixie leaned over and whispered again, "Have they always been this way?"

He nodded. "Oh, yeah. Mamma says it started when Agnes married Bert."

Agnes pointed her finger at Jack. "You two stop that whispering. I might be old but my hearing is just fine and I heard my name."

"He didn't understand why Violet was so mad at you," Trixie said.

Myrtle carried out several glasses of iced tea, stopping to put three on Ethan's table before she brought the remainder to Agnes's table. "Food will be out in a minute."

Violet came out of the bathroom, took one look at the tea and at Agnes, and shook her head so hard that her chins had trouble keeping up.

"Myrtle!" she called out. "You get me another glass of tea. This has been tampered with."

"But it's not been touched, Mrs. Prescott, I promise. I just set it down there and there ain't been nobody except Ethan around it. I don't think he would do a thing to your drink."

"My son wouldn't but someone else, and I'm not naming names, would sneak something into it. And she's just crafty enough to do it," Violet said.

Agnes fumbled with a bottle of Miralax, transferring it from pocket to purse, purposely missed, and kicked it so it would roll under Violet's feet.

Myrtle picked it up and looked around.

"It's mine." Agnes held out a hand. "Can't taste it in anything so that's my fiber of choice."

Violet shuddered. "Get me another glass. I insist, and when it is here, you can take this one back and dump it."

"Agnes!" Marty said.

"It don't hurt to come prepared, and I didn't say a damn word to her so don't you look at me like that," Agnes said.

Chapter 15

Violet took her place behind the podium, called the meeting to order, and asked if there was any old business. She wore a bright red skirt and matching jacket with the customary flag pin on her lapel, a classy scarf knotted intricately around her neck, and the smell of her hair gave testimony to the perm she'd had that afternoon.

Agnes thought she looked sweaty and flustered in spite of the brisk fall weather. Probably because Agnes had made good on her word and brought the fancy-pants Dallas lawyer along like she said she'd do. Violet could just worry and sweat some more. Agnes was there for Cathy and she would have her say if it gave Violet a stroke.

"Is this zoning thing old or new? It ought to be old since it's like that old dead horse that's been whooped plumb to death." Agnes said.

"That would be old since it has been discussed before."

"Well, I want to discuss it again. I'm thinking about putting in a shop and I want my house and the whole block zoned commercial so I won't be breaking any laws. My lawyer, Mr. Frank Watson, says that all I have to have is a paper signed by the Council. Do we need to take this to a citywide vote? The television has already been down here and there's concern everywhere about zoning laws. Small towns like ours are withering up and dying. We should zone the whole damn town commercial so we could get something in here to generate revenue."

"There are empty buildings on Main Street that could be used.

We don't need to zone our residential property commercial. Do you want McDonald's right next to your house?" Violet snapped.

Agnes pursed her lips and thought about it. "I don't give a shit if Long John Silver's goes in next to my place, and I hate fish. I'd support it if it brought money into our town treasury for things like street repairs and maybe a new jail. There's potholes in our side streets that could swallow up an army tank."

Violet ignored her and looked around the room. "Anyone else?"

Trixie stood up. "Could we just get a quick count of the folks here tonight? Those for zoning our block commercial so we can keep Clawdy's open, raise your hand."

Anna Ruth did not raise her hand.

Ethan did not.

The rest reached for the ceiling.

"I would like a word," Frank Watson said. "If there is this much proactive response, then what is this fight about? Sign the paper and let these folks keep Clawdy's open. I understand lots of folks like their beans and greens and lunch buffet as well as their breakfast. Zone the block commercial and maybe you'll see some quaint little businesses come into town. Ever been over on the eastern border to Jefferson, Texas? They have more than a dozen lovely bed and breakfast establishments in old homes. Couldn't do it without the zoning. They have built quite a little tourist town there and it generates a lot of revenue. You don't see potholes big enough to bury tanks in, let me tell you."

"As chairman of the Council committee on this, I feel that we need more time to think about it," Violet said.

"You really think that is the smart way to go, do you?" Agnes said. "The people who care anything about the town are in this room and they've voted. It's going to cost the taxpayers to have a formal vote on it, and besides, you know nobody turns out to vote on these things. Unless it's got to do with the school board or the President of the United States, folks can't even be paid to come out and vote."

"Oh, okay, give me the paper. I've been authorized to sign the thing if there was enough support for it. I'm sick of hearing about it," Violet said.

"And I want it fixed so this don't come up every time you get your panties in a wad," Agnes said.

Violet's gold fingernail glittered when pointed at Frank. "Fix it! I don't want to have to deal with that old bag over this ever again."

"Thank you," Cathy said.

Violet shot her a dirty look, but she signed the paper.

"New business?" Violet asked.

"Concession stands for the festival still in my court?" Anna Ruth asked.

"Yes, they are."

Agnes stood up slowly.

Violet rounded the podium and stood in front of it, chin up, daring her to say a word.

Ethan rose to his feet.

Cathy did the same.

"It's time for us to go now. Frank has another client he has to see this evening." Agnes turned her back to Violet, daring her to stab her in the back with the letter opener on the podium. "Thank you, everyone, for helping us out here tonight. My nieces will knock fifteen percent off anyone's breakfast ticket tomorrow morning from eight to nine for their gratitude. At the Jalapeño Jubilee, they'll have the buffet open from lunch through supper both, and believe me, their beans, greens, fried catfish, and pecan cobbler are worth stopping by for alone. And they've got the best pepper jelly and picante in the whole damn state. Remember now, Ethan, anytime your mamma has a hankering for fudge, you just call me and I'll be glad to whip up a batch for her. Let's hear it for a real good vote tonight and getting this thing settled once and for all."

The room roared with applause.

Agnes left with her lawyer, nieces, spiritual adviser, and Trixie all trailing behind her. She'd never felt more like a queen.

When they were in the church parking lot, Trixie exploded. "Who gave you the right to knock fifteen percent off the breakfast tomorrow or to make us stay open for lunch and dinner at the Jalapeño Jubilee?"

"That will be cheaper than buying a nasty old vacant building full of roaches and rats and remodeling it so you could move the business. People will remember that they got a damn good breakfast for a good price and come back later. It's a good idea, so shut up your bitchin'."

Cathy had not signed a secret paper in her own blood when she was invited to join the Blue-Ribbon Jalapeño Society. She had not vowed to stand before a firing squad to protect the members of the club. Nor had she held up her hand and recited after Violet that she would put the friendship of the other members, including Violet and Anna Ruth, before all her other friends.

It was not a college sorority but a community club that gave a small scholarship at the end of each school year to a local high school senior girl for college. Cathy had received that scholarship, so when her mother said it was time for her to give back, she'd agreed to join.

Evidently, the rules had changed from the time Cathy had been asked to join and when Anna Ruth had. Because Anna Ruth had a very different idea of what the club meant.

Cathy was flipping through a seed and plant catalog, thinking about whether begonias could survive beside the west side of the front porch next spring. Trixie was looking through a catalog where she bought her ceramic paints at good prices when she bought in bulk. Marty had just gotten a new book with car parts in it that day and she was engrossed in it.

The back door burst open and there was Anna Ruth. No knocking. No calling beforehand; she just stood there with her chin quivering and tears running down her cheeks.

Had her Aunt Annabel taken sick with a dreaded disease and only cobbler or tarts would heal her?

Anna Ruth brushed at her cheeks. "We've got to make peace. I would just die if we didn't have the club, and it's suffering from all this bickering. I'm here to forgive you, Trixie."

"Forgive *me*? You're the one who was sleeping with my husband," Trixie said.

"I'm taking the bigger part and forgiving you for slapping me. Now, let's hug and be friends. Put the past where it belongs and forget about it." Anna Ruth came at her with both arms open.

Trixie pushed her chair back and backed up. "Don't you touch me, woman. You might be making everything right with your Maker by forgiving me, but I'm not in a showing-the-love mood tonight."

Cathy bit back a giggle. Had Anna Ruth been drinking?

"Anna Ruth, you slept with Andy when he was still her husband," Marty said.

Trixie shook her head emphatically. "You forget anything you want to. I'm going to bed. Cathy, if you let her come up the stairs, I'm calling Agnes."

Anna Ruth melted into a chair and helped herself to a piece of sweet potato pie. "Oh, Cathy, I tried. What am I going to do?"

"How old are you?" Marty asked.

"Twenty-five."

"Grow up. You are not a cheerleader in high school. Trixie is not going to be your BFF. And neither am I," Marty said. "I'm going up to my room. Trixie won't have to call Agnes if you let her up the stairs. I'll kick her back down the stairs myself."

"But you are my friend. You voted for me!" Anna Ruth wailed. "Only you understand, Cathy."

The heavy stomping down the stairs left no doubt that Trixie was on her way back to the kitchen.

Cathy raised one eyebrow.

Trixie pointed at Marty. "You voted for her!"

"You didn't." Cathy gasped.

"Why would you do that? I didn't even want the damn position, but why would you vote for her? After the fit you threw over Andy and you go and vote for that hussy to be in the club with y'all. Dammit, Marty!"

"Why?" Cathy asked.

"Oops!" Anna Ruth smiled. Granted it was a weak smile but it was there all the same. "Maybe next time you'll get into the club, but I wouldn't bank on it, not after what you did to Ethan."

"You can go to hell."

"That is rude!"

"And sleeping with my husband wasn't?"

"He was unhappy, but he couldn't leave you because you have mental issues like your mother and you also have a drinking problem. I believe him. Any woman that would rather cut up paper as make Andy happy isn't right in the head."

Trixie went straight for the cabinet, took out the Jack, and poured two fingers in a water glass before she sat down at the table.

Anna Ruth stood up so fast that her chair hit the floor with a bang. "I thought he was just shooting me a line, but you just proved he was right."

Trixie held up her hand and giggled. "My name is Trixie. I'm crazy and I'm a drunk. And I cut paper up into little hearts and flowers. I'm disgusting. That's why my best friend just voted for the likes of you in her fancy-schmancy social club."

Anna Ruth stormed out the back door without a backward glance.

Trixie laughed so hard that she snorted. "So that's the story he tells his women," she said when she could talk. "Mamma has

Alzheimer's. She's not crazy. And a couple of drinks a week does not make me a drunk. Anna Ruth got screwed in more ways than one."

Anna Ruth poked her head back in the kitchen. "Don't talk about me."

"You are supposed to be gone, not eavesdropping on the back porch. Be careful—I hear insanity and alcoholism are both contagious," Trixie said.

Anna Ruth came inside but kept her distance. "It sounds like she completely lost her mind. Do you need help getting her to the institution?"

"I think I can manage on my own," Cathy said.

"My phone number is in the club daybook. Call me if you need me," Anna Ruth said seriously and disappeared into the darkness for the second time.

Marty opened her mouth as if she were about to say something.

Trixie put up a palm. "Not a word. Not a single solitary word. I'm mad at you and I may not forgive you and tonight you don't get to say anything at all. I'm going upstairs to read the latest Candy Parker novel. It came in the mail today," Trixie said.

"You'll love it. It's her best yet," Cathy said without thinking.

"You're shittin' me," Trixie said.

Marty sat down on the bottom step with a thud.

Cathy blushed. "No, it really is better than her last one about the fireman. This cowboy one will make your eyeballs fog over."

In for a dime, in for a dollar. It was harder to put a cat back in the bag than to let it out. And Cathy had just let the wildcat out of the bag.

"I can't believe you read Candy's books," Marty whispered.

"Why?"

"I never see them in your room or lying around like Trixie's books."

Cathy stood up. "My name is Cathy Andrews, and I'm disgusting. I'm addicted to erotic romance. Candy Parker's are my favorites, but I'll read any of it. That's the reason I broke it off with Ethan. I would rather take my e-reader to a back booth of the Rib Joint and read as spend time with him. Until I am willing to toss my e-reader in a trash dumpster to spend time with a man, I will not get engaged again." She raised her right hand. "So help me, God! And for the record, I do feel sorry for Anna Ruth. But I don't feel a bit sorry for you, Marty. That was downright mean to vote for that witch."

"I am Candy Parker," Marty said.

"You read it too? I thought you were too busy chasing hot cowboys to read about them," Trixie said.

"You are who?" Cathy asked.

"I don't read it, Trixie. I write it. I am Candy Parker. I chose a pen name because I didn't want to embarrass my sister. This is too rich for words." Marty laughed.

"Does that mean I don't have to wait? I can read them before they go to the publisher?" Cathy asked.

"Hell, no! You'd take a red pen to them and give me a complex. You have to wait until they are completely finished," Marty said.

Trixie started up the stairs.

"Hey, you aren't going to be mad at me, are you?" Marty hollered.

"Yes, I am, and it's going to last a long time."

"What can I do?"

"I'll think of something and it won't be pleasant. I can't believe you did that. I had to find out from that bitch's mouth. You didn't even come and tell me. Why, Marty?"

"I can't tell you."

"Well, I'm not going to forgive you until you do."

"It's going to be between us, isn't it?"

"Damn straight."

If you can't buy it at Walmart, you don't need it, was another of Trixie's mother's sayings.

She could almost hear her mother saying the words as she tossed things in her cart at the Sherman Walmart store. It had been the last time they'd gone out shopping and with very little help Janie could remember some things. That time she'd been herself right up until checkout time when she looked around her and started crying. She didn't know where she was or who Trixie was and she was terrified.

Trixie picked up a bottle of shampoo and turned the cart down the center aisle. A display of bubble bath on an end aisle took her eye and she didn't even see the cart coming around the next corner until it rammed into hers.

She looked up into Andy's dreamy eyes.

"I'm sorry. Oh!" the man said.

"Hello, Andy."

"Trixie." He nodded. "How are you?"

"Just fine. You?"

"Lonely."

"Break up with the new dispatcher or did she break up with you?"

He took a couple of steps toward her and ran a forefinger down her bare arm. "I'm lonely for you. I always came back home to you, Trixie. What's the big deal?"

She didn't feel a single tingle. No sparks. No extra heartbeat. Nada. Zilch. Should she tell him he was losing his charm?

Hell, no! If she did, she'd have to put up with his whimpering because Andy couldn't live without his sex appeal.

She didn't feel anger either. No visions of strapping him out spread-eagled in a fire ant bed and pouring honey all over his body.

She felt nothing but indifference. Marty would be so glad that she was finally, finally moving on.

She picked up his finger and dropped it. "But I'm bordering on crazy and I have a drinking problem and I read erotic books which is where I'm headed right now. I hear there's a whole new shipment over in the romance books."

He looked into her eyes. "I bet I can do a better job than any of those men in books. You still got those black furry cuffs?"

"I'm not sure you could get Anna Ruth to believe that line, and I gave the cuffs to Marty. You want to talk to her about them?"

"Come on, Trix. You know I'll never love a woman the way I do you."

"Poor baby," she said and pushed on past him toward the book section.

"I won't wait around for you forever." He raised his voice.

"I can always hope." She didn't look back.

She didn't stop at the book aisle but went on to the toys where she bought two princess coloring books and a new box of crayons. Only eight. Any more confused her mother.

After she checked out, she drove straight to the nursing home. If it was a good day, she wouldn't need the coloring books, but if it wasn't, they could color. That always calmed Janie down and sometimes it even sparked a little memory.

Trixie hoped Janie was lucid that day. Her whole world was coming apart and she needed someone outside her tight little circle of friends to talk to. She needed her mother worse than ever. Did the whole town know that Andy was cheating behind her back? And the new thing with Marty voting for Anna Ruth—that stung. Granted, Trixie had said if she did get it, she wouldn't ever put that gaudy jalapeño pin on her lapel or even on a ratty old T-shirt, but why would Marty vote for Anna Ruth? She didn't even like her, so why would she want her, of all people, in the club?

"Hello, are you new here?" Janie asked when Trixie rapped on the door.

"Yes, I am. Do you like to color?"

Janie clapped her hands. "Oh, yes, but my colors are all broken."

"I brought new ones. Do you mind if I color with you? I have two new princess books."

"What fun!" Janie patted the card table in front of her. "We can color right here. New colors?"

"That's right." Trixie swallowed the disappointment as she brought out the books and the crayons.

"I want the blue one. Cinderella's dress is blue," her mother said.

"May I have the yellow one?" Trixie asked.

Janie picked up the box, removed the yellow one, and handed it to Trixie. "What's your name?"

"Trixie," she answered.

Even hearing her daughter's name brought no response.

Janie opened the book and started on the very first page, just like she always did. Her coloring books were all beautifully done, but she never colored random pages. They had to be done in order or it upset her.

"What's your name?" Trixie asked as she colored.

"Janie. My daughter wore a blue dress to the prom when she was a junior in high school. I sewed it for her and hand beaded the bodice. It was lovely."

"What was her name?" Trixie asked.

Janie stopped for a minute. "I don't remember. Could I have the yellow? Cinderella's hair is yellow. My daughter married a man right out of high school. He had shifty eyes."

"We can trade," Trixie said. "Was your daughter's hair yellow?"

"No, it was brown, like yours."

"Just one daughter?"

"Yes, and she ran away. It was because she married that man who kept looking at other women, I think."

Janie looked up and there was light in her eyes. "Hello, Trixie! I'm so glad you came today. Did you bring me some beans and greens? I've had a hankering for some of Clawdy's cooking lately. Oh, what I'd give for a big old heaping spoonful of her pepper jelly on a hot biscuit."

Trixie swallowed twice. "Hi, Mamma. I didn't bring anything from Clawdy's, but I'll drive back to Cadillac and get whatever you want if you are hungry for that kind of food. You look pretty."

"No, just bring them next time you come see me." She smoothed the front of her dress. "I still love this dress. I told them to get it out today in case you came. It's what I wore to your wedding."

"Yes, it is," Trixie said. "That was fifteen years ago."

"It's still a good dress though, and you said I was pretty that day." Janie stopped coloring and looked up. "You look happy."

"I am. Andy and I divorced."

"I'm not surprised. Why did you leave him?"

"He cheated on me more than once," Trixie said.

"Well, then you should have left him."

"Mamma, why didn't Claudia ever put your name down to be in the social club?"

Janie smiled. "Honey, I never married your father, and I came from the wrong side of the tracks. The social club didn't want me, but that was okay. I didn't want them either."

"I left Andy because he was having an affair with a younger woman named Anna Ruth…"

Janie went back to her coloring but butted in, "Anna Ruth's mamma married the man that got her pregnant. When I got pregnant, I decided I didn't love the man I was with, so I didn't marry him."

Trixie kept coloring. "Marty voted for Anna Ruth instead of me to get into the social club. Agnes was on the ballot so she voted against her too."

"Agnes is always on the ticket. And don't hold it against Marty. She didn't vote against you. She voted against Agnes."

"But why? Agnes wants it so bad."

Janie smiled, but the light in her eyes was fading fast. "Clawdy says that if Agnes gets in the club, Violet is a dead woman. Can I please have the pink now?"

Janie's eyes went blank.

"Yes, ma'am. But remember we were coloring the princesses and you were telling me Agnes and Claudia."

"I changed my mind. Black. Prince Charming's hair is black. I don't have daughters. You must have me mistaken with one of the other girls here at the school. Some of them have daughters."

Black always meant that she'd retreated back into that dark world where she didn't know Trixie. Not once in the past had she come out of the dark shadows once she had the black crayon in her hand.

Trixie cried all the way back to Cadillac. Part of the tears were grateful ones for the tiny moment that her mother had been lucid. The rest were out of sheer frustration.

One of the two old rocking chairs on the front porch at Clawdy's creaked out a song as Cathy kept the motion going with one foot. The night air was stinking hot, but she felt cooped up in the house. Cadillac was experiencing Indian Summer, the warm days just before real fall pushed summer out of the way. She wanted to plant something, but the pansies for the winter months were in the ground already and everything was in gorgeous repair.

She missed a living room where family and friends congregated at the end of the day to watch television, play games, read, or just talk to each other. These days she felt like she lived in a hotel and worked in the hotel kitchen.

The three upstairs bedrooms were equal in size and spacious enough for Cathy to have a love seat and a recliner as well as her bed and dresser, but she missed the way things used to be.

She would have gladly shut her eyes to the clutter in Trixie's room to have someone to talk to that evening. She would have even helped glue hearts and lace around pictures in Janie's scrapbook. She wished she'd gone with her to the nursing home to see her mother. Cathy didn't mind the nursing home. It reminded her of the reference section at the library. So much information and no one even bothered knocking the dust off the books. But she was in a cranky mood and Trixie's sweet little mother picked up on the strangest vibes.

Marty had gone to the Dairy Queen for ice cream. Agnes was watching *NCIS* on television and nobody had better call, drop by, or even whisper during that time. She and Leroy Jethro Gibbs had a standing date, and death would have to stand in line until the credits rolled. If Agnes ever did commit homicide, they'd never find enough forensic evidence to convict her after she'd watched that show for almost a decade. Violet was lucky she got away with only two black eyes.

The squeal of car wheels coming to an abrupt stop put an end to the rocking chair solo. Cathy leaned forward and peered out through the crape myrtle bushes to see Anna Ruth get out of her little red car, slam the door, and stomp toward the house. Everything about her said this was not a visit to forgive Trixie but to pick another fight.

"Evening," Cathy said.

Anna Ruth came to an abrupt halt on her way to the back of the house and stormed up onto the porch. "You are not my friend. One of us has got to resign from the club, because I refuse to be in it with you."

What a wonderful idea! No more meetings with Violet, especially after the breakup with Ethan. Anna Ruth could have it. Maybe she could sponsor someone else into the club.

"I mean it, Catherine," Anna Ruth said.

"What did I do to get called by my formal name?" Cathy asked.

"You are sleeping with Andy! I thought it was Trixie and then I thought it was the dispatcher, but it was you! How could one club sister do that to another? You are worse than Marty. At least what she does, she does in public and not behind a club sister's back."

"Where did you hear that?" Cathy asked.

"Don't play dumb with me. Violet told Beulah who told Aunt Annabel. That's why you broke up with Ethan. Not because he was in love with me. But you stood by and let me make a fool out of myself with him. I've always had a crush on him and then you went after him with your prissy ways. And that wasn't enough, was it? You had to have Andy too. You are horrible." Anna Ruth sat down on the top step, put her elbows on her knees and her head in her hands, and wept like a child who couldn't have a favorite box of cereal in the grocery store.

"I did not sleep with Andy. I would never do that to Trixie."

"She's not even in the club and you have more respect for her than you do me." The wails got loud enough that a dog down the street joined her.

"Anna Ruth, you know about gossip and rumors in a small town. Wake up, girl. If you love Ethan, go tell him."

"I did!" She cried and the dog howled louder.

"And?"'

She pulled a tissue from her pocket and blew her nose loudly. "He said that he'd never thought of me as anything but a younger sister and a good friend. Can you even begin to imagine how humiliated I was?"

"Sorry," Cathy said.

"You could have had it all. Why did you break it off with him? The wedding was going to be beautiful and Aunt Annabel was so excited about making that cake. And he doesn't looove me," she moaned.

"Hush that carrying on. The neighbors are going to call the police to come see if I'm killing you. Truth is, I figured out that I didn't love him enough to sign the prenup and that I'd rather be reading a book as spending time with him. It didn't seem fair to marry a man that I wouldn't give up my job and my car for. But I didn't love him enough to do it. He's a good man and he deserves someone who'd love him that much."

"I'd give up my soul for him." The weeping stopped as if on cue, and Anna Ruth sighed loudly. "And you really did not sleep with Andy?"

"I really did not and I really will not. I can't stand the man after what he did to Trixie, and he did it with you."

Anna Ruth managed a weak smile. "But he told me they were as good as divorced and he would have already left her if he could. I'm glad that you didn't sleep with him. But I still think you need to resign from the club after what your aunt did to Violet."

"Is that legal? I thought a person had to die or move out of the county to get their name taken from the books."

Anna Ruth stood and tilted up her chin, said, "Then do one of those things," then pranced out to her car.

At least she didn't burn a thousand miles off her tires. And the dog had stopped howling. Cathy started rocking again. Why hadn't she thought of resigning from the club? Bless Anna Ruth's heart. She'd come up with an ingenious idea even if it had come from a wailing tantrum.

Teenagers were the reason that Marty never taught high school. Everything adults said to them slid off like fried eggs out of a coated skillet.

The Dairy Queen was filled with them that night. Life was good at that age. The world revolved around them. Too bad that once they graduated, reality was going to hit them smack between the eyes.

She sat in a back booth alone and imagined her mother sitting across from her.

Mamma, I would have promised you anything that day and I've kept my word. But it's killing me to see the pain in Trixie's eyes. I don't think you realized that keeping my word would hurt our friendship.

"Mind if I join you? The kids have taken over the place tonight. Jack is off to work, and I didn't want to cook," Beulah said.

Marty motioned for her to sit down across the booth from her. "Guess this warmish weather has got us all wanting to hang on to fall and not let winter come around."

"Jack is moving out in the next few days. What did I do wrong?" Beulah blurted out.

She was a large woman with short gray hair that she had permed into a curly-do popular thirty years ago. Her pantsuit was bright red and her lipstick matched it. Other than the extra bit of weight around his middle, Jack had gotten nothing from his mother. He was the image of his father, who had died right after Marty's mother.

"I know he is moving, Beulah, but it has nothing to do with you."

"It's the house that Cathy wanted. Do you think Jack is in love with her? Is he buying that place just so he can ask her to marry him when she gets over the Ethan thing? I'm just scared to death he will."

Marty dipped into her hot fudge sundae. "Would that be a bad thing?"

Beulah nodded. "Yes, it would. Violet would have a conniption if Ethan got thrown over for Jack."

"Violet has too much power," Marty said.

Beulah leaned forward and whispered, "Maybe so, but there's no way to take it away from her."

Marty reached across the table and patted Beulah's hand. "Jack, Cathy, Trixie, and I are best friends, darlin'. Jack might get married someday, but it won't be to one of us three, so don't worry your sweet head about it. Just be happy for him."

Trixie drove into the driveway and sat in her car. Darla Jean was either going over her sermon or else she was cleaning. God might strike Trixie graveyard dead if she interrupted the sermon process.

She had to talk to someone and right now she was mad at Marty. She dug around in her purse for her cell phone and called Darla Jean. When she answered she blurted out, "Can you come over to Clawdy's? I've got to talk to someone and…"

"And you are still angry with Marty over that club stuff and no one is home."

"You got it."

"Be right there."

She waited until Darla Jean was crossing the yard to get out of her car. Trixie opened the door and flipped the light switch. Darla Jean sat down at the table.

She took a deep breath. "Were you busy?"

Darla Jean shook her head. "I'm never too busy for friends. I wanted to talk to you anyway."

Trixie sat down beside Darla Jean. "Your news first?"

"I went to see Lindsey. Betty got her a job at the school. She's on the maintenance crew this summer but come fall she'll be a teacher's aide to the kindergarten teacher. She's so happy that I could just shout. I wanted someone to tell all about it, but everyone was gone. I'm thinking that God sent this child to me as a test to see if I could help more abused women. It's drawing me and my sister closer together than we've been in years and it's a good feeling to get someone out of a hopeless mess. Now your news."

"I saw Mamma." Trixie wiped a fresh batch of tears from her cheeks. "It's getting worse."

Darla Jean put her arm around her shoulders. "That's the way it happens. You are going mostly for you now, Trixie, not for her. She's locked away in the fog. Just spend time with her so there won't be regrets when the end comes."

The front door opened and Cathy yelled, "Trixie?"

"Looks like it's a group session. We're in the kitchen." Darla Jean raised her voice.

"I'm so glad you are home. Anna Ruth came and the rumors..." Cathy stopped in the middle of the sentence. "Did Janie die?"

"No, but it's getting worse and worse and she asked for the black crayon right away today," Trixie said.

"Well, I'm sleeping with Andy," Cathy said bluntly.

Trixie shook her head slightly. Was she truly hearing voices? "Would you repeat that?"

Cathy told the story of sitting on the porch and wishing they had a living room and Anna Ruth coming and what all she'd said.

By the time she finished her tale, Trixie was laughing harder than she had when Anna Ruth had burst into the kitchen wanting to forgive her. "That is the funniest thing I've ever heard."

"And you are quitting the club? I can't believe it," Darla Jean said.

"You will make history by being the first woman to quit," Trixie said.

Marty opened the kitchen door. "Hey, am I the last one at the party?"

"Group session," Darla Jean said. "Come in and bare your soul."

"I just found out that Jack bought his house so he can ask Cathy to marry him. And Violet is going to be furious because you threw over Ethan for Jack," Marty said.

"Jack is our friend. Who said that?"

"His mamma. Are you keeping secrets other than reading sexy books?"

"I am not! Is there not one thing sacred in this town? Gossip flows like a raging river," Cathy moaned.

"Couple of things must be secrets, like why you'd vote for Anna Ruth, right, Marty?" Trixie asked.

"And what's that supposed to mean?

"Mamma had about fifteen seconds of lucid tonight. She said I'm not supposed to hold it against you that you voted for Anna Ruth because you were voting against Agnes, not for Anna Ruth. But she went dark again before she could tell me why."

Marty slowly shook her head. "I cannot say a word."

"Why?" Cathy asked.

"Agnes would kill Violet and that's all I can say."

"That is exactly what Mamma said."

Darla Jean held up a palm. "We are not going to think about this problem between you two this night. Marty has her reasons, and you have a hurt in your heart. You both need time to work it out. And now we are changing the subject. I still can't believe that you are writing hot romance and Cathy and Trixie are reading it. I'm not totally sure St. Peter is going to unlock the doors for any of you."

"Funny as hell, ain't it?" Trixie said.

"Hell ain't funny," Darla Jean declared.

Cathy snickered and pretty soon they were all laughing so hard that it echoed off the walls in Miss Clawdy's Café.

Trixie wondered how she'd ever survive without her three friends. Divorce, PMS, teenagers, crazy people who thought they were your friend—all of it wouldn't be bearable without friendship.

Chapter 16

Janie didn't want to color that day and she snarled her nose at the beans and greens. She did eat every bite of the pecan cobbler but she wouldn't even touch the fish. She wanted to watch reruns of *I Dream of Jeannie* so Trixie sat beside her and laughed with her at all the right places. If she had a genie of her very own, what would she ask for?

That was easy.

Number One: that her mother was lucid and living in her own little house again.

Number Two: that Andy hadn't cheated on her and her marriage hadn't fallen apart.

And Number Three: that the awkward feeling between her and Marty would go away.

But genies didn't exist and Janie proved it when she leaned over and whispered, "You must go home now. My mamma will be calling me in to supper soon, but you can come back and play again another day. Maybe we'll cut out paper dolls. I have a friend named Clawdy and sometimes we play in her room. She has amazing things in her room. There's an old trunk in the attic and we play dress-up."

"I'd like that. I have a book that hasn't been cut out yet. Can you cut good?" Trixie asked.

"Of course, I'm not a baby!" Janie huffed.

Trixie was on her way to her car when one of the girls that kept her mother's room clean stepped out from behind a tree. She had a baby on her hip and a diaper bag thrown over her shoulder.

"Miss Trixie, I need help. And…"

"What is it, Misty?" Trixie remembered her name because the girl was a sweetheart and never agitated Janie.

The girl hung her head and wouldn't look up.

"Are you in trouble, honey?" Trixie asked. "Can I help?"

"He got mad at Layla and lit into her with a belt. She's gonna have bruises and I could go to the police but last time he broke the restrainin' order and beat me hard with that belt. I'm afraid of him and he's lookin' for us."

"How long have you been gone from the house?"

"Thirty minutes. He's already driven past here two times, but I hid in the backseat of your car. I hope that's all right."

"Get back in my car. I know just exactly where to take you." Trixie removed the scarf she'd worn to church that morning. "Put this on your head to cover up that red hair and keep Layla in your lap."

"Where are we going? He's real mean and he'll be mad. I took Layla away from him after he hit her and then he whooped me."

"And then he left?"

"Went for more beer," Misty said. "I'm scared of him. Payday was Friday. He's always mean on the weekends after I get paid."

Trixie backed out of the parking lot and drove away. "You got family?"

"Mamma died two years ago, and Daddy went to California. Last I heard he's married again. He's got a new baby of his own."

"How old are you?"

"Twenty last month."

"And Layla?"

"She's two. We never did marry. We was just living together. I don't care where you take me. I just want to get away."

"You will. I've got a friend who'll help you. She's a preacher and she knows exactly what to do. You'll have to promise her that you won't make phone calls to him or anyone that knows him."

"I'd promise anything."

Trixie found Darla Jean in the kitchen at Clawdy's with Agnes and told her the story while Misty and Layla waited in the car.

"Sorry sumbitch. Men like that ought to be shot down like rabid skunks," Agnes said. "You takin' her to Betty?"

Darla Jean nodded. "You want to come along?"

Agnes shook her head. "Girl don't need so many people all around her tonight. I'll go with you next Thursday. Looks like you just fell into runnin' an underground for abused girls. Maybe God will learn to like you after all."

Darla Jean smiled. "I hope so. Bring her around to the back door of the church and put her in my truck. It's still light so that'll keep things simple. I'll call Betty on the way. Lindsey will be glad for the company and Betty is going to dance a jig over having a baby in the house. I'm wonderin' if God ain't called me for something even more important than bringin' sinners to their knees."

Agnes shook her head. "Girl, I'm still wonderin' if God didn't understand what it was you wanted to do with that old service station. I think he thought you said you wanted to turn it into a Christmas store, not a Christian church."

Darla Jean patted her on the shoulder. "Agnes, God don't need no hearin' aid. He understood me perfectly when I asked him which road I was supposed to take. Maybe if he don't hear your prayers, it's because you ain't prayin' long enough or hard enough."

Agnes shrugged. "Get on out of here. I don't need a sermon out of you!"

Darla Jean smiled and followed Trixie out of the shop.

Misty didn't look quite as bad as Lindsey had. She had limp red hair hanging to her shoulders and a big bruise on her cheekbone. Darla Jean didn't even want to see her back and legs. Tears, both dried and fresh, were still on her cheeks, but when the baby whimpered, she hushed her with lullabies sung in a beautiful soprano voice.

"Why do you help people like me?" Misty finally asked.

"Because you need someone to help you, and God told me to help those in need." Darla Jean left Cadillac behind and headed toward Tom Bean.

"How far is it?" Misty asked when Layla was quiet.

"Ever heard of a little place called Blue Ridge?"

Misty shook her head.

"An hour at the most from Cadillac."

"That's not far enough," Misty fretted. "He'll find us, and it'll be bad."

"What's your full name?"

"Misty Waldon."

"You are now Misty Jean. There are lots of girls named Misty, and he sure won't think about you changing your name. When it's all finished, you and Layla will both have new names, new birth certificates, and new social security numbers. I can make that happen."

"God must like you a whole lot," Misty said.

Darla Jean smiled. "There's those who doubt God even knows me, but I hope you are the one who is right." She made the phone call and when they reached Betty's, Lindsey was waiting on the porch with a kitten in her arms.

"You and Layla are safe here. Go on and get out," Darla Jean said.

"Will you come in with me?" Misty said.

"Of course I will. My sister lives here, and that's Lindsey Jean on the porch."

"Your daughter?"

"Just like you are." Darla Jean smiled.

Lindsey opened the truck door. "Hello. Welcome to a brand new life."

She held up an orange kitten. "Look at what Betty got for me, Darla Jean."

"A kitten. Layla loves kittens, but we couldn't have one after the last one. He ran over it and she cried so I wouldn't get her any more. He gets real mad when she cries. Can we pet it?" Misty asked.

"You sure can. Bring the baby on inside and let's get y'all settled."

"Where is Betty?" Darla Jean asked.

"She ran down to the church clothes bank to pick up a few things and to the grocery store for an extra gallon of milk. Is she still on the bottle?" Lindsey asked.

"No. I brought her sippy cup," Misty said.

"I'm supposed to call Betty if we need diapers."

"I got enough for the night."

Lindsey gently laid a hand on Misty's shoulder. "You will think you have died and gone to heaven. Trust me."

Cathy should have gone with Marty. She loved to shop and running through clothes shops would have been so much fun, but she hadn't wanted to at the time and now it was too late.

Trixie had gone to see her mother again. Agnes was nowhere in sight. Darla Jean had said she was going to take a nap and she might be over later. Cathy had had a long bubble bath. She removed all the polish from her fingernails and toenails and redid them in bright red. While they dried, she turned on the television in her room, but that bored her. She picked up her e-reader, and even the hot sex scenes couldn't keep her attention.

Finally, she slipped on a jacket, grabbed her car keys, and left the house before the walls came crashing down on her head. She wound up at the Rib Joint, parked the car, and got out.

The shade of the porch roof offered little relief from the chilly fall wind, but she sat down anyway and drew her knees up to her chin. She wrapped her arms around her legs and laced her fingers together and sighed. Too bad John didn't open the place on Sunday. He could make a fortune with the after-church crowd.

"Hey, girl, think this norther is bringing winter or just teasing us?" John asked from the other end of the porch.

Maggie Rose ran around the end of the café, her little pink tongue hanging out and her long fur waving like a wheat field in the wind.

"I got bored and went for a drive." Cathy straightened out her legs so Maggie Rose could hop up in her lap.

"I got writer's block and thought fresh air might force me to think."

"Writer's block?" Cathy asked.

"I write mystery novels. I've sold two."

"That's great. My sister writes books too."

"What does she write?"

"Erotic romance."

"Do you write?"

"Oh, no! Not me. I was a teacher, but I don't have the patience to write books," she said.

His jeans were faded, his denim jacket worn at the seams. The wind blew his blond hair every which way. Cathy thought he was sexy as hell.

Cathy started to say something at the same time he did.

"You go first," John said.

"I was just making conversation because I don't want to go home," she said honestly.

"Come on out to the trailer. I've got cold beers in the fridge. Be a little more comfortable," he said.

She put Maggie Rose on the ground. She looked like a windup toy as she ran along in front of them.

The trailer was a long, skinny one with fading blue paint, an unpainted wood porch with no rails, and no flowers or shrubs. He held the door for her and shut it as soon as Maggie Rose finished making a wet spot in the sparse grass.

His living room was cozy with throw pillows tossed helter-skelter on the sofa and books stacked everywhere from built-in shelves to under the coffee table. Two matted and framed covers hung on the wall behind the sofa and she took a step forward to see them better.

"Yours?" she asked.

"They are. Want a beer?"

"Love one. These are very nice. Love the color in the covers. It really pops out," she said.

He opened two beers and motioned for her to sit on the sofa as he plopped down and sighed. "I signed a contract for a three-book deal, and I'm stuck on number three."

"Don't try to force it. Think about something else. Maybe that will help," she said.

She turned up the beer and swallowed twice. Any more and she'd do one of those unladylike burps. When she set the beer on the coffee table, she looked back to see his lips parting slightly as they moved toward her. The closer he came, the bigger his eyes got through those thick lenses.

It was downright sexy when his eyelids shut and the lashes fanned out on his cheekbones. His lips brushed against hers and heat shot through her body. One arm tangled up in her hair and the other snaked its way around her midriff. His tongue gently parted her lips and he made love to her mouth.

So that's what Candy Parker was talking about in her books.

"I wanted to do that since the first night you came here," he said.

"But you thought I wasn't old enough, right?" Cathy asked.

"Well, there was the possibility that you were jailbait." He chuckled.

Before she could say a word, he tucked a fist under her chin and kissed her again.

"Wow!" he said.

"I agree," she whispered.

The dimple in his cheek deepened when he smiled and made that little brown soul patch even sexier. He laid his glasses aside and drew her closer to him.

Cathy could have said no, but she didn't want to.

"You are downright hot," he muttered between kisses.

Cathy knew exactly what she was doing. There was only one way to put out the fire he'd started.

He kissed her again and she arched against him.

"Please," she murmured.

"Cathy, are you sure?" he asked.

"Oh, yes," she said.

When it was over, he propped up on an elbow on the narrow sofa. "Why didn't you tell me you were a virgin?"

She laid her fingers on her lips again. "It's not important."

Books had been written about it. Marty discussed it at great lengths. She even wrote about it. The movie industry made millions on it. But not a one of them could describe the way Cathy felt when John held her in the afterglow.

"Seconds are always better," he said.

"Nothing could be better than that," she argued.

"Trust me, Cathy, darlin', it is."

"Can we stay here all night?"

"Oh, yeah!"

It was late when Marty got back to Clawdy's. She stopped in the kitchen long enough to grab a cold can of Pepsi and carried it with her up to her room. Light filtered out into the landing from under her door and Cathy sat in the middle of her bed. She wore a pink terry-cloth robe, wet hair, and twinkling eyes.

It was a good thing she didn't have tears in her eyes or someone would be headed for a good solid ass whipping. Marty wasn't putting up with another thing that would cause her sister to worry.

"Are we having a slumber party?" Marty asked.

"I'm ready to toss my e-reader," Cathy blurted out.

Marty kicked off her shoes, opened the beer, and joined Cathy on the bed, sitting cross-legged. "So John is as good as the heroes and the best you ever had."

"No details, but yes and yes."

"Why no details?"

"Because it's too new and too important to talk about," Cathy said.

Marty smiled.

Trixie poked her head in the door. "I thought I heard voices. Private or open to the public?"

"Come on in. We're too late for the bra-burning days, but we're thinking of burning an e-reader," Marty said.

"Wow! Tell me all about it." Trixie padded barefoot across the room, leaving a string of paper bits falling off her clothes.

Cathy shook her head. "I'm not jinxing this. It feels right so I'm not talking."

"That doesn't surprise me one bit. I never did hear you say that it felt right with Ethan. You just said that it would all work out. I don't believe it."

Marty looked at Trixie. "How about you? Burning books or keeping them?"

"Oh, I'm not nearly ready to trade in my hot romances, but I've got a great story to tell you about what happened today. Darla Jean is a saint, and I've got a feeling this is just the beginning. I took an abused girl with a two-year-old baby to her, and she's on her way to her sister's."

Tears flowed down Marty's cheeks as Trixie told the story, and for the first time, there was something akin to forgiveness in Trixie's heart.

Chapter 17

"I NEED HELP," CATHY said.

"With what?" Agnes asked. Chocolate cake icing was smeared into the wrinkles around her mouth like mocha-colored lipstick.

Cathy laid a notebook on the table. "I'm listing the wedding dress in a small ad in the Denison and Sherman papers for a month. Help me describe it."

"Never been worn," Trixie said.

"Jackass fiancé. Dress not needed." Agnes put in her two cents.

"Didn't it come with a description for when you put the wedding announcement in the newspaper?" Marty asked.

"I'd forgotten about that. I've taken a picture already so folks won't be calling that wanting something else. That brochure is upstairs. I'm off to get it sent in."

"Sure you don't want to keep the thing for when you do get married? You won't get nearly what you paid for it," Agnes said.

Cathy frowned. "It was bought for Ethan. I could never wear it for another man, and besides, if I ever get married I'm going to the courthouse barefoot and in my jeans."

"Well, then sell the damn thing. If nobody wants it, I'll take it out to Violet's house and drag it behind my car round and round in her circle drive until it's nothing but tatters. One thing for sure, Marty ain't never goin' to need it and she's the only other person in the county tall enough to wear it. Besides, it's white and God knows there's enough cowboys in this state to testify to the fact she don't need to get married in white."

"Well, thanks a lot, Aunt Agnes," Marty huffed.

"Truth is truth, darlin'."

Trixie had been good. She'd helped Misty and Layla get out of an abusive situation. She'd watched *I Dream of Jeannie* with her mother. She deserved a night at scrapbooking without having to look at Anna Ruth. Cathy felt sorry for her; Trixie didn't. So maybe, just maybe, Anna Ruth would stay home and help her Aunt Annabel dust off that cake book that Cathy talked about.

Molly was already set up at the end of a long table. She barely looked up but started talking the minute she noticed Trixie. "This paper you bought last time has worked into my scrapbook so pretty. Look, the pink checks match the little dress she's wearing."

"I brought a box of buttons tonight, Molly. Mamma had them in her things and I'll never use them all up. What do you think of this one in the corner?"

"Perfect," Molly said. "Put some of those in your book. Your mamma, bless her heart, might recognize some of them and have a good moment."

"Hell-lo, everyone. I'm here!" Anna Ruth singsonged.

Shit! Some days God had his hearing aid turned completely off.

"What are you working on?" Molly asked.

"A scrapbook of my life. I bought this cute one at the Hobby Lobby this week." She held up a bright blue book at least an inch thick.

She must've had an exciting eventful life if she intended to fill that book completely up.

Anna Ruth set a new scrapbooking case on the table and folded back two sides to reveal paper, ribbons, scissors, and everything an advanced scrapbooker would need. It was arranged so neatly that Trixie shivered.

OCD and scrapbooking in the same house? What a nightmare. No more hoping that Anna Ruth would get bored and stop. It wouldn't happen. She'd sunk too much money into that kit.

"Aunt Annabel had this cute little shower invitation that she sent out when she gave Mother a baby shower so it goes on the front page." She took out a ruler and measured to get the invitation smack in the middle of the page.

"That's sweet," Molly said. "Trixie has been kind enough to bring buttons this week. Why don't we pour them out in the middle of the table so everyone can sort through them? I'll help you get them put back in the jar after we're done tonight."

Trixie poured out a long line of multicolored and various shaped buttons. Anna Ruth ignored them and carefully pasted her invitation to the middle of the page.

"Now what to put around it." She tapped her cheek with a forefinger. "Have you all heard that Cathy isn't interested in Andy after all?"

Trixie giggled.

"Oh, dear," Molly said. "We only talk about scrapbooking when we are working. That's the joy of the business. It takes our minds completely off everything else."

Anna Ruth shot a dirty look across the table.

Trixie ignored her.

"Trixie, you are the expert at this. Come see what I need. A little bit of ribbon or maybe a touch of eyelet lace," Molly said.

Trixie helped her decide on the lace while Anna Ruth pondered over which paper to start with on her first page.

Luck was not with Trixie that night. She, Molly, and Anna Ruth were the only members to show up. Molly and Trixie made a mess that took half an hour to clean up. Anna Ruth was able to shove her book back into her kit at the end of the evening in two minutes.

"Ta-da! See y'all next time," she said as she rushed outside into the hot night air.

"Think she'll ever learn to love the art?" Molly asked.

"She'll have to loosen up," Trixie answered. "I'll sweep and lock up this time. It's my turn."

"No it's not, but I'll let you. Sweeping hurts my back."

"Then let me carry your kit out to the car. You don't need to lift something that heavy."

"Thanks, honey. I sure will take you up on that too. And thanks for the buttons. Bring them back next week," Molly said.

Something damn sure did not feel right in her car. The seat leaned toward the door and the seat belt didn't want to reach.

"Well, shit!" Trixie slapped the steering wheel.

She had a flat tire. Before she was allowed to drive at the age of sixteen, her mother insisted that she know how to change a tire and change oil.

She'd never learned to like doing either one.

The steering wheel couldn't whine or fight back so she slapped it one more time before she crawled out of the car. Sure enough, it was flat as a flitter, however damn flat that was, with nothing between the rim and the street but rubber.

"Hey, got a problem?" a deep voice said from a car driving past.

"Flat tire," she said without looking.

"I'll fix it for you, Trixie," Jack said.

She whipped around when she recognized his voice. "You are a lifesaver. I mean it. I've never had to change a tire on this car. I guess it's all basic, but I'm not even sure where the jack is located. That's funny. Jack is located right in front of me."

Jack laughed. "Yes he is, and he can change a tire on this faster than you could get the lug nuts off. So pop the trunk and I'll get it done, but it's going to cost you."

"Uh-oh! What are you doing in this part of town, anyway? Oh, I forgot. You bought that house. Isn't it right around here? And Cathy got to see it first. What's up with that?" She looked around.

"Right across the street. I was over there measuring for the tile layers. Was just locking up to leave when I noticed your car. Open the trunk and I'll have the spare on in no time. You can take it down to the garage tomorrow and they'll fix it. Might have a nail in it. Nope, looks like someone removed the valve and let the air out on purpose. I hope it's not neighborhood kids."

Anna Ruth did it. Did Trixie ignore it, confront her, or tell Agnes? The latter sounded like a helluva lot more fun.

"This really is going to cost you dearly," Jack said as he jacked the car up slightly and loosened the lug nuts.

"One free breakfast coming right up," Trixie said.

"That sounds pretty good, but I had something else in mind." He backed the lug nuts off the rest of the way and slid the flat tire away.

"Lunch too? Come on, Jack, this is getting expensive," Trixie teased.

"No, ma'am. Even a bigger favor than that." He put on the spare and replaced the lug nuts.

"Okay, I'll help you in the garage all week, and I won't even start a fight with Marty over the vote she threw in the pot for Anna Ruth. It's got something to do with Agnes killing Violet, but I can't figure it out and Marty ain't talkin'," Trixie said.

"I'll take that, but I want one more thing."

"And that is?"

"Would you come into my house and give me your honest opinion of what color tile I should put in? I've never done this kind of thing and I need help. Mamma is pouting because I'm moving out, but hell's bells, Trixie, I've been home ever since Dad died, and we all know it's time for me to get my own place," he said.

"I'd love to. Why aren't you using carpet?"

"I hate to vacuum. A broom and a little mopping once a week will take care of tile. Besides, I want a dog, and carpet is a magnet for dog hair."

He finished the job, slammed the trunk shut, and together they crossed the street and walked up on the porch. He'd already locked up so he fished a key from his pocket, opened the door, and flipped on the living room light.

"Just go on through the house and get a feel for the rooms, then come back to the kitchen and look at the samples."

Trixie wandered from room to room. There were plenty of windows for light. The walls had been repainted in a light sand color, and the oak woodwork had gotten a fresh coat of varnish. The whole place smelled clean and wonderful.

"Well?" he asked.

"Something just a little darker than the walls. It won't show dirt or dog hair, and it'll blend with the walls and the woodwork. It's going to be beautiful, Jack."

"Tile next week and furniture after that. I'll fix your flat tires forever if all three of you girls will go to Sherman to pick out the stuff to go in this place," he said.

"Oil changes too?" she asked.

"You drive a hard bargain, Trixie, but I'll do it if you can talk Cathy and Marty into going with us."

She stuck out her hand. "It's a deal. Next Sunday I've got to go see Mamma in the nursing home, and afterward we should have time to look through two or three stores before they close."

He shook it. "I'll go with you to the nursing home. I haven't seen Janie in six months. I know. Shame on me. She was so good to us kids when we were growing up. I can't remember a time she yelled at us for tracking mud in the house or messing up the kitchen."

Trixie smiled. "She was a lot of fun. I hear you are buying this house so you can ask Cathy to marry you. That right?"

Jack sputtered and stammered before he finally got a whole word to come out of his mouth. "Hell no! Whatever gave you that idea? You and Marty and Cathy are like sisters to me. I love you all too much to ruin our friendship with marriage."

Trixie giggled.

"What?"

"Did you know that Beulah was scared you were going to marry Cathy and Violet would be furious that she tossed Ethan out the door for you?"

Jack chuckled. "Club! It's worse than trying to understand women."

Chapter 18

WEDNESDAY NIGHTS!

They'd changed.

Now Cathy went to the Rib Joint and didn't even come home until Thursday morning. Marty went to class, came right home, and since the cat was out of the bag about her writing, often as not, she took to her room to work on her books. If the stars were aligned right, Agnes stayed across the street and did not get into the steamer trunk for costumes that smelled like mothballs. Darla Jean had midweek Bible study with her growing flock.

And Trixie did not have sex with Andy. She still hadn't come clean about having wild Wednesdays in the past, but since the night Agnes showed up with the shotgun, everything had been crazy. There was the thing about the vote, Darla Jean's new mission, and now Jack was moving into his own house. The time had not been right; when it was, she'd confess just like Cathy had done about reading hot romance.

"Where is your mind, Trixie?" Jack asked.

"I was thinking about changes in our lives. What did I miss?"

"Nothing. I asked for a ratchet and you handed me a Phillips head screwdriver." Jack chuckled. "Want to talk about it?"

"It's all Agnes's fault."

"She caught you with Andy that night, didn't she?"

"How did you know?"

"His unmarked car was sitting in the parking lot when we arrived on the scene. He said later that he'd just pulled up to see what was going on. Didn't take a genius to figure that one out."

Trixie's face burned. "Guess not."

"Marty know?"

Trixie shook her head.

"Is it still going on?"

She wiped her hands on a grease rag. "I'm out here on Wednesday nights these days."

"You deserve better. You always have."

"Thanks, Jack. And here is the ratchet."

"It's the truth, Trixie. You deserve the very best."

"Well, hello, Miss Andrews," Lynn Woodson said from behind her desk. "I'm just finishing up here and you can have it. I was trying to get the last of this week's assignments graded." She snapped her laptop shut and shoved it into a tote bag with Ethan Prescott for State Representative printed on the side.

Marty looked down at the tote bag. "You helping with his campaign?"

"Yes, I am, but I don't guess you'll be voting for Ethan?" She picked up the bag and headed toward the door.

"Probably not. I guess you are?"

"Of course I am. We are dating, you know."

"I didn't know."

"We had broken up when he started seeing Catherine. I was heartbroken when he proposed to her, and even though she is your sister, I'm glad it didn't work out."

"Me too," Marty said.

Lynn was an outspoken political science professor at the college. Violet Prescott was about to wish she'd never pushed that prenup in Cathy's face.

Students began to arrive at the same time Lynn left the room. Marty passed out the next lesson booklet in the study. If they had problems with any part of it, they were to raise their hand and she'd come to their desk. As they started, Marty looked out over the crowd and located Derek. He was a bright young man, and with the GED, he hoped to start college in January.

When classes ended, she shut her laptop, happy with the first chapter of the book, switched off the lights, and locked the door to her classroom. The temperature dropped several degrees when she went outside. It seldom ever snowed in Cadillac, but there was that kind of feel to the night air. Thank goodness they weren't still planning a wedding in December. Not unless Lynn and Ethan decided to get married real fast. In which case, Agnes might try to sell them a morning glory wedding cake.

With Violet in the picture, Marty could easily see Lynn and Ethan having a private ceremony at some chapel in Vegas or else going to Cancun after the election. No, sir, Lynn would not be buying a cake that looked like it was oozing the bride and groom's blood.

The parking lot at the Rib Joint was crowded, but she did find a place out near the road. The noise was close to pollution level and got louder when she was inside. A line dance was going on, and the stomping on the wood floor jarred the walls.

Cathy was behind the counter, drawing beers and taking money for orders. She looked happier than Marty had ever seen her.

"Hey!" She waved.

Marty made her way around the end of the dancers who were slapping their hips and yelling, "Hell yeah!"

"Got time for a break?" Marty asked.

John wiped his hands on a towel on his way from kitchen to counter. "You two really are identical except for the hair. I'm John, and it's a pleasure to finally meet you, Marty."

Marty shook hands with him. "Pleasure is all mine, John. Can I steal her for half a minute?"

"Only if you bring her back. Go out the back door. It's easier than getting through the crowd."

"Is everyone all right?" Cathy wiped sweat from her forehead with the towel Jack laid down.

"Everyone is fine. Which way?"

Cathy led the way and Marty followed. The back of the joint was the front yard for John's trailer. It wasn't much to look at, but if that's what put the gleam in Cathy's eyes lately then it was a great place.

"What's going on?" Cathy asked.

"Remember me saying that I use Lynn Woodson's room on Wednesday nights?"

Cathy nodded.

"She's dating Ethan. I thought you should know."

It took a full minute for the news to sink in and then Cathy started laughing. "Violet has met her match."

"It doesn't mean they'll get married. They're just dating."

"Think they'd like to buy a red, white, and blue cake?"

Marty laughed with her. "That was my first thought. But you aren't ever going to unload that thing. I'm not sure that you can list an ugly wedding cake in the classifieds."

"I didn't love him, Marty. He and Lynn have so much more in common and he deserves to be happy."

"You've got a good heart, Cathy Andrews."

"So do you, Marty Andrews. Now I've got to get back to work. Don't want John to be completely worn out from cooking and waiting the front, too. I've got plans for something other than sleeping tonight." Cathy winked.

"The good twin goes bad." Marty hugged Cathy.

She and Cathy had been born two halves of a whole. Cathy had the kind soul and sweet nature. Marty had the wild streak and spoke her mind loud and clear. Marty grew up protecting her nice other half from bullies and wondering if she'd ever get a backbone. Now that she had, Marty was saddened. Would Cathy not need her anymore? Would their friendship suffer with the new roads they'd taken?

Chapter 19

CATHY RANG THE DOORBELL and waited.

Her finger was reaching to hit it again when Clayton opened the door.

"What are you doing here?" he asked bluntly.

"I would like to see Violet, please."

"I'll see if she is busy."

Clayton almost succeeded in shutting the door in her face, but she stuck a sandal-clad foot in it before it shut. "Don't be rude just because I threw a monkey wrench in your plans. I'm coming inside and I'm talking to Violet."

Her courage amazed her. Did sex make all women braver?

He opened the door and glared at her. "She's in the dining room."

"Thank you."

He motioned for her to follow him.

Cathy knew her way around the house and she'd never stolen anything. Not even an engraved paper liner for coasters. But evidently she wasn't to be trusted to walk past the credenza and down the hallway without an escort.

"Catherine is here," he said and remained by the door.

Violet's freezing stare would have intimidated her weeks before. Today it was pitiful and reminded Cathy of those women whose biggest claim to fame was being a high school cheerleader. Those poor souls who still wore their letter jackets to all the home football games thirty years after they'd graduated.

"Did you come to apologize for your behavior? If you did, you are wasting your time," Violet said.

Cathy shook her head. "I came to tell you in person that I'm resigning from the club. Under the circumstances I think it's the best thing for me to do. And besides, with two jobs, I cannot give it the time that a member should."

Violet sat a little straighter and her lips disappeared into a bed of wrinkles. "You aren't dead and you aren't moving. You cannot resign. Besides, you have to stay in the club. Your grandmother was a charter member and your mother followed in her footsteps."

"I can and I am quitting, Violet."

"No one has ever simply resigned from the club and you will not be the first. Die or move. Who will win the blue ribbons for us if you don't keep up the tradition your grandmother started? Only you know how to grow the hottest peppers in the state. We'll lose our standing if you don't enter your jelly and picante. This is not acceptable, Catherine."

"I'm not moving. I'm not dying. If I enter my pepper jelly and peppers in the fair, I intend to put the ribbons on the wall at Clawdy's. It was, after all, my grandmother who started winning the ribbons." She looked around the room at all the ribbons. Grandma, her mother, and now she had won them all, and yet there they were, in Violet's possession.

Violet gasped. "I will not allow you to leave. We are the famous Blue-Ribbon Jalapeño Society, and you are going to keep the tradition, young lady!"

"Keep me on the rolls if you want to, but I will not be attending any more meetings. Why don't you put a clause in the charter that says if a person misses three meetings in a year, they are kicked to the curb? That would take care of me and Marty both."

"I knew we shouldn't have allowed you in the club. You are more like your sister than people realize. I will not accept your resignation, but I will be very glad to talk to the club about putting a clause like that in our charter. Someone who deserves a place should be given both of you sisters' places."

"You can always sponsor Agnes." Cathy spun around and headed out of the room.

"Don't you walk out of that door, Catherine Andrews! I didn't give you permission to leave."

"You didn't have to, Violet. Good luck with your campaign and I hope Ethan is very happy. Maybe he and Lynn will wind up together yet."

"Lynn who?" Violet practically screamed.

Cathy heard her telling Clayton to find out who in the hell Lynn was as she let herself out. Guilt washed over her for letting the cat out of the bag. While the car warmed up, she dug out her cell phone and called Marty.

"Got a minute?" Cathy asked.

"Always. What's going on?"

Cathy told her what she'd done. "Do you think I should call Ethan and let him know there's a storm on the way?"

"I think you should drive away from there and never look back. He can learn to stand up to his mother. You did it so it stands to reason it is possible," Marty said.

"Thank you. Advice taken. Guilt trip over. Going home."

"See you later," Marty said.

When Cathy got home, she bypassed the garage where Trixie and Jack were busy on the Caddy and went straight to her bedroom. She changed into her overalls, kicked off her shoes, and headed for John's. Marty had always been the strong one who had Cathy's back. No one messed with Marty and only with Cathy one time. After Marty finished with them, they didn't want to cross either twin again.

Their roles hadn't changed so much that summer, but the lines weren't nearly as clear. She could see a softer side to Marty, especially since that vote had been cast for Anna Ruth. Within herself, she could feel a tougher woman emerging since she'd learned to speak her mind. Would the lines eventually disappear as they grew older? Cathy brushed away a tear with the back of her hand, leaving a smudge of dirt in its wake. She never wanted to be far from Marty. It would be like tearing half her heart out of her chest. No matter how faint the lines were, she would always need her sister.

The bed of the truck was full of groceries, diapers, and baby things bought this week with Agnes's donation to the cause. Darla Jean phoned Lindsey when she was almost to the house and she met her at the truck, Layla slung on one hip and Misty right behind her.

Darla Jean reached and Layla went right to her. "Give me the baby and you two can unload."

"Don't you be spoiling that child," Betty yelled as she crossed the yard she shared with the house next door where Lindsey and Misty lived these days. "It's my grandchild."

"Wanna bet?" Darla Jean smiled.

"Baby can't have too many grandmas." Lindsey laughed.

"But we only got one mamma and that's you, Darla Jean. Aunt Betty even agrees to that." Misty carried four bags into the house.

Her bruises were practically gone. Lindsey had cut her hair and highlighted it that week. That and the lack of fear had put a smile on her face.

"Well?" Lindsey said.

Misty grabbed Darla Jean in a fierce hug. "I got a job! I'm so excited I can't hardly talk about it. Before long we'll be on our feet well enough to take care of ourselves. Betty got me a job working from three to ten at night taking care of an elderly lady from the church. She's in a wheelchair and I get to read to her and get her ready for bed. It's a lot like taking care of your mamma because she's got Alzheimer's too."

She and Betty followed the girls into the house where she'd grown up. The floor was cluttered with Layla's toys Betty brought from the church bank, but other than that they were doing a good job taking care of it.

"And I can keep Layla in the evenings while Misty works and she'll be home with the baby in the daytime. She's been helping Betty down at the church clothes closet and everyone that comes in loves Layla," Lindsey said.

Darla Jean looked from one to the other. No more bruises. Clean hair and shiny skin. The haunted look hadn't completely left their eyes, but they'd come a long way since the first time she'd seen them.

She looked at Misty. "What would you like to do with your life? Not today or even this year. I'm glad you have a job that lets you stay home with Layla. But when she's in school, what would you like to do?"

Misty looked at the carpet. "My dream was to be a real nurse."

"Really?" Lindsey asked.

"I gave up on that years ago."

"Never give up on your dream," Betty said.

Misty raised her eyes. "I could do it, couldn't I? When Layla starts school, I could. I could go to school in the days and work at night."

"See there. Where there's a will, there's a way." Betty smiled.

"And you?" Darla Jean asked Lindsey.

"I'll be doing just what I want to do. Work with little kids."

"Want a classroom where you are the teacher? That would only take two years more."

Lindsey nodded. "It'd take a lot longer by going nights."

"I looked into a program that would let you do the rest of it by computer online courses. If that's your dream, you should save your money and buy a computer. Next year you could be taking classes and there's usually a big turnover in the Blue Ridge school system. You might work your way right into a real teaching job," Darla Jean said.

Betty changed the subject. "And what is Layla going to be?"

Layla giggled at Betty's high-pitched voice.

"Anything she wants to be," Darla Jean said.

Darla Jean was pleased with Lindsey and Misty. They'd shown remarkable signs of healing and moving on in such a short time. The bond they shared reminded her of the one Cathy and Marty had. And that was a good thing.

The list was long and the cart was full when Anna Ruth rounded the corner in Walmart and ran smack into another cart.

"I'm so sorry!" She peeked around the end of the buggy right into Andy's smiling face.

"You are forgiven, sweetheart," he said.

Her heart did a couple of backward somersaults and her pulse raced. "I couldn't see over the top of the cart. Aunt Annabel had a very long list for me to fill and…"

She always talked too loud and too fast when she was nervous, and Andy's smile made her hot, bothered, and antsy.

"And it's okay, Anna Ruth." He moved around the cart and ran a finger up her forearm. "I've missed you."

Anna Ruth was on the way to falling at his feet, throwing her arms around his knees, and apologizing for leaving him, then in an instant she realized that if she was ever to have him, she'd have to play hard to get. It was the chase he liked.

"Not one phone call, one rose, or even a note. I wouldn't know that you've missed me at all." Her voice sounded strangely normal in her ears.

"You are blocking the aisle!" a shrill voice said behind her.

"So sorry!" She whipped around to see Violet shooting daggers at her.

"For God's sake, Anna Ruth, move your cart to one side so I can get around you. What did you stop so fast for anyway?" Her look was meant to fry Andy on the spot, leaving a mess on aisle six between the laundry detergent and the soda pop. "Oh, I thought you and Catherine were involved."

Andy smiled at her, but it didn't have the same effect that it did on Anna Ruth. "Who is Catherine?"

"I guess you know her by Cathy."

"No, she's keeping company with John. He owns the Rib Joint between Luella and Cadillac," Andy said.

Violet gasped. "She overthrew my Ethan for that?"

"Hello! I thought I heard my name." Ethan started around the end of the aisle going in the opposite direction. "Are we having a reunion?"

"Looks like all of Cadillac came out for supplies tonight. We should've all made lists and just sent one of us," Andy said.

Awkward silence hung over aisle six like cigarette smoke in a honky tonk.

Andy finally asked, "How's the election going?"

Ethan smiled brightly. "Very well, I think. Lynn, honey, this is one of Cadillac's policemen, Andy Johnson. This is Anna Ruth Williams who is a teacher over at Bells, and this is my mother, Violet."

"Pleased to meet all of you. Sorry we have to run, but we're watching a movie at my house and it's getting late. We just needed Pepsi and some popcorn," Lynn said.

Ethan picked a couple of two-liter bottles of Pepsi from the shelf and pushed the cart toward the checkout counters.

"He doesn't drink Pepsi or eat popcorn," Violet whispered.

Anna Ruth shrugged. "Guess he does now."

Why didn't Violet get on around her and go about her business? Anna Ruth had moved her cart against the Tide detergent to make room.

"That haircut is horrible and she should do something with those bushy eyebrows. Did you see her fingernail polish? Of course you didn't because she wasn't wearing any."

Anna Ruth could have strangled Andy for leaving her there to sympathize with Violet. But Violet, despite her years, was a club sister and she needed her right then. So she took two steps forward and hugged the woman.

"I didn't see her nails. I was too shocked. But she does need a trip to the hairdresser. You and Aunt Annabel always taught us when our hair turned gray, we should put it up or cut it off, not wear it hanging on our shoulders."

Violet shivered. "How could he do this to me? How old do you think she is?"

Anna Ruth made a show of checking her watch. "Really, I expect she's Ethan's age and that's premature gray, Violet. It's just so tacky not to color it, don't you think? I'm so sorry but I've got to go. Aunt Annabel has an order for a cake tomorrow and she's waiting on the powdered sugar. Why don't you come by the house and talk to her when you get done in here?"

"My head hurts. I'm going home to put a cold cloth on it. I may never come to Walmart again if that woman shops here."

Anna Ruth drove to her Aunt Annabel's house with a new purpose. She'd let Andy Johnson chase her until she caught him. He needed a good wife and once they were married, he'd never cheat again. It was midlife crisis and a messy wife that sent him into her arms. Now that the dispatcher had moved on, she could control the midlife crisis.

The hankering for a bowl of red beans with a spoonful of picante sauce stirred up in them hit Agnes at nine thirty. She grabbed the thick red robe that Cathy had given her for Christmas and snapped it all the way up the front. The back door was open and the kitchen empty. She looked in the refrigerator, opened several containers, and found no beans. She slammed the refrigerator door and found half a black forest cake left on the cabinet. She sliced off an enormous chunk, put it on a plate, and was halfway to the table when Trixie jumped off the bottom step and yelled, "Boo!"

Agnes threw the plate straight up and let out a string of cussing that would have scared the hair right off of a billy goat's chin. The swearing and the scream stopped when she saw a long brown streak sliding down the yellow daisy wallpaper. The rest of the cake slammed against the floor with such force that it splattered chocolate on Trixie's bare toes.

"Look what you've done. Gone and ruined good chocolate cake, so you can damn well clean up the floor. Marty and Cathy are crazy as hell for letting you move in here."

"You clean it up. I didn't make the mess. You did."

"You caused it so you are cleaning," Agnes said.

Trixie laughed and held up her chocolate-iced foot. "Want to lick it off so we don't waste it?"

Agnes narrowed her eyes and then laughed with Trixie. "Scared the shit right out of me, girl. But I betcha I scared you with my shotgun. Own up to it. There was a man in your bedroom, wasn't there?"

"Why did you care?"

"I didn't. If I could've been sure it was you, I'd have let him slit your throat. But I was afraid he'd drug Cathy across the hall and was hurting her. I didn't know who he had in there until you came out of the bedroom. Then I was so damn mad I wished I would've stayed at home."

She leaned forward and whispered, "It was Andy."

Agnes slapped the table. "I knew it. Does Marty know? She hates that man."

Trixie shook her head.

"Hmph! I'll tell her."

"No, you won't, because she'll think you've lost your mind and have you declared incompetent and put you in a nursing home. I visit my mother every Sunday and Wednesday. I could drop by and see you."

Agnes exhaled loudly. "You'd do that, wouldn't you? Make Marty believe I was going crazy?"

"You came in here ranting again about a man in my room and threw cake at the wall when I wouldn't let you go upstairs."

Agnes bit back a grin. "I'll get even. You know I will."

"Bring it on, old girl." Trixie leaned a little more until her nose was just inches from Agnes's.

"I'm getting the rest of the cake and I'm taking it home with me, and if you scare me again, I'm throwing it at you," Agnes said.

She shifted the rest of the cake into a carryout box and carried it out into the darkness as if it were pure gold.

Trixie giggled all the way to her room. She hated Agnes when she first moved in, but since that night with the shotgun, Trixie had slowly changed her mind. They'd built a crazy friendship and she'd probably be even sadder than Cathy when the old girl died. She sat down at the ceramic table and worked on an owl for Agnes's birthday coming up in December. She intended to make a card to go with it that said something witty about an owl seeing everything at night.

A fedora! That's what her owl needed. Trixie could fashion one with some felt and craft glue. Then she'd put a couple of mothballs in the cavity and stick duct tape over the hole at the bottom.

Chapter 20

The devil that robbed Janie's memories gave them back occasionally. Usually only in five-minute sections, but Trixie was willing for anything she could get and expected nothing.

That Sunday afternoon, Trixie and Jack showed up at the door and Janie smiled brightly. "Hello. I thought you might come today. It is Sunday, isn't it? Hello, Jack. I haven't seen you in quite a while. I see you've got a bag, Trixie. Does that mean red beans and greens and maybe some of Clawdy's pecan cobbler? You still play dominoes?" She sat on one side of the card table, dominoes stacked up like Lego-blocks in front of her.

When Janie was herself, she loved hugs and she hugged back. When she didn't remember, she didn't want Trixie to touch her at all, not even pat her shoulder. That day she hugged back and then laughed. "Mercy, honey. You are going to crush me. I'll still be right here tomorrow. You don't have to get all the hugs today. I've had dinner already, but if you'll set that aside, I'll get the ladies to heat it for supper."

"I like your hugs. You smell wonderful."

"This is the same perfume I've worn since you were a little girl. Don't see that it would be any different today than yesterday."

"You are right."

Janie opened her arms. "Your turn, Jack. Remember when you were a little boy and you loved hugs?"

Jack hugged her tightly and then sat across the table, leaving the chair next to Janie for Trixie. "You are still beautiful, Janie."

"You always were a charmer," Janie said. "Now what are you two out doing today?"

"Visiting with you," Trixie said. "And then we are going to buy furniture."

"Now that sounds serious," Janie said.

Jack smiled. "I just bought a new house in Cadillac, and Trixie is going to help me with the furniture."

Janie returned the smile with a slow wink. "She's good at decorating and making things from nothing. So Jack, you are back in Cadillac?"

"I am now. I quit the military a couple of years ago and moved back."

Trixie laid her hand over her mother's. "Mamma, let's talk about you."

Janie jerked hers free and put it in her lap. "Who are you? A new nurse. I don't remember seeing you here before."

The devil had snatched back his gift after a tiny glimpse.

Trixie took a deep breath and straightened her back. "Yes, ma'am. I am your new therapist. Would you like to color? We have princess coloring books in the drawer and we have almost new crayons."

"No, I'd like to play dominoes. Daddy says I'm the best. I can beat both of you," she said.

Jack laid a hand on Trixie's shoulder as she set up the game and whispered, "You had a moment there. That's good at this stage, isn't it?"

She swallowed hard before she nodded. "It is. I'm just greedy."

Janie pushed the score pad and pencil away from Trixie and in front of Jack. "Might as well not be greedy today. I won't let you win. Young man, you keep score. Greedy people might cheat."

"Tell me all about your daddy as we play," Jack said.

Janie leaned across the table and whispered, "My daddy is dead but I have a friend. Do you know Clawdy Barton? She's my best friend. Sometimes Mamma lets me stay at Clawdy's place all night."

"My mamma knows Clawdy," Jack said.

Janie straightened up and looked at him. "Who are you?"

"I'm Beulah's son, Jack."

Janie twisted her mouth to one side and studied her hand. She laid out a double six in the middle of the table. "We don't talk when we play. We concentrate."

"Yes, ma'am," Trixie said.

Janie nodded. "Shh!"

Halfway through the game, she yawned. That meant she was ready for a nap and would grow agitated if everyone didn't leave. Then she looked up, life came back to her eyes, and she pointed.

"Would you look at that? Cathy Andrews, I haven't seen you in years. And who have you brought with you, today? It's so good to see you. Mercy me, but we're having a family reunion, aren't we? Trixie and Jack are here. All we need is Marty and we'll have everyone. We could make sugar cookies and all you kids could decorate them."

Cathy crossed the room and gave her a hug. "That would be so much fun. I remember making cookies at your house and you made the best icing for them."

"Now who is this handsome young man?" Janie held out her hand.

"This is John..." Cathy hesitated.

"I'm her brand spanking new boyfriend," John said quickly and kissed Janie's fingertips.

"Well, it's about time. Unfold a couple of those chairs and have a seat. Shall I call down for some coffee and cookies? This is a fancy hotel, you know." She winked.

Trixie touched Cathy's arm and whispered, "Thank you!"

Janie was lucid enough to talk to them for ten minutes and then she yawned again. "I don't know why they send so many doctors and nurses in to see me some days and none others. I'm sleepy now so if y'all are through, you can go so I can take a nap."

Cathy stood up first. "Yes, ma'am, we've got other patients to see. Is there anything else we can do for you?"

She pointed to Jack. "That one can cover me with my afghan."

"I'll be glad to," Jack said.

Trixie wanted to hug her again, but Janie adhered to a strict code when the life went out of her eyes. It said that she wasn't allowed to hug anyone she didn't know or take candy from them either.

Cathy wrapped an arm around Trixie's waist as they made their way slowly toward the lobby. Several of the nursing home residents were gathered in the lobby where a local preacher led them in singing "I Saw the Light." Old voices blended with young and the music echoed up and down the halls.

Cathy squeezed Trixie tighter. "She did see the light for a little while there, didn't she? Do you think us being together triggered a memory? I should come more often," Cathy said.

"Who knows what works and what doesn't, but it seems to help when y'all visit."

The Sherman city park was alive with screaming kids running from swings to monkey bars or to the merry-go-round, the tetherball pole, or the springy riding toys. Jack slouched onto a wooden bench and pulled Trixie down beside him.

"This is my favorite spot in the whole world," he said.

"I thought we were going furniture shopping," Trixie said.

"We are in a little while. Cathy and John wanted a few minutes to get an ice cream cone and Marty is running late."

"What are we really doing here, Jack?"

"Watching the kids play. I love kids. They are so innocent and rambunctious. Someday I want a dozen to bring to the park on Sunday."

"You better be getting a woman in your life pretty soon if you want a dozen," she said. "I wanted kids when I was first married. But it didn't happen. Andy never did want any. Guess he got his way and the way things turned out, it was for the best. I wouldn't want to have a kid going through what I am with my mom. Jack, who's going to take care of me when I get that horrible disease?"

Jack air slapped her on the shoulder. "Trixie, nothing says you're going to get it. And if you do, you've got all of us to take care of you."

"I love you, Jack Landry."

"I know, darlin', and I love all four of you wild girls."

"Four?"

"Yep, four… you, Cathy, Marty, and Darla Jean. Darla Jean is more like a cousin. You other three are my sisters."

It took fifteen minutes for her to finally giggle over the antics of one little four-year-old boy attempting to tame a caterpillar on a spring. Like a bull rider, he held one hand up and kicked back and forth with imaginary spurs. His father kept an eye on his wristwatch and his mother yelled, "Eight seconds and the crowd goes wild as Jason takes home the bull rider's silver buckle."

The boy fell off the side of the caterpillar, landed on his feet, swept his hat off, and bowed. His mom and dad clapped and whistled even louder.

Jack answered his phone when it rang. He said a couple of words before he put it back in his shirt pocket. "Now we can go furniture shopping. Marty and Cathy are together and meeting us at the furniture store."

"I feel better, Jack. Those kids made me laugh."

"I knew the kids could do it. If your mom hadn't been robbed of her mind, would she want you happy or sad?"

"Happy. She would definitely want me to be happy," Trixie said. "When she realized this was happening, she checked herself into the nursing home and told me to remember the good times."

"Then do it, Trixie."

Bedrooms. Living rooms. Dining rooms. Dens.

All set up in cubicles so the customer would want the whole room full of furniture, not just separate pieces. The first one in the living room section was a fancy floral sofa with carved oak legs. Trixie looped her arm in Jack's and kept walking.

"I can't see you stretched out on that thing watching Monday night football."

"But it is so pretty," Cathy argued.

"Jack doesn't want pretty. He wants a man cave," Marty said.

"If I catch a car engine in your bathtub, I'm going to shoot you," Trixie said.

Jack laughed. "Marty, your job is to hide the guns. Cathy, yours is to hide the arsenic so she don't put any in my beans and greens."

"What's wrong with flowers?" Cathy asked.

"It looks like tea drinkin' furniture and I'm a black coffee man," Jack said. "That one. What do you think of it?" He stopped in front of a buttery soft leather sofa in a rich mahogany brown with matching ottomans and an oversized recliner.

"Sit down on it and see if it fits," Marty said.

"Ahhh," he said as the leather molded to his body. "This is definitely a Monday night football sofa. Sit here beside me."

Marty plopped down on the other end, swung her legs up into his lap, and used the wide arm for a pillow. "Oh, yeah! I could definitely get into a Cowboys game on this."

"How long will this last?" Trixie asked.

"How long will what last? Sitting here? I expect until five o'clock when the store closes. The furniture? Forever. Leather ages, but it never wears out and it's so easy to clean," Cathy said.

Jack pushed Marty's legs off of his lap and stood up. "I like it. I'm a comfortable leather sofa guy, not a floral, fancy settee type of feller."

Trixie moved to another sofa. "Like this one any better?"

"I do," Cathy said. "It's a lighter color and doesn't look so man-cavish."

"That sounds like a disease," Marty said.

"It is," Cathy agreed. "You won't ever catch a wife if you don't put a few feminine touches in the house."

"I'm not out to catch a wife. Why would I need one? I've got you three to help me when I need advice."

"Good Lord, Jack. You aren't going to become a player, are you?" Cathy gasped.

"Become?" He laughed and motioned for a salesman. "I want this sofa, the matching recliner, and that oversized rocking chair that goes with it. We'll keep looking."

"Marty, I like your taste better than Cathy's. What about the tables?"

"I like the ones that are sturdy and well made and I'm partial to oak if it's not got flowers carved in the woodwork like that first sofa did."

"You don't like florals? They are really in this season," the salesman said.

"See?" Cathy said.

Marty looked at his name tag. "Tom, I like flowers in vases but not on furniture. I like things that never go out of style, not things that are in for a season. And I think Jack and I agree on that."

Trixie grabbed his arm and steered him toward two oak tables. "These would be perfect in your cave."

Cathy rolled her eyes. "They look like you could butcher hogs on them."

"Or fix an engine?" Jack teased.

"I swear, Jack, I'll shoot you," Trixie said.

"Shall I add them to your list?" Tom asked.

"Yes. The two end tables and that coffee table to prop my boots on at the end of a long shift." Jack nodded.

"Lamps?" Tom asked.

"Not today," Trixie said.

"What else can I help you with?" Tom asked.

"We'll browse awhile," Trixie answered.

"I've got this order written up. Call me if you want to add to it." Tom headed toward a young couple looking at a dining room table.

"No lamps? I like lamps and the house doesn't have an overhead light in the living room. Kinda hard to read by candlelight," Jack said.

"There's a Western store on the other side of town that has some really neat accessory items. I saw a couple of lamps that would go perfect with this furniture," Trixie said.

Marty clapped a hand on Jack's shoulder. "Oh, I love that store. The man who owns it is one sexy cowboy."

Cathy rolled her eyes.

"Hey, don't give me that look. I can probably get Jack a damn good discount."

"I bet you can," Cathy said.

"Speaking of which," Jack's eyes twinkled, "shall we take a look at the bedroom furniture?"

"Nothing pretty and fancy, right?" Cathy asked.

"Something sturdy so in case he meets a hot little cowgirl sales clerk when we go to the Western store, it won't break down when he takes her home." Marty looped her arm in his.

The four of them moved to the bedroom section and Jack pointed at a king-sized bedroom suite. "I like that one. King-sized bed, oversized dresser with two mirrors. And none of those fancy curls and whirls for dust to settle in."

Tom was immediately beside them. "That's our new missionary design. Plain lines and it is easy to maintain."

"I'll take the whole outfit. Now let's go buy ice cream, ladies."

That evening when she got home to an empty house, Trixie sat down at her scrapbooking table and went to work. A card would never express what it meant for Cathy to show up at the nursing home, but it would let her know that her gesture hadn't gone unnoticed.

Trixie found a picture of the three of them back in college and cut, glued, and pasted for more than an hour before it was exactly the way she wanted. Then using her calligraphy pen, she wrote a message inside:

Some friends are in your life for a season.
Some friends are in your life for a reason.
Some are there forever to double your joys
and halve your sorrows.
Thank you for being a forever friend
and helping me today.

She signed her name with a flourish and slipped into Cathy's room, laid it on her pillow, and went back to her room. Lord, what would she ever do without Cathy, Marty, Jack, and Darla Jean? They were all kin, not by blood, but by heartstrings.

Chapter 21

Small towns in Texas are famous for their festivals. Burnet has a Bluebonnet Festival in April; Commerce has a Bois D'Arc Festival in the fall; Whitewright puts on its Grand Street Fall Festival; and General Granbury's Birthday Party is held on the courthouse lawn in Granbury once a year.

Other than the name and locale, they were pretty much all the same. Vendors sold barbecue, hot dogs, cotton candy, and hamburgers as well as jewelry, cowboy boots, trinkets, and purses. Local organizations sold Indian tacos, chili, baked goods, and handmade crafts. There was always a parade and sometimes even a beauty contest and a carnival.

Cadillac hosted the Blue-Ribbon Jalapeño Society Jubilee the second weekend in November, and even the sign on the Baptist church said, "Pray for pretty weather this weekend." Folks didn't mind a little nip in the air, but they didn't want rain. In Cadillac, the Jalapeño Jubilee was an even bigger splash than the Super Bowl, and everyone talked about it for weeks.

There were framed awards given for booths, floats, bicycles, and horses all decorated for the parade. Tables were set up in the community room with samples of all kinds of jalapeño dishes for folks to sample. If they liked something, they could purchase the recipe for a one-dollar donation to the Blue-Ribbon Jalapeño Society, which was earmarked for the scholarship fund. There were pepper poppers, kabobs, several kinds of pepper cheese dips and cheese balls, jalapeño soups and chili, jalapeño pizza, corn bread, and even chocolate-covered jalapeños and jalapeño banana muffins with cream cheese frosting for those with a sweet tooth. Cathy had promised half a dozen jars of her pepper jelly and she delivered them early that morning.

Excitement was in the air. Everyone parked their lawn chairs in front of their houses or had copped a spot on front porches to watch the parade that morning. The fire siren sounded the message that it was beginning and conversation dropped to a low buzz as the first car in the procession made its appearance on the east end of town.

The weather cooperated—sunshine, no clouds, and sixty-five degrees. Absolutely perfect. Cathy, Agnes, Marty, Darla Jean, and then Trixie were all lined up in lawn chairs that Marty had dragged from the garage. They were sitting right on the edge of the sidewalk that ran in front of Clawdy's. Kids darted out to grab candy that Ethan threw from the sunroof of the long white Cadillac limo as the car made its way ever so slowly down the three blocks of Main Street.

"It's a good thing them kids can't vote next week or that man would be in office slicker'n scoopin' scum off a swamp," Agnes said when the limo passed the café. "Guess he's still mad at you, Cathy. He's throwing his candy on the other side of the road. Too bad." She cupped her hands around her mouth and yelled. "If I don't get a lollipop, I don't vote for you, Ethan."

He didn't even look her way.

She poked Cathy on the arm. "Damn, I'm glad you got out of that mess. You could have spent the morning riding in that car with that old witch."

"Aunt Agnes, we have to be nice!" Cathy said.

"You be nice. I'll wait until I'm dead to be nice." Agnes caught Violet staring from the back window of the limo and stuck out her tongue.

The Cadillac High School marching band stopped smack dab in front of Clawdy's and put on their famous halftime show. Flags spun around in a blur; batons twirled and flipped in the air as the band played the national anthem and then the Caddy High fight song.

People all along the street stood up and placed hands over hearts as the band played the first song and then yelled, whistled, and clapped as they played the school song. The fire truck was the next item in the parade, with firemen tossing even more candy and then twenty horses prancing along with cowboys from six years old to ninety-six riding them.

"Look at that Milford Jones. Still sits a horse mighty fine, even if he is way up over ninety years old, doesn't he?" Agnes said.

"Are you coveting your neighbor's husband? I do believe that is a sin," Darla Jean said.

"No, I'm not coveting Milford Jones, so don't you go preachin' me a sermon."

"I save the preachin' for Sunday, Agnes, but you are welcome to sit on one of my pews anytime you want to come to my church," Darla Jean whispered.

Cathy was struck speechless when she saw Anna Ruth and three other members of the club popping up an eight-foot table right behind them. Surely the Blue-Ribbon Jalapeño Society wouldn't be so rude as to put up a bake sale table right in front of Miss Clawdy's Café.

Agnes heard the noise and turned around. "What the hell?"

"Hello, ladies. Go ahead and watch the parade. We are getting set up for our bake sale. We're selling chips with your choice of picante, salsa, or jalapeño cheese dip. And Annabel made her famous jalapeño banana muffins for the folks who've tasted them over at the community room and want more. And there's lots more. We have ham and cheese sandwiches with your choice of plain cheese or pepper cheese. We fully well intend to get the prize for having the best booth at the jubilee. Don't mind us. We'll be real quiet." Anna Ruth put a finger over her lips and said, "Shh."

Agnes sat down and watched the antique cars parading past. "Cathy, would you look at that one? I remember when my daddy bought one like that. It was our first automobile. Mamma said he parked it under the shade tree out to the side of the yard and when he came back, the old red rooster was sittin' on the top of the hood crowing like it was his car. Daddy picked up a hammer lyin' on the worktable attached to the tree and threw it at the rooster. Hammer went right through the window. I miss seeing the queen candidates riding down the street. It was that damn Violet's fault that it all had to stop. She was too old to be a candidate and was jealous over those crowns."

Trixie leaned over toward Marty. "Now what?"

"I have no idea. We paid for that big ad in the newspaper this week saying we'll have an open buffet until six o'clock. Now the people will stop at their table and grab and run rather than coming inside and sitting down. Betcha we are going to have a hell of a lot of leftover food," Marty whispered.

Agnes pointed out a 1958 Chevrolet truck all tricked out with shiny paint and chrome running boards. "Reckon they'd sell that to me?"

"Aunt Agnes, I told you to be nice, but you're acting like you don't even know what we're talking about when it was your idea to advertise and to serve both lunch and dinner," Cathy said.

"Always remember the story of the hammer. Now look at that car, would you? It's an old Studebaker. I wanted one of those, but Bert wouldn't let me have it. I remember when a queen candidate rode on the hood of one. Let's see… that would have been the last time they had a queen. Damn Violet's meddling ways anyway!"

Nothing made a lick of sense. Agnes was always ready to go to war with the whole Blue-Ribbon Jalapeño Society. They had just deliberately snubbed Clawdy's and she was interested in old cars and past queens? Something was definitely wrong with the picture.

Little kids on their brightly decorated bicycles rode down Main Street after the antique cars, with Andy bringing up the rear right behind them in the newest police car in town. A poster was affixed to the passenger's door with black glittery words: *Last Year's Celebrity of the Year, Andrew Johnson.*

"Great parade," Agnes said. "Best we've had in years. Only way it would've been better was if we'd had queen candidates riding on them old cars."

"Are you all right? Do I need to lay hands on you and pray for you?" Darla Jean asked.

"You touch me and I'll break your fingers," Agnes said.

"Aunt Agnes! You said you'd be nice," Cathy whispered.

"Nice don't mean I have to let this woman start chanting over me," Agnes snapped and trotted across the street, her bright red sneakers smacking the hot pavement.

"Cathy, you are going to help, aren't you?" Anna Ruth yelled.

"I resigned."

"But you are still on the roll. You still have responsibilities."

Cathy folded her chair and handed it to Marty. She crossed the yard in half a dozen long strides. "This is downright mean, setting up in front of our shop. You were in charge of vendors. You could have put someone selling crafts or purses in this spot."

Anna Ruth smiled sweetly. "I could have, but I didn't. Isn't our booth beautiful?" She waved a hand over a whole table full of food. "And what do you think of the prices?"

The poster board Anna Ruth had pasted to the front of the table matched the one on Andy's car, leaving no doubt about who'd glittered and glued the thing the night before. Was that why Anna Ruth was so interested in scrapbooking? The prices were ridiculously low. There was no way Clawdy's was going to make a profit that day.

Anna Ruth chirped on like an excited canary. "I suppose we could have gotten more, but we just want to make a hundred dollars today. Aunt Annabel and I worked all day yesterday, and Violet came over to help us make the sign with all the pretty peppers on it. And she helped make the icing for the muffins too. Don't you just love the way we did the signs in glitter to match our club pins and last year's Jubilee celebrity?"

Cathy clenched her fists. "I'm not helping. No matter what Violet says, I'm not a part of the club anymore, and I've got a café to run."

"Good luck with that," Anna Ruth said coldly.

The limo crawled to a stop in front of the shop, and the driver, all dressed up in a black tuxedo, held the door for Violet. That day she wore navy dress slacks with a matching blazer over a red and white striped blouse. Her signature flag pin glittered on her lapel, and her makeup did a fine job of covering up the last of the bruising around her eyes.

"I'm making a stop at all the vendors to be sure all is going good. How are you, Catherine? I'm glad to see you helping. I knew you wouldn't really resign."

"Oh, but she did." Agnes trotted right across the street and headed toward the table of goodies.

Violet held her tiny little red purse up in front of her. "Agnes Flynn, you stay away from me. I will call Andy to put you in jail if you start anything."

"I promised Cathy I'd be nice so I'm buying chips and picante from y'all. I went to get my money to pay for it," Agnes said.

Violet lowered the purse and took two steps backward.

"How much you plannin' on makin' if you sell everything on the stand today?" Agnes asked.

Anna Ruth beamed. "Our goal is a hundred dollars, but the money isn't as important as getting the award to go in the sunroom with the blue ribbons. My first year in the club and my very first award. I'm just so excited I could cry."

The Andrews house sat on a slight rise, just enough to tilt the long table forward an inch or two. Two little boys were in front of it with Agnes. One pointed at a paper saucer with a muffin on it then drew his finger back and pointed at a plate with chips and picante.

"Which one?" Anna Ruth asked.

"He'll have both." Agnes turned her head to the other child. "What do you want, honey?"

He looked at his mother who nodded and chose a muffin. Their mothers yelled their thanks to Agnes who waved them off with a flick of the wrist.

"That will be two dollars," Anna Ruth said.

Agnes moved around to the back of the table, fished a bill from her purse, and handed it to Anna Ruth. Then she grabbed the edge of the table and with a shove sent the whole thing flying out across the yard and into the street. The wind stuck the glittery sign to the front windshield of Violet's limo. A jalapeño banana muffin with thick cream cheese frosting flew through the air and smashed with great force against Violet's flag pin. A Styrofoam bowl of salsa wound up in Anna Ruth's blond hair. And the whole place looked like a major crime scene by the time the red picante, cream-cheese-covered muffins, and everything on the table had mixed together in the air and come crashing down on the sidewalk and street.

"What have you done?" Violet screamed.

"Guess I'm clumsy. Got it from my daddy. He aimed for a damned old rooster one time and knocked out the windshield of his new car. I was reaching for some picante and lost my balance. Guess you better keep that whole hundred dollar bill I just gave you, Anna Ruth. I wouldn't want it said I didn't pay up when I make a mess."

"You did that on purpose so we wouldn't win the award for the best booth." Violet brushed the cream cheese icing from her jacket and then wiped it on the butt of her slacks before she thought. "Now look what you made me do!"

"You might want to call the cleaning crew to come take care

of this before the fire ants find it. They go to stinging the kids and their mammas are all going to get pissed at you, Violet, since you're in charge of the whole Jubilee. Or worse yet, the kids will start using those pepper poppers like footballs to kick up and down the street and food will wind up on all those antique cars. I don't know if hot peppers can ruin the paint or not, but I wouldn't take no chances. You're lucky I'm clumsy. Violet's muffins would probably taste like shit anyway. She never did learn how to cook."

It started as a snicker, turned into a giggle, and then was a full-fledged roar that Cathy could not control. If Agnes had planned what would hit Anna Ruth and Violet, she couldn't have done a better job.

Trixie stepped out on the front porch seconds before food peppered through the air like bullets from a machine gun. Her laughter brought Darla Jean and Marty on the run and just in time to hear more of the argument.

"You are evil and vile," Violet hissed.

"And you look like shit," Agnes said. "Go on home and put on that red, white, and blue dress you wore to church. It looks like a circus tent so it will go right along with this jubilee."

"What are they fighting over now? Oh my God!" Marty saw the upturned table and the mess. "Please don't tell me there is a dead body in all that mess."

Trixie wiped her eyes, smearing mascara everywhere. "Agnes did it. God, I hope I grow up to be just like her."

Violet took a step toward Agnes.

Agnes bowed right up to her. "You don't really want to do this, do you?"

"Why don't you lie down and die?" Violet asked.

"You first. I got to see where you go before I die. I'd go to hell before I'd go to heaven with you. Now get on out of here and make yourself presentable. In about ten minutes, that boy of yours is getting on his stump to promise the citizens of Cadillac a better life. I don't reckon you want to miss it. Just lick the icing off your fancy bitch pin and go on now." Agnes laced her arm in Cathy's and marched her up the driveway to the back door.

"I reckon that will pay for part of the food I've eaten the past two years," she said when they reached the back porch.

"Your bill is paid in full, Aunt Agnes!" Cathy hugged her tightly.

At noon, Jack arrived to buy takeout lunches for the break room at the police station.

"Heard that Agnes tipped the club table out into the street and then paid for everything on it," he whispered to Trixie.

Trixie nodded. "Agnes is my new hero."

"What happened?"

Trixie told him between giggles.

"I may not go home tonight. Mamma is going to fret about all that something horrible."

"Is your new furniture at your house now?"

He nodded. "But I haven't formally moved out of Mamma's place."

"So stay at your new place tonight, and it'll make the permanent move less traumatic for her. Call and say that you are planning to be out very late and you're not coming home."

"Why didn't I think of that?"

"Think of what?" Marty asked.

"Jack is going to stay in his new house tonight because Beulah is going to be in a tiff over what Agnes just did."

"I wouldn't go home either," Marty said. "And it will ease the way for the real move."

"We could bring Agnes and help you finish moving tomorrow evening. Beulah sure wouldn't cry in front of her," Trixie said.

"If things get too sappy, I just might take you up on that." Jack grinned.

The rest of the day went fast. When it was time to close the shop, the kitchen was a complete mess, there was no food left in the pots, and the grill looked worse than it ever had. Trixie would throw up her hands and quit if Marty said they had to start serving dinner and supper every day. The buffet was wiped out at six o'clock and all the desserts were gone except one slice of black forest cake. Trixie boxed up it up and laid a card on the top that she'd made weeks before to give to Molly. She'd put it aside and never taken it to scrapbooking, but she could always make another one for Molly and the sentiment fit perfectly: *You are one in a million!*

She quickly glued a big yellow silk sunflower to the top of the box and added a long green paper stem and a couple of leaves. Then she trotted across the street and rang Agnes's doorbell.

"What do you want?" Agnes grouched when she opened the door.

"Special delivery for the old fart who should've been the celebrity this year." Trixie handed it to her and hurried back across the street before Agnes could say a word.

The bathroom was steamed up. That meant Marty and Cathy had already had showers and Trixie could take as long as she wanted, and she did. When she finished, she flung open her closet doors and was pondering over which jeans to wear to the street dance when Marty knocked and stuck her head inside the room.

"Got a minute?" she asked.

"Got as many as you need. Next Chamber meeting, I'm going to see to it they'll change the Jubilee to the first week in October so it won't be so close to the Craft Fair. Or maybe we could combine the two," Trixie said.

"Won't happen. Not as long as Violet and the old dogs are in control. You don't buck tradition in Cadillac. You know that, Trixie."

"It's worth a try."

Trixie sat down on the bed and patted the spot next to her. "Sit down and spit it out. Never known you to beat around the bush. You sure you're Marty or did you and Cathy trade places?"

"I'm mad as hell at you. Almost to the point of throwing you out of this house," Marty said.

"Good Lord, what did I do?"

"You've been seeing Andy and sleeping with him. God, girl, don't you remember how bad he hurt you? And you had the audacity to get mad at me over that damn vote that I had to do or else Mamma would come haunt me."

"How did you find that out?"

"It doesn't matter how I found out."

"I've got a question for you before you throw me out. Why didn't you tell me he was cheating on me even before Anna Ruth?"

"I didn't know, Trixie. I knew he was a skirt chaser in high school and that he flirted, but it wouldn't have surprised me to find out he was still up to his old games. But I didn't know for sure and I wasn't going to hurt you with gossip. I would have told you, I promise," Marty said.

"I *was* seeing him. I *was* sleeping with him. I'm not seeing him anymore, Marty. It's over. I swear it is."

"I don't believe you. First time he winks, you'll fall over backward and drag him down on top of you. I'm going to feed him poison and go to his funeral to be sure that he's really dead. That's the only way you'll ever be rid of him. You can mourn and then finally move on."

"You are a good friend. I know beyond a shadow of a doubt that you'd shoot him for me! But I really am over him. That night with the shotgun was the last time he's been here. I couldn't have made it through the horrible times without y'all. I can't explain but I really, truly am over Andy. He can do whatever he wants. I don't give a shit. Now help me decide what to wear and please don't throw me out of the house."

Marty poked her on the arm. "You know something else. You've got another secret and you haven't told me. I can see a gleam in your eye. Do you have a boyfriend? That's why you are over Andy, isn't it? You've got a new lover!"

Trixie cocked her head to one side. "Sorry, darlin', I don't have a new boyfriend and if I did have a secret, it wouldn't be something like not voting for you."

Marty's eyes widened. "Then what is it?"

Trixie giggled. "I do not have another secret, I promise. You really would poison Andy, wouldn't you?"

"Damn straight!" Marty stuck out her little finger and they did a pinky-promise like two little girls.

"Now do I get a pretty card like Cathy?"

"Maybe in a couple of days. What do you want your pretty card to say, Marty?"

"Men and catastrophes come and go. Girlfriends are forever," she said.

"And Jack. Don't forget that Jack is our friend too, even if he is a man."

"Good friends are forever then," Marty said. "That's what I want it to say. Now let's go to the dance. I've already spotted a new cowboy and he's going to dance with me until the Jubilee shuts down."

Chapter 22

Cathy really meant to turn her cell phone off, but in the aftermath of an all-day buffet at Clawdy's, rushing to the Rib Joint to help John close up, and then a wonderful hour of passionate sex, she had fallen asleep. When it rang the next morning at eight o'clock, she thought the noise was the alarm. She reached across John's body and slapped the off button on top of the clock. It rang again. She figured she'd hit the snooze button so she slapped the clock one more time. On the third ring, she realized it was her phone, rolled over, and grabbed it from the nightstand on her side of the bed.

"Hello," she said groggily.

"Good morning!" a voice that sounded vaguely familiar chirped. "I'm calling about the wedding dress you have posted in the Denison newspaper. My boyfriend proposed last night and we're getting married in three weeks and I'd love to see this dress. The picture shows it to be very basic, but my aunt and I can dress it up with some satin flowers, and we're making our own detachable train with a big J embroidered in seed pearls on the train inside a heart."

Cathy didn't need a play-by-play of the woman's whole life. She just wanted to sell the dang dress. "I live south of Sherman, Texas. How do you want to take care of payment and seeing it?"

"I live in the same area. Could we meet in the Walmart parking lot? The weatherman says it could rain so if you could come right away, that would be very nice."

Cathy dropped the phone and scrambled to retrieve it before her buyer thought she'd hung up on her. She was finally awake enough to recognize Anna Ruth's voice. Now what did she do? J meant that Andy Johnson had proposed to her. She'd seen them flirting like teenagers at the street dance, but surely Anna Ruth wasn't that crazy. Andy's track record had proven that he wasn't capable of "forsaking all others."

"What time?" Cathy asked.

"In an hour? I can't wait to get to work on it."

"I'll be there."

"How will I recognize you?"

"I'll be the one standing beside my car holding up a wedding dress," Cathy said quickly and hung up.

She dressed and left John sleeping soundly. Fifteen minutes later, she tiptoed upstairs, rapped gently on Trixie's door, and whispered her name. When no one answered, she opened it a crack and looked inside. Trixie threw a pillow at the door and pulled the covers up over her head.

Cathy looked over and saw Marty's door open so she poked her head inside and whispered, "Hey, are you awake?"

Marty growled.

Cathy went into her room and sat down on the edge of the bed. No way was she selling that dress to Anna Ruth before talking to either Trixie or Marty.

Trixie made her way to Cathy's bed. She crawled up into the middle of it and sat cross-legged. "This had better be good for you to wake me up this early on Sunday morning. It's too early to even get up for church."

"I sold the wedding dress," Cathy said quickly.

"Well, hot damn. Where's it going?" Trixie came alive.

"Probably to the Cadillac Baptist Church and I'm ninety-nine point nine percent sure that Anna Ruth is the buyer and Andy is the groom. Is that going to be a problem? She didn't recognize my voice when she called so I can just not show up at the Walmart parking lot."

"Oh, yes, you will show up. I don't care if she buys it. I don't care if she's marrying Andy. I'll even go to the wedding with bells on my toes. Is that all?"

Cathy nodded.

Marty poked her head in the door. "What's going on?"

"Cathy sold the wedding dress to Anna Ruth, who is going to marry Andy."

"I'll be damned." Marty joined them on the bed. "I'll even help carry it out to your car and then I'm going back to bed."

It took all three of them to put the dress inside the car. Marty and Trixie both stood on the porch in their pajamas and waved as she drove away from Clawdy's. She parked on the outer fringes of the lot, not far from the gas pumps, and waited until she saw Anna Ruth's little red car whip in off the highway. She held up a hand.

Anna Ruth pulled in beside her and rolled down her window.

"Do you need help? Has that old car finally gone its last mile? I can call someone or come back, but right now I'm looking for a woman holding up a wedding dress. I shouldn't even offer the way your aunt acted at the Jubilee yesterday but I'm happy. Andy proposed last night and we're getting married in three weeks. He's gotten a job with the Bells Police Department and we are moving since I'm already teaching there and it's going to be so wonderful and I don't even have to give up the club." True Anna Ruth style, she rambled on and on.

Cathy reached inside the car and held up the wedding dress.

"Oh!" Anna Ruth gasped.

"What do we do now?" Cathy asked.

"I love it, but I can't. Who's seen it?"

"Trixie, Marty, Darla Jean, and Aunt Agnes."

"It'll be six inches too long, but Aunt Annabel and I figured we'd use what we cut off to make flowers with little satin leaves for the train. And she's already got the train cut out. It's going to fasten onto the back of the dress with hook and eyes with the same satin as the flower leaves and… what am I going to do?"

"Your call," Cathy said.

"I never did love Ethan, you know. I just thought I did. It's always been Andy, but I don't know about wearing a dress that was bought for Ethan's bride. Somehow it doesn't seem right."

"Okay." Cathy opened the car door to put it in the backseat.

"Wait! I'll take it. No one will even recognize it when we get done dressing it up."

The check she handed Cathy was made out for the exact amount she'd listed it for. At least she didn't try to negotiate a cheaper price.

"But you have to promise me something," she said.

It was kind of late to be asking for promises after she had the dress and Cathy already put the check in her purse.

"You got to promise not to tell everyone. I don't want Violet to know for sure. She'd be a real pain about it," Anna Ruth said.

"I promise."

"Thank you, Cathy! Like they say in the movies, this never happened. Oh, and you'll be getting your invitation for you and one guest in the mail next week. Club is giving us a shower. I don't suppose you'll want to come to it under the circumstances, but please come to the wedding. You do know that Violet is livid about that new boyfriend of yours, though, so be prepared."

"Ain't that nice." Cathy smiled sweetly.

Anna Ruth carefully draped the dress over the passenger seat in her car and waved out the driver's window as she drove off.

Cathy drove straight to McDonald's, went inside, and ordered a cup of coffee. She carried it to a booth by the window. The first sip was hot enough to burn and it hurt so she wasn't dreaming. She'd just sold the dress to Anna Ruth who was really marrying Andy in three weeks. That made it the first Saturday in December, the very day she was supposed to have married Ethan.

All of Cadillac would be busy either with preparations for Andy's leaving the force, the wedding, or at least the gossip. Things couldn't get any crazier.

Her phone rang. She checked the ID before she answered and said, "You are supposed to be asleep."

Trixie giggled. "Andy just called Jack and he called me so he could be the first to tell me that Andy is marrying Anna Ruth. Jack is going to step up into Andy's job. Did she buy the dress?"

"Oh, yeah, but believe me, when she gets done with it, you'd never know it was the one I bought. And we're sworn to secrecy about it. If Agnes finds out, she'll taunt Violet, and even though Anna Ruth is a pain in my ass and I'm still mad at Andy, I don't want to pop her bubble on her wedding day. Andy can have that job all on his own and I'm real glad that she'll be in Bells when it happens so she won't come whining to me. That's not very nice, is it?" Cathy asked.

"I can't believe you said ass. And darlin', you don't have to be nice all the time."

Andy had one more bridge to cross before he moved to the other side of the county and went to work in Bells as Chief of Police. Whether he burned the bridge or rebuilt it was totally up to Trixie. But it had to be done on Monday morning before Anna Ruth got involved with the wedding preparations. After that it would be impossible to bring the wedding train to a screeching halt and jump off.

Cathy was working the tables in the dining room at Clawdy's and when he sat down at a table, she scowled. Thank God it was

Cathy and not Marty. She'd have done more than give him dirty looks. He wiped sweat from his face with a handkerchief. So what if it was fifty degrees outside? His life was on the line here.

"I'd like to talk to Trixie," he said.

"No. Go away," Cathy said.

"Trixie," he raised his voice. "I need to talk to you!"

She came from the other room and popped her hands on her hips. "What do you want?"

"Can we talk in private?"

"Trixie." Cathy lowered her chin.

"I'll be fine. I promise."

"Five minutes and then Marty and I are both intervening."

"Won't take that long," Trixie said.

She sat down at the table.

Andy reached across and laid his hands on hers. "I asked Anna Ruth to marry me last night."

She jerked her hands free and put them in her lap. "Congratulations. I heard about it first thing this morning."

"I took a job in Bells this past week."

"Congratulations on that too. Why are you here?"

"I'm moving. I'm starting all over and I'd rather it be with you. We could go to Bells. We could start again, and this time we could get it right."

"Why did you ask Anna Ruth to marry you?"

"I want a wife. I like being married. I like coming home to a woman in the house. But after I asked her, I realized I want that wife to be you."

"Go upstairs and look at my room. I haven't changed."

"Neither have I, but we made it work those first years. I can undo this thing with Anna Ruth. It was just a thing of the moment. She'll be mad but it can be done."

"The answer is no and won't ever change, Andy. I'm moving on and I'm happy. I'd never trust you. And besides, Anna Ruth bought a wedding dress yesterday morning. I think it's too late to back out, Andy, but I do feel sorry for her."

"I'll marry you again and swear on the Bible that I'll be faithful. We can fly down to Cancun for a week. You can give your part of Clawdy's back to Marty and Cathy. I won't even fuss about the money you took out of our savings to buy a partnership in a café," he said.

"You did marry me and you swore before God that you would be faithful and you weren't. Cancun wouldn't make any difference. And the truth is, Andy, you aren't worth giving up Clawdy's for. Go marry Anna Ruth. She might not kill you the next time you cheat. I would."

"When I walk out the door the offer is off the table. Think about the sex, Trix."

"Don't let the door hit you in the ass," she said.

He stormed outside, slamming the front door behind him.

Cathy patted her on the shoulder as she walked past. "I heard every word. Lord, what a mess."

"We are going to be all right." Trixie smiled.

Agnes was in the kitchen when Trixie got back. She looked up with a scowl on her face and said, "What the hell was he doing here?"

"I should have let you shoot him that night. He came to give me one more chance," Trixie said.

"And what did you tell him?"

"I told him he was out of chances."

"What about shooting him?" Cathy asked.

"I wasn't seeing things. She had Andy up there in her bedroom," Agnes tattled.

"But it's over now, isn't it?" Cathy frowned.

"You heard what I told him," Trixie said. "I meant every word."

Marty threw six pieces of bacon on the grill. "For real?"

"He can give all the rest of the chances he's got in his pocket to Anna Ruth. I'm done with him."

Marty went back to her job. "Good!"

Chapter 23

Agnes loved Saturday morning cartoons. Not those new ones with robots and machines that transformed from cars into monsters. No, she liked the old ones with Sylvester and Tweety Bird and Wile E. Coyote. Those were the real McCoys. She'd gotten up early because that's when the good ones came on. She'd made her Saturday morning hot chocolate and saved back a bowl of peach cobbler from the day before for breakfast. When a woman got past seventy, she didn't pay much attention to all the folderol about six servings of vegetables and fruits. She just took her liquid fiber every night and ate what she pleased.

Wile E. Coyote was about to pluck the roadrunner's tail feathers when the doorbell rang. No one ever came to Agnes's house on Saturday morning. Pretty often on Thursday, Darla Jean popped by to ask if she'd like to go see Betty and the girls, but never on the weekends. She grumbled all the way across the living room to the door.

"Good God, Lanita, what happened to you? Did you have a wreck? I didn't hear a thing but I was watching television." Agnes stepped out and looked up the street and down the street but she didn't see a vehicle anywhere.

Lanita was married to Jim Washington, a high-powered real estate agent in Denison. He was originally from Cadillac and had brought Lanita home with him when he retired from the Army. She was a small, dark-haired woman in her early thirties and a trophy wife for Jim who was in his mid-fifties. The two of them attended church in Cadillac every Sunday and sat on the far end of Agnes's pew.

"Can I come inside?" Her voice carried a soft southern accent.

Agnes backed up and motioned her into the house.

"Have a seat. You had breakfast? I'll share my cobbler."

Lanita sat down on the edge of a chair. "I'm not hungry. Jim is in Vegas for a conference. He'll be back this afternoon. I need help and I have no idea where to turn. I left him once and went to my friend's place in Arkansas. He found me and it was awful, but I can't take much more. They're getting suspicious at both the Sherman and the Denison hospitals in their emergency rooms. Last time the doctor kept asking questions. It made things worse when we got home and he said next time he'll kill me."

She pulled off a denim jacket and Agnes inhaled sharply. "What he use? A whip?"

"Fists and a belt. I want you to help me die."

Agnes really sucked air that time. "Ain't no sense in that, girl. I got a friend just down the street that can help take care of this thing."

"I just meant that I was going to stage a suicide and I need you to pick me up and give me a ride to the bus station. I'll get a plane ticket somewhere."

"That will leave a paper trail. Way Darla Jean does it, you are a new person and that man will never find you."

"You trust her?" Lanita asked.

Agnes didn't hesitate a second. "I'd trust her with my life, but don't tell her I said it. Now how were we going to kill you?"

"I was going to take his boat out on Lake Texoma and blow it up. I was going to stop at the gas station and the marina and any other place I could so people can see me with it. Then I planned to slip over the side and swim to shore where you'd pick me up while it burned. I saw it on a television show."

"It's too damn cold to be swimming to shore. You'll catch

pneumonia and really die. Did the man in the movie find her?" Agnes asked.

Lanita nodded.

"How did you get here?"

"I drove my car."

Agnes reached over to the end table and picked up her phone. Darla Jean answered on the third ring.

"I got another abuse case over here in my house and we only got a little while to take care of it. And her husband ain't a sack of shit. This is a real hard case. What do we do?"

"I'll be right there. Don't let her leave."

Darla Jean jerked on a pair of jeans, a shirt, and Nikes. Betty had an empty bedroom left in her house, so yes, there was room for a woman in need.

Agnes had the door open before she had time to ring the doorbell. "I don't know about this one, but we got to help her."

Darla Jean sat down on the sofa. "Tell me what happened."

Lanita poured out the whole story.

"Where are you from? I hear a southern accent."

"Louisiana. Down in the Cajun country. I met Jim when he was just about to retire out of the service."

"Where is your car?"

"I parked it two blocks down in front of one of those old empty buildings. I didn't want anyone to see it in front of Agnes's house."

"Go get in it and go home. Don't do a thing out of the normal on the way. How far from a store or church parking lot do you live?"

"It's six blocks to the parking lot at a doctor's office. I can give you his address."

"Walk out of the house with nothing but what you are wearing. Don't take money, credit cards, your purse, or even jewelry. Dress like you would if you were going for a Saturday morning walk and I'll be parked at that parking lot. We'll go to my sister's place for a few weeks. You will be our cousin who's come from Louisiana for a visit. Your name is Nita Jean until you decide who you want to be and where you want to go."

"Thank you." Lanita reached over and touched Darla Jean's hand. "You are an angel."

"Hmph! I damn sure wouldn't call her that," Agnes said.

It taxed Agnes's ability to keep her mouth shut and her fists to herself the next morning in church when Jim showed up and sat on the pew down from her. When the preacher stood up and asked everyone to pray for Jim because his wife had gone missing, perhaps kidnapped, she had to bite her tongue to keep from shouting out to the whole congregation the real story.

Violet reached him first after services and gave him a hug. The line behind her was long, but Agnes didn't join them. She shook the preacher's hand and was almost to her car when Jim yelled her name.

"I've hired a private detective and I had a tracker on her car. She came to Cadillac yesterday morning. Did you see her?" Jim talked as he walked toward her.

Agnes turned around and looked him right in the eye. "Yes, she did. I heard the preacher talkin' about it and hurried out here to get my cell phone and call the police. She came by my house because I asked her to drop in sometime to talk about the ladies' auxiliary. We do all kinds of work like get the Bible school things ordered and have bake sales to pay for it."

"Did she seem anxious or upset?"

"No, she did mention a headache. Said she'd taken a nasty tumble down the stairs in your house. Reckon she got amnesia and wandered off somewhere? She said she might take your boat out to the lake because that relaxed her. Did you check to see if it's missing?

Maybe she's run out of gas and just floating around. Should I go on and call them or will you?"

"I'll take care of it and thank you." Jim had his phone out and was talking as he walked away.

Cathy was helping in the kitchen when Agnes popped in the next morning. It was a slow Monday, but the middle of the month often was.

"I hope there's chocolate in heaven," Agnes said.

"What makes you think an old renegade like you will ever go to heaven?" Trixie asked.

Agnes pointed at Trixie. "I got something to say and it ain't got a thing to do with you because I wouldn't leave you a dime of my money."

"Can I stay or should I go to my room and cut out paper dolls?" Trixie teased.

"You can stay but mostly I want Cathy and Marty and Darla Jean to hear this."

Trixie threw a hand over her heart. "I'm hurt."

"Don't give me that shit. This don't have anything to do with you so stir that pot of beans and hush. Now here's the deal. I was going to leave my entire estate to you, Cathy. I'm going to change my will and use the money to help Darla Jean run her abused women thing." She went on to tell them the whole story of Lanita and what had happened at church.

Cathy hugged Agnes. "I think that is a wonderful idea. It might help keep some women alive."

"Good, now let's talk about this gawd-forsaken wedding about to come off. I'm thinkin' about moving my membership over to your church after the wedding. I'm looking for a sign from God as to whether I should or shouldn't. But this wedding is what I want to talk about. Y'all are all going with me and you're going to sit beside me on my pew."

"Not me," Trixie said. "That would just be too weird. And besides, you don't even like me."

"Not me!" Cathy shook her head. "That's the day I was going to marry Ethan. I don't care if I do get an invitation that says plus guest; I'd rather stay home and clean the trailer house with plus guest as go to that wedding," Cathy said.

"Hell if I'll go to that damned thing. I went to his first wedding. That was enough," Marty declared.

Agnes sat back and smiled at the argument she'd started.

Darla Jean laid her hand on Agnes's arm and whispered, "God bless you, Agnes. Betty and I could do this on our own, but we appreciate your help."

For the first time in her life, Trixie saw Agnes blush. The old girl wasn't nearly as tough as she'd like everyone to think.

Chapter 24

Agnes was sitting on her porch enjoying a rare sunny day in the middle of November. She'd put on her jacket and fuzzy house shoes and carried a cup of steaming hot chocolate outside with her.

"Well, shit!" she mumbled when Beulah Landry headed across the street. She'd heard all she wanted to hear about that damned wedding. She didn't care if Andy and Anna Ruth blended sand from each of their little glasses together and poured it into a crystal bowl signifying that forever they would be one. Or if the unity candle was engraved with pictures of angels. She didn't even care if the dress was the fanciest thing since the last royal wedding over in England. If Trixie couldn't make him walk the chalk line, Anna Ruth didn't have a chance in hell.

Beulah sat down in the rocker beside Agnes. "Beautiful day, ain't it? Don't reckon we'll get many more of these. It'll get blustery and cold pretty soon."

"Want some hot chocolate?"

"Oh, no, I can't stay long. Violet just called me. One of the club ladies was down at the Dairy Queen having a hot fudge sundae and she saw Marty and a man get out of an old Chevy car. One of those like Bert had in the fifties. Guess her man kissed her right there in public. Don't reckon that's the way a woman her age ought to be behavin'. I swear, I hope Jack don't start doin' crazy things now that he's in his own house."

"He's past thirty. He's old enough to sleep in whatever the hell bed he makes up, but don't be holdin' your breath, Beulah, that he's never going to take a woman in his house. Or that someone won't see it when he does."

Beulah shivered. "There'll be gossip."

"Yep, just like right now. Have you seen that man that Marty was kissin' on?" Agnes asked.

Beulah shook her head.

Agnes blew into her cup of chocolate to cool it. "Well, when you do, grab hold of your under-britches and hang on real tight 'cause they're going to start to crawlin' down. Hell, I keep mine up with suspenders when he's around."

Beulah gasped. "Lord, Agnes, I swear you get worse with every passing year."

"Gettin' old ain't for wimps, Beulah. Only the strong and the mouthy get to do it. You been feelin' good lately? You look a little poorly to me."

"I'm just fine. I've got soup on the stove. I just thought you ought to know what was going on."

Agnes waited until Beulah was in her house before she went over to Clawdy's through the back door.

"Marty, what the hell are you doing kissin' on some man at the Dairy Queen?" Agnes huffed.

"Who said I was kissing a man at the Dairy Queen?" Marty asked.

"That would be me, not Marty. I saw Beulah coming over to your house." Cathy laughed. "John and I were at the Dairy Queen last night and he bent me over just like in the movies and told me that he loved me. First time he's said those words and he said them right out in public. It was wonderful, Aunt Agnes."

"Well, shit! I let on like I knew the man and he was so sexy he gave me hot flashes. He'd damn sure better be that good lookin' when you introduce him to me, girl."

"Oh, he is," Cathy said.

That Sunday afternoon John was on a roll with his new book so Cathy played with Maggie and reread one of her sister's first novels.

She finished the book and looked out the window. The sun was bright and beckoned her to come outside. She looked over at Maggie Rose and whispered, "Want to go for a walk?"

The dog didn't even wag her tail. She just shut her eyes and ignored Cathy.

"Have a good nap then." Cathy reached for her jacket and shoes. She had barely stepped off the porch when she heard a car out in front of the restaurant. The engine stopped and a door slammed.

She hoped whoever it was hadn't come from far away only to find the restaurant closed, but she was glad that John wasn't open on Sunday. Folks needed one day in the week just to play catch-up with the rest of their lives. She listened for the car's engine to start up again, and when it didn't, she walked out across the yard and around the end of the joint.

"Well, dammit all to hell!" she said and instantly felt guilty for cussing on Sunday, especially when she hadn't gone to church that morning. Anna Ruth was sitting on the porch, her arms wrapped around her body trying to stay warm. If she'd come back to return the dress, she was shit out of luck. Cathy had already deposited the money and she wasn't the Walmart store where satisfaction was guaranteed and you could bring anything back with no questions asked.

"There you are," Anna Ruth said. "I saw your car and decided to wait here on the porch for you. Where have you been?"

"John lives behind the restaurant," Cathy said.

Anna Ruth stood up slowly. She wore jeans, a jacket, and a purple hickey right below her left ear. "It's cold out here. Warm one day, cold the next. I wish it would make up its mind what it wants to do. But I really, really want it to be nice for my wedding so I shouldn't complain. Let's go back to your place." She came to a stop so fast that her hair flopped around to her back. "My God! Cathy, you gave up the Prescott Plantation for a trailer house?"

"Happiness can be found in a grass hut as well as a mansion," Cathy said. "What are you doing here?"

"Aren't you going to invite me inside?"

"No, I'm not. John is working. He's a mystery author, and he's having a good day so we aren't having company. We can go through the back door of the restaurant and sit in there or we can sit on the porch in front."

Anna Ruth did not hesitate for a nanosecond. "Inside, then. This north wind is cold. I hope Andy has booked a honeymoon somewhere warm, like one of the islands."

Anna Ruth was like an unlucky penny. She just kept showing up at the weirdest times.

"Can I get you something to drink?" Cathy asked.

"I'd love a sweet tea."

"Don't have any of that made up. We've got beer and soft drinks."

"Pepsi, then." Anna Ruth sat down at the nearest table and waited.

Cathy drew up two large Pepsis and carried them to the table. "You never did say why you came out here. I've never seen you eating in this place, and how did you know I'd be here?"

"I don't eat food without a fork and I don't like the taste of barbecue. And it's all over town that you are practically living with the cook out here. Sometimes I wonder about you, Cathy. You had everything at your fingertips and were too stubborn to sign the prenup. Now look at you. It's a shame."

"You came out here to lecture me?" Cathy sipped her Pepsi. It wasn't nearly as good as the beer she'd left sitting on the porch.

"No, I'm sorry. It's just that you disappoint me so bad sometimes that I don't even know what I'm saying. I sure didn't come out here to upset you or hurt your feelings. I came to ask you about that wedding cake you ordered. Aunt Annabel will have to start making the morning glories tomorrow morning. She always allows two weeks for a big cake like that."

"Okay. She is aware that it goes to the Christian church that Saturday, right?"

Anna Ruth's chin quivered. "I've been mean to you. Telling you to get out of the club and all, and now I'm here to beg. I wouldn't blame you if you said no."

"What are you talking about?" Cathy asked.

"Here." Anna Ruth handed Cathy a folded check. "Aunt Annabel never puts the check for a cake in the bank until the day of the wedding. You can have it back if you won't make her do your cake. She needs the full two weeks to make mine, and she can't do two in that time."

Cathy opened the check. Sure enough, it was the very one she'd written to Annabel. Marty was wrong! She had managed to sell her cake. Well, in a sense anyway. At least she'd gotten her money back. Aunt Agnes might be disappointed because she had visions of filling her freezer with the ugly thing and serving slabs of it at her Sunday school meetings.

Anna Ruth dabbed at a tear with a paper napkin from the dispenser in the middle of the table. "Will you please tear up that check so Aunt Annabel doesn't have to make your cake? You don't need it and she needs all the time to get mine done."

"Sure." Cathy tucked the folded check in her pocket.

Anna Ruth clapped her hands. "Oh! I was so afraid you'd say no. My cake is going to have life-sized red sugar roses trailing up from the bottom all the way to the top where we'll have a gorgeous topper. The whole thing will be over four feet tall."

"Want to buy a topper? I've got a crystal one for sale that I ordered from New York," Cathy asked.

"What does it look like? Did Ethan or Violet see it?"

Cathy shook her head. "No, they didn't. It's cut glass crystal, eight inches tall. It's on the Internet at Tiffany's if you want to see it."

She'd offered it as a joke. She sure hadn't thought about unloading that expensive chunk of glass. But Anna Ruth's expression said she was very interested.

"And I bought the matching mold for a miniature ice sculpture that I thought would be pretty rising up out of the punch bowl. You'd have to set it on a square cube at least six inches tall to get the effect," Cathy said.

She should feel strange selling off her dress, her cake, and her topper, but all she could see was the look on Marty's face when she told her that she'd gotten her money back for the whole shittin' shebang.

Anna Ruth nodded. "Can we go see it now? It sounds beautiful."

"Sure. I'll meet you there in ten minutes. I'll have to get my purse."

"Oh, Cathy, you are such a good friend. We are like sisters, aren't we? We have our fights, but we always make up," Anna Ruth gushed.

The girl was nuts, but there wasn't a cure for her brand of nuts. To be cured, a person had to realize they had a problem. If Anna Ruth did that, she wouldn't be planning a wedding with Andy Johnson anyway.

Without commenting on the bit about sisters, Cathy hurried out the back door with Anna Ruth on her heels, going on and on about how wonderful things were going and it had to be fate, and how happy she and Andy were going to be on the other side of Grayson County.

Thank goodness she parted ways with Cathy a few feet from the café and trotted around to the parking lot. Anna Ruth was waiting by the back door when she pulled into the driveway at Clawdy's and waved as she got out of her car.

Marty was in the garage with Jack. Her frown when she saw Anna

Ruth dropped the temperature another ten degrees. She headed right for the house with a big wrench in her hand.

"What is going on here?" Marty asked.

"I sold her my cake," Cathy said quickly.

"You going to sell her your honeymoon too?" Marty asked.

"Oh! Do you have tickets to somewhere wonderful?" Anna Ruth asked.

Marty laughed even harder.

"I do not! Lord Almighty, Marty! That's not even funny!" Cathy said. "I'm going upstairs to get the cake topper for her."

"You really sold that hideous red cake with morning glories on it?" Marty asked. "And you really bought it?"

Anna Ruth slapped a hand over her mouth. "Oh, no! I just gave her check back so Aunt Annabel could have the time to make my cake. Mine is Hawaiian wedding cake and pure white on the outside with red roses. I could never do morning glories. Violet would just die."

"Who's killing Violet?" Agnes pushed into the kitchen. "God, this weather is going to be the death of me. Turnin' off colder than a witch's tit out there. You killed Violet, Anna Ruth? How'd you do it? If you didn't drive a stake through her heart, she'll come back alive."

Cathy rolled her eyes. "She's buying my cake and my topper. Give me a minute to go get it and she'll be gone and Violet is alive."

"Well, shit!" Agnes said.

Chapter 25

Brother Arnold Smith went down to the church on Thursday morning to unlock it so the ladies could begin decorating for the wedding. It must be a woman thing, because he never could see all the time, energy, and money they put into a wedding. But women set great store by all the foo-foo. So he'd do his two jobs. One was unlocking the church so they could get inside to decorate. The other was officiating at the wedding and attending the reception. His wife, Estella, said weddings and receptions were the social life of a preacher's wife. Far be it from Brother Arnold to prevent his wife from having a proper social life.

This wedding, he'd heard, was going to top anything Cadillac had seen since the day Violet married Ethan Prescott the third. Annabel Williams had enlisted the help of everyone in the church since she only had three weeks to get a wedding ready that should have taken six months at the very least. Even Estella was helping hot glue silk roses and crystal wedding bells to the middle of huge puffs of filmy stuff to attach to the pews.

His wife said that his hearing was going bad, but there wasn't one thing wrong with his ears. In her old age, she'd started whispering just to make him think he couldn't hear. He slung open the door and started singing "Rock of Ages" at the top of his lungs. There, he could hear every note! Proving that he didn't have a hearing problem but that she was getting chronic laryngitis in her old age.

He made it to the middle of the church before he realized his feet were wet. When he looked down, the carpet was completely soaked and he was standing in two inches of water. The musky smell of wet carpet and the old wood beneath the carpet wafted up to his nostrils at the same time. That's when he stopped singing and heard a bubbling noise. He turned around and hurried back to the bathrooms. The men's room was fine, but the ladies' room was gushing water from one toilet and the hot water tank both.

He flipped the lever on the potty and nothing happened. He spun around to check the hot water tank sitting in the corner. The pipe bringing the water into it from underneath the church had rusted plumb through and water was spraying everywhere.

The preacher grabbed his cell phone from his pocket and it slipped out of his hands. Like a football player trying to recover a fumble, he battled with it, snatching and grabbing until he lost his footing on the slippery, water-covered tile. His hip hit the toilet on the way down, and he heard the crack before he felt the horrible pain. He'd finally gotten a hold on the phone, so he immediately dialed 911 and then called his wife.

"Did you get the church unlocked? Anna Ruth just called and they're on their way with the first load of pew bows," she whispered.

He yelled, "Speak up, woman!"

"Stop yelling at me!"

"I'm dying!"

"You are not. You're just hard of hearing. I said Anna Ruth is on her way with bows."

"I am dying. I think I've broken my hip, and I'm lying in three inches of water waiting for the ambulance. Tell Anna Ruth to go back home and take her beau with her."

Darla Jean looked forward to her trips to Blue Ridge on Thursday and that week was extra special. She had the papers for Lanita all signed and sealed, ready to deliver. Lanita was ready to get out of

Blue Ridge and start a new life. Darla Jean had a friend from the business who had retired about the same time she did and moved to the Bahamas. After a year, she moved to Canada and bought a small bookstore. She kept in touch with Darla Jean and offered to give Lanita a room above the store and a job.

They were planning a special lunch for Lanita at Betty's place and then Darla Jean was putting one Cheri Jones on the plane to Ontario, Canada, out of DFW Airport in Dallas. Now there would be an empty bedroom for the next woman in need.

Darla Jean tied her brown hair back into a low ponytail and dressed in jeans, a sweatshirt, and sandals that morning. She found business as usual in the kitchen over at Clawdy's. Marty was cooking. Cathy and Trixie were waiting tables. Agnes was sitting at the table having biscuits and sausage gravy.

"Hey, girl. What are you up to today?" Marty asked.

"I'm on my way to Blue Ridge. Today Lanita is leaving the nest," Darla Jean answered.

"You are doing a good thing," Marty said.

"I think I've found my true calling. Not that I'm giving up the church, but this feels right. I'll miss her, though. The girls and Betty have enjoyed having her."

"Your sister is a saint. You've got to bring her up to meet us sometime," Marty said.

"That would be nice, and I don't mean in an 'ain't that nice' way either, Trixie. I'm sure she'd love to meet my friends. She's never asked and I ain't never told what business I used to be into, but it would set her mind at ease to meet y'all."

Darla Jean poured a cup of coffee and sat down at the table. It was amazing how many problems had been solved around that old wooden table. But after the wedding cake and the topper business, the drama had come to a halt. Maybe the world was finally tilting back toward normality.

She split open a biscuit and slathered butter inside. The first bite was still in her mouth when the back door burst open and there was Anna Ruth, dressed in jeans and a Western cut shirt, and with tears running down her face.

Like flying debris in the middle of a class five tornado, drama constantly whirled around Anna Ruth. The past week must have just been the calm before the storm, because until that hussy moved to Bells, there was always going to be something going on in Cadillac.

She fell on the floor beside Darla Jean's chair and laid her head on Darla Jean's lap. "Oh, Darla Jean, you've got to help me."

"What has Andy done now? Or was it Trixie?" Darla Jean asked.

"I didn't do jack shit. I been minding my own business and helping run this café," Trixie said.

Anna Ruth wailed. "The church flooded. I mean, it really flooded. It must have started right after the service on Sunday, and the preacher and his wife have been out of town seeing their kids so we didn't have a Wednesday night service and..." She stopped to inhale, but her chin still quivered. "When the preacher went to open the church this morning, it was all covered in water because the toilet was overflowing and the hot water tank pipe broke and was spewing and what am I going to do?"

Agnes looked up toward the ceiling and said, "Thank you!"

"For what?" Anna Ruth frowned.

"I wasn't talking to you. I'm talking to God, and you aren't supposed to interrupt a woman when she's talking to God."

"Why would you thank God for this mess? It's just awful. It won't be aired out for a week so there won't be services Sunday morning, and my wedding, my beautiful wedding, is on Saturday!" That set her off on another crying jag.

Agnes slapped the table. The noise stopped all the crying. "Shut up, woman! This is my sign."

"What are you talking about?" Anna Ruth asked.

"I been askin' God to give me a sign if he wanted me to move over to Darla Jean's church. I can't ask for a bigger sign than the one he gave Noah. So I'm moving. Sunday I'll be over there at your church, and I don't want to hear a damn thing about the Good Samaritan. I'll be on the front pew, and if Violet shows up, she can sit on the back one because I said I was changing churches first."

"I don't care where you and Violet go to church on Sunday. I just need to use the church on Saturday," Anna Ruth said. "Please, Darla Jean."

"If you'll hush crying and settle down, you can use my church on Saturday, but I don't have a reception hall. And Agnes, I'm preaching on the 23rd Psalm on Sunday, not on the Good Samaritan."

Anna Ruth's tears dried up and she smiled. "Violet says we can use the community building, and it is right across the street so the people can leave their cars in the parking lot at your church. And we're having a little rehearsal tomorrow night. So we'd need it then, too, and we need to start decorating right now."

"Okay," Darla Jean said. "I'm on my way out of town, but I'll go show you how to lock up when you are done."

Anna Ruth stood up and hugged Darla Jean. "Thank you so much. Aunt Annabel is waiting in the van."

Darla Jean stood up and her cell phone rang. She pulled it out, pushed the button, and answered. But then she heard another ring. She looked around the room.

"Not mine," Trixie said.

"Oh, that's my new ringtone," Anna Ruth said. She put the phone to her ear, turned white as snow, and gasped.

"What now?" Trixie asked.

"The preacher really did break his hip. He will be in the hospital for a week. I don't have a preacher." She wailed out the last word pitifully.

Agnes grabbed her ears. "God, say you'll marry them just to shut her up."

"God wouldn't marry them if he lost a bet with the devil, Agnes," Trixie said.

"I'll preach at your wedding if you won't faint right here on the kitchen floor," Darla Jean told Anna Ruth. "Now let's get on out of here so these people can get their work done. Lord, what an unholy nightmare."

She ushered a shaking Anna Ruth out to the van, put her inside, and slammed the door.

It would all be over on Sunday, and they could settle down into routine again. The plumbing at her church was fine and tile covered the floors, so if it did flood, nothing would be ruined. And all she had to do was preach the wedding, which she'd do in the middle of a snowstorm to get Andy and Anna Ruth out of town so neither of them would interfere with her friends' lives anymore.

With Lanita's help, Betty had made gumbo, boiled shrimp, rice, and beignets for lunch. Five women sat around the table with good food in front of them and tears in their eyes.

"Okay," Darla Jean said. "Enough of this sadness. I've already seen enough tears to last a week today. And this is a happy day. This is a day of jubilee. A woman is going to the Promised Land to get a brand new start. She's been saved from an abusive man and she is starting a new life."

"Yes, I am, but I hate to go and leave this wonderful home," Lanita said. "If it's not too sad, tell us about the tears you've already seen today."

"It's a long story," Darla Jean said.

"We've got two hours until we have to leave," Lanita said.

Darla Jean filled a bowl with gumbo and entertained them with the story as they ate, from the first of the summer when she'd fallen on her hind end out in the street trying to see who Agnes had shot, to that morning.

She finished her story and reached for another beignet just as the clock struck twice. Betty stood up, picked up Lanita's suitcase, and carried it toward the door. "Hugs but no weeping. That's the rule, girls."

Lindsey hugged Lanita tightly. "I'll miss you and every time I look at the moon I will remember you."

Misty hugged her. "Layla and I'll remember you every time we sing the Cajun lullaby."

"Me too," Lanita said past the lump in her throat. "You two take care of Betty and Layla."

Lanita walked out of the house.

Cheri Jones got into the pickup with a suitcase full from donations to the church clothing bank. And she looked straight ahead as they drove south out of Blue Ridge.

Darla Jean could feel her pain.

"You want to know why I chose that name?" Lanita asked.

Darla Jean nodded.

"My grandmother never called me by my name. She always called me her sweet little *cher*, which is a Cajun endearment. And Jones is such a common name and so far removed from Landeaux, which was my maiden name."

"Very good," Darla Jean said.

"They won't ever leave," Lanita said.

"Who?"

"Your new daughters. They've found a home. I would have liked to but it's just not far enough from him. I'm a little nervous but I trust you, Darla Jean. God walks right along beside you. I know it. I can feel it."

Agnes was watching her afternoon soaps when the phone rang. She waited until the commercial started and picked it up.

"You got five minutes to talk and then I'm hanging up because my show will be back on," she said.

"Good grief, Agnes, you are a snappy old thing today. It's this changing weather. It's gettin' to all of us. Did you hear about the church?" Beulah asked.

"I did. It's a sign from God that I need to start going elsewhere. So I'm going to put my dollar in the collection plate at Darla Jean's church on Sunday. Violet can have the church that God flooded."

Beulah gasped. "God didn't flood our church. The toilet did."

"You think God ain't got a message in that? Floodin' the church with shitty water? Sounds like he's tellin' me to find another place. You and Violet, y'all go on and buy some new carpet and redo the bathroom. I'll be goin' to the one I can walk to from now on."

"Agnes, you have gone plumb crazy."

"Way I see it is that the rest of you are the crazy people. If God rains down shit from the clouds, y'all will probably stand out there and let it fall on you. Now my show is back on so good-bye."

Marty and Jack washed up after getting the last of the latest remodel done on the Caddy.

"If it don't get cold and stay cold, we're all going to die of pneumonia. This changing back and forth is tough on the allergies," Jack said.

"Amen to that. Are you bringing a plus one to the wedding?"

"No, I'm bringing a plus three. You, Cathy, and Trixie."

"Your mamma is afraid you're going to take women into your house and there will be gossip."

"It won't be gossip, darlin'; it will be the unadulterated gospel truth." Jack grinned. "Hey, I heard there was a new chapter in the Andy and Anna Ruth wedding book?"

"That damn book is going to go on until three days past eternity."

She went on to tell him about the church and the preacher. "Next thing you know she'll be sick and want one of us to stand in her place and marry Andy by proxy for her."

John dove under the covers with Cathy. It had been warm that morning so he'd turned the heat off and now it was really cold.

"We are pretending it's December and we are in Colorado in the mountains. We're snowed in and we can't do anything but have sex for a whole week," he teased.

Cathy snuggled up next to him. "Then keep me warm. Speaking of warm, don't plan anything for Saturday afternoon. We're going to the wedding I've been talking about. Aunt Agnes swears she's going and I don't want her to have to sit alone. She's a salty old girl and after the Jubilee upheaval, I owe her big-time. And besides, Darla Jean will be officiating, and it will take me and Marty both to keep Agnes out of trouble. Lord, she might ruin the whole wedding."

"Honey, long as you don't make me put on a three-piece suit, I'd be glad to go to a wedding with you. I'd even be glad to go to our wedding with you."

"I know, but when we do this, it's not going to be with all that fanfare, and it's not going to be right before Christmas. I'm thinking maybe just the two of us on a mountaintop in Colorado or on a tropical beach in the wintertime with the white sand under my bare feet."

"Yep, my kind of woman. Now let's make some heat of our own," he said.

Jack removed his gun, badge, and radio and locked them in a desk drawer, untucked his shirttail, and unbuttoned it as he headed for the shower. Holidays always caused a whole rash of crazy things. People bitched about their neighbors' dogs or their cars making too much noise. Tonight a whole block of people were without electricity because someone plugged in too many Christmas lights and blew out a transformer.

One woman called to complain about her neighbor's blow-up Christmas decoration blocking her view of the road. So much for spreading love in the season!

Love!

He wasn't opposed to finding a special someone someday, but he'd be damned if he dressed up in a tux like Andy had brought by the station that day. It had a cummerbund and a vest, plus a cravat. The policemen were supposed to show up in dress blues. Jack already dreaded wearing that tight uniform, and the wedding was two days away.

Trixie knocked on the door and waltzed right in without a "come on in, the door is open." "We had leftover fried chicken so I made you up a platter, and Marty made her blackberry cobbler so I brought a chunk of it for you."

"Beans and greens?" He opened containers.

"Oh, yeah. Dinner ain't worth havin' without beans and greens. You are going to the wedding, right?"

"Yes, I am. In my dress uniform," he groaned.

"I'm going too. I've decided to go to prove to you and Marty and everyone else that it's over between Andy and me."

"That's bullshit," Jack said.

She raised an eyebrow.

"You want to see just what kind of god-awful show Anna Ruth has orchestrated. And it's payback for the way Andy treated you. Nothing like watching him have to stand there in that monkey suit and vow to be faithful, is there?"

Trixie laughed. "Well, there is that too! And Agnes swears she's going. It'll take all of us to keep her out of trouble."

Chapter 26

On Friday night, Ella's Beauty Shop stayed open until eight o'clock. She liked to close at noon on Saturday, so in fairness to her customers, she put in a long day on Friday. Her granddaughter, Kayla, did fancy nails in the corner of the shop, and to generate some business she was running a two-for-one special that week. If one person came in for a manicure, they could bring a friend and she'd do their nails for free.

There was no way in hell Agnes was going to a wedding with her roots showing. Violet would definitely be invited, since she was the head she-coon of Grayson County and the president of the Blue-Ribbon Jalapeño Society. Wild horses couldn't keep her away from a social function, and if her roots were showing, it might hinder a vote. Ethan had lost the election, but it hadn't slowed her down one bit. She was already talking about the next one.

Agnes made an appointment with Ella to get her hair done and dyed. And to help Kayla out, she made arrangements for Marty, Cathy, Trixie, and Darla Jean to accompany her and have their nails done. It was not because she liked any of them, but poor Kayla needed money so she could get her full-fledged cosmetology license. Besides, since it was the night before the big wedding, if Violet was at the beauty shop, Agnes would need her spiritual adviser and her bodyguards. Two manicures was a small price to pay for that kind of protection.

Ella and Kayla were looking at magazines when all five women traipsed in together. Ella, a tall thin woman with blond hair, laid her book to the side and went straight to the washing sink.

The beauty shop wasn't as big as Miss Clawdy's pantry. Right inside the door to the left was Kayla's nail salon station. Four folding chairs were lined up to the right. Between the chairs and two hair dryers, magazines were scattered on an old coffee table that Ella brought from her house. Behind Kayla's nail desk, two beautician stations were situated. Across the back wall, two shampoo sinks were set up.

"Who's first?" Kayla asked.

"Me," Trixie said. "I want the French manicure."

The other three pulled chairs up around her and were picking out their fingernail polish from a wide assortment when the door opened and Violet breezed in. She went straight to the back, picked a floral duster off the rack, and put it on over her bright blue pantsuit.

"Ella, I'll need the complete workup today. Trim, wash, touch-up, and of course comb-out. Oh… my… God! What are you doing here?" she gasped when Agnes sat up.

"Uh-oh!" Trixie said.

When Agnes sat up, she and Violet were barely three feet from each other.

"I'll get Agnes's touch-up started. While it's setting, I'll get yours washed," Ella said.

Violet backed up slowly and sunk down into a drier chair.

"If they get into it, you get Aunt Agnes and I'll corral Violet," Cathy whispered to Marty.

Marty nodded. "Darla Jean, you will help me, and Trixie, you help with Violet," Marty said out of the corner of her mouth.

Agnes Flynn had worn her shoulder-length hair ratted and styled up on her head in the same style for fifty years. It had been red from the day of her birth and had never thinned with age like some women's had. She'd sworn when it started going gray that she'd come into the world a redhead and be damned if she wasn't leaving the world the same way, so she'd started getting it dyed.

Violet ignored everyone and looked at a magazine while Agnes got her "touch-up." Then Ella motioned her back to the chair right opposite Agnes. She removed the pins from Violet's hair, brushed all the rats out, and nodded toward the shampoo chair.

"So how is Ethan?" Ella asked.

"Just great. This was really just our trial run, you know. We didn't expect to really win but next time, it will definitely be his year," Violet said. "And he's got a new lady friend. She seems nice, but she's headstrong. I think that's what happens when a woman reaches forty and still isn't married. They get set in their ways. That's why God intended that women get married young so that they are willing to do what their husband thinks is best."

"I don't know," Ella said. "Young girls this day and age aren't mature enough to handle a house, kids, and a job, and it takes two incomes this day and age for a couple to get by. So is Ethan serious about her?"

Violet whispered, "I'm afraid he is and she is two years older than my Ethan and she has gray hair! And she wears it down to her shoulders."

Ella rinsed the soap from Violet's hair. "I'm seeing more of that. Women today don't keep up with the old standard that gray hair should be worn up or cut off."

"It's a shame," Violet said. "But what is a mother to do? She is a political science professor and she's mature. She wouldn't ever be flighty and break it off with him over a…"

Agnes cleared her throat loudly.

Violet mumbled the rest of the sentence.

Ella squeezed the water from Violet's hair with a towel and said, "There you go. Now let's go over to the chair and I'll get those roots done. While you let them soak, I'll get Agnes rolled and under the hood.

Agnes could see every move in the mirror without actually looking right at Violet. That would be downright rude, and besides, the girls wouldn't want to mess up their fingernails pulling them apart like they did at the football field.

Didn't Violet know that stovepipe black hair and the ratted flip look had gone out with the hippies? She'd moved forward with her dress style, but her hair still looked like shit.

Agnes looked at her own hair in the mirror and made an instant decision. She was sick of wrapping it in toilet paper and putting that net over it every night. Sometimes her head itched between beauty shop appointments and she'd like to be able to shampoo it in the shower like the girls did theirs.

"I want it cut today," Agnes said.

"It is due for a trim." Ella finished with Violet and nodded toward the rinsing station.

Agnes sat down and leaned her head back into the sink. Ella grabbed the sprayer and rinsed until the water ran clear and then draped a towel over her wet hair. "Okay, let's go trim a couple of inches off and roll it up."

"No, I don't want a trim. I want a full-fledged cut. I want it to look like that. No more rollers, just a couple of twists of the curling iron and a shot of hair spray." Agnes pointed to a poster hanging above the mirror. The woman in the picture wore her hair cut in a stylish neckline with enough on top to fluff up a bit. Surely to hell it couldn't be too hard to take care of that hair-do, and if it was she'd take her curling iron across the street and make one of the girls help her.

"You sure about this, Agnes?"

"Yes, I am. Cut it off!"

"Aunt Agnes!" Cathy said. "Think about it. You've worn your hair ratted ever since I've known you."

"Yes, I have. But some of us can change with the times."

"Are you talking to or about me?" Violet said.

"Of course I am. You look like shit with that hippie style. I don't want to look like you so I'm getting my hair cut off short, and besides, I'm tired of messing with this ratted hair. Last week I killed a spider right above my head on the wall. What if that damned thing dropped down into my hair and built a nest? Why, it could kill me dead, and I'm not dying until after you do, so I know which way you go. So off it goes and if I don't like it, it's only hair, and it'll grow back by next summer."

Ella picked up the scissors. "I'm going to ask you one more time. Are you sure, Agnes?"

"If you don't start cuttin' pretty soon, I'll go home and take the electric knife to it," Agnes said.

Ella made the first cut.

Marty and Cathy held their breath.

She cut some more.

"I'm going to like it," Trixie said. "It'll take twenty years off you, Agnes. And it'll be so much easier to fix."

Violet glared at the red hair falling on the floor. "You have lost your mind."

Marty cocked her head to one side. "Trixie is right. If you need someone to curl it and pick it out for you, I'll do it."

"I'll hold you to it, and if you are off shackin' up whatever next sexy cowboy you chase down, then Darla Jean can do it. Trixie, you ain't about to get near me with a hot curling iron," Agnes said.

"Ah, come on, Agnes. If I miss and put a burn on your neck, all the girls at your Sunday school will think you got a hickey and they'll be jealous," Trixie teased.

"I swear, Agnes, you do look younger. How does it feel?" Ella said.

"No pins. No rats. Feels light and breezy. I wish to hell I'd done it years ago. Don't be looking at me like that, Violet. You could never pull it off. Your hair is too thin and your face is too round. Accept it. You look twenty years older than I do. Just be careful about spiders getting close to you."

Violet had her mouth open to answer when the door burst open and Anna Ruth's bawling preceded her into the room. Her hair was in little pink sponge rollers and she didn't have a smidgen of makeup on her face.

"Oh, Cathy, I've been looking everywhere for you. It's horrible. Just horrible. We can't have the wedding." She threw herself in a dryer chair and covered her eyes with the back of her hand.

"What now? Did my church burn down?" Darla Jean asked.

"Maybe God is trying to tell you that you shouldn't marry Andy," Trixie said.

"No, he is not!" The weeping stopped and she shot dirty looks across the beauty shop at Trixie.

"They get into it, me and Cathy will take Trixie. Darla Jean, you and Marty get a hold of Anna Ruth," Agnes said loudly.

"What's the problem now?" Cathy asked.

"My cousin was going to be my bridesmaid. She came to rehearsal and to our little private dinner at Aunt Annabel's. She's seven months pregnant and on the way home she went into premature la… bor," she screeched.

"And?" Trixie asked.

"I don't have a bridesmaid and I've got to have someone walk down the aisle before me and scatter the rose petals and hold my bouquet and take pictures with me and all that."

Cathy sighed.

Marty shook her head.

"So you want me to be your bridesmaid?" Cathy asked.

"Nooo!"

Cathy heaved a bigger sigh of relief.

"You are too tall to ever fit into the bridesmaid's dress. My cousin is my size."

"Then why in the hell are you in here carryin' on like a dyin' coyote?" Agnes asked.

"I want Cathy to make Trixie be my bridesmaid. The dress will fit her," Anna Ruth said.

Trixie held up both palms. "You are crazy, woman. Andy would run out of the church if he saw me walking up the aisle."

"Does he even know you are here?" Agnes asked.

"Nooo! He kissed me, and we agreed we wouldn't even talk until we say our vows. I can't call him or anything, and he doesn't know."

"What color is it?" Marty asked.

"What?" Anna Ruth asked.

Marty whistled loudly, and the whole room went silent. "The dress that won't fit Cathy. Trixie wouldn't do that job for all the dirt in Texas, so all the whining in the world isn't going to do a bit of good. Stop carryin' on and tell me, what color is the dress?"

"Red satin."

"I've got a red satin dress that I wore to the Christmas party at the college last year. I'll do it," Marty said.

"Really?" Anna Ruth said.

Trixie gasped. "You have got to be kiddin' me. After the way you've hated Andy all this time."

"Yep, I'll do it. What time are you going to the church to get dressed?" Marty answered.

"The wedding is at two. I'll be there at one."

"Then that's when I'll arrive," Marty said. "Go on home and get a good night's sleep so you'll look decent for your wedding."

"Marty, you are a true friend."

"No, I'm not. I just happen to have a red satin dress."

"Thank you, thank you!" Anna Ruth floated out of the beauty shop like a butterfly, humming the wedding march.

"Why in the hell did you do that?" Trixie looked at Marty.

"Can you see Andy's face when he looks down that aisle and I'm coming at him? It will be absolutely priceless. And she'll scatter pictures all over their house and I'll be right there in them. It's a real Kodak moment, and besides, I was feeling downright left out. She's got Trixie's ex-husband. Darla Jean is preaching the ceremony, and Cathy's cake topper and ice sculpture is part of her wedding. I hadn't contributed a thing. And remember, I voted for her," Marty said.

"And don't forget she's got Cathy's dress that she was going to marry Ethan in," Agnes piped up. "You voted for that hussy when my name was on the ballot! Dammit, Marty! What were you thinkin'?"

Cathy's eyes bugged out. "How did you know about the dress?"

"Annabel let it slip to Tandy Jones who is helping convert it into a dress fit for a princess—her words, not mine. And Tandy whispered it to me at the Sunday school meeting this morning. Now ain't that nice?" Agnes winked at Trixie. "Now y'all are getting to help dear little Anna Ruth out. I even get to be part of the whole thing because I got my hair cut so I'll look better than Violet tomorrow. Now, answer me, Marty. Why'd you do a stupid ass stunt like vote for that woman?"

"Aunt Agnes, I could tell you why I voted for Anna Ruth, but then I'd have to kill you."

"What are you? CIA?" Agnes asked.

"No, something even more secret than that, darlin'. Now sit down and let Ella put some curls in the top of your new hairstyle."

Kayla giggled. "Your turn, Marty. What color fingernail polish do you want? Fire engine red to go with that dress? I remember it from last Christmas. You brought it in here to match your polish."

Marty touched her arm. "That is exactly what I want. Don't tell anyone about my dress. We want it to be as big a secret as the bride's new and improved version of my sister's elegant dress."

"Oh, honey, it will sure be that."

Ella finished curling the top of Agnes's hair and then picked it out and sprayed it. "What do you think?"

"I love it. Reminds me of my hair when me and Bert married. He always did like it short," Agnes said. "Your turn, Violet. Are you going to the wedding?"

Violet looked down her nose at Agnes and said, "Anna Ruth is a club member. I wouldn't miss it for the world, but Ethan won't be able to attend. He and his lady friend flew to Las Vegas for a long weekend. He'll be back on Sunday night."

While Kayla finished Marty's nails, Ella rinsed Violet's hair. She draped a towel over her head and took her back to the chair. "Time to roll it up and set you under the dryer."

"No! I want it all cut off like that." She pointed to the same picture that had taken Agnes's attention. "Annabel will help me if I have trouble styling it every day."

"You can't cut her hair like mine. I won't have it," Agnes said emphatically.

Darla Jean and Trixie stepped between the two old ladies.

Ella shrugged and looked at Cathy.

"Aunt Agnes, she can have her hair cut any way she wants," Cathy said softly.

Agnes popped her hands on her hips. "Are you going to dye it red next week too?"

"I am not! I wouldn't have that horrible color you were born with for nothing!"

"Okay, Ella. Cut it all off. If she promises not to dye her hair red then you can cut it like mine. She'll look like shit but go ahead and let 'er fly," Agnes said. "Come on, girls. I don't want to see how bad she's going to look."

Agnes escaped out the door with the four girls while Violet was still gasping. When they were outside, she giggled. "Well, that went well, didn't it?"

"Aunt Agnes!"

Agnes touched her hair. "Don't know why I didn't have it cut twenty years ago, and it did go well, Cathy! I got Violet to cut her hair. The only reason she wore it like that was one time Bert said it looked very nice. It was all he could think to say when she asked him outright if he liked it. And Marty is going to scare the shit right out of Andy! It was a wonderful evening! Well worth every single dime I spent. Let's go Clawdy's and eat ice cream right out of the carton to celebrate."

Chapter 27

THE DOORS OF THE church opened right into the sanctuary, so Marty, Anna Ruth, and Annabel had to walk outside in the cold from the back door to the front to make their appearance. The cue was that Marty would go around the building when they heard the first notes of "The Sweetest Thing" and take her time getting down the aisle, scattering rose petals from the white satin basket on her arm. She should end her walk on the last note and set her basket on the front pew.

Marty could not hurry in four-inch spike heels that put her well over six feet tall, and she'd styled her hair as high as she could get it that morning to make herself even taller. It truly was one of those priceless moments when she stepped inside the church and Andy's smile disappeared. He raised an eyebrow and set his jaws so tightly that she hoped his face was too sore to even kiss Anna Ruth at the end of the ceremony.

Whispers and tongue-clucking were wasted on her. She knew exactly what effect she'd have on the congregation when she offered to be the bridesmaid. Her long red satin dress had thin diamond straps, hugged her curves like an expensive leather glove, and was slit on one side all the way to her upper thigh. And she did not wear panty hose.

"Wow!" someone said.

She didn't blink but just kept smiling at Andy.

The song had been planned for the Baptist church where the

aisle was much longer than the one in Darla Jean's church, so she set her basket down when there was still another minute of the song left. She turned around and smiled at the crowd.

"Is this a joke?" Andy hissed.

"The cousin went into labor," Marty whispered. "I'm the replacement. She begged Trixie to do it, but she refused. Count your blessings, Andy."

Anna Ruth's music finally began. Annabel fluffed out her train so everyone could see the seed pearl J and the hearts and then she quickly cut a circle around the outside of the pews to take her place on the front pew.

Fresh roses were laced into Anna Ruth's hair, styled like a medieval princess with a crown braid. She carried an enormous bouquet of red roses and it would take an expert to ever find Cathy's simple dress under all those flowers and pouf. She set her eyes on Andy and didn't even look at the crowd.

Agnes leaned over to Cathy and whispered, "Were you really going to wear that thing? It looks like shit."

"It's sure not the dress I bought. She's made lots and lots of adjustments to it," Cathy answered.

John slipped an arm around her waist. "I hope you were serious about running away to the beach. All this stuff is making me claustrophobic."

"Very." She kissed him on the cheek.

Bows the size of blow-up beach balls graced every single pew. And in the middle of each was a silk red rose with wedding bells hanging on white satin ribbons below it. Arched white iron candelabra entwined with illusion, greenery, and red roses and burning brightly with dozens of candles decorated the pulpit.

"I hope all those candles don't set the church on fire. Can you imagine how hot it is up there?" Trixie whispered to Agnes.

As if he could discern her voice in the midst of a packed church,

Andy's eyes left Anna Ruth for a second and looked at Trixie. She locked gazes with him and winked.

Midway through the wedding, the sky darkened outside and thunder started grumbling off in the distance. Trixie leaned over and whispered in Agnes's ear, "It's going to rain."

"Bullshit! That's just God telling Anna Ruth to run one final time," Agnes whispered back.

Cathy whispered in the other ear, "If it rains, John brought his truck and it's parked close to the door. You head straight for it."

"We need rain. I might do a stomp dance right out in the middle of the street. If I'd known all it took was a ridiculous wedding to get us a good soakin' rain, I would have paid Andy to marry her sooner," Agnes declared. "I don't give a shit if he cheats on her tomorrow if we can get a good rain out of the deal."

It took a unity candle, two prayers, three songs, and the sifting of the sand in addition to exchanging rings and traditional vows where Andy promised his fidelity, love, respect, and protection before the personal vows were said.

Andy had written them the night before when he'd had no idea that his ex-wife would be sitting on the third pew and he sure wasn't expecting Marty to be standing three feet from him. He took Anna Ruth's hand in his and could have dropped down on his knees in thanks when several loud claps of thunder kept his vows from echoing off the walls. Marty couldn't even hear them, much less Trixie.

Anna Ruth had just begun her vows when a clap of thunder sounded like someone had set off a nuclear bomb right outside the church. She dropped Andy's hands, looked at Darla Jean, and squealed, "Just finish it!"

"I now pronounce you man and wife. Andy, you may kiss the bride," Darla Jean said just before the next rumble hit.

"The couple has asked that everyone join them across the street at the community room for the reception," Darla Jean said. "And I believe you'd better rush because it's going to rain any minute."

The bride and groom rushed down the aisle without the planned wedding music. She picked up her train and he held her hand as they jogged over to the community room. A whole entourage followed behind them. Some of the folks actually made it inside the room before the clouds opened up and rain fell in waves.

Marty was on her way out of the church when she heard her mother whisper right behind her. *Why haven't you told Trixie? Your friendship is more important than fifty-year-old gossip, and besides, she won't tell.*

Marty looked over her shoulder and felt disappointed when Claudia wasn't there.

Agnes picked up her umbrella. "Come on, Marty. You can share with me. I brought Bert's big old umbrella, and it's big enough for both of us."

Jack popped up an umbrella and held it above Trixie's head. "Hurry up, and we won't be soaked."

"But the backseat and trunk of my car is loaded with food," she said.

"Then I'll help you get to your car and then go on ahead to get my garage door unlocked. Y'all sure you don't want to go to the reception?"

"Hell, no! I've had all the sticky sweet wedding shit I can stand for a whole year." Trixie laughed.

Darla Jean locked the church doors and motioned for her family to follow her. They left by a side door with Lindsey and Betty under one umbrella and Misty, Darla Jean, and Layla under another one.

"You all look pretty spiffy today," Darla Jean said.

"Thank you for inviting us," Lindsey said.

"I'm so excited to be going to a party," Misty said.

"Hard rain don't usually last. It'll be over by the time the party is done," Betty said.

"It's really not a party, girls. It's just a little get-together at Jack's new house so we can all see it."

"I thought we were going to the wedding reception," Lindsey said.

"Trust me, this will be a lot more fun than that reception," Darla Jean told her.

Jack raised a glass of champagne that Cathy had poured and said, "Welcome to my new home, where the door is always open to my old friends and my new ones. Before we get busy eating all this wonderful food my dearest old friends have fixed, I have a toast. To old friends and to new beginnings and new friends."

"That is enough of that old shit." Marty laughed.

"You are as old as we are," Cathy told him.

"Then to new beginnings for us all." Jack grinned.

"Yes, sir!" John said.

Glasses clinked and everyone took a drink.

Agnes raised a glass of sweet tea. "To the end of the best year of my life. And you are all welcome!"

"For what?" Trixie asked.

"I protected your sorry ass, and that shotgun blast changed your life. Admit it," Agnes said.

Trixie smiled. "Okay, I'll admit it, and it changed for the better."

Agnes looked at Darla Jean.

"What'd I do?"

"I got God to like you, so you owe me big-time. And you, Marty, I've got calluses on my knees from praying for your soul. And Cathy, where do I start?"

Cathy raised her glass. "Girls?"

They touched their glasses together and chimed at the same time. "Thank you, Agnes."

Agnes smiled. "Now ain't that nice."

Later that night, Marty slipped into Trixie's room. "You asleep?"

"No, I'm wide awake. Who could sleep with all that thunder still going on? Don't it know it's supposed to snow in December, not flash lightning and rattle the windows?"

Marty sat down on the edge of the bed.

Trixie sat up and wrapped her arms around her knees. "Did you see someone at the wedding that interested you?"

"Nope, did you?"

Trixie shook her head. "I'm not ready. But I'm glad that Andy is out of my life, Marty. I really am."

"Me too. I voted for Anna Ruth because I promised Mamma on her deathbed that I would do everything in my power to keep Agnes out of that club."

"Okay, I understand." Trixie hugged Marty.

"But you deserve to know it all, and you've got to help me keep Agnes out of the club by whatever means it takes."

"Okay. I will. You are forgiven," Trixie said.

"Mamma's mother and Agnes were sisters," Marty said.

Trixie laid a hand on Marty's shoulder. "You don't have to explain. You've got your reasons and it's all right. I promise. It won't be there between us anymore."

"I know, because I'm going to explain. Grandma told Mamma the story before she died, and then Mamma told me. Agnes has no idea, but if she did, she'd kill Violet."

"What did Violet do that was that bad?"

"Violet was always the queen bee in Cadillac, even as a young girl. When Grandma finally grew the best peppers and won the blue ribbon at the Texas State Fair, it was Violet who came up with the idea for the club so that put her instead of Grandma in the spotlight. Anyway, back when they were young, she got pretty upset when she wanted Bert Flynn and he chose Agnes. She tried to seduce him, but he wasn't having any part of it."

Trixie whispered, "But how would she find out? Violet damn sure wouldn't tell that kind of thing on herself."

"Mamma said that the war between them got stronger every year and she always feared if Agnes got into the club that Violet would say that Bert really did sleep with her after he and Agnes were engaged just to get even with her. She could just see a night when Agnes was praising her precious Bert for something or another and Violet would tell her that she knew from experience that he hadn't always been faithful."

"How in the world did that ever get kept a secret in Cadillac?"

"Other than Bert and Violet, Grandma was the only one who ever knew and she wasn't about to tell her sister because she didn't want Agnes to spend the rest of her life in jail."

"How'd she find out?"

"She overheard Violet begging Bert to break it off with Agnes and come back to her the day before Bert and Agnes got married. She promised him anything he wanted if he would. And that's the reason I voted for Anna Ruth."

"Why did your grandmother ever let herself get roped into that club, anyway? The way Agnes and Violet have been at each other's throat, it's like she was taking sides against her sister," Trixie said.

"Agnes told her to join when Violet came around with the idea of starting the club. She said that Grandma could get Agnes in the club and together, they'd take Violet down. It didn't work. Every time Grandma nominated Agnes, Violet used her clout to make sure Agnes did not get chosen. By the time Mamma got into it, Violet had so much power that Agnes wasn't about to get into the club. But this last vote could have been disastrous. It was pretty damn close."

"You really think Agnes would get mad enough to kill Violet after all these years?"

"Bert has been dead more than thirty years. She hasn't changed a thing in her house and still has all of his clothes. He was a total saint in her eyes. What do you think?"

Trixie giggled.

"It's not funny. I've been worried sick since that stupid vote and you are laughing?" Marty said.

"It is funny! I just realized that Violet Prescott's wings and halo are as fake as her gold fingernail. Ain't that the funniest thing ever?"

"What is the funniest thing ever?" Agnes marched through the open door and plopped down on the bed.

"Nothing." Trixie winked at Marty.

"Well, it's not the funniest thing ever, whatever the hell it is. Beulah just called me all in a tizzy. Prissy Parnell has done decided that she's had enough of Buster, and she's come back to Cadillac. She's filing for divorce tomorrow morning, and Beulah is terrified that she's going to go after Jack. Lord, the world would come to a screechin' halt if Jack married a divorced woman."

Marty smiled. "Why?"

"Hell if I know. God knows he ain't goin' to find a thirty-five-year-old virgin like Beulah wants him to have. And there's more. Ethan and his teacher friend done got married in Las Vegas. I'm sure that since she's Violet's daughter-in-law, she'll fill the place that Cathy left behind when she was the first ever to quit the club. God, I'm proud of that Cathy. No more blue ribbons for that stupid-ass club. They might have to change their name to the Used-To-Be Club. Guess the Jubilee will always be the Jalapeño Jubilee, though. It's too late to change it after all these years, and besides, Cathy does grow the best peppers in the whole state. Anyway, Prissy will probably take over your spot."

"I didn't quit," Marty said.

"Hell, yes, you damn sure did. You just didn't know it. They ain't keepin' you without Cathy. Violet can have the club. Hell, she could get down on her knees and beg me, and I wouldn't be in it. I don't need that shit in my life. I got my hands full keepin' all y'all out of mischief."

Marty gasped. "You wouldn't join the club if they asked you?"

"Hell no! Never would have. I just wanted to be voted in so I could tear the hell out of her stupid club to pay her back for trying to talk Bert into leaving me high and dry at the altar. Today couldn't have been any more perfect. Now I'm going home and eatin' that piece of chocolate cake I talked Jack into letting me bring away from his place," Agnes said.

"How'd you know about that?" Marty asked.

"Bert told me. We didn't keep secrets," Agnes said on her way out.

Marty waited until she heard the back door slam and pulled out her phone. "I'll call Jack. You call Cathy. This is too damn good to wait until morning."

Trixie giggled as she dialed the phone.

Blue-Ribbon Jalapeño Society—who gives a shit?

Friendship—always and forever priceless.

The End

Read on for a look at
The Shop on Main Street

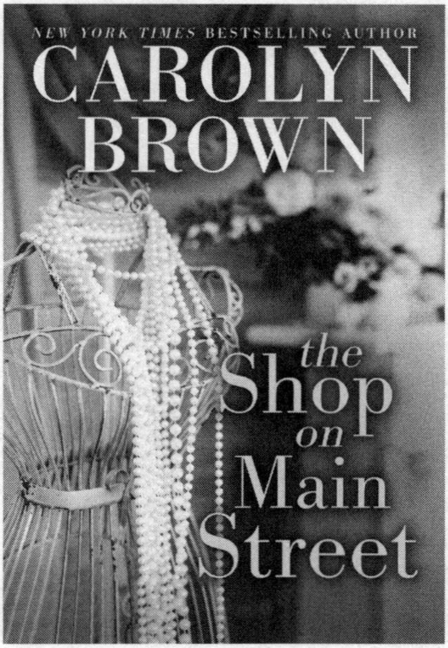

Available now from Sourcebooks Casablanca

Chapter 1

Some men are just born stupid. Some don't get infected until later in life, but they'll all get a case of it sometime. It's in their DNA and can't be helped.

Carlene could testify with her right hand raised to God and the left on the Good Book that her husband, Lenny, had been born with the disease and it had worsened with the years. Proof was held between her thumb and forefinger like a dead rat in the form of a pair of bikini underwear. They damn sure didn't belong to her. Hell's bells, she couldn't get one leg in those tiny little things. And they did not belong to Lenny, either. Even if he had become an overnight cross-dresser, his ass wouldn't fit into that skimpy pair of underbritches, not even if he greased himself down with bacon drippings.

They were bright red with a sparkling sequin heart sewn on the triangular front. They'd come with a matching corset with garter straps and fishnet hose. Carlene recognized them, because she'd designed the outfit herself at her lingerie shop, Bless My Bloomers. They belonged to a petite, size-four brunette with big brown eyes who had giggled and pranced when she saw herself in the mirror wearing the getup.

Carlene jumped when her cell phone rang. The ring tone said it was Lenny, but she was still speechless, staring at the scrap of satin in her hand.

She dropped to her knees on the carpet and bent forward into a tight ball, her blond hair falling over her face. She felt as if someone had kicked her firmly in the gut and she couldn't breathe. In a few seconds she managed a sitting position, wrapped her arms around her midsection, and sucked in air, but it burned her lungs. The noise that came forth from her chest sounded like a wounded animal caught in a trap. Tears would have washed some of the pain away but they wouldn't flow from her burning green eyes. Finally, she got control of the dry heaves and managed to pull herself up out of the heap of despair. Dear God, what was she going to do?

The brunette who'd bought the red-satin outfit had told her that she and her sugar daddy were going to Vegas, and she wanted something that would make him so hot he'd be ready to buy her an engagement ring. What was her name? Bailey? Brenda? No, something French, because Carlene remembered asking her about it. Bridget…that was it! Bridget had been to Vegas with Lenny. On how many other trips had he taken a bimbo with him and how many of them had been ten or fifteen years younger—and a size four, for God's sake?

In seconds, the phone rang again. She picked it up and said, "Hello." Her voice sounded like it was coming from the bottom of a well or, maybe, a sewer pipe.

"Carlene, I left my briefcase in my office. I slept on the sofa to keep from waking you, since I got in so late last night. Bring it to me before you go to work, and hurry. There's a contract in it that I need and the people will be here to sign in ten minutes. I'll hold them off with coffee until you get here."

No good-bye.

No thank you, darlin'.

Not even a please.

Did he talk to Bridget like that?

Anger joined shock and pain as she dropped the panties back in the briefcase and then removed the little card she'd made for him to find that morning. She'd written that she was sorry she had fallen asleep before he got home and that she'd make it up to him that night with champagne and wild sex. She stood up, straightening to her full statuesque height of just a couple of inches under the six-foot mark. Damn that sorry bastard to hell. How could he do this to her?

Ripping the note into confetti-sized pieces and throwing them in the air did nothing to appease her anger. Dozens of questions ran in circles through her mind. Had Lenny brought his twenty-something-year-old bimbo to her house for a romp on her bed while she was at work? Did that sorry sucker have sex with his mistress at noon and then with his wife that same night? Just how long had the affair been going on, anyway?

Among them all came one solid answer. She was not living in the same house with a lying, cheating, two-timing son of a bitch. She was leaving his ass and nothing or no one could convince her to stay another night under the same roof with him.

Five Red-Hot Chili Cook-Off trophies looked down from the mantle at her. She picked them up one by one and hurled them across the room. Not one of the damn plastic things broke, which made her even angrier, but she didn't go to the garage and get a hammer to work them over. Instead, she turned into a feverish packing fiend. In less than half an hour her van looked like an overflowing Salvation Army donation hut. Clothing and shoes were stuffed into the back like sardines. Plastic grocery bags filled with items from her dresser drawers were stacked in the backseat, and the briefcase sat right beside her on the front seat.

She gave it looks meant to fry holes through the leather, but it just sat there as cool as Lenny. Damn his black soul to hell for all eternity. She hoped that he was given a place sitting naked on a barbed wire fence and every time he fell off the devil shot him with a cattle prod.

From their house in Cadillac, Texas, to Lenny's car dealership in Sherman was exactly seven miles and she made it in a little less than five minutes. If it hadn't been for good brakes on her van, she would have plowed right through the plate-glass windows and rammed into that pretty brand-spanking-new red Corvette in the showroom. Some days started off bad and got worse as they went along.

Tears begged to be turned loose but she blinked them back. Be damned if he'd see her cry or reduced to a heap on the floor, either. It might happen, but he wouldn't bask in the glory of seeing it.

Her hands shook and her jaw ached from clenching her teeth. She took a deep breath and pushed open the door of her van, remembering to grab his briefcase before she slammed the door shut. Her bravado left when she looked through the window and caught sight of him through the glass windows in his office right off the showroom floor. Her stomach churned and nausea set in again. Could a person love and hate someone at the same time?

Her legs felt like they were filled with steel when she pushed open the glass door and headed toward Lenny's office. He looked up from behind his desk and with a flick of his wrist motioned for her to come on in.

She was still staring at him trying to figure out whether to beat him to death with the briefcase or just set it in the middle of the floor and get the hell out of there before she started weeping, when she saw a movement in her peripheral vision.

"Well, hello!" Bridget appeared from behind the Corvette parked just inside the doors. "It's good to see you again."

Either the woman did not know Carlene was Lenny's wife or she was a fool who'd caught an acute case of stupid from Lenny Joe Lovelle. Either way, she was crazy as hell and didn't value her hair or eyeballs. Anyone with two sane brain cells in their heads could see that Carlene Lovelle was a time bomb with a lit fuse.

Bridget's eyes twinkled and she lowered her voice to say, "The red outfit drove my sweet sugar daddy right up the walls. Honey, we had the honeymoon suite and we didn't hit the blackjack tables one time all weekend. He didn't even leave to go to his business meetings. We spent the whole two days in that big round bed or else in the heart-shaped hot tub. It was our five-month anniversary and he said that he got luckier in that room than he ever did at the gambling tables. I'll be back in to buy something else for the sixth month. We're going to Florida to celebrate my twenty-second birthday as well as our anniversary. I'm thinking naughty nurse so get the bling out and I betcha I get my ring on that trip. Oh, and guess what else? We are both members of the mile-high club now."

Carlene plopped the briefcase down on the hood of the Corvette and wished that she'd bought one of those shiny metal ones for Lenny's birthday instead of one made of soft kid leather. Hell, if she had a metal one, she really could beat him to death with it, but that fancy leather thing wouldn't even leave bruises.

Bridget's eyes widened out to the size of saucers when she saw the LJL initials on the top of the familiar case and had trouble staying in their sockets when Carlene popped it open. Right there on the top of a big manila envelope were the red panties.

Using a pen with the car dealership logo, Carlene picked up the underpants and threw them at the woman. Then she dumped documents, pens, sticky notes, and everything else in the briefcase onto the tile floor and stomped holes in the papers with her spike heels.

Bridget caught the scrap of red satin and all the color drained from her face. "What are you doing with my panties? And why do you have Lenny's briefcase? Who in the hell are…oh, my, sweet Jesus!" She slapped a hand over her mouth. The panties hung on her pinky finger, and it looked like she was trying to swallow the evidence.

Carlene picked up the empty briefcase and lobbed it like a rocket toward the window between her and Lenny. It lost momentum and didn't even crack the glass but it made him drop like bird shit behind his desk.

"I…I…" Bridget stammered.

Well, praise the Lord, her vocabulary now had two vowels. Maybe by the end of the day, she could add a consonant or two and be able to speak in whole sentences again.

Lenny must've jumped up as fast as he dropped because suddenly he was beside her. "My God, Carlene, what in the hell…oh!" He stopped dead.

His eyes darted from Bridget to Carlene. "I can explain. Bridget, honey, tell Uncle Sam to close the deal with Mr. and Mrs. Reynolds. He'll have to reprint the contracts. And would you please clean up this mess before anyone sees it? Carlene, we'll go discuss this over some coffee in the lounge."

Then he proved just how damned stupid he was by reaching out and touching her shoulder as if he could charm her into forgiveness. Well, Lenny Joe Lovelle wasn't charming jack shit out of her that morning, and it would be a cold day in hell before she ever forgave him. Even Alma Grace, with all her religion and praying, would agree that the Good Book did not condone adultery or fornication—even though it didn't mention skimpy under-britches.

She doubled up her fist and landed a good right hook in his left eye. He went down on his knees and yelled, "Why in the hell did you do that?"

"Because you touched me, you son of a bitch. If you ever lay a hand on me again, I will snatch you bald-headed and then start on your bimbo over there," she yelled.

Shit! Had she really raised her voice right out in public like that? Carlene Carmichael Lovelle was a lady who did not air her dirty laundry, but dammit, he'd broken her heart, twisted it up into a pretzel, and now he was acting like it was nothing. She glared at him, hands on hips and back as straight as steel.

Bridget instinctively covered her hair with her hands, the panties now looking like dangly earrings as they floated down from fingertips to shoulders.

He stood up and narrowed his eyes. "Come on, Carlene, we have to talk."

"You can talk to my lawyer."

He laid a hand on her shoulder and smiled. "Darlin'..."

She slapped him with her open hand hard enough to put a blaze of red on his cheek, but he didn't drop to the floor. "Dammit, Carlene. You are making a scene."

"A scene. You want a scene? I'll give you a damned scene that a sugar daddy can appreciate." She placed the toe of her high-heeled shoe on the bumper of the Corvette and marched up across the hood, leaving dents that looked like hail had peppered down on the pretty red car. When she was standing on the top of it, she looked right at Bridget.

"Bridget, *honey*, you had better never show your face at Bless My Bloomers ever again."

"Get off that car. You've already done thousands of dollars worth of damage. Sam is going to sue the hell out of you for this," Lenny shouted.

Sam, a robust man with a rim of gray hair, a belly that hung out over his belt, and five-thousand-dollar eel cowboy boots, rushed out into the showroom. "My God, Carlene, have you lost your mind?"

"She's gone crazy, Uncle Sam," Lenny said.

"You want to see freakin' crazy? I will show you crazy." She stepped down to the hood and did a stomp dance. By the time she finished, the showroom was full. She took a deep bow and hopped down from the hood. "When I'm done, you'll be damn lucky to have potatoes with your beans once a week, much less plan little weekend trips to honeymoon suites where you wallow around in a round bed with office girls rather than going to meetings. Dock his pay for the damage, Sam. You'd be wise to fire his ass, but since he's your nephew, that won't happen, will it?"

"Come on, Carlene, it was just a fling. It only happened one time and I'll never do it again," Lenny whispered.

"Fling! Just a fling?" Bridget's voice was as loud as a fire siren. "You promised me that you were leaving her. You promised me an engagement ring with a two-carat diamond as soon as you left your fat wife. You promised me we would have our own apartment by the time the chili cook-off happens and I could be your cheerleader for the event and you'd hang our picture above all those trophies in your office."

"Well, he's not leaving his fat wife. I'm leaving his cheating ass and he's all yours. Better keep him on a short leash. He charming, but he's a two-timin' son of a bitch." Carlene's high heels sounded like fire crackers as she stormed out of the dealership.

She drove until she reached the outskirts of town, pulled over, and laid her head on the steering wheel. That lyin' cheating bag of shit didn't deserve her tears but they flowed down her cheeks anyway as she sat there with the engine running and the air conditioner turning her warm, salty tears as cold as her heart felt.

Monday morning was Josie Vargas's favorite time of the week. She'd cooked all weekend, put up with whining grandkids and great-grandkids, sons in her living room arguing about football on the blaring television set, and daughters-in-law sipping iced tea at her kitchen table while they gossiped about people she didn't even know. The most beautiful sight in the world was the taillights as they all went home Sunday night after supper. Maybe by Friday she'd be glad to see them again, but right then she rolled her eyes toward the ceiling and gave thanks that she'd only birthed two sons.

"Okay," she muttered at the ceiling. "They say they are bringing the kids to see me so I don't get lonely since Louis died. Me, I think they are coming home to be waited on and to eat my cooking. Tell me I'm wrong. No? You can't lie?"

She warmed two leftover waffles from the day before in the microwave and drizzled a mixture of hot butter and maple syrup over them. That and coffee would keep her until she arrived at Bless My Bloomers where she sewed fancy lingerie for all sizes of women. Crazy women who wanted pearls and ribbons and fancy crap all over their under-britches. Josie couldn't imagine wearing the things that she made. Plain old white cotton panties were good enough for her butt and Louis had never complained one time when he took them off.

He would turn over in his grave if he knew she'd gone back to work. She'd retired at sixty-five and she and Louis had twelve good years together before he died. But she got lonely after he was gone, and when Carlene came to ask her if she wanted a job at Bless My Bloomers, she'd jumped at the chance.

She was ten minutes early and parked her twenty-year-old car around back, leaving the curb space and driveway for customers. She was a short woman with a touch of gray in her hair and brown eyes set in a bed of wrinkles. She was eyeballing her eightieth birthday in another year and she loved those three girls she worked with as much as her own granddaughters. Before she got out of the car, she took out the little compact that Louis had given her for their first anniversary and reapplied her trademark bright-red lipstick.

No one else had arrived yet so she let herself in the back door with her key and headed straight to her little room. It had been the library when the house was a residence but nowadays it was her sewing room. The living room was the store. The parlor had been divided into four fitting rooms. The dining room was the stockroom and the walls were lined with basic bras, corsets, and panties in all sizes, shapes, and colors. There were three bedrooms upstairs, and sometimes the owners, Carlene, Alma Grace, and Patrice, kept extra stock up there if the dining room overflowed.

She'd been working on a fancy corset for a bride when she left Friday evening. She pulled up her rolling chair, picked up the pearls, and started sewing them one-by-one onto the lace panels between the boning. She'd always liked intricate work. Even as a child she was the one who loved embroidery and needlepoint.

"I don't remember Carlene ever being out sick before. I hope she ain't sick today. Alma Grace will have a prayin' fit if she has to fit all those choir women from her church without any help."

Alma Grace stopped by her mama's house on the way to work every morning so they could have a mother/daughter devotional. They read the daily pages from the study Bible, said a prayer, and then had breakfast.

Few people in Cadillac even remembered the Fannin sisters' real names. Sugar's birth certificate said Carolina Sharmaine, but she'd always been called Sugar. The same with Gigi; her real name was Virginia Carlene. And Tansy had started out life the day she was born as Georgia Anastasia. They'd each had a daughter within a year of each other twenty-seven years before. Alma Grace belonged to Sugar, Patrice to Tansy, and Carlene to Gigi.

"Are you planning a surprise for the Easter program this year?" Her mother pushed a strand of ash-blond hair back behind her delicate ears. Diamond studs glittered in the morning sunlight. Both of her sisters told her that the television show *Good Christian Bitches* had really been modeled after Miz Sugar Magee. Those women damn sure hadn't given up a bit of their bling or their style to be religious and neither had Sugar or Alma Grace.

Alma Grace's curly blond hair, the color of fresh straw, was held back that morning with a silver clasp. Cute little cross earrings covered with sapphires matched the necklace around her neck and her blue eyes.

"Now Mama, you know I never give away all my secrets about the Easter program. That's why we have such a crowd. Everyone knows it'll be spectacular and even bigger than the year before. But I will tell you this much. The teacher from the drama department at the school is working on a gizmo to make me fly as I sing the final song and there will be sparkles on my wings. It's going to be breathtaking. They'll still be talking about it at the chili cook-off. Maybe even at the festival this fall."

Sugar's eyes misted. "It will be the best thing that's ever happened in our church, and when your sweet voice starts to sing the final song, it will be like the heavens open up and the angels are singing."

Alma Grace dropped a kiss on her mother's forehead. "Thank you, Mama. I've got to go to work."

Sugar sighed. "Lord, I wish you wouldn't have…"

Alma Grace laid a hand on her mother's arm. "I prayed about it, remember? And God told me it was just underwear. Carlene, Patrice, and I are making a good living at Bless My Bloomers. And just think of all the happy men in the world who are staying home with their wives because of our jobs."

Sugar nodded seriously. "That's the only thing that I take comfort in, darlin'. Now let us have a little prayer before you go. We'll pray the blood of Jesus will keep you pure as you work on all those hooker clothes."

"Mama!"

Sugar tilted her chin up. "Well, God didn't tell *me* that those things were fit for decent God-fearin' women so I intend to pray about it every day."

"I've got to go or I'll be late. Dinner at Miss Clawdy's at noon?" Alma Grace asked.

"Not today. Gigi and Tansy and I are going up to Sherman to look at a new car for Gigi. She's still driving one that's four years old. It's a disgrace, I tell you. She's got a son-in-law in the business and she drives a car that old. Why, honey, it's almost a sin. I guess I should be happy that she's driving a car instead of a truck, but honestly, four years old!"

"Well, y'all have a good time and bring the new car back by

the shop for us to see. That Lenny is so good to his family. Maybe someday I'll find a husband like him. Carlene is one lucky woman."

Sugar waved from the front door. "Yes, she is."

Alma Grace parked the car beside Josie's and went in through the back door. "Hey, no coffee? Where's Carlene?" she yelled.

"Ain't here yet. Hope she ain't sick. Y'all have got all those church women coming for a fitting today."

Alma Grace rolled her eyes toward the ceiling. She'd forgotten about that appointment. Thank goodness her mother was tied up with Aunt Gigi's new car business or she'd have had to cancel lunch with her. Sugar Fannin Magee pouted when she got all dolled up and didn't get to go out and it was not a pretty sight.

"Think I should call her?" Alma Grace asked.

"Hell, no! She'll call us if she's sick. Maybe she's finally pregnant and got the mornin' sickness."

"A baby." Alma Grace almost swooned.

"I didn't say that she was. I said that she might be, and if she is, she'll tell us when she damn well gets ready. Why don't you make coffee?"

"Because Carlene says that my coffee isn't fit to drink. I'll get the lights turned on and the doors opened. I'm sure she'll be along in a little while. Patrice is late all the time but I've never beat Carlene to work since we opened the shop last year."

The alarm rattled around in Patrice's head like steel marbles banging against the edges of a tin soup can. She groaned and shoved a pillow over her eyes with one hand and used the other hand to slap the hell out of the clock, sending it scooting across the floor. That the plug came loose from the wall was the only thing that saved the damn clock from being stomped to death that morning.

Damn Monday mornings after a weekend of hell-raisin' sex and booze. Wine, beer, Jack Daniels, and half a gallon of rocky road ice cream after the fight with her boyfriend did not make for a good start to a new week. Hangover, bloat, and tears were poor bed partners, especially on a Monday morning.

She kicked the covers off, took a warm shower, drank a cup of tomato juice laced with curry, ate half a can of chilled pineapple, and popped two aspirin. It was her special recipe to cure a hangover.

Her job at Bless My Bloomers was keeping books, inventory, and anything to do with a computer. Lord, she hated to face columns of numbers and deal with the wholesale sellers all morning with her head pounding like she was standing next to a jackhammer.

No one at the shop could help her, either. Alma Grace, bless her heart, could sell a blinged-out corset to a saint, but she could not add up a double column of figures even with a calculator. Carlene, God love her soul, could design something so sexy that the devil would hock his horns to buy it, but she was all thumbs when it came to keeping track of what went out and what came into the shop. If things got hectic in the sales room, Patrice could talk to customers, show them the merchandise, and even make a sale, but she didn't enjoy it.

The bathroom mirror brought about a loud groan. Her aqua-colored eyes looked like two piss holes in the snow and her platinum blond hair, straight from a bottle down at the Yellow Rose Beauty Shop, was only slightly better looking than a witch's stringy strands in a kid's movie. Hell, next week, she might cut it all off and wear it in a spike hairdo. It would damn sure be easier to fix than getting out the curling iron every damn morning.

"Grandma Fannin would have your hide if you did that," she whispered to her reflection.

When she'd done enough to cover up most of the hangover, she pulled a pair of skinny jeans from her closet, along with a tight-fitting shirt that hugged her double Ds and black, shiny, high-heeled shoes that she could kick off under her desk.

Evidently Lenny had brought Carlene to work that morning, since her car wasn't parked out behind the shop. Patrice laid her head back against the headrest for a minute and shut her eyes against the blinding sun, vowing that she'd find her sunglasses before she stepped out into the sun again. She needed coffee, good black strong coffee, and lots of it. Thank goodness Carlene always started a pot first thing in the morning.

Her head throbbed so bad, she'd almost be willing for Alma Grace to lay hands upon her and pray that God would heal her, but then she'd have to listen to her asking God to forgive her for drinking. She just needed something to relieve the headache. She hadn't killed her boyfriend, so she didn't need forgiveness, and even Jesus drank wine, so Alma Grace could keep her preaching to herself.

Shading her eyes with her hand against the bright sunlight, she made her way to the porch. Coffee! She needed coffee and lots of it. Bless Carlene's heart; she always had it brewing first thing in the morning. But that morning the wonderful aroma of fresh coffee did not greet her when she opened the door.

"Dammit!" she swore.

"Carlene?" Alma Grace yelled from the front of the house.

"It's Patrice, not Carlene. Where is our cousin? She's never late," Patrice said.

Josie poked her head out of the sewing room. "From the looks of your eyes, I'd say you have a supersized hangover."

Patrice held up a palm. "Guilty. Don't tell Alma Grace or she'll start praying."

"Come on in the kitchen. I'll fix you up," Josie said.

"I already did my magic."

"Did it work?" Josie pointed at the kitchen table.

Patrice shook her head and it hurt like hell.

"No." She sat down, put her head down on her arms, and poked her fingers in her ears when Josie started the blender.

"What is it?" she asked when Josie set a green drink that looked like ground-up bullfrogs in front of her.

"Don't ask and don't come up for air. Drink it all down without stopping," Josie said.

Patrice did and then slammed the glass on the table with enough force to rattle the salt shakers. "Holy damn shit! That's hotter than hell's blazes."

"Yep and it'll burn that hangover right out of you in five minutes. Now let's go to work. Carlene's not here. I hope she's not sick. Y'all have the church choir coming today for fittings."

"Dammit all to hell!" Patrice groaned. "I'm not in the mood for praisin' God and blessing souls or fitting bras to those holier-than-thou gossiping women."

"Me neither but they've got boobs that have to be roped down, so suck it up. Must have been a helluva a weekend that you had." Josie smiled.

"I don't even want to talk about it until my head stops pounding. God, I hope Carlene isn't sick. I don't want to wait on customers today."

Alma Grace poked her head in the kitchen door. "I hope she's not sick, too, but it would be wonderful to have a baby in the family. My mama and your mama and Aunt Gigi are going to Lenny's this afternoon to look at a car. It'd be a shame if Carlene isn't here when they drive it by to show us."

About the Author

Carolyn Brown is a *New York Times*, *USA Today*, *Wall Street Journal*, and *Publishers Weekly* bestselling author and also a #1 Amazon and #1 *Washington Post* bestselling author. A RITA finalist, she's received the prestigious Montlake Diamond Award, is a three-time recipient of the National Reader's Choice Award, and has won the Booksellers' Best Award.